Saving
Saffron
Sweeting

Saving
Saffron
Sweeting

Pauline Wiles

Author's Note

According to the famous quote, Britain and America are 'two nations divided by a common language'.

Saving Saffron Sweeting is set mostly in England and uses British English. If you would like a guide to the expressions used, please visit www.SavingSaffronSweeting.com for a free download.

You'll find further bonus materials there too.

Acknowledgements

I count myself exceptionally lucky that not a single acquaintance told me how nutty I was to attempt a novel. Nonetheless, certain individuals provided more than a splash of support and deserve special thanks.

Feddy Pouideh was undoubtedly the catalyst who got me started and also served as cheerful proof that one can indeed write a book and live to tell the tale. The talented Kristin Harmel was gracious enough to supply the encouragement I needed to venture beyond Chapter one. And I learned a huge amount about indie publishing from the information shared by Joanne Phillips on her blog.

Intrepid beta readers Jennifer Cunningham, Marissa Tejada and Julianne Lawrence helped me smooth off many rough edges, and proofreader Jude White brought the quality of the text to a standard fit to be seen in public. Any lingering errors are mine.

My parents, Philip and Ann Dendy, willingly accompanied me on treks around Cambridgeshire villages to ensure my description of Saffron Sweeting was authentic. It's true this willingness evaporated when they found they were also required to research the vertiginous roof of the Varsity Hotel, but they swallowed their fate with equanimity and a glass of white wine.

My husband Darius earns immeasurable gratitude for technical support, cover design and trusting that his wife had not lost her marbles entirely. He bore the indignity of reading his first ever Chick Lit novel and still managed to give constructive feedback. Moreover, as far as I'm aware, he has never cheated on me at a conference in Las Vegas. Not yet, anyway.

Saving
Saffron
Sweeting

Chapter 1

I was balanced on an eight-foot ladder with a mouth full of curtain hooks when I realised that my husband was cheating.

The individual pieces of the picture suddenly came together, making terrifying sense. I blinked hard, then stared at my knuckles, which were now white from gripping the ladder. But the image wouldn't subside. The picture I saw was James with another woman.

I was hanging curtains in my client Rebecca's bedroom, and the project was almost complete. This was great, as she'd been excited to give the room a whole new look after she'd recently come to the end of a long relationship.

'I'm ready to move on. Grace, I want a totally fresh look,' she'd told me when we met to discuss how I could help her. 'Something luxurious, maybe a little sensual. I don't plan on being single forever.'

I was still new in the design business and it was a huge deal for me not only to land a new client, but also one who had money to spend and some kind of clue what she wanted. My first few months had been a real struggle and I was starting to question my talents. Other business owners had stressed the importance of tapping my personal network to get things rolling, so James had spread the word around his office. Apparently, he had done a good job of promoting my abilities to Rebecca, his company's marketing manager. She had been great to work for and seemed appreciative of my suggestions. The only slight issue was that in the last few weeks she had been anxious to speed things up and get the bedroom completed.

Eager to please, I had been beavering away and attempting to charm my suppliers into hurrying. After getting the curtains up, I planned to hit the shops for accessories, and then the room would be ready for whatever action she had in mind.

My work had been interrupted by a knock on the front door of Rebecca's condo. I'd opened it to find a bubbly young woman, who presented me with a pair of pink stilettos.

'Oh!' she said. 'I was hoping Becca would be home. Can you let her know Kerry returned these?'

'I think she's at work,' I said, taking the shoes. 'I'm her bedroom designer.'

'Ooh, you mean the love nest? Can I see it?'

'Er, it's not finished yet,' I replied. 'I expect she'd rather show you herself.'

Kerry shrugged. 'Okay. I'll catch up with her.' She turned and was a few steps down the hall before she added, 'And tell her I want to hear all about Vegas and this James guy. He sounds delish!'

My mind was still on the curtains. I'd shut the door and put the cute shoes down, before returning to the bedroom.

Climbing back up the ladder, I thought, No wonder Rebecca wants to hurry this room. She's met some man in Las Vegas and needs her bedroom back. I was stretching to try to hook the edge of the curtain to the last ring on the pole when the dark feeling began to slither over me.

Did the ladder wobble? Had one of San Francisco's famous earthquakes nudged it? Or was the lurch, the sway, the feeling of my stomach dropping to the new wool rug, due to something else? I checked the new tear-drop chandelier hanging above the bed. As a British transplant to the Bay Area, I had spent the first couple of years diving under our dining table at the slightest tremor. But by now I had learned that if the light fixtures weren't swaying, the seismic jolt was all in my head. The glass drops of Rebecca's chandelier stared back at me steadily, not even winking, let alone dancing.

I had the presence of mind not to swallow my curtain hooks as I took a huge gulp and slid down the ladder. I slumped onto the new and naked mattress as I thought about my husband's recent conference trip to Las Vegas and how edgy he had been since. I remembered our paths crossing briefly in the kitchen, the first morning after his return.

'How was it?' I'd asked, digging through the drawer for my favourite cereal spoon.

'Okay, I guess.' He reached for the tea bags.

James seemed dispirited and I thought perhaps the industry analysts had given his company, a mobile security start-up, a tough time.

'Are you home this evening?' he wanted to know.

'Probably,' I called over my shoulder. I was already heading to my computer to check whether anyone had emailed for decor advice. Even at that hour, my mind was firmly on my fragile business.

But that day I'd been called by a potential customer to discuss her family room and, as was typical, she could only meet me in the evening. I was hard at work researching inspiration pictures when James came home, and within minutes I headed out to my appointment. After more than an hour of fruitless discussion on the merits of contemporary versus rustic style, I drove the forty minutes home across the Dumbarton Bridge to find my husband was already asleep.

With an uncomfortable feeling, I also recalled the previous evening, when he'd come home from work early and asked to talk to me, but I'd been flying out of the door to my women's networking group. This had been the pattern of life recently: we seemed to pass each other fleetingly, our schedules never lining up for longer than it took to brew a pot of tea.

And now I had learned that Rebecca had hooked up with someone called James in Las Vegas. My James had been acting oddly since he had returned from there. Keep calm, I told myself, it's probably fine.

But it wasn't fine. The third and ugly part of the truth was literally staring me in the face. Rebecca's favourite colour was purple and despite some reservations on my part, she had been adamant about using a strong shade of aubergine. We'd finally agreed on a sophisticated tan for three walls, painting the dramatic colour as an accent behind her bed. And although James usually showed precious little interest in any of my decorating ideas, we had been talking about Rebecca's project just before his trip, when we'd been in the kitchen long enough to empty the dishwasher together.

'How is your client list coming along?' he'd asked, shaking leftover water from a wine glass.

'Slowly,' I'd replied. 'Rebecca's bedroom is nearly finished but I don't have anyone lined up after her.'

He didn't say anything but had stretched over my head to put some plates away.

Happy to talk about my work, I'd let my brain run on. 'I hope it all comes together okay. That accent colour was such a bold choice.'

He'd pulled a slight face. 'Yeah, purple always reminds me of something my grandad would have had.'

I had dropped the topic, as I'd learned during our years together that James based most of his interior design dislikes on the vivid avocado and orange combinations in his grandfather's house. He thought any room featuring retro patterns or an accent wall was hideous.

Now, I leaped off the mattress as though it had bitten me on the behind. I was convinced I hadn't mentioned purple, aubergine or any other arty description for the colour behind the bed.

He knows what colour this room is. He's been here.

I was out of the house and into the car before I knew it. Days later, it occurred to me I should have stuffed Rebecca's hollow curtain poles with frozen shrimp. Of course, the clever moves always elude me at the time.

~~~

By the time I arrived at the Palo Alto office where James and his team were trying to create the next Silicon Valley success story, all dignity had abandoned me. I think my tears were already beginning as I lurched through the front desk area, empty because the company was too small to have a receptionist. In my haste, I then collided with the *foosball* table, which appears to be a required toy at every start-up with venture capital funding.

I spotted my husband – cropped, dark brown hair, shirt half untucked as usual – hunched over his keyboard, at the end of an untidy row of T-shirt clad computer coders. This gaggle looked barely old enough to have gained admission to Stanford University, let alone already graduated.

James looked up and noticed me. Surprise crossed his face, but was replaced with something I assumed was guilt. I could see how deep the lines in the middle of his forehead were getting these days, and how weary he looked.

'Purple,' was all I managed to utter at first. Terrific. Millions of wives over the centuries have faced this situation and all I could say was *purple.*

'Grace –' He stood and took my arm, trying to get me to sit.

I wrenched myself free. 'How did you know her bedroom is purple? How did you know?'

'Listen.' He shook his head. 'It's not what you think'.

Okay, so *purple* may not have been eloquent, but at least it was original. I saw red – as well as crimson, magenta and every shade in between.

'How could you?' I hissed. 'I know what's going on. And all the time, I've been decorating that sodding room!'

'Please,' he glanced sideways at the line of coders. 'Calm down!'

Fingers had frozen over keyboards. Curious youthful faces were turned towards us: James was a popular boss.

'You knew her bedroom is purple because you've been sleeping with her, haven't you? You've been sleeping with my client!'

'No, look, it wasn't like that.'

'No, you look. Look at this purple and tell me you've never seen it before.' I pulled the paint sample from my purse and unscrewed the lid. Dark and liquidly sinister, I waved it dangerously close to his computer.

'Okay, okay, I'm sorry. Please – calm down and let me tell you.' By now his dark brown eyes were wide with panic.

The whole office had fallen silent, but I saw that not everyone was watching us. Instead, some of them had turned to the far side of the room, as Rebecca stood and began heading our way. I realised most of them knew she had a part in this drama. And what about Rebecca? Was she half expecting this to happen? There I was, a total mess inside and out, and she appeared to be perfectly composed.

She came closer and I caught the eye contact between her and James. He had now turned paler than I'd ever seen, including the time he got food poisoning in Turkey and couldn't stand for three days. As she walked behind the desks of her co-workers, most of them didn't seem to know whether to freeze or flee.

'Look,' she said, 'let's not do this here.' Not a blonde hair was out of place.

'Where would you rather *do it*?' I snapped back, but my voice was quivering. 'Your bedroom? With my husband?'

James reached for me again, but seemed to change his mind and let his hand drop. 'I know you're furious right now, but it was just one stupid mistake in Vegas,' he said quietly.

'I don't believe you! You've been in her bedroom!' I was looking wildly from one to the other, sick with the thought of them wrapped around each other.

'Well, actually,' Rebecca had the nerve to put her hand on his arm, 'it's probably best that you know, Grace. It wasn't a mistake.' She glanced at me and I noticed for the first time an intense determination in her face. 'I'm so sorry, we didn't plan it this way. It happened after I hired you. But we can't help how we feel.' In her strappy beige sandals she was nearly as tall as James, and she barely needed to lift her pointy little chin upwards to gaze at my husband adoringly. 'The thing is, I care about you and I want to be with you.'

A collective gasp flew round the office, almost loud enough to drown my yelp of pain. I could sense the techie crowd reaching for their phones to post *Wild and crazy work love triangle* on their Facebook pages. I felt like I'd been whacked in the ribs with a cricket bat, but I registered through my tears that James was shaking his head in defeat. The little pot slipped from my fingers before I could think of throwing paint in their faces. Instead, it added a permanent souvenir of the demise of my marriage to the carpet and his Hush Puppies. Rebecca sidestepped smartly and her sexy sandals escaped the shower. Too bad.

Failing entirely to live up to my name, I turned and fled with as much poise as a double-decker London bus.

~~~

We spent the next two days in an ugly blur of sobbing, shouting, and silence. Not all the tears were mine: James followed me straight home and begged me to hear his side of the story. I heard but I didn't listen and I certainly didn't believe his lame attempts to blame his cheating on a drunken night of clubbing at the conference in Las Vegas. Did he really think I was that gullible?

He tiptoed around me for the first evening, then slept in our guest room and left early the next day. That was worse than the awkwardness of him being in the apartment: I knew he was going to see Rebecca and I was tormented by the thought. I wasn't even sure he'd come home again. But he did, to find me curled up on the sofa with a blanket, in pointed denial of the California sunshine outside.

'Will you please talk to me?' He approached hesitantly. 'I know this was really, really stupid but I need to tell you my side of things.'

'You mean you've got something original to say?

Because up to this point, it's all looking like one big cliché to me. You cheated, you got caught, you're a lying bastard.'

He sat down at the other end of our Ikea sofa and I immediately tucked my legs under me, as if it would burn me to touch him. 'Grace, I didn't lie to you, I was trying to tell you!'

'Well, you didn't try very hard.' I could feel my eyes welling up yet again.

'Look, ever since I got back, I've been trying to get you to sit down.' He did at least have the decency to look distraught. 'But you've been so caught up in your business recently – there wasn't a good moment.'

He was staring at me intently and I could see the beginning of tears in his own eyes. He clearly hadn't shaved that morning and his shirt was even more of a crumpled disaster than usual.

'Well, excuse me for turning my back for five minutes to try and make some money.' I was firmly on the defensive, one hundred per cent the injured party. 'And in case you hadn't noticed, I was slaving away to finish a project for the woman you're sleeping with!'

'I'm not sleeping with her. It was just one time. One stupid bloody time. I'm so sorry.'

'I don't believe you. You knew about that goddamn purple wall.' I was looking around wildly, seeking my escape route. I didn't want to be in the same room with him.

'All right, so I happened to see her bedroom! That doesn't mean anything.'

'No, it means everything.' I was sobbing now. 'It means I'll never trust you again.'

I wish I'd had the panache to storm out of our apartment in an expensive cloud of Chanel perfume. I wish I'd owned a Louis Vuitton bag to grab on my way to check into a luxury hotel, where I'd instigate a passionate revenge fling with a nineteen-year-old bellboy. Unfortunately, I clambered off the sofa with pins and needles in my legs and tripped over my blankie instead. Then I trailed soggy tissues across the floor and locked myself in the bathroom, where my only company was a dog-eared copy of *National Geographic*.

I had followed my British husband – and his job – from London to California, but my own attempt at the American dream had flopped. I'd been working crazily, had failed to see my marriage falling apart, and felt like a total fool.

I certainly couldn't afford to kick James out and stay in our apartment on my own. My so-called business was barely breathing. I had no idea how many months or years of scraping by might be ahead of me, if I attempted to build a list of design clients who weren't going to thank me by stealing my husband. Did I have the energy to move out, find a job, and rebuild my life in the fast-moving world of Silicon Valley? What the heck was I doing in this country, anyway? All I wanted was to crawl under the bed covers and hide, preferably with a packet of imported Cadbury's biscuits.

In the small, mocking hours of the next morning, I found myself unearthing a suitcase from the closet. With safety, seclusion and comfort food as my primary motives, I booked a flight home to England.

Chapter 2

'Quick! Hop in before they shoot us!' Jem released me from a bear hug and started trying to stuff my suitcase into the boot of her Mini.

Despite my fatigue, I smiled. My best friend since university, now my brother's wife, she'd come to a halt at a jaunty and probably illegal angle by the arrivals building of Heathrow Terminal Three. We were already drawing beady looks from the police officers patrolling the area. I told her that she and six-month-old baby Sebastian presented minimal threat to Queen and country.

'You wait until he wakes up,' she replied ominously. 'His screams could bring down the government.'

After my long flight, seeing Jem spring from her car was the boost I needed. I knew she wasn't finding motherhood easy, but her spirit was clearly alive and well. One of the reasons I adore Jem is her optimism, which, frankly, I lack.

'I bet you're tired so we'll go straight home. Okay?' She still had one eye on the nearest policeman and gave him a coy wave.

'Perfect. Thanks for coming – the Tube might have been the end of me.'

Every time I arrive back in London, I wonder what kind of impression England makes on new visitors. From the air, the countryside looks so green and peaceful, with its patchwork of hedges, fields and winding rivers. Then, you come down to earth with a bump amidst the bedlam of Heathrow Airport. Today, we had performed nauseating circles above Essex waiting to land, then lurked for twenty minutes on a taxiway until another aircraft departed and made room for us to park. When released from our tin-can prison, there was a hike of about a mile through the terminal building. My reward at passport control was a scrum similar to the first day of the Harrods sale, only without the designer goodies. By some miracle, I was reunited with my suitcase and thanked the baggage gods that, unlike last time, my underwear had not spilled over the reclaim belt in a Lycra impression of road kill.

'Nope, won't fit.' Jem was defeated in her attempts to shoehorn my bag into the small boot, but got away with stashing it on the back seat beside the sleeping tyrant. And then we were off, Jem piloting the Mini fearlessly through the airport maze. She seemed able to carry on a conversation directed at me, the baby and London's aggressive drivers in equal measures.

'How was the flight? Did you sleep?' she asked, making an X-rated gesture at a double-decker bus.

'A bit.'

I was looking out of the window. Even at the best of times, I found coming back to London after being in the US a bit of a shock.

Everything looked incredibly familiar and yet surreal, like watching a favourite TV show for ages, then finally getting to visit the set. We were on the wrong side of the road, of course, traffic was brutal, and hazards like zebra crossings, mini roundabouts and speed cameras littered our path. Even though it was June, definitely one of the best times to visit Britain, the sky was gloomy and so were the faces I saw on the streets. My mood was equally low. I had left my husband and bundled myself onto a plane without any clear idea of what to do next. Now, I was technically home, but it didn't feel like it.

'Your hair's longer. Suits you. Damn, who put that camera there?' She had just steered the Mini up a bus lane in Hounslow and probably had her number plate snapped.

'Uh-huh.' I knew she was just being kind. Jem is one quarter Pakistani and has the most beautiful, sleek dark hair I've ever seen. Mine, on the other hand, is mousy and goes limp at the first sign of trouble. If Jem had noticed my red eyes too, she didn't say anything. Normally hazel, they're my favourite feature, but lack of sleep and more or less constant sobbing had left them puffy and dull.

I felt grubby, too, from the long overnight flight, where I'd folded myself into the window seat and tried to avoid all conversation with the older couple next to me. I don't know if they were curious that I'd cried for an hour after we left San Francisco, and then some more as we flew over the Houses of Parliament and up the Thames to Richmond, but they hadn't pried.

As for Jem, I had emailed her with just a little of what had happened and, bless her, she stuck to small talk as we drove to the flat she and my brother owned in Ealing. She entertained me with Sebastian's little ways, including his liking of outings by car, bus or train. Only when still was he prone to vigorous exercising of his lungs.

'And Harry's fine, just very busy at work,' Jem said, as the houses lining our route changed from totally depressing to only slightly grungy. I couldn't help mentally comparing the grey streets and kebab shops with the sunny tree-lined avenues of Menlo Park.

'He's in Aberdeen for a few days,' she continued. 'I should be irritated at him leaving me with Seb but really, I haven't got a leg to stand on. We're reliant on his income now.'

I nodded. She was on maternity leave from her job in human resources and I knew she was wondering whether to go back to work at all.

~~~

How could this worn, sagging sofa be so comfortable? I must have dozed off for a few minutes as I woke to find Jem placing mugs of tea and a plate of chocolate Hobnobs in front of us. I doubt she intended it as a gesture of sisterhood and solidarity, but for me it was the first sign of hope in several days. I couldn't actually remember when I had last eaten.

My brother and Jem had managed to scramble onto the London property ladder with a top-floor Edwardian flat. Although small and not furnished in the latest style, it had a bay-windowed lounge and other original features which would trigger heart palpitations in most Californian designers. It smelled of pine floors and clean washing. I was glad to be there.

Jem slurped her tea slightly and planted her feet in their striped socks on the coffee table.

'Well then,' she said, tilting her head in my direction and frowning. 'Want to spill the beans?'

Tongue-tied, I nibbled on my biscuit and wondered if dunking it would cause it to disintegrate. Jem knew me well enough to keep quiet and wait.

'One minute we seemed fine ...' I said awkwardly, 'and the next I found out he's in love with someone else.'

'And she's someone he works with?' Jem pursed her lips and I suspected she was choosing her words carefully. She'd known James almost as long as she'd known me and had always liked him. We sometimes compared notes on our husbands and although I knew my brother won for charisma and romantic gestures, there was a thoughtfulness about James that was hard to beat. His everyday willingness to do the washing up and put laundry away – things that were invisible to Harry unless Jem nagged him – had meant more to me than Friday night flowers.

'Not only does he work with her,' I swallowed and bit my lip, 'but she was basically my only good decorating client. I was doing her bedroom.'

'Wow. That's horrible. What can she have been thinking?'

'I'm more gutted by what James was thinking.' The chocolate biscuits were disappearing remarkably fast. Surely I hadn't eaten all those? Regardless, I took another: this was a crisis and everyone knows you don't count calories in the middle of a crisis. 'It's just so humiliating. I'm pretty sure they were doing it in that bedroom. I was working so hard to make it beautiful.'

'Oh, Grace, I'm sorry,' Jem said.

I could tell she was upset on my behalf and I loved her
for that. Without doubt, she's the non-existent sister I would
have liked as a teenager. Only now, it's better, because we
share gossip and nail varnish without stealing each other's
boyfriends and losing borrowed shoes at parties.

'Were there ... other problems?' she asked.

'I don't know.' I chewed my lip. 'We've definitely been
less patient with each other, recently. Less affectionate.
Maybe I wasn't making enough effort. Huh. Easy to be wise
now.'

'It's rough on your relationship, when you're both
running on the hamster wheel.' Jem gave me a worried
smile.

'And seeing him with – her –' I gulped, 'makes me think
I've really let myself go.'

'Tosh,' said my sister-in-law immediately.

But Jem hadn't met the other woman and I was busy
comparing myself unfavourably. At five feet four, I would
never be willowy like Rebecca, and although I'd lost weight
recently, none of it seemed to have gone from around my
hips. Having always been more interested in home
accessories than fashion, I had to admit that in the last
couple of years my wardrobe had become especially boring.
I lived in black jeans and my shoes were all practical, with
nothing even half as sexy as the sandals Rebecca had been
wearing on the fateful purple paint day. Combine all this
with limp hair and a totally deflated ego, and I knew I wasn't
exactly alluring to come home to.

'You haven't let yourself go.' Jem shook her head
fiercely. 'And even if you had, I don't think James would
cheat just because of that. You two were a team.'

I wriggled my shoulders in the hope that the stubborn
knots caused by tension and cattle-class travel would melt.
'Well,' I said, 'I mucked up somewhere.'

'What will you do now?' she asked.

'I dunno. I really don't know.' I sighed. 'I told James I wanted to spend time alone in England and think things through. Frankly, I was working so hard and the business was in such a mess, I'd love to just have a break.'

'You walked away from your design work too?' Jem seemed surprised.

'I asked another designer to finish off a couple of things for me. But I literally had almost no clients so there wasn't much to hand over.' If I was honest, one reason the thing with Rebecca hurt so much was because she'd walloped me not just as a wife but as a professional too. She'd been the only glimmer that clients liked my work and that my business could succeed.

'And, um, where will you stay?' Jem wasn't saying what she meant. Three adults and a baby in a flat this size would be impossible. She and Harry didn't have space for a dishwasher and Sebastian's room was smaller than the walk-in closet I'd taken for granted in California. There was no dining room or even a dining table, and the sofa bed was the only option for guests.

'Don't worry, not here. At least, not after tonight.'

'So you'll go to your parents?'

This made me screw up my nose. 'Yikes, I don't think that would work.'

I have a cautiously affectionate relationship with my family and I know they love me from top to toe. But we never discuss tricky issues or emotional stuff. I hadn't even told them I was flying back, let alone what had happened with James. And, since retiring, my parents had developed some quirky habits that would drive me round the twist.

'In any case,' I added, 'there's something so predictable about women running home to their mothers.' I gave a small smile. 'I'd rather avoid becoming a total cliché.'

Jem looked at her watch and got to her feet reluctantly. 'I need to give Seb his feed. The bottle steriliser is broken so that's a whole extra hassle.'

I followed her through to the postage stamp kitchen,

which, due to the influx of baby paraphernalia, now seemed even more cramped than before.

'So where, then?' She returned to our previous topic as she juggled bottles and gadgets in the microwave. I hadn't been around babies much and James and I had talked in only vague terms about a family of our own. Sebastian hadn't been any trouble so far, but the amount of kit he required looked pretty daunting.

'Dunno.' I shrugged. 'I just want to go somewhere very quiet, very English, and hide for a while. The Cotswolds, maybe?' I fancied the poetic imagery of heartbreak under a thatched roof, perhaps including country pursuits like long misty walks and picking flowers. To be totally upfront, the scenes inside my head bore a distinct resemblance to a Jane Austen novel.

'The Cotswolds are pretty. Would cost you an arm and a leg, though.' Jem was now doing something with powdered baby milk. Breast-feeding had not gone well for her and for sanity's sake, she'd eventually given up. 'And presumably, your mum and dad are going to want to see you.'

'True.' I put the kettle on, thinking another cup of tea might keep me awake until we ate dinner. 'But I can hardly pick Norfolk and not stay with them. They'd be hurt.'

Meanwhile, sounds like a mewing kitten were reaching the kitchen. I was about to ask if they'd adopted a cat, when I realised I was hearing the first stirrings of a hungry baby.

'And I'd be hurt 'cause it wouldn't be so easy to meet up for calorific treats.' She squeezed my arm. We'd missed each other and our afternoon tea ritual while I'd been in San Francisco. Earl Grey with our husbands just couldn't compete with dainty cucumber sandwiches, or scones topped with jam and cream, and girl talk. 'So that's easy,' she continued. 'Just find a hotel halfway between here and Norfolk.'

The mewing kitten had turned into a screeching hyena. Jem scooped up some baby gear and headed out of the kitchen.

~~~

Later, after we'd microwaved a Tesco's lasagne and I had unwisely downed my share of a bottle from Harry's wine collection, I asked for a map. This sparked a hunt down the sides of the bookcases, during which we found a baby rattle and a dusty relic that had started life as a sock. Eventually, we unearthed an out-of-date road atlas. It seemed the straight line from my parent's home to Ealing ran just east of Cambridge.

'There you go.' Jem stabbed an unsteady finger at the page. 'That's halfway. Go and lick your wounds there.'

'Where?' I hoped it was only jet lag that was making the map so fuzzy.

'I dunno, it's upside down. Under my finger.' We had clearly overdone the Pinot Noir as both of us were struggling with the small font.

'Saffron Sheeping?' I asked.

I wasn't sure I wanted a load of smelly sheep in my scenic Jane Austen fields. But the area around Cambridge was worth considering: we'd lived in the city when I was young and I remembered it was pleasant enough. Presumably, it was also less costly for visitors than the picture-perfect Cotswolds.

'No, wait, it's Saffron Sleeping.' She peered at it and I'm sure her eyes crossed slightly.

'That sounds better. Maybe if I sleep for long enough, I'll wake up and find this is all a horrible dream.'

'Yeah,' she agreed. 'And I can bring Seb up there to visit. He might learn how to go through the night without terrorising me every three hours. We should Google it, see what it's like.'

We failed completely to find Saffron Sleeping on the internet and I assumed that was the end of the idea. Jem, however, consulted the map again, which took a couple of minutes as she still had it the wrong way up and began her quest in Cornwall. 'Hah!' she announced. 'It's not *Sleeping*, it's *Sweeting*!'

'What?' I was digging through my suitcase, wondering if my frenzied packing had included anything that could pass as pyjamas. It was a good job Harry was away, as it seemed I might have to sleep in an Alcatraz T-shirt and my knickers.

'We had it wrong, it's Saffron *Sweeting*. Well, that's an excellent omen,' she declared.

One thing I find amusing about Jem is her belief in omens, horoscopes and reading tea leaves. 'It is?' I yawned back, starting to arrange pillows on the sofa.

'Grace, it's perfect! It's a village named after sugar. Definitely give it a try. After all,' she beamed at me, 'how bad can it be?'

Chapter 3

It's a good thing Jem was no longer breast-feeding, as our red wine consumption that evening would probably have got Sebastian drunk too.

However, by ten the next morning, we were only slightly hung-over as she drove me to a local car rental office. Squeezed between a launderette and a branch of Barclays bank, they appeared to have just three cars outside. Sure enough, I got the midget-sized jaunty yellow one. Never mind: it would use less petrol and inflict less collateral damage whenever I tried to park it.

'Are you okay?' Jem looked anxiously at my pale face as I heaved my suitcase from her Mini.

'Yes, I think so.' I tried to keep my voice brave and normal. 'Seeing you has helped no end.' I wasn't generous enough to include Sebastian in this compliment. He was, of course, now sleeping angelically in his car seat, recovering from his nocturnal wailing which had roused Jem multiple times. I had been glad of my freebie airline earplugs and had stayed welded to the sofa bed.

'I'm still not quite sure what the plan is,' Jem said, as we made a cursory attempt to check my car for scratches.

Our tipsy map reading of the night before had degenerated into finding English villages with silly names. We'd started with Six Mile Bottom and progressed via Ugley to Piddletrenthide.

'Well,' I smiled, 'Bacon End was tempting, but on balance I think Saffron Sweeting just has the edge.'

'Really? You're actually heading for a place you've never been? I was just mucking around last night, you know.'

'It's okay, I'm pulling your leg. I think I'll drive up through Cambridgeshire on the quieter roads, and maybe stop for a look at some of the villages. If they're all horrible, I'll swallow my pride and call my mother.'

Jem handed me last night's road atlas and a Kit Kat. 'Okay, well, phone me, wherever you decide. And let me know when you're ready to meet for afternoon tea.'

'Absolutely. Say hi to Harry.' I leaned into her car and gave Seb a parting wave. Jem gave me another of her big hugs and I squeezed her back in silent thanks.

~~~

I don't believe in fate, or omens, but I admit that sometimes life moves in mysterious ways. Despite our antics of the previous evening, I had no intention of spending the night anywhere with a wacky name. Things didn't quite work out like that, though.

The London skies had been smoggy and oppressive, but as I turned off the M25 to head north, the sun came out and I could appreciate the green countryside. At Bishops Stortford, I left the motorway and continued on the old Cambridge road. The gentle winding from village to village was a soothing change of pace. Uneven hedges and lush fields lined the road, a few rabbits were playing on the verge, and I passed handmade signs including *Pick Your Own Strawberries* and *Village Fête Saturday*.

By the time I reached Saffron Walden, I was ready for a break and some elevenses. I already knew the bustling market town was named from growing the saffron crocus, which yielded an expensive yellow dye. In our research the previous night, Jem and I had learned that Saffron Walden's success had overshadowed Saffron Sweeting's earlier fame. By the seventeenth century, the newcomer was dominant while Saffron Sweeting languished. I'm pretty sure yellow dye is no longer a big part of Saffron Walden's economy, but it still enjoys a cheerful affluence.

Having inched my appropriately saffron-coloured vehicle into a parking space, my first purchase was a new phone. My US cell phone always refused to work in England and, in any case, a different number would mean James couldn't call. To be honest, I desperately wanted to know if he had tried to reach me, but I squashed that thought and headed for the tourist information office. There, I armed myself with *Things to Do in East Anglia* and some leaflets on local bed and breakfasts. These I took to a cafe, to ponder my next move.

'What would you like, love?' The waitress greeted me as she cleared my table of the debris from previous occupants.

I ordered a pot of tea and a sausage roll. The latter wasn't strictly necessary, but the stress of my business had meant I'd skipped too many meals in recent months, and since discovering James's affair I seemed to have lost my appetite completely. If I was going to keep morale up, I'd better eat. The tea came immediately, strong and hot. As she returned with my food, the waitress spotted the hotel information.

'You're visiting, then?' She put down a fork wrapped in a paper napkin.

'Yes ...' I wasn't about to share my circumstances. 'Just looking for a place to stay for a few days. Somewhere near Cambridge, maybe.'

'Ah, you're visiting the colleges. Lovely.' She'd made an assumption, but it didn't matter. 'You might look at the Red Lion in Whittlesford. My friend runs it and it's very good.'

'Thanks.' My attention was on the tempting sausage roll. Sure enough, moist, spicy sausage meat was wrapped in warm, golden pastry which was flaky on the outside but gooey on the inside. Heaven. The tea was also reviving my spirits. We Brits don't really do therapy; we just put the kettle on. I turned my thoughts back to my pile of literature. There it was: a leaflet for the inn she'd mentioned.

The Red Lion was founded as a priory in the thirteenth century, I read. *Rooms are comfortably furnished and often have character features such as low-level beams and wonky floors.* Yes, they actually said 'wonky'. *Eight miles south of Cambridge, Whittlesford is a classic English village where cricket is played regularly on the green. The*

Red Lion offers a range of home-cooked food, but you may also enjoy the Tickell Arms and the Bees in the Wall.

Jem would definitely get a kick out of pub names like that. I studied the pictures and decided the Red Lion was perfect. I would call them from my car.

The man who answered their phone, however, had other ideas. 'Sorry, we're fully booked. There's an air show at Duxford.'

'Oh.' Nerdy plane-spotters had trampled all over my cricket-gazing fantasy. I was deeply disappointed.

'But I can recommend my cousin's bed and breakfast. Oak House. She's just a few miles outside Cambridge, on the way to Newmarket.'

'Er, right.' Did everyone in the English hospitality industry know each other?

'She does a first class breakfast. I can give you her number.'

Well, I thought, for top notch bacon and eggs it might be worth a try, especially to delay facing the music with my parents. 'What village is that?'

'Saffron Sweeting. Do you know it?'

I didn't need Jem here to proclaim that this coincidence was a huge omen.

'No,' I told him, 'but I think I'm about to.'

~~~

It was just after lunch time when I drove into Saffron Sweeting, a little early for checking in, but I'd phoned ahead and been told to come on over. Oak House was a wide, cream-painted building, with pairs of latticed windows symmetrically placed each side of the front door. I couldn't tell how old it was, but the front wall bulged a little and was restrained by cross-shaped wall ties. Moss covered the patchwork tiles of the roof, which sloped at a friendly angle over the eaves. As I got out of my car, I caught a summery, floral scent, possibly from the clematis which was climbing around the front door. To the side of the house was an impressive tree – undoubtedly the oak – and in the garden I glimpsed a handful of extremely plump chickens.

'You made it! Come in, dear, come in!'

The owner of Oak House appeared to be in her mid fifties. She had shoulder-length grey hair pulled back by a wide band, and a rosy complexion. I thought it was highly promising that she was wearing an apron in the early afternoon.

'Did you drive far? Your room's all ready.' She didn't pause to allow me to say anything, so I lugged my suitcase into the large hall and looked around discreetly. The old house had a solid, comforting feel. A heavy wooden staircase was in front of me, and to one side a grandfather clock ticked solemnly. Through an open doorway, I could see a formal sitting room. From here, a tortoiseshell cat dashed across the black and white tiles of the hall, then disappeared. Best of all, my nostrils detected both furniture polish and baking cookies. This place certainly had reassuring potential for the next forty-eight hours.

'I'm Lorraine,' she beamed at me now, offering me the visitors' book to sign.

'Grace Palmer,' I replied, although I think she already knew that from the phone call.

'I'm glad you're here, Grace. I hope you'll have a wonderful stay with us.'

I was grateful she didn't ask what brought me to the village. I needed to practise my explanation, before it was ready for general consumption.

Instead, she continued in a business-like manner, 'What time would you like breakfast in the morning? Is between eight and nine all right?'

'Fine, yes, thanks.' I made a mental note to set my alarm clock, as jet lag was always worse for me the second night than the first.

'Righty-ho. Lovely. Let's go on up.'

By American standards, my room was not luxurious.

The bed was a small double which sagged alarmingly when I sat on it, and there was no sign of a television or radio. The en-suite bathroom was absolutely minuscule: I had to squeeze around the door and then found it necessary to sit side-saddle on the toilet. However, the bedroom had a pretty view of a field behind the house and the decor wasn't bad, especially if Lorraine had been aiming for a floral English look. I was pleased to discover a tin of home-made shortbread on the tea tray, which explained the enticing aroma downstairs.

Even more delightful was the basket of magazines in the corner, including copies of *Ideal Home* and *Country Living*. I had left California in too much of a hurry to bring any of my precious design magazines and I was already regretting it. Later, I would probably curl up in bed and mentally redecorate the room, weighing the merits of Laura Ashley compared with Cath Kidston.

For now, though, I decided a walk around the village would be a good plan. I had booked into Oak House for two nights without any idea what Saffron Sweeting looked like. This seemed a good time to find out.

I was pleasantly surprised to discover that Saffron Sweeting, though not postcard pretty, wouldn't bring shame on any tourist brochure. As I walked from Oak House towards what looked like the village centre, I passed a number of attractive cottages and a few larger, detached homes, before coming to a crossroads by a small pond. Here, the village sign, depicting agricultural activity, was set proudly into a millstone. My arrival caused noisy excitement amongst the resident ducks, who made a fuss in anticipation of food. Some offended waddling and tail-shaking then followed, when it became apparent I had nothing to offer.

To my left, I spotted a medieval-looking church a short way up a slight hill, complete with yew trees at its gate. Most of Cambridgeshire is pancake flat, so a hill of any size is a big deal. I chose instead to carry on, past what I assumed was the vicarage, curiously located next door to a pub, The

Plough. Surprisingly, I found I was hungry again, but, like the ducks, I was out of luck, as the pub was closed for the hours between lunch and evening. I passed a couple of gorgeous pint-sized cottages, where pink hollyhocks bloomed beside stone front steps, but couldn't see any sign of a cafe or food shop.

Despite the pleasantness of the street, the whole village seemed strangely quiet, with just the occasional cooing of a wood pigeon. Either Saffron Sweeting was enjoying a Mediterranean-style siesta, or the economy was hurting. Spotting a woman walking her dog, I called out to her.

'Excuse me – is there anywhere I can buy something to eat?'

She looked at her watch, as her golden Labrador came to greet me and shove its nose in unwelcome places.

'Well,' she replied, 'the bakery should still be open.' She gestured to a road on my right. 'Otherwise, the post office is your only option.'

'Thanks,' I said, untangling myself from the Labrador's lead and crossing the street briskly to turn in the direction she'd pointed. I'd never heard of post offices serving lunch before and wasn't going to explore that suggestion today.

This new road yielded a small bank on the corner, which, from the sign advising all customers to use the Newmarket branch, seemed to be completely closed. Next to that was an adorable terracotta-coloured thatched cottage, declaring itself to be the Old Forge, and then a tiny estate agency. I peeked in the window just long enough to ascertain that prices here were as crazy as in the Bay Area, but presumably without the luxury of two-car garages and walk-in closets.

And then, opposite, I spied a brick shop with a big bay window and a faded *Sweeting Bakery* sign above the door. I wondered how a village this size, which clearly wasn't thriving like Saffron Walden, could sustain such a business. Nonetheless, here it was and that was fine by me.

Five minutes later, I sank onto the bench by the duck

pond, with a ham sandwich for me and a loaf of yesterday's bread for the ducks. They showed their appreciation with a riot of quacking and flapping, during which the prettiest one narrowly missed pooping on my foot. I resisted the temptation to talk to them, noting the irony of my transformation from happily married Californian entrepreneur to crazy lady scoffing carbs and making friends with birds.

Suddenly, I felt really alone and questioned whether I was coming unhinged. Not wanting to be in the same room as James was one thing, but fleeing to a random English village was surely a little weird. In my shock and confusion over my husband's affair, I had put my hands over my ears and galloped away from my problems. Now, I had temporarily stopped running, but the pain had pursued me and seemed to be settling itself firmly on my shoulders.

For the first time since discovering I was the third person on a bicycle made for two, I had an urge to hear my mother's voice. I reached into my bag and pulled out my new phone.

'637939.' My father followed the old-fashioned convention of answering with their number.

'Hi, dad, it's me.' My voice was far stronger than I felt.

'Gracie! Hello, pet!'

'How's things?' This was my standard greeting, whether five thousand miles away or fifty.

'Oh, we're grand. And you? It's early, isn't it?' My dad has a mathematical mind and he was correct: it wasn't yet seven in California. Or did he have an inkling that I was no longer in that time zone?

'Well, um, yes, that's why I'm phoning. Is mum around?'

'Yes, hang on, I'll get her. NOR-AH!'

I instinctively held the phone away from my ear before this shout, aimed at my mother whose hearing is much better than dad realises. He is getting pretty deaf himself and tends to assume everyone else needs a higher volume too. Likewise, I heard his barely concealed announcement that it was me on the phone.

'Hello, poppet!' My mother sounded her usual chirpy self.

I gulped, emotion welling up as the reality of the last five days infiltrated my armour of denial. I was determined not to start crying; or at least, not yet. I looked up instead at the horse chestnut tree which shaded the bench and tried to focus on the barely-formed little fruits.

'Hi, mum.' Good, my tone was reasonably steady.

'Are you in England?' She came straight to the point.

'Yeah.' The ducks were looking for second helpings, eyeing my barely touched sandwich. I took a long breath. 'You know I'm here?'

'Yes, love, we knew you were on your way. James phoned.'

I hadn't thought of that. 'Uh, did he?'

What had he told them? Surely not: *I'm a lying scum bag who cheated on your daughter and she's left me.* They had been so thrilled when James and I got married, and as far as I was aware, they hadn't changed their minds since.

'That's right. Yesterday. He asked if you'd arrived.'

Ouch. 'Really?' My mind was racing, trying to deal with a conversation that had more spin on it than a first serve at Wimbledon.

'He said you were feeling a bit down and you thought England might cheer you up. Lovely idea, June's such a nice month.'

My mouth was dry. 'Was that all he said?'

'Oh, and that he's sorry he couldn't come on the same flight as you, but he's managed to finish things at work now. He said he'll be arriving here the day after tomorrow.'

Chapter 4

I swear I hadn't meant to kick that poor duck. I'm not an animal abuser or anything sinister. It's just that I sprang to my feet when my mum dropped this bombshell, and I hadn't realised a female duck was pecking about under the bench, hoping to find fallen morsels. She gave an outraged squawk, shook herself from beak to webbed feet, and huffed her way back to the safety of the pond. I kept an eye on her for a few minutes and am pretty sure no lasting damage was done.

I finished the conversation with my mum as quickly as I could, still not prepared to tell her the full story. Instead, I told a white lie and implied I was still in London. I hinted that I wanted a couple more days to catch up with Jem and Harry, plus time for some shopping, before I headed to sleepy Norfolk. Mum seemed to accept this, or, if she did smell a rat, she was diplomatic enough to say nothing. I knew I'd have to fill my parents in soon, but meantime I had a bigger problem on my hands: I desperately wanted to stop James coming.

I looked at my watch: still early in California, but it was hardly my problem if I woke him up. A kick in the gut reminded me he might not even be at home, but curled up instead in the purple love nest with Rebecca. With tears in my eyes, I punched out his number, only to hang up immediately as I realised I didn't want him knowing how to reach me.

Sighing, I walked the few minutes back to the village and found a phone box near the post office. It was the traditional kind, red with little windows, which at one time had been sentenced to death by British Telecom. Clearly, this one had been spared. I squeezed inside, lined up a stack of coins, and took a deep breath.

'It's me,' I said when James answered, hoping he wouldn't have to ask who *me* was.

'Grace! Hi!'

Did he sound pleased? I wasn't sure. He didn't sound especially sleepy, but nor did I get the sense I'd interrupted anything.

'Um, how are you?' James adjusted his voice to be more neutral.

'I'm okay,' I replied. A huge pause followed. I had absolutely no idea what to say next and in any case was fighting a lump the size of Windsor Castle in my throat.

'I'm glad you called. I've been worried about you,' he said.

You weren't worried about me when you screwed Rebecca, I thought bitterly. Aloud, I managed a more dignified, 'I told you, I just need some time to think.'

'I spoke to your mum. I told her I'm coming over.'

'I know. Please don't.'

'But Gruff, look, I can't just sit here and do nothing. I need to talk to you.'

Did he realise he'd just called me by the pet name only he used?

We'd met in my first term at Durham, accidentally bumping trays in the canteen one evening. James seemed shy and his attempts at flirting were dismal, but Jem had taken one look at my blushing face and had moved away to sit with the girls of the college rowing team. During a drunken late-night philosophy session with friends, we'd created nicknames for each other based on characters in children's books. Jemima was unlucky – she got lumbered with Puddle-Duck. I, apparently, resembled a Gruffalo. Fourteen years later, James still called me the same thing, but he never embarrassed me with it in public.

'We're talking now, aren't we?' I fed the phone a few more fifty pence pieces.

'Yes, but we haven't … I mean I haven't explained. I want to make it up to you.'

White-hot pain rushed into my head. I couldn't believe he was treating his affair so lightly. 'What? You can't just make it up to me! You slept with someone else.' I was gripping the phone so tightly, my fingers were cramping. 'It's not like forgetting a birthday or something.'

'Please ... I'm *so* sorry. I thought – well, if I came over, we could spend some time together and work this out.'

'Smooth it over and forget it? Not likely,' I snapped back. 'Anyway, there's no point in you coming. I'm not staying with mum and dad.'

'Oh. You're in London, then?'

'No. I'm not telling you where I am. I want to be on my own for a bit.' My voice was jerky from tears now. 'Can't you understand that?'

He seemed to consider this. 'Okay,' he sighed. 'If you need space, I owe you that. But please, don't shut me out. When you're ready to talk, I'll come.'

'All right,' I said. The phone started beeping for more money and since it had already gobbled half the daily output of the Royal Mint, I decided our conversation was over. Just as I hung up, I think I heard him say *I love you*, but I'm not sure.

~~~

When characters in books say they cried themselves to sleep, I am sceptical. That night, I drenched several tissues, gave myself the hiccups and emptied the complimentary tin of shortbread. Sleep, however, was certainly not on the agenda, at least not until long after the Saffron Sweeting church clock had chimed two.

Roused rudely by my alarm clock, I wondered how on earth I could face Lorraine's famous breakfast. However, I reckoned without the assistance of the tiny shower, which was pleasantly hot for the first four minutes and then turned abruptly icy while I still had conditioner in my hair. I emerged brutally lucid, realising why some eighty-year-olds are so fanatical about swimming in the sea daily. My thoughts were clearer, my skin was glowing and my appetite wasn't too shabby, either.

Lorraine was upbeat as she brought me some orange juice and an enormous pot of tea. I mused that being a morning person is part of the job description, if you run a bed and breakfast.

'Good morning, Grace! Did you sleep well?'

'Yes, lovely, thank you,' I lied tactfully. I also avoided mentioning my cold shower. Not the assertive choice, but, in common with many English friends, a hotel has to be absolutely terrible before I consider complaining.

'It's a lovely day for sightseeing.' Lorraine delivered toast in a silver rack and a dish of glossy marmalade.

'Yes, lovely,' I agreed lamely. I wasn't in the mood for floating past Cambridge colleges in a punt.

By the time Lorraine brought a flowered china plate boasting a pair of fried eggs, some bacon and even a famous Newmarket sausage, I had decided the risk of going to my parents was too great. I was still nervous James might turn up, and I dreaded that kind of showdown. Here in Saffron Sweeting, I felt anonymously safe. The village was quiet and attractive, and would make a restful hiding place while I attempted to get my thoughts together.

I dipped the sausage in the egg yolk and watched with satisfaction as it oozed all over my plate. At this rate, the weight I'd lost recently would go back on fast. I'd better give some thought to taking up jogging again. Not today, of course, but soon.

It seemed I was the only guest at Oak House that morning and Lorraine made a couple of other cheerful comments which were possibly intended to engage me in conversation. To discourage her, I picked up a National Trust handbook and pretended to browse as I ate.

In reality, though, I was trying to come up with a plan that went beyond visiting historic houses and their accompanying gift shops. After my conversation with James yesterday, I realised I had no strategy at all. I was completely adrift, looking at a blank sheet of paper representing the rest of my life. I was terrified: never before had I faced so many choices all at once. Sorting out my future might take more than a few days and a couple of cream teas.

My American bank account was empty, but I still had some meagre savings in England. If I was careful, I probably had enough funds to take several weeks off, but it would certainly help if I wasn't paying for bed and breakfast each night. And I had no great desire to stay at Oak House indefinitely, listening to the grandfather clock ticking my life away. Even if I didn't know which road to take, I couldn't just sit and do nothing.

Before this sliver of courage could desert me, I got to my feet and thanked Lorraine for breakfast. Squaring my shoulders, I went upstairs to grab my handbag.

~~~

Normally, I wouldn't pass a bakery without going in to lend my support to a small business. However, even after walking into Saffron Sweeting, I was still so full of breakfast that I wondered if I'd ever eat again. So I crossed the road instead to the little estate agency, announced as Hargraves & Co by dark green swirly lettering. All the houses in the window seemed to be large, expensive and for sale, not rent.

Nonetheless, I ventured inside, causing the bell attached to the door to clang loudly as I stepped down into the bright but narrow office. It was barely more than ten feet wide, although it stretched back quite a way, and three desks were huddled into the space. Only one of these desks was occupied, by a chic auburn-haired woman who was currently on the phone. She waved a hand at me without making eye contact; hesitantly, I took a seat.

'No, darling, I don't think they will,' she said into the phone, which was tucked under her chin so she could work her keyboard at the same time. 'They told me six eighty is as high as they can go. I don't think seven hundred is at all reasonable, especially given this economy.'

I eyed the large colour photograph of the featured listing on the wall next to me. It looked like a converted barn, complete with triple garage and a paddock. The asking price was well into seven figures. It was stunning, but I suspected those lofty rooms would get lonely without a massive family to fill the space.

'Their mortgage is in place – I think you should consider the offer very seriously.'

Another phone began to ring and she frowned at it. All three desks were piled high with papers.

'Okay, yes, just let me know, darling. But don't think for *too* long.' She had picked up her smartphone and her fingers were flying at the speed of a concert violinist. 'Yes, all right, I'll call you tomorrow.'

The other phone stopped ringing, but began again immediately.

'Sorry to keep you.' The estate agent flashed me a smile which lasted a tenth of a second, before propelling herself across the room on her wheeled chair to answer it. As she did so, I got a glimpse of a short skirt, shapely legs and an impressive pair of leopard print heels.

Another brief conversation followed, which of course I could hear. The caller seemed to have approval to spend four thousand a month, as long as the place was fully furnished and ready immediately.

'Right, super,' the agent finished up, twirling her shoe on the end of her foot. 'Yes, absolutely, Saturday is fine. Let me know what time.'

Finally, she stood and came towards me. She was older than me, maybe by ten years. Above the long legs were ample but undeniably attractive curves. 'Hello, I'm Amelia Hargraves. How can I help?' She held out her right hand, adorned with a large cocktail ring, to shake mine briskly.

'Hi.' I felt like an irritant in her busy morning, where time was presumably money. For such a sleepy village, this had come as a surprise. 'Sorry to bother you, but I was wondering if you have anything for short-term rental?'

'What type of property did you have in mind?' Amelia returned to her desk and consulted her computer screen.

'Er, small, just for one person. And just for a few months,' I said.

Her phone buzzed and she consulted it before turning back to me. 'Well,' she shook her head, 'there isn't much – most of the places I have are family homes. I do have a cottage in Bottisham, though.'

She thumbed through a file and passed me a flier. The photo showed a depressing looking brown house, with a car resting on bricks in the front garden.

Amelia was apparently good at reading faces and I'm sure mine had fallen.

'Do you want to be in Cambridge itself, or out here?' She was searching through another file.

'Out here, preferably,' I replied.

'Good – competition is fierce in Cambridge for short-term rentals, even though it's summer.' She pushed a wavy auburn strand behind her ear. Even if the colour had received considerable help from her hairdresser, it suited her beautifully. My own was dull and lifeless in comparison.

'Here's a garden flat in Newmarket. You'd have racehorses going past each morning, on their way to training.'

That sounded fun and the picture looked much better. Regrettably, the monthly rent was so high that I would be better off staying at Oak House.

'Thanks, but I don't think my budget can go quite that far,' I apologised.

It seemed the implications of leaving my husband were going to be economic, as well as emotional. I hadn't expected accommodation to be so scarce. Saffron Sweeting obviously wasn't bustling with activity, so who, apart from fleeing wives like me, was so keen to live here?

Amelia gave me a quizzical look. 'You're not on a relocation package, then?'

'No.' That was an odd question. 'Why?'

'Just thought I'd check. Most of the people arriving in the village are being transferred by their employers.' The phone on her desk rang but she ignored it. 'You realise we're only five miles from the Science Park?' Her tone was matter-of-fact.

'Oh, right.' I had heard of the Cambridge Science Park but didn't know much about it, other than it being an out-of-town location for technology companies.

'Yes, three American bio-tech firms moved in this spring. Cambridge is the hot place now for genetics and all that. They're bringing a lot of staff over.'

This explained why she was so busy and the high prices of the houses in the window. Perhaps I would have been better off in the postcard-perfect Cotswolds, after all.

'That's ironic. I've just come from America, but I'm not a gene scientist.' I gave a small smile.

She shrugged and turned her attention back to her computer.

'Actually, I just left my husband,' I blurted. So much for keeping a low profile.

Amelia's carefully groomed eyebrows shot up, and now I had her full attention. 'Oh, you poor darling.' She tutted and shook her head. 'That explains why you look so shell-shocked.'

'Do I?' I knew I wasn't exactly radiant, but jet lag could be blamed for that, surely.

'I'm afraid you do. I was the same, all through my divorce,' she added carelessly, as if a divorce was as troublesome as a pair of too-tight shoes. She looked at me again, and her expression softened. 'Listen,' she said, 'I'm not promising anything, but I'll keep my ears open for you. Take my card and call me in a couple of days, all right?'

~~~

I had just passed the duck pond on my way back to Oak House, when I heard a squeal of brakes. I turned around in time to see a large red estate car come hurtling down the hill from the church, and there was a horrible crunch of gears as it failed to make the left turn at the crossroads. I winced as it shot straight across the road instead, only to hit the wooden bench with a splintering bang. This was probably the only thing that prevented the car from ending up in the water with the ducks, which rose up as one in an almighty flap.

I jogged the fifty yards back to the scene – there, that counted as my exercise for the day – and saw two little boys looking out of the car's rear window with wide-eyed expressions of glee.

'Mommy!' one of them cried out. 'What did you *do*? Dad's gonna be so *mad*!'

A blonde woman clambered shakily out of the driver's seat, crying but apparently unhurt.

'Goddamn it,' she wailed. 'Which jerk came up with the idea of a stick shift?'

I detected a definite American accent.

She thumped the bonnet – now crumpled and hissing steam – with her hand. 'Can't they even make a car that works in this frickin country?'

Chapter 5

They say that misery loves company and, sure enough, it cheered me up to talk to Mary Lou while we waited for the breakdown service to come from Newmarket. Neither she nor her boys were hurt, but her pride was as dented as the car and she seemed to think this was yet another way that England was conspiring to challenge her. The family had been here only six weeks and initial excitement had given way to confusion and homesickness for Pennsylvania. I realised that although I was feeling adrift and confused, at least I hadn't wrapped my little car around a village bench.

'I had awful trouble with the gears when I was learning to drive,' I offered in support.

'Automatics are the sign of a civilised society,' she grumbled. 'Randy, quit hassling that duck!'

The younger boy seemed intent on bullying the waterfowl. Of course, with a name like that, if he was attending an English school, he was probably receiving similar grief from the other kids. The elder, quieter boy had his nose in an iPad.

'Do you need a lift somewhere?' I offered. 'I have a car at the bed and breakfast, just up there.'

She sighed. 'Thanks, that would be great. We were heading home anyways.'

I walked back to Oak House to get my car. When I returned to the duck pond, the breakdown crew had arrived and their unhurried efforts were being supervised by a small crowd, including an elderly man with a walking cane, a woman on horseback and the village postman.

After the sorry-looking tangle of red metal had been loaded and driven away, Mary Lou gave me directions to her house, just beyond the far edge of Saffron Sweeting. As we drove through the village, I realised I hadn't yet explored this far. On the right, we passed a huge, low building with a decaying roof. This, presumably, was the malt house which Jem and I had read about.

According to our internet research, nobody is sure how the village got the Sweeting part of its name, but one theory is that *steeping*, part of the malting process, got changed accidentally over time. Many villages had a malt house in the eighteenth century, supplying the needs of local publicans and home brewers. The Saffron Sweeting malt house looked as if it had received little attention since then. It had a forlorn air, which was a shame as its solemn architecture was appealing.

'So, the boys aren't in school?' I hoped I wasn't being too nosy.

'It didn't seem worth it, with just a few weeks before school gets out here. I've been trying to give them classes at home. But they're going in September, for sure ... if I don't strangle one of them before that.'

'Have you made plans for sightseeing during the summer?'

'We sure have. We've been to London, which they loved. We're going to Oxford and Bath next week. Then there's Ireland – yeah, and Paris and Amsterdam, for sure. And Italy. I gotta see Florence.'

I blinked as she rattled off these destinations, remembering that by American standards, the distances in Europe are tiny. And if they were only going to be here for a limited time, it did make sense to see as much as possible.

'Right here,' she announced. 'On the left.'

Despite the confusing instruction, I got the right house: beautiful brick, with a dark red door. It had a genteel character and a weather vane perched on the roof. There was even a dovecote in the front garden, although I didn't see any sign of occupants – probably a blessing, with Randy around.

'Wow,' I said. 'This is gorgeous.'

'I guess,' Mary Lou sighed. 'But it's only got one and a half bathrooms and I hate sharing with the boys. I miss my mud room and media room too. And the closet space sucks.'

I could imagine the acres of space she had enjoyed in Pennsylvania, and had to admit that an extra bathroom was the thing I had loved most about my California apartment.

'Okay, guys, say thanks to Grace.' The three of them climbed out of the car. As they did so, I saw net curtains twitch at the cottage opposite.

'I hope your husband isn't too cross about the accident,' I offered.

'He won't freak out. He has too much going on at work.' She shrugged. 'So, Grace, where are you headed now?'

'Well, I'm not sure. I only arrived a couple of days ago. I might go and explore a bit.'

'We appreciate the ride.' She picked up Randy's jumper, which he'd dropped carelessly. 'Hey, lots of the wives meet Tuesday lunchtimes at the pub. There's not much else to do here. You're welcome to join us.'

'Thank you, I'd like that.'

As I drove away, the irony wasn't lost on me. The first friend I'd made in Saffron Sweeting was an American.

~~~

Taking a drive around the local area did indeed seem like a good plan. I could keep my eyes open for places to rent which Amelia Hargraves might not know about.

I wasn't hungry for lunch, but I drove back into the village and walked around. Mary Lou was right – the only shops were the estate agency, the bakery, and the combined post office and general store. I stopped at the bakery for a hot chocolate before venturing to the post office, hoping to buy a map of the area.

A bell tinkled, announcing my presence as I stepped over the awkward doorstep and down into the shop. All the buildings in Saffron Sweeting seemed to be lower than the street and I wondered whether the village ever flooded. If so, the ducks would have the last laugh.

'Afternoon,' came a rough female voice from the back of the store.

'Hello.' I headed for the display of newspapers and magazines, in the hope that maps would live there too. Having a choice of one meant my quest took no time at all, and I turned to see the elderly shopkeeper watching me closely. I added some salt and vinegar crisps and a carton of Ribena to my selection while she waited to serve me, fingers tapping gently on the counter. There was no one else in the shop.

'Staying at Oak House?' she asked, peering through bi-focal glasses to ring my purchases up on an old-fashioned till. Her hands were swollen, presumably from arthritis.

'Er, yes,' I replied, taken aback that she knew this, but then realised that this was a reasonable assumption.

'American?' she sniffed.

Goodness, had my accent changed that much in four years? I'd barely said two words. Then I remembered Amelia telling me about other newcomers from across the Atlantic.

'No, um, just visiting Cambridge,' I mumbled.

'Right,' she said. 'Four eighty-eight, please.'

I paid her and made the mistake of trying to further our conversation. 'I'm glad you were open. I thought it might be half-day closing.' I knew for a fact that some English villages still picked one afternoon per week to close at lunchtime, to make up for working on Saturdays.

She folded her arms and looked at me severely. 'We're not dinosaurs here, you know. I'm open every day except Sunday. And the library has broadband internet, if you want it.'

'Great ... thanks.' I turned to go.

'And one more thing, young lady.'

That didn't sound good. My mum called me *young lady* when I was in trouble. I turned back guiltily.

'You can tell your friend she'll have to pay for that bench,' the shopkeeper said sternly. 'Saffron Sweeting won't tolerate joyriders.'

I realised she must mean Mary Lou. That news had certainly travelled fast, although 'joyrider' seemed a bit strong to describe someone who hadn't quite found second gear in time. But I just nodded meekly and made a tactical retreat from her shop.

I knew it wasn't logical to expect everyone in the village to be friendly to strangers, and I was over-sensitive at the moment in any case. I tried not to let this old lady and her spy network influence my feelings about Saffron Sweeting. However, after such a chilly conversation, I drew comfort when I returned to my car, parked outside the tiny library a few yards along the High Street. According to the posted opening hours, it did indeed offer Wi-Fi, but not on a Tuesday afternoon, Thursday morning, or any time at all on Friday.

~~~

If it hadn't been for the glass of evil-tasting dandelion and burdock, I don't think I'd have set foot over the threshold of Bury estate agency Miller & Mullet.

I had driven across to the market town of Bury St Edmunds, appreciating with prodigal eyes the lush trees, narrow roads and tiny villages of my route. Once there, I had been snared by the formal quaintness and white-aproned waitresses of Harriet's tearoom, where the promise of baked goods was too much to resist. A hot, buttery crumpet took me back to my mum's warm kitchen, homework after school, bickering with Harry about the lyrics in Freddie Mercury songs, and wet socks. I'm not sure where the wet socks came from, but that was the image I got as I bit into the crumpet and dripped butter onto my plate.

As for the drink, I wasn't even sure I liked dandelion and burdock, but I was certain it wasn't available at a San Francisco drive-through and I was determined to revel in all things English. Looking back, I believe it had fermented a little and instilled me with false confidence.

As with Hargraves & Co in Saffron Sweeting, I was the only client in Miller & Mullet. However, while Amelia seemed to work on her own, here were three young men who looked barely old enough to hold driving licences, wearing carbon copy shiny suits and predatory smiles. One of them leaped to his feet and crossed the electric blue carpet to shake my hand vigorously.

'Hello, I'm Darren, how can I exceed your property expectations today?'

Ouch. Clearly, he had just come back from sales training. I withdrew my hand and put it out of his reach.

'Well, I'm looking for somewhere to rent. Somewhere small.' I glanced at his companions who seemed nonchalant, but had the air of being ready to move in if Darren mucked things up.

'Yes, of course,' he said enthusiastically. 'How many bedrooms?'

'Oh, just one, I think.'

'Excellent, let me show you some options. I think you'll like these.' Darren bounded across the room to a sagging filing cabinet, from which he pulled a stack of property details. 'Sit down, sit down, let's see what we have.'

I quickly ruled out three houses which were too expensive, two dismal flats, and a caravan. This left a tiny box, which he proudly told me was a 'railway cottage' and a granny annexe, apparently located in 'Bury's finest avenue'.

'Let's go and see your new home!' He was on his feet, nodding encouragingly and jangling car keys.

Darren drove carelessly, but not dangerously enough for me to abandon our mission. He also used the word *excellent* at every opportunity, including for the damp, unfurnished 'railway cottage' which boasted views of both the tracks and a dual carriageway. In its pint-sized sitting room, I felt I could reach out and touch opposite walls simultaneously. Meanwhile, the kitchen was a grimy slum with an ancient boiler and electric sockets which looked like you should wear rubber boots to operate them.

Darren bounded upstairs to the *excellent* bedroom and I trudged behind. I wasn't sure there was room for a double bed in the space, and although the Victorian fireplace was a nice feature, it was also the only source of heat. With several thousand pounds and lots of imagination, the room could become a cosy nest, but in the short term, I would rather sleep in a tent.

In the bathroom, with cracked white bath, high level flush toilet and worryingly bouncy floorboards, I watched a black, hairy spider trying to hide in the overflow of the sink.

Darren, however, was beaming. 'Well,' he enquired, 'can you picture its potential?'

Yes: I pictured the bath, with me in it, crashing through the rotten floor to the kitchen below. Instead of asking him if the house came with free life insurance, I gave a polite smile. 'Of course it has great potential, for a buyer. But for a rental, I was hoping for something more welcoming.'

Darren nodded, undeterred. 'Ah, you should see York Road, then. Beautiful, very homely. Excellent avenue, very exclusive.'

I wondered where he lived, and decided it was probably with his parents in a post-war semi, somewhere on the edge of town.

We left the railway arachnids to their own entertainment and made the short journey to a suburban, tree-lined avenue dotted with detached houses. I noticed that the residents were in no hurry to take down their 'Vote Conservative' posters, even though the elections had been last month. We walked up the driveway of a mock-Tudor house, with diamond-patterned double glazing and clashing pink roses in the flower beds. Darren then led the way along a narrow path to the side of the garage.

'The grandmother died quite recently, so the owners are renting the flat out,' he explained, opening a narrow front door. 'He's a dentist, they're a lovely couple.'

I tried to look impressed, but stalled as the smell of old

lady hit me. It was part cabbage, part lavender and, I'm sorry to say, part incontinence. The studio room was a good size, but the air, combined with floral wallpaper, swirly brown carpet and pink velvet curtains, made me feel instantly nauseous. The furniture was obviously the old lady's and I winced at the thought of sleeping in her bed.

By the time Darren tried to show me the *excellent* kitchenette and bathroom, I had abandoned being polite.

His smile faltered. 'It's a beautiful street, very safe, very quiet.'

'I think I've seen enough. Thank you anyway.'

On the way back to his office, Darren talked cheerfully about the possibility of sharing with other 'young professionals'. I didn't say much, partly because I was so disheartened by the options I'd just viewed and partly because I was too scared to talk. I was worried that if I opened my mouth, the dandelion and burdock would make a bid for freedom. Darren probably wouldn't think it was excellent if I threw up all over his company car.

Chapter 6

Next morning, the dandelion nausea had subsided, but was replaced with a different headache: increasing disappointment over my marriage and fear for the future. Realising I could either stagnate sorrowfully in the lounge at Oak House and be glared at by the tortoiseshell cat, or make an effort to pull back from the brink of despondency, I lugged myself into Cambridge for sightseeing.

Locals complain about the parking, the lunatic cyclists, and the shortage of affordable housing – amen to that last one. Visitors to Cambridge, on the other hand, are unanimously bowled over by eight hundred years of history and stunning architecture, packed tighter than a Tetris grid.

As a teenager in the city, with my mind on lipstick, exams and shopping, I had failed to appreciate it, but now I paused at every corner to drink in a new vista. Camera in hand, I wandered past the touristy shops on King's Parade, down Silver Street to the throng at the Mill Pond, and then north along the Backs. The gentle exercise, mild June air and centuries-old postcard views calmed me and renewed my optimism.

Pausing on Garret Hostel bridge, I watched the punts glide down the river past Clare College and Trinity Hall. Some were professionally chauffeured, expertly steered by attractive male students, no doubt hoping for large tips. These guys made it look effortless: they had perfected the art of steering by leaving the pole in the water at the end of each stroke. They also knew the dangerous parts of the river, that is, the bits with mud which could hold the pole hostage unless it was given a sharp twist before being pulled up.

Other punts, however, were self-propelled by tourists who had clearly never set foot in such an odd flat-bottomed boat before. These were making chaotic progress, the punter wobbling madly as he or she tried to balance on the rear platform, with absolutely no control over direction. I saw one lose his pole, causing much hilarity amongst his group. The emergency paddle was found and they manoeuvred the twenty-foot-long boat back upstream to retrieve the defiant pole from the mud.

The metaphor wasn't lost on me. Yes, I was wobbling, direction-less and probably going against the flow. But at least I was afloat. I had a little money and a few friends, and enough skills to muddle through. I might not be gliding elegantly, but I could keep paddling. It would take more than an unfaithful husband to sink me.

~~~

My soul and spirit were further boosted when I stumbled upon an elegant cafe, housed in a church nave in Trinity Street. After lunch, I phoned Jem.

'Grace! Where are you? How are you?' she asked in one breath.

I filled her in: I had indeed made my way to Saffron Sweeting and was hoping to stay for a while.

'Are you sure you want to be stuck in a small village?' she asked. 'I feel bad about steering you there – I had too much to drink the other night.'

'I think it's okay,' I replied. 'I like that it's quiet. And the bakery's great.'

The welcome I'd received from Brian, the baker, had certainly been warmer than in the post office.

'Wouldn't it be easier to get work in London?' Jem asked. 'And I'd see you more often.'

'It's only an hour on the train,' I smiled. 'But if I can't find somewhere to stay, I'll rethink.'

'How are you feeling?'

'Okay, I guess. I spoke to James – he was on the brink of coming over here but I persuaded him not to.'

'Wow. Interesting, that he was going to drop everything

and follow you.'

'You think?'

'I do. Things can't be all cosy with the other woman, if he was on his way here.'

'Oh.' I hadn't thought about his motives for coming to England.

'Grace ...' Jem said, 'I'm behind you, whatever you do, but, well, do you think maybe you were a bit hasty? You and James have such a lot of history; shouldn't you at least talk to him?'

I didn't want to think of our history: fourteen years, two countries, multiple jobs. Thirteen Valentine's Days, a dozen summer holidays, hundreds of Sunday mornings. Two written-off cars (me), one broken arm (also me), one broken marriage vow (him).

I swallowed. 'I can't. I just can't deal with seeing him.'

'Okay,' she said, after a pause. 'That's understandable. What about your mum and dad? Have you told them?'

'No ... but I'll visit them soon. They think I'm with you, by the way.'

'Right, no problem, I won't say anything. But promise you'll come and see me,' she said. 'I could do with some adult conversation.'

'All right,' I said. 'We'll do afternoon tea soon.'

~~~

I didn't expect Amelia to remember me as I pushed open the bottle-green door of Hargraves & Co and stepped down into the office, but to her credit, she did.

'Hello there,' she called from behind a mountain of papers. 'I've been keeping a look out, but I haven't found anything for you.'

Today, she was wearing a neat pencil skirt and an amazing floral silk blouse which made her hair look as shiny as a racehorse. I made a mental note to find a good hairdresser, and soon.

'Oh, well, that was kind,' I replied. 'I realise I'm asking a lot, to get something cheap and short-term. I just looked at some awful places in Bury.'

'It's not easy for renters at the moment, darling. Demand is so strong, you're getting slim pickings.'

'You're certainly busy,' I smiled at her, thinking I should get out of the way and let her do some work.

'Yes, totally hectic and I love it, but sometimes I'd give anything to stop for a cup of coffee.' She started stapling and stuffing house details into green Hargraves presentation folders. 'And between you and me, some of the American clients can be so critical ... They just don't understand that houses are different here.'

I spotted a prominent listing displayed next to the door. The asking price was close to two million pounds. 'That's gorgeous,' I said, taking note of the sweeping driveway, conservatory and even a small stable block. There was a glossy, dark creeper on the outside of the house, giving it the kind of stately look which takes decades to achieve.

'Wonderful, isn't it,' she agreed. 'But unfortunately it only has two bathrooms and the heating needs an exorcist. My clients aren't thrilled by cold baths, it seems.' Once again, her shoe made restless circles in the air.

My gaze was still on the glossy photos on the wall. Even without that kind of money, I would have enjoyed a good nose around any of the houses. For me, trying on real estate was far more exciting than trying on clothes.

The phone rang and Amelia lunged to answer it, scattering fliers on the floor as she did so. I picked up the ones I could reach, before deciding to leave her in peace.

Retreating quietly from the office, I crossed the street to the bakery. It was half past three and I had to wait behind a couple of mothers with young children in tow, presumably buying after-school treats. As they squeezed around me with their bags of goodies, I asked Brian for a hot chocolate and then remembered what Amelia had said about coffee. On impulse, I added a latte and a couple of Bakewell tarts to my order.

Hands full, I returned to the estate agency. A middle-aged couple were now seated by Amelia's desk, details of several houses spread in front of them.

'To be real honest,' I heard the man say, 'we weren't blown away by anything we saw yesterday.' His accent was definitely west of Cornwall. Three or four thousand miles west.

'The rooms were kind of poky,' his wife added.

'Well, the house on Damson Lane is listed. It's two hundred years old,' Amelia smiled at them. She spied me hovering near the door and I gestured to the coffee as best I could, as the hot chocolate started to burn my other hand.

Her eyes widened. 'For me? You sweetie, thank you!'

I approached her desk and excused myself to her clients as I leaned across with the drink and pastry. The man was tanned and looked like he had outdoor hobbies – tennis or golf, perhaps. His wife had been careful not to catch as much sun, but her hair was tastefully streaked with blonde highlights and her manicure was immaculate. I imagined she spent a fair amount of time lunching at their country club.

'Well, sure it's listed,' she said. 'It's for sale, isn't it?'

Amelia looked quizzical and sipped her coffee.

'Excuse my overhearing,' I ventured. 'Amelia didn't mean it's for sale. In England, a listed property means it's protected for historical value and interest. It can make approvals for alterations hard, but you're rewarded with living somewhere with centuries of character.'

Mrs Country Club tilted her head to one side. 'Oh, really?' she licked her lips and glanced at her husband. 'You mean, like some famous historical figure could have lived there?'

Amelia caught on fast. 'Well, in this case, we don't know,' she said, 'but being so close to Cambridge, kings and princes have certainly roamed these parts.' Did she wink at me?

The husband was studying the house details again. 'Why does it say the bedrooms are on the first floor?' He pointed at the paper. 'They weren't. They were all upstairs. That's just misleading. You're supposed to check your facts when you're selling houses.'

There was a pause; Amelia seemed taken aback.

I felt the sugary courage of my hot chocolate. 'Pardon me again,' I ventured, talking to Amelia. 'In the US, the first floor always means the ground floor.' I looked at Mr & Mrs Country Club now. 'That's just a British quirk,' I said apologetically. 'I'm afraid we count a little differently. By first, we mean second.'

The husband looked from me to Amelia, and back again. 'Do you work here?'

I started to say *No, of course not*, but Amelia was quicker.

'This is Grace,' she said smoothly. 'She's British but lived in the States for several years. My clients adore her.'

Her what? Adore who?

Mrs Country Club looked at me doubtfully, but her husband was already nodding.

'Well,' he said, 'perhaps we should go take another look at this place. And I'd like for Grace to accompany us this time.'

'Perfect,' Amelia beamed. 'Would you like to go now?'

~~~

Their real names were Ted and Betsy and they were from Thousand Oaks, outside Los Angeles. He was Vice President of something unintelligible for one of the bio-tech companies and they were expecting to be in England for at least five years. Betsy refused to rent for that long and since money wasn't a primary constraint, they planned to buy a house.

I had tried to take Amelia to one side to ask her what on earth was going on, but she had disappeared for all of twenty seconds into the back room, returning with a set of keys. She handed these to me cheerily, before bundling me and her American clients out of the front door. Before I could blink, I found myself in the back of Ted's vast beige car, complete with delicious smelling leather seats. I hoped my shoes were clean.

I had no idea where our intended property was, but fortunately Betsy had a good memory and directed Ted up past the church to Damson Lane. The car crunched on the gravel driveway and I slid from my seat to find myself in front of the house I had been admiring in the photo. It was even more charming in reality.

'Wow.' I stood stock still and drank in the facade with its mellow bricks, the colour of ripe wheat. The house wasn't huge but it had majestic presence. It had either been the manor house or home to a wealthy farmer. The trunk of the ancient Virginia creeper was as big as a small tree. Being a little outside the village, there was total peace and the only sound came from a few birds singing in the hedgerow.

Ted and Betsy were looking at me oddly as I didn't move.

'Sorry,' I shrugged to them. 'I feel like I'm in a Jane Austen novel.'

'Which one?' Betsy asked, as we all crossed to the front door and I prayed the lock wouldn't be tricky.

'*Pride and Prejudice*, I think. That's my favourite, anyway.'

Ted yawned but Betsy nodded agreeably. 'I just love Keira Knightley.'

The front door yielded and I stepped back to allow them into the house first. This was their second viewing and I could tell they were interested but uneasy. By English standards, it was gorgeous, but I could see that the formal rooms might feel constraining. Ted and Betsy were probably accustomed to a 'great' room, or open space living. Happily, the kitchen had been modernised and was spacious enough to accommodate a casual dining space too. It even had a big red range cooker, which Betsy was eyeing with suspicion.

'That's an Aga,' I told her. 'I've never cooked on one, but I understand that once you get used to it, you're hooked.' Coincidentally, I had been reading an article about them in bed at Oak House the previous night. 'Apparently, they're enjoying a renaissance, even though they cost thousands.'

Ted was in a little sitting room, where French doors opened onto the sweeping lawn at the back of the house.

'I suppose we could use this as the den,' he called to Betsy.

We joined him and I noticed the attractive stone fireplace. Betsy glanced at it too.

'Do you think it would be cold in winter?' she asked me.

'Well, if you're used to Los Angeles, you'd probably want some nice heavy curtains.' I pondered. 'But it's not too big, so wouldn't cost much to heat.'

Upstairs, I asked them if two bathrooms for six bedrooms was a problem.

'We don't have kids,' Betsy said – sadly, I thought. 'So I think it's okay.'

'If guests all come at once, they can share,' Ted shrugged. 'Good of you to mention it, though, Grace.'

I revised my initial opinion of him – he wasn't as irritable as I had thought.

'I don't understand the complete lack of closets.' Betsy gestured round the master bedroom with some frustration. 'What in the world do English people *do*?'

'Well,' I said, 'mostly we have stand-alone wardrobes. You might want to go shopping for a couple of those.'

'Great,' said Ted. 'More to buy.'

'But if I were you,' I told Betsy jokingly, 'I'd grab that small bedroom next door and make the whole thing into a giant walk-in closet.'

She giggled and I realised I'd stumbled on a great idea. Perhaps she owned mountains of clothes.

We didn't spend long looking around outside the house, which was a shame, as I could happily have brought a picnic and spent all day. But they said they'd seen it last time and had liked the stables.

'Do you ride?' I asked Betsy.

'Not much,' she said, 'but I wanna learn. English style. With the velvet hat and jacket and all.'

I smiled at her and silently hoped she didn't plan to take up fox-hunting.

As I made sure everything was locked up before we got back in the car, I could hear them discussing the house in hushed tones. I wasn't sure how they felt, but I knew I was smitten. I told them I'd be thrilled to go back with them, if they wanted to view it a third time.

'Do you mind if we drop you on the edge of the village?' Ted asked. 'We've got dinner with friends this evening and need to run back to our hotel in Cambridge first.'

I didn't mind one bit. They pulled over next to the duck pond and I slid squeakily from my leather seat before saying good bye. I doubted Amelia would lock up her office much before six, and I made my way back at a leisurely pace. The afternoon shadows were lengthening and Saffron Sweeting was glowing gently. A tractor rumbled by, but otherwise the High Street was deserted.

As I crossed the road by the post office, I noticed the elderly woman who ran it turning the sign on the door from open to closed. I waved at her and I'm sure she saw me, but she didn't wave back. Obviously not a cheerful soul. I put her deliberately from my mind and wondered what to say to Amelia. It all seemed pretty unorthodox – after all, she hardly knew me, yet she'd sent me off with strangers and the keys to a two million pound house. Still, I had to admit I'd enjoyed the outing.

Amelia was leaning against her desk, arms folded, looking stern. Was I in trouble?

'There you are, Grace,' she said. 'We need to have a bit of a talk.'

So, I *was* in trouble, but I couldn't quite think what I'd done.

'Are you still planning to stay in Saffron Sweeting?'

'Um, well, I'd like to, I suppose.'

'Good.' She nodded approvingly. 'Ted and Betsy just called. They've made a generous offer on that house.' The smile started in Amelia's eyes and spread rapidly across her face. 'You're hired.'

Chapter 7

Amelia treated me to a fish and chip supper at The Plough, which, considering the commission I'd just made for her, was fair enough. It was a beautiful evening and we sat in the garden, accompanied by the pleasant blended aroma of warm beer, fried food and honeysuckle. It was early enough in the evening that children were eating, not bickering, and early enough in the summer that wasps weren't climbing into everyone's drinks. In other words, it was as good as it gets in an English pub.

Amelia was demolishing her battered cod as though she hadn't eaten in three days. Actually, she was so busy, this might be true. I was on my second glass of Sauvignon Blanc and taking secret delight in my sudden success. Previously, I had felt like an awkward thorn in Amelia's side; now I was flavour of the month and she was enthusiastic.

'Grace, darling, you clearly have a bit of a talent for this.' She paused to take a swig from an enormous glass of gin and tonic.

'Oh, I don't know,' I said modestly. 'That house is so gorgeous, it basically sold itself.'

'Not true, they were eating out of your hand. Bloody marvellous. So,' she continued, 'I need an assistant and I'd like you to consider it.'

I dipped a chip in ketchup, smiled politely, and waited.

'Not full time, and you'd have to do some of the boring stuff in the office, but I'd like you to, well, *translate* for the Americans, show them that we understand their needs.' She waved her ring-adorned right hand expressively. 'The fact that you've lived there is excellent.'

I couldn't remember a time when someone had tried to persuade me to work for them. Previously, it had been me doing all the running, either applying for jobs with multiple other grey-suited candidates or, recently, pitching my ideas for design work, trying to sound confident and capable. Now, after just one afternoon, Amelia was telling me I have a talent. This was a pleasant change, but scary too.

'The thing is,' I replied, 'I was sort of planning to just take a few weeks while I think about what to do with the rest of my life.' I shrugged sheepishly. 'You know, my marriage and all that.'

'I understand completely.' She paused for a respectable instant before adding briskly, 'But you might as well do something useful while you think. If you only help out for a few weeks and then disappear back to California, I won't hold it against you.'

She was right: I couldn't just sit around and mope. And I'd been surprised how much fun it was to look around the house and fantasise about how the other half lives.

'But I haven't found anywhere to live. I can't afford to stay at Oak House indefinitely.'

Amelia saw that I had placed my knife and fork together and stole a few remaining chips from my plate. Technically, she was overweight, but she didn't seem to care. The curves suited her well and her energy was attractive.

'Yes, I hadn't forgotten. I might be able to help with that. But I need to make a couple of calls in the morning.'

This was surprising news, based on her previous assessment of my chances of finding accommodation. I smiled amicably but wondered what she had in mind. Suspicious, I pictured myself in a sleeping bag on the floor of her office, or in a tent by the duck pond.

'Come into the office tomorrow morning,' she suggested – or commanded, I'm not sure which. 'We'll sort the details out then.'

I had to admire her headlong style. Where I saw only problems, she cleared obstacles out of her path in favour of immediate action. I was inclined to hesitate and deliberate, whereas she was boldly blithe. I nodded my agreement.

'Super!' She picked up the menu with gusto. 'Want to share a sticky toffee pudding?'

~~~

I slept badly that night, not helped by the early June dawn and the cacophony of bird song which burst forth at 5 a.m. I snoozed for a couple of hours, tied the duvet in knots around my feet, then phoned Jem for advice.

'Hope it's not too early,' I apologised.

'Don't be daft, we've been awake for hours. At least, Seb's awake, I'm not fully conscious yet. Harry just left for work.'

I pictured her glugging instant coffee in their little kitchen. Then I told her what had happened yesterday.

'So, she's offering you a job and you're in a tizz about taking it.'

'Yes. It just feels a bit sudden. I'm still such a mess,' I said.

'But she'll pay you to look at houses and translate American?'

'It looks like it. But not much, I expect. And I came here to think, not work.'

'Er, but the money would come in handy, right?'

'Right, yes, it would.' That was definitely true.

'And she's not forbidding you from thinking at the same time?'

'Well, no, I suppose not.'

'Grace, honey ...' Jem paused. 'I mean this very kindly, but honestly, what have you got to lose? Give it a try.'

She had a great point. Compared with what I'd already lost, this was nothing.

~~~

A little before we reached Mary Lou's house, Amelia turned left along a road I hadn't yet explored. Slowing almost immediately, she made another turn and bumped her dark green Mercedes along what appeared to be a farm track. Through a thick hedge on our left, I glimpsed a large but uninspiring house. To our right was swaying cow parsley and a field which contained a crop I didn't know. After a couple of hundred yards, we turned sharply left and Amelia parked the car on a rough patch of gravel in front of a little cottage.

Originally of brick but now painted white, the cottage had small, irregular windows. The dark slate roof was pitched at a strikingly steep angle. At both ends of the cottage were tall chimneys, neither of which looked perpendicular to the horizon. The front door appeared to be no more than six feet tall, with its own little pitched roof to protect it. On either side, a straggling yellow rose clung to the wall. The overall impression was like something out of a Beatrix Potter story and I looked around for Mrs Tiggy-Winkle.

'It's very cute,' I said as we got out of the car. 'Is it one of your listings?'

Amelia hadn't yet explained why we were here. She had shown me a few of the clerical tasks at Hargraves, declined to commit to an hourly rate of pay, but promised a significant bonus if I landed new clients who purchased houses. Then, she had locked the front door of the office, twirled around the sign to read *Back Soon*, and bundled me into her car.

'Not exactly,' she said. 'The solicitors dug up some God-awful problem about access, so it's off the market.'

She scrabbled in her beautiful leather handbag and pulled out door keys.

'It belongs to Grey Stoke House.' She waved the keys at the hedge which separated us from the bigger house. 'But it turns out the track we just used is on the land of the farm next door. So, technically, a buyer would be purchasing a house with no legal means of getting to it. The farmer's smelling money and is demanding an exorbitant sum for that twelve-foot strip of land. The legal beagles are having a field day.'

I was having trouble keeping up. 'So, you can't sell it?'

'Not yet,' she said. 'It could take several months to sort out. Anyway, I suggested to the owners they might fancy a spot of rental income in the meantime.' She looked pleased with herself.

'Wow,' I sighed, as a swallow swooped past us into its nest under the eaves. 'It's lovely, but I don't think I could afford it.'

Undeterred, Amelia picked her way across the crunchy gravel and began unlocking the front door.

'Hargraves & Co will cover your rent,' she called to me. 'But understand, darling, you'll get booted out when I can sell it.'

Cover my rent? To live in this beauty, with actual roses round its door?

'Can you do half days at the office, Tuesday to Friday, and all day Saturday? I'll make sure you don't starve,' Amelia added, as the big black hinges of the door opened squeakily. 'What do you say?'

'Thank you so much,' I croaked in a voice as rough as my new front door. 'It's adorable.'

~~~

When I moved in the next morning, I quickly understood that the cottage wasn't completely adorable, but I didn't appreciate its full repertoire of quirks until I had lived there for forty-eight hours.

My first impression when Amelia had allowed me time for a quick look around was of white-painted walls, low ceilings and oak beams. The kitchen was sunny and not too dated, plus there was a working fireplace in the living room, which might make for cosy evenings as summer slipped away. The cottage was partially furnished, with timeless, sturdy pieces.

My subconscious interior design voice had declared it a fabulous blank canvas, and asked for a five-figure accessories budget to transform sparse into stylish. My practical, just-left-my-husband voice had promptly replied that a set of sheets, some towels and a few kitchen tools would be fine.

I had driven into Newmarket to procure these basics, for once taking little pleasure in choosing between blue or cream sheets and striped or dotted towels. My non-existent budget meant my options were limited, and the act of buying a cheap set of Argos china made my split from James more final. By the time I had arrived back at Oak House to tell Lorraine that this would be my last night under her roof, my mood was sombre.

Curled up in bed with the complimentary shortbread tin for the final time, I wondered what James would think of my new job and home. He had always been supportive of my career ambitions, even the ill-fated decision to leave my safe, dull job at the university and start my own design business.

Now, I was sufficiently removed from recent events to know the self-imposed stress of launching a business hadn't helped our marriage. I second-guessed every decision I made, and when James and I were together, which wasn't often, I was insecure and anxious. Whenever questioned, he'd simply said, 'Don't worry so much, Gruff. Do what makes you happy.'

Clearly, these had been empty words, as he could hardly expect me to be over the moon about his purple-tinted affair with Rebecca.

As I switched off the light and listened to the gentle summer breeze ruffling the leaves of the oak tree, I recalled the weeks before his trip to Las Vegas. I had certainly been wrapped up in my own problems, but how on earth had I missed what was going on? I couldn't help but wonder at what precise point my husband had given up on us.

~~~

It took just one trip in the little yellow car to move my entire possessions from Lorraine's bed and breakfast to the cottage. Even as a student, I had owned more gear than this. However, it certainly made the whole moving process less painful: an hour after leaving Oak House, I had unpacked and was drinking tea in my own kitchen, determined to tackle the coming days like a strong, calm, single woman.

I was strong and calm through the afternoon as I stocked up on essential groceries, evicted spiders from the bathroom and managed not only to find the ancient boiler, but even to rekindle its pilot light. But in the early evening, when I entered the kitchen to fix a snack, I spotted a brown tail disappearing under the cooker. My composure deserted me and I bolted halfway up the stairs, then sat down abruptly and sobbed.

Just at the point where I had soaked a couple of tissues, searched my pockets in vain for more, and remembered I hadn't bought any toilet paper, my mobile phone rang. It was Amelia, to ask how I was settling in.

'I'm sorry,' I gulped at her. 'I don't think I can do this.'

'Why ever not?' she asked. 'What's wrong?'

'I'm no use to anyone at the moment.' I hiccupped. 'I shouldn't have said I'd work for you.'

'Darling, you're just a bit stressed. You're making some big changes.'

'I forgot to buy toilet paper.'

She laughed heartily. 'Well, that's hardly the end of the world, is it?'

I pictured her at her desk, twirling a shoe on the end of her foot.

'Grace, I know it's not easy when your marriage ends. Give it some time and don't worry so much.'

'But ...'

'But what?'

'I saw a rat. In the kitchen.'

'Darling, you most certainly did not. It was probably a mouse.'

Of course, I thought, she would say that: she's an estate agent.

'Just a little mouse,' she continued. 'He didn't mean you any harm. But if you're troubled by it, I'll get a man out there tomorrow.'

'Right.' From my vantage point on the stairs, I kept my gaze fixed on the spot where the rodent had disappeared.

'Now, why don't you go and have a hot bath and maybe open a bottle of wine? Things will look better after a good night's sleep.'

I said nothing, hugging my knees and sniffing pathetically.

'Okay?' Amelia asked.

'Yes, okay,' I said, wondering if the post office would still be open to sell me toilet paper. And rat poison.

Chapter 8

The draughts were terrible, the hot water was a lottery, and if I turned on too many lights at once, the fuses blew. No matter how many times I trundled my car up the driveway, I shook my bones to bits as we fell into every single pothole, and I mentally renamed Grey Stoke Cottage to Pothole Cottage. Nonetheless, I quickly bonded with my quirky little abode and learned to get along with its foibles. I saw no more evidence of rodent occupation and decided perhaps the mice had moved out the same day I moved in. Either that, or they were too clever to get caught in the peanut butter baited trap I left for them.

I felt especially safe in the angular bedroom with its creaking bed, sloping ceiling and tiny dormer window. For the next twenty-four hours, I hid out there, crying a little, sleeping a lot and trying not to wonder what James was doing. Once, I picked up my phone and had dialled half his number before catching myself.

But I knew I couldn't hide for ever. Nervous, excited, with just an edge of sadness, I took a brisk shower, smoothed the creases out of my smartest clothes and turned up for work.

~~~

Amelia greeted me with business-like enthusiasm, and proceeded to extract more than her money's worth that first afternoon. I purged paper piles, printed property handouts, sorted invoices and more. Together, we unearthed the wood of her desk from below stacks of files. We created a to-do list for each of us, filled a recycling box and found three large cheques which had never been paid into the bank. The phone rang more or less constantly and I stumbled through the enquiries as best I could.

At five minutes to five, Amelia pointed to the clock with a shriek. 'Quick!' she cried. 'Can you pop across to Brian at the bakery?' She pulled a ten-pound note from her purse and pointed apologetically to her shoes, which were not ideal for a last-minute sugar sprint.

When I returned with hot drinks and sandwiches a few minutes later, I saw with satisfaction the progress we'd made.

'So, how are you doing?' Amelia asked, sinking into her chair with relief. She seemed less frazzled than before.

'Okay, I think. Shouldn't you be the judge of that?' I offered her first pick of either cheese or tuna.

'Well, the sooner you can get to know the properties we have available, the better.' She was tackling her tuna roll with as much enthusiasm as if it had been caviar. This woman loved her food.

'In fact,' she continued, 'tomorrow you should start viewings; that will help a lot.'

'Okay,' I agreed, 'and I could make sure these are current.' I waved my cheese sandwich at the display of glossy property photos on the wall by the door.

'Perfect,' she nodded. 'People keep wanting to buy that thatched house and it's been sold for weeks.'

'Can I add square footage to each description?' I asked. 'That might be a big help.'

'I'd love that. So many of the Americans ask and I'm hopeless at maths. Just make it clear you're estimating, not promising.' She grinned. 'Don't get me sued.'

~~~

The next day was Saturday. After nine hours of property viewings, I was shattered but content as I bumped the yellow car up the track to my quirky cottage. Its solid timelessness reassured me and the windows glowed warmly in the evening sun.

I had visited ten different homes with three American

families. The first two were on short work contracts, looking for year-long rentals. Their questions had covered everything from the strangeness of the plumbing and the hygiene of carpet in the bathroom to the impracticality of a detached garage and how to get cable television. Did I know about the local schools? Was it better to buy a car and sell it after twelve months, or hire one?

I had been reminded how hard it is to move thousands of miles and how mundane activities like buying groceries or doing a load of laundry became challenges. Unlike the States, England had adopted metric measurements for food and the shops now expected a PIN number to verify credit card purchases. Many of the newcomers were finding it hard to complete even basic transactions. I found myself smiling, explaining and apologising in equal measures.

The third family, a couple with a little girl and a toddler, were ready to buy a house. They, too, were experiencing culture shock and were just as bemused by the homes we saw, but they were treating the experience as a delightful adventure.

'We're thrilled to be here,' the mother told me. 'Bruce is part Irish and we're going to track down all his relatives.'

Bruce ignored this, and told me they'd need four bedrooms.

'I'm so pleased Bethany is going to an English school,' his wife continued. 'I want her to grow up with beautiful manners. English women have such poise, don't they?'

I had a flashback of my poise on the recent day when I had stormed into my husband's office, yelled at him in front of his team and tipped purple paint onto the carpet.

'Um, well, if you say so,' I muttered. 'Now, isn't this a beautiful staircase?'

~ ~ ~

At six o'clock, they had thanked me heartily and promised to be in touch early the following week. I'd dragged my weary bones back to the Hargraves office and made sure I hung up the keys on the correct hooks. Amelia was tidying up, humming to herself but in a hurry.

'Sorry, darling,' she'd said, 'but I hate this time of year.'

'Why?' I'd asked, surprised. She had seemed upbeat until now.

'It annoys the hell out of me to work during Wimbledon fortnight.' She winked. 'All I want to do is drink Pimms and ogle the Aussies in their white shorts.'

I'd grinned. I loved the way the British media supported their chosen hopeful, appearing to believe their own hype that a Brit could win the tournament. The inevitable national tragedy, somewhere around the quarter-finals, was a British summer tradition. This year the hopes of Britain's housewives were pinned on the delectable Bobbie Middleton, whose long legs covered the tennis court at astounding speed. He was extremely dishy, but unfortunately young enough to be my son.

Rummaging in her desk drawer, Amelia had pulled out the Hargraves cheque book and reached for her favourite Tiffany pen. 'Do you have an English bank account?'

'Er, yes.' I wondered why she was asking. 'I never got round to closing it when James and I moved.'

'Good,' she'd said, writing busily, then blowing on the ink to dry it. 'I owe you your bonus for the sale to Ted and Betsy. Obviously the deal isn't final yet, but I thought an advance might come in handy.'

I'd smiled politely and put her cheque in my bag.

Now, though, in my little cottage kitchen with golden evening sunbeams flooding across the floor, I took it out to inspect it and did a little jig on the uneven terracotta tiles. It was far and away the easiest money I'd ever made.

~~~

Finally, I felt ready for the eccentric embrace of my family. The drive from Saffron Sweeting to my parents' home in

Norfolk was little more than an hour, so even though I had slept late on Sunday morning, I arrived before lunch time.

Dad was in the front garden, tending his roses. As I opened the car door, the pong of manure welcomed me.

'Gracie, pet, hello!' He downed shovel to greet me with an affectionate and only slightly stinky hug.

'Hi dad.' We released each other quickly, enough affection for one visit already shown. 'Poo, you know how to have a good time.'

'Top grade stuff, this, courtesy of your mother's new chickens. Little sods are playing havoc with my lawn but at least the roses are lapping it up.' He wiped his forehead with his handkerchief. 'How are you, love?'

'Fine, thanks.' I gave him a bright, non-committal smile. 'Mum's inside?'

'Yes, in the kitchen – doing lunch.'

I headed into their small bungalow with trepidation in case I found my mother wringing the neck of something feathery. Happily, the roast was already in the oven and she was snipping up mint, so I concluded it was probably lamb.

Once again I was wrapped in a brief but surprisingly strong hug, before she released me and scrutinised me.

'It's lovely to see you.' She pushed her glasses back up her nose with a minty finger. 'We've missed you, poppet.'

'Me too,' I said, stealing a raw carrot and perching on the little stool at the end of the counter. Their kitchen had been designed in the eighties. It boasted patterned tiles, Flotex carpet and even a serving hatch to the dining room. Usually I get a strong urge to redesign it, but today the familiarity was comforting.

Mum looked at me a little longer, but said nothing and reached for the olive oil. I hadn't really thought how I was going to break the news about James. Would it be easier to tell her while we were on our own in the kitchen, or wait until later? As usual, I chose to postpone the difficult conversation.

'So, how are the chickens?' I asked instead.

'Oh, wonderful! So funny, they all have their own personalities.' She manoeuvred a roasting tin of potatoes into the oven and kicked the door shut. 'Would you like to meet them?'

I didn't especially want to add my mother's chickens to my circle of best friends forever, but it reduced the chance of awkward questions and I could tell she was proud to show me her *ladies*. So, off we went outside, where I was introduced to each chicken in turn. My garden tour also included the compost heap, where a badger had been spotted last week. I wondered privately if the tourist board should be informed and whether there was any danger of this overshadowing Buckingham Palace on the tourist trail.

As we came back inside, my father appeared. Thankfully, he had scrubbed up a bit and changed his chicken-poop shirt for a clean one.

'Fancy a sherry before we eat, Norah?' He tipped smoky bacon crisps into a bowl to accompany their aperitif.

I sank quietly into their Sunday routine, and dutifully had two helpings of lamb. We also made a huge dent in a rhubarb crumble and both of them had two glasses of wine.

'Thank you, that was lovely,' I said politely.

'You're welcome, love.' Mum smiled at me and picked up the custard spoon to lick. 'We're sorry James couldn't join us.'

I decided I might as well get it over with.

'I don't know quite how to say this.' I looked down at my lap and twisted my floral napkin. 'I think I've left him.'

There was a shocked pause and my father shuffled his feet under the table.

'Oh, Gracie.' My mother recovered first. 'We thought maybe something was wrong.'

In for a penny, in for a pound, I thought.

'He had an affair,' I blurted. 'With someone at work. I was designing her bedroom. I'm going to spend a couple of months over here.' This all tumbled out in a rush.

A short, inscrutable look passed between my parents,

then dad patted me on the hand and stood up. 'I'll put the kettle on,' he said, and retreated to the kitchen.

Now my news was out, I felt calmer. It was better they knew.

My mum seemed to be searching for the right words. Eventually, she said gently, 'Gracie, I know this might seem like the end of the world, but it isn't. Things will turn out okay.'

'Thanks, mum.' That was all I could manage, before the tears filling my eyes rushed down my cheeks.

Mum gazed out of the window for a couple of minutes, either pondering her next sentence or admiring the feathered ladies. Then she asked, 'So you're with Harry and Jem? Some girl time and shopping?'

'Not exactly, no,' I confessed, and explained briefly that I had stationed myself in solitude in Saffron Sweeting. 'And, mum ... I really don't want James to know I'm there.'

'Grace! Why —' She began to interrupt me, but stopped, nodding slowly. Her face was compassionate.

To acknowledge her support, I volunteered a few more details about my new living arrangements. By the time I could tell I'd eased my mother's concern, dad was back with our tea.

'It's a shame, I always thought James was such a clever chap,' he said mildly. 'The only thing I didn't like was that he took you to America. At least you're not five thousand miles away any more.'

Leaving my family to move across the Atlantic had been hard, but James and I had been determined to treat our move like the incredible opportunity it was. We'd been able to try things, like skiing and wine tasting, that weren't common in England. James was sportier than me, but he'd led me down the green runs at Squaw Valley and slowed his pace for bike rides at Crissy Field. His career had thrived in the innovative culture of Silicon Valley and even though I'd struggled to find a job I enjoyed, California had been a fun place to live. Throwing in the towel had never occurred to me until the stepladder day of a few weeks ago.

Mum shot my dad a sharp look. 'Well, you know how misguided men can be, Geoffrey. He's not as clever as we thought, if he did this to our beautiful Gracie.'

Dad looked suitably chastised and busied himself tormenting the tea bags in the pot. I wiped my eyes on my napkin and averted them from my wedding photo on their sideboard. I didn't know if it would still be there next time I visited. From my mother's stern expression, I suspected I would return to find professional portraits of her new poultry instead.

Chapter 9

My emotions concerning my marriage may have been raw, but at Hargraves & Co, my head was clearer. I could already see I had made a positive contribution to Amelia's working life. The office was now tidy, with flowers and quality magazines in our small reception area. We had US-friendly details for all our houses. Messages – and cheques – were no longer buried. Amelia had more time to do what she did best, which was to negotiate great deals for her sellers.

I had asked her why she hadn't hired an assistant before.

'Had one,' she'd replied breezily. 'She walked out in the middle of Easter weekend, when she found out her fiancé was shagging her twin sister. Total nightmare.'

'That's horrible!' I was shocked. 'Ugh, what a betrayal!'

Discovering James was having an affair with a client was one thing, but I couldn't imagine the pain of him cheating with a sister.

'You're telling me. Busiest weekend of the year. Cost me a sale, I'm certain.'

Clearly, our definition of the ultimate betrayal was a little different. Nonetheless, a smile tugged at my cheeks. Amelia might have been a self-declared mess after her divorce, but she was strong and sassy now.

My unofficial role at Hargraves was to act as buyer's advocate, touring homes with them, answering questions and pointing out the advantages of each property. This I did with enthusiasm and honesty, but I didn't disguise the drawbacks, either. Some of my clients probably found that strange, but others thanked me for being 'on their side'.

In the short time since starting work, I had helped sell another house, and Amelia was threatening to take me shoe shopping to celebrate.

'I know your trainers are practical, but they don't really

convey success, darling,' she chided me with a good-natured wave of her toe.

We were doing market research on the internet while keeping one eye on the tennis scores.

'But they're *smart* trainers, not like something the ballgirls are wearing,' I replied. It was true: mine were a slim style, pale blue with suede details – not a sexy shoe, but respectable for the office. I distracted Amelia by pointing to the slide show accompanying one of our competitor's listings. 'Do you think this yellow kitchen will sell?'

For a few minutes, we discussed the merits of magnolia over sunflower paint.

'Ever considered a career in home staging?' Amelia asked me. 'It's a close cousin to interior design and you certainly have an eye for what buyers want.'

'Well, obviously, I love that kind of stuff ...' I rubbed the crease which had involuntarily appeared on my forehead. 'But I wasn't much good at getting people to pay me for it.'

She raised one perfect eyebrow. 'Maybe you just didn't give it long enough.'

'Yeah, well, my courage kind of left me when my husband slept with my best client,' I sniffed defensively. 'Puts you off, you know?'

'Sorry,' she said, and studied her cocktail ring.

I knew she didn't mean to upset me; it's just that Amelia didn't strike me as very empathetic about the challenges of owning a floundering business. It was fine for her, all she had to do was twirl her shoe a few times, like Dorothy clicking her heels, and wealthy American home-buyers lined up at her door. She and her twirling Blahniks were probably responsible for the weak pound too.

'So, your husband wasn't supportive of you running your own show?'

'Um, no, he was really sweet about it, actually,' I said. 'I just couldn't make it work.'

'How so?'

There, she was doing that shoe thing right now.

'Well, let's see ...' I wondered if I wanted to discuss this. I found maybe I did. 'I wasted a ton of money on glossy advertising, which got me precisely zero clients. That was stupid; everyone told me not to do print ads but I didn't listen.' I chewed on a biro, thinking back. 'And I went to no end of networking groups. They were fun, but full of women with equally desperate situations, flogging nutritional advice or life coaching or other stuff nobody really *needs*. We all smiled gamely but I think we were all struggling.'

'But people value great design, surely?'

'I suppose so. But I wasn't moving in the kind of circles that have big budgets. The people I pitched to seemed to think I could transform their room with five hundred dollars and a trip to Ikea.'

Amelia nodded sympathetically. 'Not quite your target niche?'

'No ...' Another sigh. 'And once I lost confidence, I got so anxious, I was kind of consumed by it.' I had made deep tooth marks in the biro and saw my hands were inky blue. I chucked it in the bin and wiped my fingers on the *Cambridge Evening News*. 'Plus, it meant I was out most evenings.'

'So?'

'So ...' This was harder. 'I think James and I maybe got a bit ... disconnected. He saw how scared I was and he couldn't help.'

'Hardly an excuse to start sleeping around, though,' she said.

'No, of course not, absolutely not.' I shook my head hard, to make sure I believed it. To my relief, I found I did. 'But I don't suppose I was much fun to live with.'

The phone on my desk rang and I jumped, then summoned up one of the brave smiles that were becoming my speciality.

Amelia tilted her head, drumming her fingernails on her desk. 'Right. Well, I don't care if you're fun to live with or not. We're still going shoe shopping.'

~ ~ ~

Later that afternoon, Amelia was on the phone when the door opened and a woman in her late thirties came into the office. Tall and wiry, she had shortish, curly dark hair held back by a headband, and was dressed simply in chinos, striped shirt and loafers. She picked up the glossy Cambridgeshire property magazine and began scanning the photos in our *Rental* display.

'Hello, can I help?' I stood and came towards her, noticing her keen, bird-like dark eyes. I thought she reminded me of a raven, then decided no, a jackdaw: her overall look was cuter and without menace.

'Hey there. I just arrived from Boston and I'm looking for somewhere to rent.'

Her origin was no big shock. 'Okay,' I replied, 'I can help with that. What kind of thing do you need?'

We discussed her requirements briefly: small, outside the city, preferably with character. Not unlike my own hopes when I had arrived in Saffron Sweeting. But unlike me, her company was picking up the cost for the first six months. She named a figure which gave her plenty of options.

'And you're looking to move ... when?' I was busily taking notes.

'As soon as possible,' she said. 'I arrived here Thursday and start work next Monday.'

'And you're in bio-tech?'

Nancy – that was her name – blinked, a little surprised. I awarded myself only half points for such an easy guess.

'I don't suppose you have anything with a thatched roof?' she asked. 'They are so *adorable*.'

I clicked my tongue, thinking hard. 'Sorry, I don't think so,' I replied. 'Not unless you're ready to buy. Thatched anything always goes fast, but especially the rentals.'

'Too bad,' she said. 'Never mind, can you show me what you have?'

'Absolutely.' I collected keys for a couple of older homes

which I felt had some charm and murmured 'See you in a bit' to Amelia, who was by now pushing hard on her phone call. From the speed of the accompanying shoe twirling, I suspected an agreement was imminent.

In the street, I pointed my car out to Nancy. 'It's that yellow one,' I told her. 'Some clients prefer to drive themselves, but you're welcome to come with me.'

'Yours is great.' She climbed in without fear, once she'd remembered the passenger seat was on the left.

'There's only one option at the moment in this village,' I told her, 'and the other is in Dullingham, which is still pretty convenient for the Science Park. I assume you're based at the Science Park?'

She was. 'At first,' she said, 'I schlepped around looking for a flat in downtown Cambridge, but I would still need a car to get to work and the parking was just awful. Plus, I was kind of freaked out by the swarms of kamikaze bikes weaving inches from my fender the whole time.'

I wasn't sure where 'downtown' Cambridge was, but the middle of the city certainly wasn't the place for newly imported wrong-side-of-the-road drivers. For a moment, I considered an abrupt career change to offer driving lessons for American newbies. No, that was ridiculous, and my nerves probably couldn't stand it either. Whatever colour my elusive parachute turned out to be, it wasn't that.

~~~

After just two hours, Nancy and I were friends. She had told me of her stout enthusiasm for the Royal Family, and I had shared that I had moved back to England following my marriage break-up. Unfortunately, our conversation had been more enjoyable than the viewings.

The first cottage had been wonderful: sloped ceilings, beams everywhere and, in the kitchen, even a two-part stable door. The bedroom was large, although admittedly it lost a third of its space due to the acutely sloping ceiling.

Outside, the cottage boasted an original coal chute and purple petunias.

Nancy had loved it, but not the location. 'I dunno about driving these narrow roads in winter,' she mused.

Sure enough, the death knell came for the Dullingham cottage when we encountered a distressed tractor during our return to Saffron Sweeting. It had got one wheel stuck in a ditch and was leaning ominously. After a minute of indecision, I squeezed the car past. Nancy and I both held our breath for fear that the unglamorous cargo of sugar beet might come raining down upon us.

The second little house, near the river in Saffron Sweeting, had spadefuls of character but was unfurnished and impractical. Amelia would be hopping mad to learn it hadn't been cleaned thoroughly, either. The dishes piled in the kitchen sink alerted Nancy to the lack of a dishwasher. This discovery led us on a general appliance hunt, which revealed an ancient twin-tub washing machine in an adjoining outhouse.

'Oh boy,' was Nancy's reaction.

'Mmm, not good,' I agreed. 'A girl needs her creature comforts.'

The most direct route from this cottage back to the Hargraves office was through the ford. The village had a bridge, of course, but that was up near Mary Lou's house. I thought Nancy might find it a novel way to end our tour. I hadn't been through it before, but had watched other cars splash through easily. After the fine weather we'd been enjoying, the water seemed to be only about six inches deep.

'I don't know if you do this in the States,' I said to her, 'but in English villages, it's still fairly common to be able to drive through a shallow river as the most efficient way to get where you're going. We call them fords.'

'No way!' she laughed. 'That's totally nuts.'

'Not really,' I replied. 'I think it's rather fun.'

'Cool,' Nancy said. 'Let's do it!'

My mistake was to approach the ford and enter the

water in second gear. We were just halfway across when I realised the little yellow car was struggling with our low speed. It seemed Mary Lou wasn't the only one whose gearstick awareness was lacking. I tried to change down into first and promptly stalled.

'Shit!' I exclaimed, followed by 'Excuse my French' to my new client.

'Jeez,' said Nancy. 'Will it start again, or are we screwed?'

I tried the engine and was rewarded with indignant spluttering sounds, followed by a couple of gurgles.

'Okay, no problem, not to worry,' I said to Nancy, as much for my benefit as hers. I would deal with this calmly. 'I'll just give us a push.'

'You're gonna get your feet wet.' Nancy grinned as she stated the obvious.

I was already wriggling out of my maligned suede trainers. 'Can you skooch over and take the wheel?'

I opened the car door. It was well above the water level: this would be a piece of cake. Gingerly, I lowered myself down into the shallow river. The water was chilly, but not unpleasantly so, and under different circumstances would have been refreshing. It flowed happily around my calves, certainly not presenting any danger. I was standing on smooth stone, presumably laid on the river bed to stop cars sinking into the natural gravel or mud.

Grateful none of the Saffron Sweeting ducks were present to observe my predicament, I held onto the car as I paddled carefully round to the back. Nancy wriggled over the gearstick, into the driver's seat.

'Do I need to steer?' she called.

'I doubt it,' I replied. 'Just hold it steady in case the water tries to take us.'

With that, I placed both hands firmly on the yellow boot and pushed. Nothing happened. The small car was disproportionately heavy and there was resistance from the water.

This will teach me to join a gym, I thought. I bent my knees further and pushed off hard with my feet.

'Yay!' cried Nancy, as the vehicle started to move through the water.

With gritted teeth, I tried to take advantage of the momentum. But as we inched closer to the river bank, the smooth stones became covered in weed, and without warning my bare feet swished out from under me. For a startled moment I was weightless, before I toppled sideways with a resounding splash. The soothing footbath became a frigid shock.

'Bollocks,' I gasped, sitting up in a hurry. 'Sod!'

'Oh my God.' Nancy opened the driver's door and looked back at me. 'Are you okay?'

'Yes, fine, sorry, fine!' I scrambled to my feet, determined to make the best of it. And I *was* fine, apart from a bruised elbow and dripping clothes. I was wearing a short beige linen skirt and pale pink T-shirt, both now clinging to me. 'Sorry,' I called to her again. 'All under control.'

It was at this point I realised that the ducks might have been absent, but we had an audience nonetheless. Up on the road, above the bank we had almost reached, was a dark blue sports car. The driver, a man, was holding a mobile phone to his ear.

'Hang on a minute,' I heard him say. Then he called out, 'Are you ladies in a spot of bother?'

Was he laughing? How long had he been there?

I looked down at my wet clothes. Hell, my T-shirt had gone see-through. I was wearing a bra, of course, but still ...

'No, thanks, we're doing great!' Nancy shouted back cheerfully, before I could respond.

Rats: some help would have been fantastic. Still, I shrugged and tried to look as though I cavorted in small rivers for fun.

He was definitely laughing now. 'Right, okay then, I'll leave you to it.'

And with a growling roar from the twin exhausts of his flashy car, he was gone.

I tugged my sodden T-shirt down over my waistband, set my lips in a defiant grimace, and got back to pushing.

Chapter 10

By the time Nancy and I arrived back at the office, I was a little drier but shame-faced. Amelia, clearly disgusted by my appearance, but chirpy from closing a sale, shooed me out with both hands. 'Nancy, we'll keep our eyes open for you,' she promised. 'Perhaps you'd consider something a bit more modern too?'

Nancy admitted that she would, then invited me to the pub for a restorative drink. Since we'd abandoned my car on the river bank to dry out, I decided I could afford to get mildly legless.

'Sorry you took a swim,' she said as we sat down in the garden, eyeing the sky for clouds. 'But you were awesome.'

'I didn't feel very awesome.' I opened a bag of prawn cocktail crisps to share.

'And that guy who stopped! Too funny! Do you know who he was?'

'No idea,' I said. 'Didn't really look at him. I was distracted.' And I preferred not to think about the view he'd had of my bra. I nursed my Pimms moodily.

'I know what I'm reminded of!' Nancy declared suddenly. 'It was just like that movie!' She sniffed at the crisps before licking one cautiously.

'Uh?'

'Which one was it ... I know – *Emma*. Remember? Gwyneth Paltrow's carriage got stuck in the river and the cute hero came to help.'

Huh. I'd seen it. 'Yeah, but he didn't come to help, did he? He laughed and drove off.' I tutted and wondered if it was too early to order dinner. I had surely earned dessert tonight.

Nancy, however, took a sip of her wine and said pleasantly, 'Am I being a jackass, showing up with my English fantasies? Thatched cottages and romantic heroes?

You must be hacked off at yet another dumb American.'

'Not in the least,' I replied, my tone more friendly. The booze was making me feel better. 'Anyway, our cottages might not be up to scratch, but I can promise you several guys in Saffron Sweeting look just like Ewan McGregor.'

Good, she realised I was taking the mickey.

'Technically,' Nancy smiled now, 'I have a guy lined up already.'

'You do?'

'Well, a man. He's older. We've been seeing each other off and on for about six months.'

'That's great,' I said. 'Someone you work with?'

'No ... I met him at a conference. He's a professor in genetics at Cambridge.'

'Wow. Good for you!' I admit it, I was impressed.

'So, obviously, when the chance came to work here, I leaped at it.'

'I bet he's thrilled,' I said encouragingly, wondering if it would damage my professional image to eat the fruit out of my glass.

Nancy's smile faltered. 'I think so.'

I looked at her with what I hoped was enquiring kindness.

'It's just that now I'm here, I'm not totally sure Elijah had factored me into his plans,' she said eventually.

I pondered this. Two careers, two continents: that was never going to be an easy puzzle.

'Well, yes, it's tough if you're both successful in different countries,' I agreed.

She nodded.

'I originally moved to California because of my husband's job,' I told her. 'It was like being on holiday – vacation – for a while, but I didn't settle until I got a work permit. And then we came unstuck nonetheless.'

Nancy watched me.

'Sorry if this sounds old-fashioned,' I said, 'but I'm beginning to think it's really hard for two people to have different career paths and still stay in sync.'

'Grace, that's mighty depressing,' she said in return. 'I think Jane Austen would expect you to be more optimistic.'

We laughed and I made an effort to lighten my tone. 'Okay, don't listen to me,' I said, 'I'm just a bit freshly bruised.'

~~~

By the second of July, a few Stars and Stripes flags had started to appear outside Saffron Sweeting's larger properties. Everyone assumed they were in support of the American tennis players at Wimbledon, and the pub was nearly the scene of an ugly confrontation when the world number one – an American player – dispensed with poor Bobbie Middleton in a fourth set tie break.

Next day, yet more flags had appeared and were the cause of some muttering in the bakery. I had stopped by to pick up coffee for Amelia and me, as had become my habit each morning. The grumbles were led by Violet, the grumpy old woman from the post office.

'We're proud of *our* sportsmen too, but you don't have to go shoving it down people's throats,' she was saying.

I smelled the sweet, yeasty air and wondered if a flapjack was suitable breakfast food. Brian, the mild-mannered architect of my emerging gluten addiction, made diplomatic noises to Violet.

'And isn't it an affront to the Queen, to fly another nation's flag on English soil?'

'Yes, well, maybe it isn't very tactful,' Brian shrugged, 'but it cheers the village up, doesn't it?'

'Poppycock,' retorted Violet. 'We don't need cheering up – we've won Best Kept Village twice.'

'Morning, Brian!' I took the risk and interrupted, giving Violet a wide smile. 'I expect the flags are for the Fourth of July, rather than the tennis,' I added.

Violet sniffed and put her cheque book back in her

ample handbag.

Her friend, a chubby woman with tightly permed hair, chimed in. 'What, you mean Bastille day? Celebrating the guillotine – hmmph.'

I caught Brian's eye and swallowed a giggle. 'Um, I think that's France,' I responded, adding, 'Two coffees, please,' to bring us back to business.

'Well, wherever it was, I hope they're not bringing their Republican ideas to Saffron Sweeting. We're loyal to our monarch here.' With a regal flounce, Violet tucked her handbag over her arm and exited the bakery, her friend trailing like a lady-in-waiting.

I wasn't sure of Brian's allegiances, so I gave him a bland smile in response to his conspiratorial wink. It was a long time since a man had winked at me, but as I had met his gorgeous wife, who taught Pilates in the village hall, I assumed I was safe enough.

'Anything to eat?' Brian asked me. 'French croissant, perhaps?'

'Only if you'll promise not to report me for treason.'

He slid two plump golden croissants into a white paper bag and winked again. 'On the house.'

~~~

The following evening, the long summer shadows had faded to dark and I was yawningly thinking of going to bed when a sharp burst of terrifyingly loud bangs split the night in two. Gunfire in the sleepy safety of Saffron Sweeting was unthinkable, but the possibility of a gas explosion crossed my mind. Within seconds, the bangs were followed by hisses and fizzles and it dawned on me that our American cousins were celebrating Independence Day.

I scampered upstairs and looked out of the bedroom window, but saw nothing. Undeterred, I tried the bathroom and found that by climbing on the toilet seat, I could enjoy a partial view of the display. I've always loved fireworks and wished I had known in advance. For an amateur display, both size and height were impressive and I guessed they had taken considerable planning and funds. There were several of my favourite kind: simple white stars shooting out from multiple centres.

The hissing and fizzing from the direction of the village was loud, but not loud enough to drown out a sudden and insistent wail from close at hand. I froze and listened. Were the rats back? Was this some kind of mating call?

Gingerly, I ventured back downstairs, wondering if I would witness an erotic rodent rumpus on the kitchen table. No, the room was still and just as I'd left it. Another wail, however, led me to the back door, which I opened just a crack.

Instantly, a wet black nose pushed the door wider and a blur of black and white shot past me. Before I could let out my own surprised yelp, four determined paws and a long tail had disappeared into the living room.

I followed at considerable speed and found my canine interloper had taken up residence in the middle of my sofa, where he was now panting with delight at his escape from the evils of the night. He was some kind of large spaniel, no longer a puppy, but still young. His legs and tail were beautifully feathered and his feet only slightly muddy. Improbably long ears framed a pair of melting brown eyes. He looked both smug on his sofa throne and a little beseeching, in case I turned out to be a cat person. Lucky for him, I'm not.

Mungo, as his collar told me he was called, was now considerably calmer and rested his head contentedly on his front paws. I perched beside him and patted his glossy coat while I wondered if it was too late to phone the number on his tag. No, I decided, his owners were probably crazy with worry. I located my mobile phone and dialled.

'Thank you for calling Saffron Sweeting post office,' the message greeted me.

My wail was as anguished as Mungo's original barking.

My spare hand flew to my mouth.

'We are open from nine to six, Monday to Saturday. Please leave a message ...'

My intended cheerful announcement of Mungo's whereabouts deserted me and I hung up, looking at him in horror. The stupid mutt had the audacity to wag his tail.

'You can't be,' I told him sternly, shaking my head in disbelief and foreboding. 'You can't be Violet's dog.'

But he was, and I was now an accomplice in his escape.

Chapter 11

Of course, I was being over-dramatic. With the clarity of thought which often seems to come with a new morning, I concluded I was unlikely to be thrown into prison for harbouring Mungo for a single night.

After I'd turned out all the downstairs lights, he had trotted happily up the stairs behind me, and stationed himself on the landing to oversee me brushing my teeth. We then had a battle of wills when he'd made preparations to spring into bed beside me.

'No way,' I had told him. 'I'm not that desperate for male company just yet.'

Despite the soppy eyes which greeted this refusal, I stayed firm, and he circled the room a couple of times before settling for the thin cotton rug beside my bed. There, he had snored happily for most of the night.

When I arrived groggily in the kitchen next morning, Mungo was stationed by the back door, gazing at the handle. A small 'woof' and a swish of his tail made his request crystal clear. I opened the door, and instantly he was gone.

'Well,' I thought, 'either I'm conveniently off the hook, or in even bigger trouble when he gets squished on the road between here and the post office.' But short of sprinting after him in my nightie – which was not going to happen, for reasons of both decency and fitness – there wasn't much I could do. I took a calm, capable breath and put the kettle on.

~~~

I was in the habit anyway of calling at the bakery on my way to Hargraves & Co, but that morning I was hopeful of hearing more about last night's fireworks.

My eagerness for gossip was rewarded when I pushed open the glass-paned door and found two oldish women deep in discussion. I suspected they played bingo with Violet in the village hall on Tuesday nights. It soon became clear they were not debating the merits of granary versus wholegrain.

'Independence is all very well, but they don't have to rub our noses in it,' said the taller one in the blue showerproof coat.

'Yes, if they're so proud of their country, I don't know why they're camped out in ours,' replied her friend with the jaunty golf umbrella.

I winced; I happened to admire American national pride. It contrasted nicely with the British tendency to grumble about everything from the government to the weather.

Brian felt compelled to chime in. 'Well, ladies, taxation without representation was a daft idea on our part, you know.'

Tall blue coat looked down her nose at him, not really understanding the reference, but refusing to be sidetracked. 'As for the fireworks, I'm sure they broke at least three by-laws. My husband's on the council: something will have to be said.'

'Ooh, I know!' Her friend seized the topic. 'Fireworks belong in November. Decent folk were already asleep last night when that dreadful racket began. We get up early in these parts.'

I thought to myself that the only truly dreadful racquet of recent days had been Bobbie Middleton's, but resisted the urge to say so. As far as I was concerned, the more fireworks the merrier. Watching them light up the San Francisco Bay each Fourth of July had been one of the highlights of my time in the States.

'Violet said her poor dog was so terrified, he bolted into the night,' added tall blue coat. 'Disappeared completely. Didn't come home until this morning.'

I let out a silent sigh of relief and my shoulders dropped an inch. Mungo had made it back safely.

Golf umbrella seemed ready to say something more, but we were interrupted as the door flew open with a crash and a child-missile hurtled into the shop. I recognised Randy from his behaviour as much as his looks: sure enough, he was followed by Mary Lou, another woman and finally, trailing, Randy's elder brother.

The little shop was now full and the two Sweeting natives wasted no time in gathering themselves and their bread. They departed with noses high, sparing just a couple of stiff nods and a curt 'Good morning' for the newcomers. I used the intervening few seconds to ask Brian for my usual two coffees.

'Hello again,' I smiled at Mary Lou. 'How's the car?'

'Oh God,' she said, 'don't ask. It's determined to mock me.' Then, to Brian, 'I'll get a large coffee, please. No Randy, you may *not* have a doughnut.'

Her friend asked for the same and then yawned as she said, to no one in particular, 'I could sure use some caffeine this morning. The kids were too excited to sleep.'

I looked around for more children. Perhaps they were tied up outside, like dogs?

'They're in school,' Mary Lou said to me, 'where mine should be.'

'I enjoyed what I saw of the fireworks,' I said pleasantly. 'I wish I'd been there.'

'We had quite a crowd,' said Mary Lou's friend.

'Where were they held?' I asked.

'The field next to that deserted barn. The sad-looking one,' said Mary Lou.

'The malt house,' said Brian. He had poured a total of four coffees and set them on the counter.

'Such a pity, history just falling apart.' Mary Lou paid for her drinks. 'Do you have any sweetener by chance? Randy, stop that.'

Brian searched behind the counter and came up with a couple of dog-eared sachets. 'It's been like that for a while,' he said. 'The village doesn't have the funds to restore it.'

'Well, too bad,' said the friend. 'England has so much awesome architecture. Mary Lou, are we still heading to Waitrose in Newmarket?'

Mary Lou grabbed hold of Randy by his shirt collar. 'Don't forget to join us, Tuesdays at the pub,' she called to me, as the four of them jostled their way out of the bakery.

Brian sighed. 'I wish the village was a bit friendlier to them,' he said.

'Well, her boy is a bit of a tearaway,' I replied in polite understatement.

'No, I mean all the new families. The Sweeting shops are struggling and it would be so nice if they shopped here rather than in Newmarket.'

'Things aren't so bad, surely?'

He looked down at the floor. 'They're not good, Grace. So many people just get in their car and go to Tesco's or Sainsbury's for everything. Violet would never tell you this, but she's been threatened with closure at least twice.'

Poor Brian. 'Sorry to hear it.' I eyed the sausage rolls and decided I would play my part in supporting the local economy. 'Amelia's so frantically busy, I thought things must be going well.'

'We like Amelia ... but she's the exception that proves the rule around here. And she's pretty determined when she has to be.'

What did that mean? Had Amelia trodden on some toes in the village?

'Speaking for myself,' he continued, 'business rates just keep going up and the insurance is horrendous. Apparently, other bakers keep getting sued for allergies.' He furrowed his brow.

I asked for the sausage rolls and as he put them in a bag, Brian said, 'I wonder what would keep the gaggle of mums in the village, rather than going to Newmarket.'

'You could try free refills,' I joked.

'Come again?' He looked surprised.

'Er, I meant that coffee shops in the States often give a

second cup for free.'

'Do they really? Good heavens.'

'It encourages people to hang around. And buy something to eat, of course. You'd probably need to put up the price of the first cup, though.'

Brian looked thoughtful. 'What else?' He fixed his gaze on me.

Oh dear, what had I started with my big mouth?

'Oh, gosh, well, you know,' I stalled. Whatever I said next would probably offend him.

'Yes?' He wasn't letting me off the hook.

Right then, in for a penny and all that. 'Well, Mary Lou wanted sweetener, so you should have some of that available. Maybe over there, so people can help themselves.' I gestured towards the door. 'And could you offer an alternative to milk? Soy, perhaps?'

'Soy ... soy ...' he rolled the words around a little. 'Allergies again.'

I looked at my watch and realised that Amelia would not be amused if I showed up late with cold coffee. It was time to make a diplomatic retreat.

'And how about a couple of tables outside? Umbrellas? Cushions, even? That would be nice.'

I fled before he could tell me to take a running jump.

~~~

It was too good to last. For the first time that I could remember, the fine weather held right the way through Wimbledon, instead of turning disgusting for the second week. But almost as soon as the last trophy had been presented, the wind swung around to the north and things turned filthy. Every day brought heavy clouds and dark downpours and The Plough switched its special offer from strawberries to soup.

I tried to stay positive and, not having seen rain in California since April, declared I was grateful for the onset of wet weather. I found some polka-dot wellies in Marks and Spencer and gamely planted a bucket under the leaking roof in my bedroom. The wistful side of me, however, took melancholy delight in gazing out of the misty cottage windows, as fat raindrops trickled down the panes.

Unfortunately, no Willoughby appeared to console my Marianne Dashwood sensibilities and I began to wonder whether forbidding James from coming to see me had been such a clever move. Despite outward assertions that my marriage was over, I wasn't quite ready to wish James and Rebecca a long *or* happy life together.

~~~

'I wanted a stove, not a space ship.' Nancy was peering at the oven in the kitchen of the little house we were viewing.

Since we hadn't found her somewhere to live the last time, we were out looking again, despite the ugly weather. This time, the houses were modern, with unthinkable conveniences like microwaves and tumble dryers.

As I joined her to examine the oven, I realised that the control symbols were completely different from those used in the States.

'Well, even so, I think this is the one. It's in great condition.' She stood up, apparently satisfied that this house met her needs.

'You like it?' I was surprised.

We were in a modern cul-de-sac, on the edge of Saffron Sweeting. The chalet bungalow with its smooth cream-painted walls and double glazing wasn't what she'd initially specified at all. But I could see that a kitchen that didn't threaten carbon monoxide poisoning was a plus.

'One thing I've learned is that when I'm wrong, it's best just to forget it and move on. Dwelling on stuff rarely helps.' She looked around contentedly. 'If I'd been stubborn about Hollywood's idea of an English cottage, I'd be washing my panties in the sink for the next year.'

Chapter 12

'I love him to bits, but it's so blissful being able to go to the loo without a nappy bag.'

A few days later, Jem and I met for tea at our favourite London hotel. I don't know which of us was more excited. She had splashed out on a babysitter, and was relishing the freedom of being able to navigate Tube station steps, go upstairs on a London bus, and even go to the toilet without squeezing self, baby and nappy bag around impossibly tight corners.

I, on the other hand, had missed both her and the English tea experience desperately. Naturally, I had been to cute and cosy Lovejoys in San Francisco and even dabbled with the splendour of the Palace Hotel, but I had lacked a tea soulmate in the States. James, to my eternal frustration, didn't see the point of eating between meals. He had tolerated our infrequent tea outings with the same expression I wore for Giants baseball games. And, to be blunt, a scone in San Francisco just didn't taste the same as one served in Piccadilly.

Jem and I had spent some time on the phone in an excited discussion of which tea venue was worthy of this special occasion. The Ritz was ruled out quickly, for being too glitzy and ostentatious. Fortnums, I speculated, would be full of tourists and hence disqualified for that reason alone. We both liked the Dorchester, but our long-time favourite was the little-known Dukes Hotel, hidden away in a tiny street next to Green Park. Small and friendly, we loved that it was classy, but not so intimidating that you couldn't undo the button of your jeans if the generous portions of sandwiches and pastries required it.

Apart from a couple of French ladies, we had the serene pale blue Drawing Room to ourselves. We were working our way steadily from top to bottom of the tiered cake plate, while tipping limitless quantities of loose-leaf tea down our throats.

Over delicate sandwiches of mature Somerset cheddar and tomato, cushioned between squishy white bread, we discussed my brother's well-being, which didn't take long, and Jem's career concerns, which were more troubling.

'So many women in the world don't have careers, I'm lucky to have a choice,' she said. 'Thing is, I can't imagine getting my act together enough to go back to work, but staying home with Seb for the next five years scares me witless too.' She looked torn. 'I feel like I should be contributing to society.'

'You are contributing, you're raising Seb.' I wasn't qualified to advise her, but I had seen enough of life with a baby to know that getting everyone fed, dressed and out of the door by eight each morning would be a mental and physical miracle.

'Could you do something part-time, maybe?' I asked.

'I guess,' she sighed. 'I suppose I could go back on that basis, if I make a strong case.' She dabbed with her fingertip at the stray pieces of grated cheese on her plate, before licking them off thoughtfully. 'But I'm not sure it's fair on my team, if I'm always disappearing when Seb's ill.'

'What does Harry think?' I asked.

'We haven't talked about it properly. I suspect he thinks I should go back to work.'

'For the money?'

'Well, the money would be nice, but more for my sanity, actually.'

'But he hasn't said so?'

She shook her head and eyed up our tower of treats. The middle tier beckoned with toasted teacakes and plump sultana scones.

'Some evenings, I have absolutely no conversation to offer, except the number of times Seb puked, or how loudly he screamed. I'm not very brilliant company.'

'Well, in my humble opinion, you should discuss it with

Harry. But I don't think your first concern should be how brilliant your company is. Do what's best for you and Seb.' I followed her gaze to the scones.

'Fair point.' Jem nodded, then perked up as she asked, 'Do you think we can justify the clotted cream and jam?'

'Oh, absolutely. Well, it's rude not to, right?' I sat up a little straighter and poured some more tea for us, being careful with the hot handle of the silver teapot. For once, I remembered to use the strainer too, so I didn't fill our cups with soggy tea leaves.

Jem sipped her Darjeeling and leaned back on the plush silk sofa. Then she said kindly, 'You're looking brighter, my friend.'

'Am I? Oh.' For the first time in ages my jeans felt tight, which hardly seemed a good thing.

'Well, for starters, I can't get over your hair.'

'Oh. Thanks. Amelia sent me to her hairdresser in Cambridge.'

The terrifying Jean-Claude had bullied me into an angled bob and some lovely ash-blonde highlights. He knew his stuff: I felt lighter and swooshier as a result. Right there, in his twirling leather chair, I'd promised myself I'd go back regularly.

'And you seem more ... peaceful. I'm thinking that's a good sign.'

Now Jem mentioned it, I realised I had been sleeping much better. My skin looked healthier too.

'You know,' I said, 'the last few nights have been easier. Most mornings, I still wake up and calculate the time in California and wonder what he might be doing. But at least I'm no longer spending half the night thinking the same thing.'

'So, you're feeling a tad better?'

I chewed my scone while I contemplated this. 'The initial shock has worn off. It's sinking in now: what happened and that my marriage is over.' I swallowed. I'm not sure I'd said those words out loud yet. Tears gathered at the back of my eyes like ballet dancers backstage, but to my relief they dispersed without fuss. I exhaled.

Jem said nothing, but touched my arm lightly and waited.

'And then I upended my life by fleeing here,' I continued. 'That was probably a bit crazy.'

'No, you did what you had to do.'

'As for the future, I've absolutely no clue,' I said. 'But I like the interim solution just fine. For somewhere to tread water and work out what comes next, I did okay.'

'I'm dying to see Saffron Sweeting. We'll come and visit you next time.'

The waiter brought yet more tea and asked if we wanted anything else. Only the delicate pastries on the bottom tier awaited our attention.

'That was amazing, better than a spa day. I'm in scone-shaped bliss,' Jem told him.

'Thank you, madam,' came the discreet reply.

'Do you think they'll mind if we take a quick nap?' I asked longingly, after we'd made valiant attempts to polish off the mini chocolate eclairs and teeny individual portions of apple crumble.

Jem looked at her watch reluctantly, probably calculating Tube time back to Ealing and the babysitter's hourly rate.

'So ... Grace,' she said, 'I didn't want to spoil our tea but you obviously have a right to know.'

'Know what?' My thoughts of a quick ten minute nap on the squishy sofa evaporated.

'It's just that James has called me a few times. He's been asking – well, pleading really, to get in touch with you.'

'Oh. Has he?'

'You're surprised?'

'Um, I dunno. Maybe I thought he'd just give up on me?'

'Grace, you're worth more than that.' Jem tutted and I made a little 'maybe' shrug.

'It was kind of awkward, actually,' she continued.

'Right, yes, sorry,' I conceded. They had been friends before this. All of my family had liked James – yet it seemed the whole lot of us had been wrong about his character. I added quickly, 'You didn't tell him where I am, did you?'

'No, don't worry, I just said that it was up to you when you made contact with him. And that you're fine, obviously.'

'Thank you so much.' We hugged awkwardly, partly because we're British and somewhat reserved, but mainly because we were so full of calories.

~~~

We said goodbye at Green Park station and I hopped on the Piccadilly line to King's Cross. The evening rush hour was starting and I allowed myself to be swept up in the zealous herd making their exit from London. I was glad to match their brisk pace, not pausing until I had tucked myself into a precious corner seat on the commuter train to Cambridge.

But then, as we rocked and rolled our way through grimy London suburbs, small towns and eventually green fields, I pondered our tea and Jem's news. Was my self-esteem so low that I was surprised James had been trying to contact me? Did I really think the man who had looked into my eyes and promised *Till death us do part* wouldn't want to know where his wife was? I had steeled myself for the possibility that if he was in love with Rebecca, he'd be too swept up with her to worry about me. Yet here he was, trying to make contact.

Of course, talking to him was pointless because I had absolutely nothing to say.

Did I?

~~~

July drew on: the cow parsley grew ever taller and inbound families felt the urgency of settling into new homes before school started again. I wasn't even looking beyond the end of the summer; for once in my life, I was living firmly and busily in the present.

My enthusiasm for looking at houses – big, small, and quirky – was undiminished. I had showed up nervously at the pub for lunch with Mary Lou's gang and been rewarded with an extrovert, friendly group of women. These personal connections had led to me selling a couple more homes to American transplants. Amelia was pleased, and we increased my hours. Money was still tight, but free rent was a blessing. I was almost living within my means, not counting the loan from my parents to buy a car when the rental company had demanded the return of their yellow peril.

To Amelia's exasperation, I was now driving an old white VW Beetle, acquired from a chicken-keeping friend of mum's. The elderly friend, suffering from cataracts, had given up driving after a 'teensy incident'. This unfortunate occurrence turned out to be the traumatic squishing of one of her own flock. Amelia christened it my murder-mobile, which I thought was a bit strong, considering the glee with which she guzzled chicken and chips at the pub.

Of course, the Beetle didn't exude the kind of Mercedes-driving success that Amelia herself favoured, but my American clients declared it was wonderful, praising the vintage 'European' style. Even so, many of them were reluctant to actually ride in it, preferring to drive themselves to our viewings.

My loneliest time of day was the evening, after I'd made a simple dinner, cleared up the kitchen and found my body was weary but my mind still alert. This was when I missed snuggling with James on the sofa, my head on his shoulder as we scrolled idly through the latest offerings from Netflix. The gap beside me each evening was echoed by the hollow space in my chest.

So, at first I found it ironic, then amusing, then welcome, that Mungo the crazy spaniel found his way to my cottage with increasing regularity. Sometimes, he was there when I got home from work, panting as he lay on the doormat in the evening sun. Other evenings, he arrived with laser-like precision just as I had finished dinner and was wondering whether leftovers were worth keeping. These I denied him, as his illicit visits made me feel guilty enough and I didn't want to add to his incentive. Whatever his reasons, he kept coming and as the July evenings began to shorten a little, he decided his favourite place was on top of my feet in my basic but comfortable living room.

~~~

A couple of weeks after I'd met Jem for tea, I arrived outside the Hargraves office one Tuesday morning and got the nebulous impression that something was different. I scanned our facade to see what was amiss. Then I realised my eye was telling my brain to notice the reflection in the window. Behind me, over the road at the bakery, two tables, a cluster of chairs and – yes – yellow umbrellas had mushroomed. A blackboard proclaimed *NEW!* and its swirly text promised not only *Free Refills* but also *Free Wi-Fi*.

Crikey, I thought, Brian took my advice. Pride swirled through my toes and up my legs, but by the time it reached my knees, apprehension took over.

I skipped our coffee pick-up and went directly inside. Amelia was already there, checking her messages.

'What's up?' she asked distractedly.

'I'm feeling the guilt of interfering with Brian's business.' I threw my car keys on my desk, turned on the computer and sat down heavily.

'Why, what did you do?'

I told her about my chirpy suggestions for bringing some Seattle coffee house chic to Saffron Sweeting. 'What if nobody's interested and Brian's wasted his money?' I fretted. 'Or even worse, what if everyone buys just a cup of coffee, blags endless refills and camps out with their laptops all day?'

'Well, it doesn't sound like the end of the world,' Amelia laughed and threw several sticky notes of messages in my direction. 'And even if you gave advice, it was up to Brian whether or not to take it.'

I humphed, my face of impending doom still intact.

'Grace,' Amelia shook her head at me impatiently, 'you fret too much, darling.'

It was close to lunchtime when I returned from showing a far-too-small house to a family with four little girls and a baby boy (had they kept going until the longed-for son arrived?). As I parked the Beetle, I was pleased to see a couple of women occupying one of the bakery tables. One of them even had a laptop. Were they having some kind of business meeting? That struck me as a little high-powered for Saffron Sweeting. No offence, but this was hardly Palo Alto's simmering cauldron of innovation and venture funding.

With stomach rumbling, I was forced across the road to face the music.

'Hello, stranger,' Brian greeted me. 'Like the changes I've made?'

A delicious scent of coffee assailed my nostrils. Had he been grinding it this morning?

'Well, gosh ...' I was hesitant. 'It looks great out there.'

He nodded. 'Yesterday and this morning were both extra busy.' He inclined his head towards the serve-yourself milk and sugar by the door. 'The refills seem popular – probably made a loss on those today ...'

Oh. Why hadn't I kept my big mouth shut, instead of idly throwing out my opinion? I clearly had zero business sense, now proven on two continents.

'... which is fine by me, as the cakes and savouries have more than made up for it,' he added cheerfully.

'Really?' *Really?*

'Yup. Had to bake a second batch of most things.'

'Oh!' I didn't know what to say, but if I'd had a tail, I

would have wagged it. 'Well, once people taste your stuff, of course they'll buy more.' I recovered my manners.

'And tell their friends, hopefully,' he said, then broke off to serve another customer.

I selected an egg mayonnaise sandwich from the chiller cabinet and made a tactful retreat.

'You're looking pleased with yourself,' Amelia commented, as I plunked myself in my chair and attacked my lunch.

'Brian says people like his new offerings.'

'Good,' she said. 'So I take it impending disaster is averted?'

I chewed in silence.

'Told you it wasn't worth getting your knickers in a twist.' Amelia waved her hand airily as she picked up the phone. 'But I'm pleased. The better the local businesses do, the better it is for house prices.'

'And it's terrific for Brian too,' I reminded her.

'Hmm? Oh yes. Terrific.' She was already dialling her next prospect.

~~~

'Don't take this the wrong way,' I said, 'but lots of older people haven't forgiven Mrs Simpson for seducing our king. You're implicated, simply because of your nationality.'

To my relief, Nancy just laughed, and asked for clarification of Prince Harry's chances of getting on the throne. She didn't seem to have noticed any animosity towards the Americans in Saffron Sweeting.

Considering Nancy had a demanding job and was also having an intellectually passionate fling with a Cambridge professor, I saw her around the village surprisingly often. We had met up at The Plough for a Friday night drink and, since the rain had eased for a few days, we'd agreed we should seize our chance to sit in the garden. Happily situated at a picnic table next to an apple tree, my clumsy attempt to explain succession rights within the Royal Family had accounted for the disappearance of our first glass of wine.

Since our arrival, more customers had trickled into the pub garden and, judging by the deep-fried smell now wafting from the kitchen, food service had begun. I wondered if I could talk Nancy into staying for another drink and something to eat.

'Well, hello, how are you?' came a friendly call.

I looked up to see Lorraine from the bed and breakfast advancing across the grass. I introduced her to Nancy and invited her to join us.

'Oh, thanks, no, my brother's inside getting drinks, he'll be out in a minute. With his kids – they're a bit of a crowd.' She laughed. 'Nobody's staying tonight, so I seized my chance for an evening out.'

I explained to Nancy that I had been a guest at Oak House for my first few nights in the village.

'Actually, Grace, I've got a bone to pick with you.' Lorraine raised a finger as if to waggle it at me, but didn't quite go that far.

'I stopped at the bakery to get tomorrow's bread,' she continued, 'and they're all sold out. Croissants, pastries, all of it. Gone.'

I didn't know what to say – how could this be my fault? I hadn't been near the bakery today.

Lorraine twinkled at me. 'Brian is singing your praises. He says you suggested a few changes and they've made a world of difference.' She lowered her voice a little. 'Apparently, he's selling twice as much to the Americans as he ever did to the Brits.'

Nancy looked intrigued. I just looked embarrassed, then felt thankful as a male version of Lorraine and three small children spilled out of the pub into the garden.

But I wasn't quite off the hook yet. Lorraine's next words bowled me for six.

'So I was wondering,' she said brightly, 'since so many

of my guests are American, can you come and do the same for me?'

Chapter 13

This was the last thing I'd been expecting. My mouth dropped far enough to catch any summer flies buzzing around the pub garden.

'Well, um, I don't know.' How could I manage this tactfully? Oak House bed and breakfast had been a friendly place to stay, but it did have room for improvement. 'Have you had advice from anyone else?' I asked Lorraine.

'No, unless you count what people put in the visitors' book. That can get lively.' She laughed.

Lorraine apparently had the thick skin that was necessary to welcome strangers into her home.

'I'm really not sure I'm qualified.' I started to wriggle out of her request, then felt a kick on my shin. Surprised, I looked across the table at Nancy. Sure enough, she widened her eyes in mock innocence and began humming meaningfully.

'Could you just come over for a cup of tea and let me know what you think?' Lorraine's tone was almost pleading now.

I remembered guiltily what Brian had said about businesses struggling in the village.

'Well, if you think I can help ...'

'Oh, that's terrific, thanks so much. How's next Thursday for you?'

~~~

Amelia was a fabulous negotiator, sticking strictly to the principle that in a real estate transaction, the person in a hurry pays the price. I had seen her wrangle for days over the fine points of a deal, then pull her client away cheerfully if the terms weren't to her liking. At that point, the other side usually caved in.

'They get invested, darling,' she had told me sanguinely. 'Once people have put a lot of time and effort into something, they have a tough time backing out altogether.'

I had stored this piece of information away for future use, wondering if James's zeal to get in touch with me stemmed from his long-time investment, or just stubbornness.

But another reason for Amelia's success was research and preparation. She seemed to know the local real estate market back to front, and never missed an opportunity to delve her nose into details of a transaction.

'Fancy a little excursion?' she asked me. 'There's a property auction tomorrow and I'm planning to go.'

'Ooh,' I said, ears alert. 'Are you buying something for a client?'

'Not yet,' she replied. 'Just want to see how the cookie crumbles.'

'I'd love to come,' I said, picturing an auctioneer in a tweed jacket and ruddy-cheeked bidders in green Wellington boots. 'Can we both be away from the office?'

She consulted her computer screen. 'Looks like it starts bright and early. We'll be back here by eleven.'

~~~

Located in a cluster of tastefully converted farm buildings on the road to Grantchester, the auctioneers were clearly making a tidy profit from their dealings. Half barrels overflowing with red geraniums marked the entrance to the car park and the way into the auction room itself. There were no tweed jackets or Wellingtons in sight and the clientele had arrived in gleaming Range Rovers rather than muddy Volvos. In fact, there were rather too many fancy cars for Amelia's liking. The manicured gravel parking area appeared full, and a helpful *Overflow* sign pointed to the adjacent field.

'I don't think so,' my boss sniffed, and prepared to

parallel park her Mercedes in the last few feet of space next to a navy convertible. I felt a soft bump as she completed the manoeuvre.

'Whoopsadaisy,' she said carelessly, but she did have the decency to check for damage on the other car's bumper. 'No harm done,' she pronounced, before hurrying me inside.

The atmosphere which greeted us was low-key. The auction hadn't yet started, but I suspected that when it did, this crowd would need a lot more caffeine to get them excited. Most of the attendees were middle-aged men wearing sensible coats over shirts and ties. There was, however, a scent of money in the air.

Amelia strode down the centre aisle, looking for good seats. Heads turned, possibly because of her height and hair colour, but more likely due to her lime green summer dress and shapely long legs. Once seated, I buried myself in the auction catalogue while she sat up like a meerkat to see who else was in the room. Just as the auctioneer arrived at his podium, I saw her exchange waved greetings with a man in the same row as us, but across the aisle. A glance in that direction told me he was much younger than most of the other buyers, with fair hair and an attractive profile. Something about him was familiar, but my attention was pulled back to the stage, where the auctioneer had begun brandishing his gavel. Things were getting under way.

For a few minutes, I followed the lots carefully, mentally weighing the merits of nine acres near Huntingdon and a former pub in Linton. The auction covered a wide area and all types of land and property seemed to be represented. I would quiz Amelia later on her area of interest.

But as the auctioneer moved on to yet another piece of boringly flat farmland, this time located on the unfortunately-named Grunty Fen Road near Ely, my attention wandered around the room. I found my eyes drawn again to the man Amelia knew. I couldn't shake the feeling I'd seen him somewhere before. I was eyeing up his profile and noting that his nose wasn't quite straight, when his head swivelled suddenly in my direction. Damn, he'd caught me. I coloured instantly and looked away, but not before he grinned at me. Trying to look nonchalant, I nodded back.

'Young lady, are you trying to bid?' The silver-haired auctioneer was scrutinising me over half-moon spectacles.

Scarlet by now, I shook my head, appalled at my blunder. I was well aware of the consequences of flapping body parts or other items around in an auction house. The last thing I needed in my life was to buy a dilapidated farmhouse near Stansted Airport by mistake. I faced front and succeeded in not looking his way again.

After about an hour, Amelia grew restless. 'C'mon,' she whispered. 'I've seen enough. Let's head back and grab a coffee.'

As we brushed past the knees lining our row and made our way to the exit, I was surprised to see her acquaintance follow us. I had noticed at one point he'd bid on a large house in Ipswich, but as far as I could tell, he didn't win it. Perhaps that was his only reason for being here.

We were nearly at the car when he caught up with us. 'Hello, Amelia.'

'Scott! Hi, how are you?'

They exchanged pleasantries and I noted Scott was a few inches taller than her, even allowing for her heels. He was wearing a dark suit which fitted his athletic build perfectly. His white shirt was open at the neck and showed off a light suntan. For an irrational moment, I pictured him in cricket gear, forearms tensed to grip the bat.

Amelia turned to introduce me. 'This is Grace,' she said. 'My new assistant.'

'Hi.' I shook his hand and found my fingers were grasped firmly. Looking up to make eye contact, I fell into a pair of eyes the colour of denim, accentuated by just a hint of fine lines. From the mischievous smile he was now throwing my way, I could see how he'd got them.

'You look different, Grace,' Scott smiled. 'With dry

clothes.'

I frowned; he grinned and waited. When the penny dropped, I wanted to hide in the nearest hedge. Cringing, I asked, 'It was you at the ford?'

'I'm afraid so.' He didn't look at all afraid. He looked like he might be enjoying himself, and I got the distinct feeling he was checking that all my clothes were, in fact, dry. For the second time that morning, I blushed.

'Oh, you two have met?' Amelia asked, pressing the button on her key to unlock the car.

'Um, no, not really.' I nipped smartly around to the passenger door to put some distance between this man and myself. I was mortified at the thought of the wet T-shirt view he'd had last time he'd seen me.

I was saved by Amelia's cheeky parking.

'God's teeth, Amelia, did you have to land on top of my car?' Scott had spotted that the bumper of the Mercedes was kissing his convertible.

'Oh, don't be a fusspot.' She tossed her head as she hopped into the driver's seat beside me, although she did slide down her window to continue the conversation. 'I didn't want to walk across the grass in my heels.'

'Of course you didn't. Perish the thought.' He tilted his head to catch my eye through the car window, and winked conspiratorially.

I couldn't help but smile back, and felt myself breathe out as I did. I was clearly out of practice at chatting with gorgeous men. There was nothing going on here, he was simply a friend of Amelia's.

'Well,' he said to Amelia, 'since I'm trapped until you move, be a doll and get a wiggle on.'

With parking pressure like that, I would most likely have found the wrong gear and crumpled both cars. Fortunately, Amelia had no such difficulties and reversed out of the space smoothly.

As we turned out of the car park onto the narrow country road, she threw me an appraising look.

'So, what was all that about?' she asked. 'Did you fail to mention there was an audience for your frolic in the river?'

I shook my head and fixed my eyes on the Cambridgeshire landscape. 'If you don't mind,' I said through tight lips, 'I'd really rather not talk about it.'

~~~

Having put the auction encounter firmly out of my mind, I directed my thoughts towards my appointment at the bed and breakfast. And once the day arrived, I found my enthusiasm for the conversation had increased. Not only had Lorraine been kind to me when I'd first arrived in Saffron Sweeting, but Oak House did have wonderful potential.

Remember to be tactful, I told myself sternly, as I parked my car by the cream-coloured walls. I checked my watch to make sure Lorraine had had enough time to finish serving breakfast and do any housekeeping that was needed.

She welcomed me with a big pot of tea and fresh cheese scones. Was she related to Brian, or was there something in the water around here which resulted in such delectable baked goods?

We sat in the breakfast room and I asked what had triggered this request.

'Well ...' She took a deep breath and I realised she was nervous. That made two of us. 'People seem to enjoy staying here, but I'm rarely full, and it doesn't really pay to just have one or two guests at a time. Most of the comments in my visitors' book are kind, but occasionally somebody says something quite blunt. Are Americans more demanding, do you think?'

'Not necessarily,' I said. 'But I think they're often less frightened to complain than Brits.'

'So, a few months ago, my father died. That's why my brother was here – we were just going over a few loose ends.'

Saving Saffron Sweeting

'I'm sorry.'

'It's okay. He'd been ill for a long time.' She paused. 'Anyway, I've inherited a decent amount – not a fortune, you understand – and I'd like to invest it in Oak House.'

'That makes sense,' I nodded. 'Especially since this is your home too.'

'I thought you would have a good sense of what would make my American guests happy.'

It was time for me to sing for my supper – or rather, scones. 'One thing you might not know,' I began gently, 'is that in the States, bed and breakfast is usually a luxury experience, and people expect top quality – with liberal sprinkles of history, antiques and so on. But they'll pay top price for it. English B&Bs are very different, usually more of a budget option.'

'I'd much rather be high-end,' Lorraine said quickly. 'I can do the history thing easily.'

'Absolutely, that's a real strength. And your cooking is definitely a plus.'

'Thanks,' she smiled. 'So ... I was thinking about adding a conservatory, for guests to enjoy when the weather isn't so wonderful. Do you think that would be nice?'

I chewed my lip, and the grandfather clock in the hall ticked by a few seconds. A sunroom addition to the house would cost many thousands of pounds. And how many of her guests sat around all day? Surely they were out, visiting the Cambridge colleges, or going off into the Suffolk countryside?

'Well, that would be lovely,' I said slowly, 'but I'm not sure it would be the best use of your money.'

I glanced at her for a negative reaction, but Lorraine was waiting receptively.

'I looked at some of your online reviews,' I continued. 'The biggest criticism seems to be for your bathrooms.'

'Oh,' she said. 'Well, it's an old house, you know?'

'I know, and it's beautiful, but Americans do love a powerful, hot shower. Could you have a plumber take a look? Maybe install power showers?' I didn't mention my own experience of the alternately freezing then dribbling water.

'I could do that,' Lorraine said.

'The other thing in the reviews is soft beds. If you were to upgrade your mattresses, that's definitely something you can add to your promotional materials.'

'Mattresses? Really?'

'Oh yes,' I confirmed. 'They won't be cheap, but if you go with a famous name, you can list it on your website and people will know you take comfort seriously. They'll infer that you're a quality place to stay.'

'I never would have thought of that.'

Right, here goes. I took a deep breath. 'Ideally, you should spend the night in each of your rooms, and see what you find.' Or feel in your spine, I thought. 'If there is a bath, lie in the bath too. You'd be amazed at what you can see from down there. Cobwebs and stuff.'

Lorraine was taking notes, which I found hugely flattering. I couldn't remember the last time I'd given an opinion and someone had written it down.

'I did that when we first opened,' she acknowledged. 'I suppose I haven't got round to it for a while. What else, Grace?'

'Your website is nice and I like it,' I told her, 'but when you've made these changes, you should get new photos. They should be professionally done. So many of your competitors have narrow-angled, dingy photos.'

'Right, super,' she said, still writing.

Was she actually going to go ahead with my suggestions?

'I can give you the name of the photographer Amelia uses, so that's easy.' I accepted another scone. 'And we should find out how to add online booking to your website.'

'Online booking?' she echoed.

'Yes – two reasons. You can update your prices easily, by season, if you like. Graduation dates in Cambridge should cost more – that kind of thing. And it's such a pain for people to contact you to find out if you've got space. I'm sure some potential guests go elsewhere, rather than take the trouble.'

'Well, I wouldn't mind not having to answer vacancy questions,' she agreed. 'Do you think that's hard to do, though?'

'I'm sure we can figure it out.' I sounded more confident than I was. Fleetingly, I thought how great it would be to ask James for help – he could probably do that kind of stuff in his sleep. But no, that was out of the question. Lorraine and I would just have to muddle through.

'Shall we take a look at each of the rooms you have?' I asked. My designer's eye was curious to see what tweaks we could make.

We visited the four guest bedrooms. All had pleasant proportions and attractive furniture. The fabrics were a bit girly, but that was hardly the end of the world for a bed and breakfast. However, there was room for improvement in the accessories Lorraine had chosen. As we went from room to room, I pointed out several spots where bigger lamps, local art or new cushions could make a big difference.

As we came back downstairs, the grandfather clock told me nearly two hours had passed. I'd been so wrapped up in our tour, I hadn't noticed the time at all. Lorraine's energy, however, was clearly on the wane.

Anxious, I bit the bullet. 'Lorraine, you've gone a bit quiet. Did I overstep the mark?'

'Oh no, Grace,' she said. 'I do see what you mean. It's just, I'm a bit daunted by all that decorative stuff. I'm better at shortbread.'

'It's important,' I said kindly. 'Those little touches really finish the room.'

'I know, it's just … my domestic goddess talents don't quite go that far.' She paused. 'I don't suppose you could help me buy what we need?'

'Oh my gosh.' My face lit up. 'I'd love to. Absolutely.'

'I'd pay you for your time, of course. On top of your fee for today.'

Pay? Time? Fee? The words floated in through my ears clearly enough, but turned immediately to marshmallow in my brain.

My grey matter was still getting over the shock of being paid for my 'consulting', as Lorraine called it, as we said goodbye outside Oak House. Otherwise, I would have been quicker to leap into my car when I saw the formidable figure of Violet approaching from the direction of the village. A dog lead dangled from her hand and sure enough, ten yards in front, trotted Mungo.

Too late: he had seen me, or smelled me, or whatever it is that canines do to target their prey. His tail accelerated from waving to frenzied wagging and the jaunty trot became a flat-out gallop as he flew down the pavement to greet me. He was running delighted rings around Lorraine and me, but mostly me, when Violet caught up. I have to say, she was sprightly for her age.

'Sorry, ladies,' she said breathlessly. 'Mungo seems to have forgotten his manners.'

'No problem,' I shrugged and tried to appear nonchalant. Time to escape. 'Well, thanks Lorraine, I must go. But we'll plan a day for our shopping trip, okay?'

Lorraine nodded effusively, then turned to Violet. 'Grace has been suggesting some changes to appeal to the Americans.'

'Has she, now?' Violet's lips made a thin line.

I found my keys and tried to untangle myself from the doggie force field around my legs.

'He's super-friendly,' Lorraine said.

Violet narrowed her eyes to match her lips. 'Yes, he's not usually like this with strangers.'

'Okay, must be off,' I attempted, as Mungo thrust his nose into my groin.

'Then again, he's not been himself recently.' Violet was undeterred. 'Acting strangely, going walkabout, that sort of thing.'

She was still looking at me. Had she rumbled that Mungo was being unfaithful and that I was the other woman? It wasn't a role I ever imagined myself playing, but the trouble was, I was really fond of him. Ugh, I bet that's what Rebecca had said too.

As Lorraine asked Violet if she'd like some eggs, I took my chance to make a low-key exit. Well, as low-key as possible, when driving a vintage Volkswagen with a clunky gearstick. At least it didn't backfire and give Violet a heart attack. That would really give her reason to dislike me.

Chapter 14

When six o'clock came and Amelia left the office, I was still buzzing with energy. It had been a fantastic day: Lorraine was delighted with my suggestions for her bed and breakfast and I'd even made some pocket money.

I tidied up a bit and took a message from the scary solicitor handling one of Amelia's pending sales. Watering the plant on the coffee table, I looked out of the window and saw Brian taking in his yellow cushions and umbrella. He was late closing tonight. I soon understood why, as a large red car jerked to a halt outside the bakery, hazard lights flashing. Mary Lou leaped out and they disappeared inside together. She re-emerged speedily with several big white cake boxes and, with only minor complaints from the car's gears, sped off.

Absent-mindedly, I tidied the newspapers and magazines, then emptied my inbox. Should I start browsing online for Lorraine's accessories? No, I decided, that kind of thing was best viewed in person. We had the Cambridge shops, including the blissfully comprehensive John Lewis department store, at our disposal.

Still, I didn't feel in the mood to go home. I checked my personal emails and found there was another from James: *Just wanted you to know I'm thinking about you. All is fine here. When you are ready, I'd love to talk. I miss you.*

He sent me messages like this a couple of times a week, but I usually didn't respond. Firstly, I didn't know what to say, and secondly, I didn't want him thinking I was sitting around with nothing to do except write to him. Better for him to assume I was busy, happy and moving on.

Wait a minute: today I really *was* busy and happy. On reflection, I'd been feeling more content for a couple of weeks now. Life in this funny little village had taken on a pleasant rhythm. I liked it here and they seemed to like me too. Well, except Violet, that is.

I hit Reply: *I'm fine, thanks. Summer is my favourite time in England and I'm enjoying myself.* Was that suitably upbeat and general? I decided it was and pressed Send.

Almost instantly, a message came back: *Can I Skype you?*

Whoa. This was more than I'd bargained for. It was just after ten in the morning in California – wasn't he at work?

I was still dithering over my response when my computer announced his incoming call. I shot back a couple of feet in my office chair. Should I answer? Could I ignore it? What would Amelia do?

I was pretty sure she would tell me to buck up and stop being a cowardy custard.

With amazing presence of mind, I remembered to answer without video. After all, it was ten hours since I'd put any make-up on.

'Grace, how are you?' Unmistakably his voice. So familiar to me, but so strange at the same time.

'I'm fine, thanks,' I replied. Neither pithy nor original, but a respectable start. Truthful too.

'Are you in London, or Norfolk?'

'Neither.' Too blunt. 'Somewhere in between,' I added. 'With friends.'

'Oh. Okay. As long as you're okay, that's good.'

There was a pause, probably of the awkward sort, but I doubt many broken marriages enjoy comfortable pauses.

'Have you decided when you're coming home?' he asked.

'Um, no.' I didn't have a home in California any more, did I? I spoke slowly and carefully. 'I think, for now ... this is home.'

'Oh. Right.'

I let the transatlantic silence stretch.

He tried again. 'Can I come and see you?'

'No.' My voice was clipped, too terse for diplomatic relations, but I couldn't help it.

'I just want you to know ...' He sighed. 'I'm really, really sorry. I'll do anything to make it up to you.'

I could hear emotion building in the back of his throat.

'I wish I could wind back the clock,' he said. 'Whenever you want to talk about it, I'm here. Or I'll come there. I just need to see you.'

For my computer-geek husband, this was an eloquent speech. I was almost impressed. 'I don't want to talk about it,' I said. But what I really wanted to know was, *Are you still with Rebecca?*

'If you change your mind, I'm ready.' He paused. 'Is there anything you need? Have you got enough money? Can I send you some?'

Considering we didn't have kids, this was decent of him. I was glad to be able to refuse with dignity.

'No thanks. I have some ... consulting work.' I was stretching the truth there, but it felt good to say it. Really good.

'That's great.' He sounded genuinely pleased. This was typical: he always had been a loyal cheerleader for me. Until the day he'd committed adultery, that is.

'What about your stuff?' he continued. 'Is there anything you want me to send? Eeyore, maybe?'

Oh, this wasn't fighting fair. Tears came out of nowhere. Out of – what? – seven billion people in the world, James was the only one who knew I still liked to sleep with a cuddly toy. Or had done. Eeyore hadn't made the cut in my frenzied packing efforts.

'Okay.' These two syllables were all I could manage. Like it or not, I was talking to my closest friend.

'And if you think of anything else, just email me. Or call. Any time.'

We said goodbye and I shut down the computer. It was kind of him to offer to send Eeyore. And a couple of other eccentric but well-loved items, like my favourite bone china mug and stripy slipper socks, wouldn't go amiss either. In the morning, I would send a carefully worded email to request them, and ask him to use my parents' address.

Standing up, I shook myself, and decided it had still been a really positive day, despite the emotional, donkey-shaped ending. I collected my things together and drove back to my cottage. Mungo was waiting on the doormat, unapologetic for his earlier exhibitionism.

'You fool,' I greeted him. 'You practically gave the game away.'

He wagged his tail heedlessly and followed me into the kitchen. 'Anyway,' I told him as I looked in the freezer for something tasty and ideally high in both fat and carbs, 'you're going to have competition soon. Eeyore's on his way.'

Unimpressed, Mungo flopped down in front of the kitchen sink, from where he kept an eye on my dinner preparations. I had just punctured the film on some frozen macaroni cheese when a sudden thought formed in my head. My contented bubble deflated as surely as if someone had stuck a fork in me too. By offering to send my stuff, James was accepting that I wasn't coming back.

'Mungo,' I sighed, 'go and fetch a corkscrew. We're going to need some wine.'

~~~

A couple of days later, Amelia started to pack up earlier than usual. 'Well, it's a tough job, but someone has to do it.' She looked decidedly cheerful.

I looked at her in puzzlement. I was re-sizing photos to use on our website and was boggle-eyed from concentrating.

'Hargraves is sponsoring the pub quiz,' she explained. 'That means I have to show up, schmooze and present prizes. And probably buy a few rounds of drinks too.'

'That's nice.' Bother, I'd stretched that house so much it looked like a dachshund's kennel.

'You should come,' she said. 'Do you good to expand your social life.'

'I have a social life,' I replied defensively. 'My best

friend's in London and I went for a drink with Nancy the other evening.' What did she want me to do, go clubbing every night?

'And the rest of the time you sit in that cottage and feel sorry for yourself, darling. Reading romance novels and talking to that dog, I expect.'

Was it that obvious? I had felt especially listless since the call with James. 'I like the cottage.' My tone was sulky now.

'Great, so it'll still be there when you get back from the quiz tonight.'

'Oh, Amelia, I dunno ...'

'Relax, will you? It's not *Mastermind.*'

~~~

Naturally, the first five minutes were the worst. My awkwardness on arriving at The Plough subsided when I found myself randomly allocated to a team by Amelia. She plonked me down on a little round stool with a glass of Chardonnay in one hand and a pencil in the other.

'This is Grace,' Amelia introduced me. 'She lived in California so she should be a big asset.'

My teammates introduced themselves.

'Hello, Grace. I'm Marjorie. I used to work in the bank before it closed; now I do a spot of cleaning for Lorraine. You know Lorraine, at the bed and breakfast? And this is my son, Eddie. He's home from college for the summer, aren't you, Eddie?'

I could see the family resemblance: both mother and son were round of face and body, with curly blond hair and freckles. Eddie nodded at me obligingly. As the evening progressed, I learned he was a young man of few words, probably because Marjorie supplied them all.

A dark-skinned man in his late fifties shook my hand. 'I'm Kenneth; pleasure to meet you.' With great care, he placed not one, but two sharpened pencils and a little notepad on the table.

'Kenneth runs the Sweeting Library. Takes our pub quizzes quite seriously.' Marjorie looked nervously in Kenneth's direction.

Oh dear, I thought, the last thing I need is somebody getting ants in his pants over each wrong answer.

'And I'm Peter. Hi, Grace, glad you're joining us.'

'Hi.' I took a quick look – forties, slim, attractive. Hair a bit too long, dark red sweater, probably cashmere. I had a soft spot for cashmere. 'What do you do?' I asked him.

'I own the antiques store, the barn, on the main road to Waterbeach.'

'Oh yes, I think I know. I've been meaning to come and look round.' Clearly, I hadn't yet fully explored the attractions of Saffron Sweeting. I wondered if Amelia had chosen this team for me randomly, after all.

'You like antiques?' he smiled.

'Very much – but I'm not at all knowledgeable,' I replied truthfully.

After a pause, Kenneth said, 'I suppose we have to see the funny side of Amelia sponsoring a drinking event.'

Peter gave a tight smile and shrugged. 'She's fine now.'

What did that mean? I waited for Kenneth to say more, but he just sniffed and made himself busy rolling the pencils under his fingers.

Marjorie, however, caught my eye and leaned closer. 'Amelia was a bit too fond of the bottle at one stage,' she whispered loudly. 'Almost got done for drink driving several winters back.'

Peter frowned at Marjorie. 'It was Valentine's Day. Just after her divorce was final.'

I nodded. I could well imagine a bleak February evening, her marriage cold in its coffin, and Amelia's desperate need for oblivion. But I wasn't going to sit here and gossip about my employer. By any measure, she'd been really kind to me.

Seeking a change of subject, I looked around the pub.

There were six teams assembled, with four or five people in each. Fergus, the pub landlord, looked delighted to have so many patrons on a Wednesday night. I saw Brian the baker in the far corner, and Nancy appeared to be on his team too. Making up another team, I saw Violet and her two women friends, plus a man who I think was the village postman.

'I know a few of the faces, but not many,' I said. 'I've only been here a couple of months.'

'Not many newcomers are here,' Marjorie said. 'It's basically word of mouth to be invited.'

'They probably wouldn't feel very welcome.' Peter caught her eye. Then he said to me, 'It takes a while to be accepted around here.'

I couldn't tell whether he was making a general observation, or trying to warn me, but it didn't matter as I'd mostly shrugged off Violet's iciness. I looked again at Nancy's group, but they showed no signs of resentment towards her.

'The pop culture questions and modern history are usually British focused,' Kenneth chimed in earnestly. 'Although heaven knows why we have a pop section. Some international politics wouldn't go amiss.' He adjusted his wire-rimmed spectacles.

We were a strong team. Kenneth, of course, knew a lot about a lot. Marjorie had apparently become a fan of daytime television since the bank made her redundant. And Peter showed deep knowledge of the arts and English history. I filled in where I could, with the capital of Idaho and the number of Elizabeth Bennet's sisters, but I wasn't needed much. That suited me: I was happy to keep quiet unless my team was stuck. Besides, I didn't want to draw Kenneth's wrath for getting Eric Clapton's star sign wrong.

Our weak area was science and technology. Judging by the groans that greeted these questions, this was a failing the other teams shared. By contrast, as the only person in the room with a biology PhD, Nancy was much celebrated by her accomplices.

The quiz was boisterous but light-hearted. I was surprised to discover how the clock had advanced while we had been busy drinking, thinking and munching Twiglets. Fifty questions resulted in a tie between Nancy's team and a group of Cambridge graduate students who had infiltrated the event. Unhappily for them, the tie-breaker was to name all the US presidents who had died in office. The Cambridge grads put up a good fight, but floundered after the three juiciest assassinations and FDR. As Nancy told me later, 'I've always been a sponge for facts like that. We had those names drilled into us in grade school.' She aced the question and Amelia presented Marks and Spencer vouchers to Nancy and her exuberant teammates.

As the quiz participants dispersed, I heard Marjorie debating with Eddie which of them had had less to drink. I too was wondering whether I was under the limit to drive home. Then she turned to me to say goodbye.

'Very nice to meet you, Grace. Lorraine told me she's looking forward to making the changes you recommended.'

Peter overheard this. 'Aha!' His expression became animated and he turned to me. 'The penny's just dropped – that was you?'

'Er, yes.'

'Of course it was,' he said. 'It makes perfect sense now. Good for you.'

I still felt shy about the advice I had given Lorraine. In the hope of escaping the conversation tactfully, I joined Nancy at the bar. But it seemed the topic was a hard one to shake off.

'How was your visit to the bed and breakfast?' she asked immediately.

I told Nancy a little about my morning at Oak House and how much I'd enjoyed it.

'I undercharged her, of course. I was so surprised to be offered money at all; I thought I was simply doing a neighbourly favour.'

Nancy laughed and tore open a pub-sized bag of

peanuts.

'Amelia was cross with me,' I continued. 'She huffed and puffed and gave me a lecture on valuing myself.'

'I read something about women having a hard time talking about money.' Nancy munched on her nuts.

'It was just such a shock. I'd enjoyed the morning and then she wanted to pay me for it.'

'Grace, that's how work is supposed to be. Enjoyable, I mean, and doing what you're good at, for money.'

It didn't sound so bizarre when Nancy said it. Why did it feel so strange to me, then?

'Talking of work,' I said, 'you were impressive tonight.'

'Thank you, ma'am,' she laughed. 'Too bad none of my countrymen are here – that would have been much fairer.'

'Apparently, they weren't invited.' I was only half joking.

'Are you driving home?' Nancy asked.

'Whoops, can you tell I'm squiffy?' I giggled. 'No, I'll leave the car here and walk.'

'I can drive you,' she said. 'I only had a glass.'

Nancy shifted her gaze to my left shoulder and smiled politely. I realised Peter had joined us at the bar and introduced them. Thankfully, I wasn't so tipsy that I couldn't remember his name. Nancy gave him a quick once-over, taking in his floppy brown hair and friendly face. He wasn't quite the local Ewan McGregor I had joked about, but he wasn't bad at all.

'Do either of you ladies need a lift home?' he asked us.

'No thanks, I think we're good,' Nancy replied.

'Well, in that case, I'll wish you a pleasant evening.' He turned from us before apparently remembering something. 'Er, sorry.' He swallowed. 'Grace, could I trouble you for your phone number?'

Chapter 15

'Really? I always thought he was gay.'

I blinked slowly and stared at Amelia. Whether or not she liked a drink, she was far more alert than me this morning.

'Sorry?' My grey matter struggled to catch up.

'Peter. I thought he had a boyfriend. Partner. Whatever.'

Oh, shoot me, now.

Nancy had driven me home, affirmed that she found Peter attractive, and airily dismissed my protests that it was far too early to think about going out with someone.

'Grace, honey, you're not getting engaged to him. He's cute. See what happens.'

'It's just so unexpected,' I'd said.

'Well, it shouldn't be,' she'd laughed at me. 'You're not going to be a nun for the rest of your life, are you?'

'I hadn't thought about it.'

'Well, cross that off your list, babe. Did I mention he's cute?'

I'd thanked Nancy for the lift and made an unsteady beeline for bed. I'd fallen asleep in mere seconds – all that wine – but then found myself wide awake at 3 a.m., thinking about the evening and Peter asking me out. Shocked, flattered and confused, I kneaded the questions around in my mind.

Did I like him? Was I ready to start seeing someone? What were the norms of dating these days? Was he too old for me? What would James think? Why did I care what James would think? What would my mother think? That last one was the most disturbing of all.

In short, I'd worked myself up into a tangled mess of sheets, pillows and self-reflection. By the time the sparrows and blackbirds started trilling outside my window, I was muzzy-headed and irritated with myself. Possibly just a little hung-over too.

Realising I had once again fallen victim to nocturnal over-thinking, I'd taken a chilly shower, applied extra under-eye concealer and affected a breezy air as I arrived in the office with two large coffees. Slicing open the envelopes of our morning post, I'd told Amelia about Peter chatting me up.

Now, her words sunk in. I wanted to crawl under my desk and throw up, not necessarily in that order.

'I think they run the antiques shop together. Partners in both senses,' Amelia continued.

'Blimey,' I groaned. 'I – am – *so – embarrassed*.'

'Are you all right? You've gone a bit green, darling.' She was looking at me with great amusement.

'How could I –?' I gulped and shook my head. 'Thank God you told me!' I put my forehead in my hands.

'Look, you weren't to know.' Amelia got up from her desk to perch side-saddle on mine. 'Easy mistake to make.'

'I can't believe I was daft enough to think he fancied me,' I said, followed quickly by, 'You won't tell anyone, will you?'

'I won't tell anyone. But why shouldn't men fancy you? You're lovely.' Amelia nudged the letter opener out of my reach.

Mortified, but not actually suicidal, I shook my head mutely.

'Yes, you are,' she insisted. 'I'm pretty sure Brian has a crush on you, for starters.'

'Brian? He's married,' I countered.

Amelia snorted indelicately. 'Oh, and that stops them, does it?'

Ouch. There was a short silence before I said quietly, 'Low blow.'

'Sorry, Grace, that wasn't very sporting of me. But really ... which world do you live in?' She hopped off my desk and started to change the toner in the printer.

'Yeah, okay. I get it. As for Peter, I'm still absolutely humiliated.'

'At least you didn't dress up sexy and throw yourself at him.'

'True.' That would have been too much to live down.

'Look on the bright side. Now you can spend all day wondering what it is he wants.'

~ ~ ~

In fact, I had to wait almost a week for the ironic truth. It was a perfect August evening when I parked the white Beetle outside Peter's antiques barn, but I was focused on business, not pleasure. His eagerness to see me again had been based on recommendations from Brian and Lorraine. Apparently, it was common industry knowledge that Americans loved to buy antiques, and Peter couldn't understand why his sales weren't stronger.

'Here you are! Thanks for coming!' Peter came out of the barn to greet me.

I had some difficulty meeting his eye, but reminded myself that if Amelia and Nancy could be trusted, only the three of us knew of my slip-up. James used to tease me that my gaydar was terrible, but compared to some of the interior designers I had met in San Francisco, Peter was anything but camp. Warm and kind, yes, but not camp. He led me inside the barn, where another man was just leaving.

'Excuse me,' he said, 'I'm toddling off.'

'Grace, this is Giles, my co-owner,' Peter said.

'Lovely to meet you,' Giles shook my hand. 'Peter's over the moon that you're here.'

Okay, my gaydar was working just fine now. It wasn't the patterned pink and grey sweater Giles was sporting, nor was it his tastefully trimmed moustache or the lilt in his voice: it was the sum of these details and many more. Grace Palmer, I thought, you nearly made a five-star idiot of yourself.

We said goodnight to Giles and I looked around the barn. While my eyes adjusted to the dim light, my nose explored instead. I inhaled a wonderful blend of beeswax, mahogany and history. There were under-notes of camphor and leather. I breathed deeply and contentedly.

'Oh, there are some stories here,' I said, once I could see the array of treasures.

Amongst the large furniture were dozens of smaller items, all begging to be touched. My first glance found a pile of patchwork quilts, a wine crate full of printing blocks, and agricultural tools sitting next to ancient, cracked suitcases. Open drawers revealed bundles of postcards and silver spoons tied with black ribbon. On the floor were cloudy glass chemistry jars and a worn but dignified rocking horse. Looking up, I found vintage bunting and even a garden gate hanging from a beam.

'It's fantastic,' I said longingly. 'I could take most of it home with me, right now.'

Peter smiled. 'I'm glad you like it. Giles and I buy what takes our fancy, and we hope for the best.'

'And ... it isn't going all that well?'

'No. Not considering our local market and what others in the industry are saying.' He rubbed his jaw thoughtfully. I tried to forget how inappropriately I'd been thinking about that jaw just the other night.

'We thought maybe it's too untidy,' he suggested. 'Too random?'

'Hmm, I don't think that's the trouble.' I shook my head. 'Correct me if I'm wrong, but I assume most of your customers are browsing for things they *like*, not things they *need*?'

'I suppose so, yes.'

'I'm thinking it's more likely to be your marketing.'

'Ah, right, yes. We did advertise in the post office window – is that what you mean?'

Be tactful, Grace. 'I think we can do better than that.'

An hour later, we had brainstormed a dozen ways for

Peter and Giles to generate more interest. Their website was uninspiring, but Peter said they simply didn't have the skills or money to keep it up to date. Instead, we decided they would create a page on Facebook, and promote 'new' items with photos. They were going to have a cheese and wine party at the barn, inviting the whole village. And they would start offering free in-home consultations.

'I don't think the Brits do this as much, but Americans seem to like expert advice,' I told him. 'Everything from their taxes to where to hang their art. So don't be shy in telling your Yankee customers what they need.'

'Really? How interesting.' He smiled at me. 'And when we're rushed off our feet, we'll hire you to do that part for us.'

He was kidding, I assumed.

'You'll need a photo album full of example pieces for the consultations,' I told him. 'To show people what you're suggesting. Not everyone knows their Queen Anne from their elbow. Start tearing pictures out of magazines too: anything that might inspire people.'

'Right, like a portfolio?' Peter asked me.

'Precisely. Now, what else?' I was in full flood, the ideas just kept coming. Peter was obviously highly intelligent, but there was so much more he and Giles could do to promote themselves. 'You should get a sign out on the main road too. Make it friendly: *Browsers Welcome.*'

I had a further idea for promoting his business, but thought I should discuss it with Amelia first.

Like Lorraine, Peter had been taking notes, in a lovely brown leather portfolio on his desk. I couldn't imagine James ever owning anything so stylish. I said another silent thank you to Amelia for saving me from total shame and ploughed on with my ideas.

'You take credit cards, don't you? No? Okay, you have to fix that.' Too bossy? Hopefully not – he didn't seem to mind. 'And you do free delivery?'

'Er, we don't usually arrange delivery,' Peter said. 'Is

that a problem?'

'Well, put it this way. Picture an American wife, recently arrived here, her husband's at work, she's bored, she's exploring all the English shops.' I paused to make sure he was still with me. 'She finds a darling antique console table for her new house, which will be perfect in the front hall and impress her new friends. But there's no way it'll fit in the boot of the ridiculously small English car that she's got stuck with.' I took a breath. 'Don't you think we should make it as easy as possible for her?'

Slowly but surely, Peter began to nod. 'Brian was right,' he grinned. 'You're worth every penny.'

~~~

Nancy and Mungo were engaged in a fervent tug-of-war in my living room, doing battle over a tatty grey stick he'd been treating like a best friend.

I was on the sofa with legs tucked under me, hunting through a cookbook from the library. Nancy had hinted that she wanted to learn to make an English roast, so she could impress the super-discerning Elijah with a dinner invitation. Hence, there was a lump of silverside in my fridge and I wasn't sure what to do with it. Despite my love of great food, I much prefer it when someone else does the hard work.

It was the Sunday of the Bank Holiday weekend; rain clouds had lurked ominously over Saffron Sweeting for the last four days and were now giving us a solid drenching. The tables outside the bakery were deserted as villagers scuttled to do essential errands only. The annual cricket match against Bottisham was a wash-out. By contrast, the ducks at the pond were thrilled. They had started to form raiding parties to explore the exotic puddles of the High Street and I wondered if they were considering a full-scale coup, or at least running for a seat on the local council.

Nancy and Mungo's game ended with an abrupt crack as the unhappy stick broke. Mungo retreated to the hearth to chew up the longer half, scattering drool-covered bark over my floor.

Nancy collapsed back in an armchair. 'He gives a great arm workout,' she laughed, then looked around. 'Have you made some changes, Grace?'

'Hmm?' I wasn't keen on any of the recipes: too fancy for a couple of novice chefs. 'I think we should just shove it in the oven for a couple of hours.'

'This place looks more homely,' Nancy carried on. 'Have you been buying stuff?'

'What? Oh yes, I have.'

After a bit of awkwardness, I'd agreed to let Peter pay me in goods. He had helped me pick out a lovely antique sewing table, a mantel clock with a solemn tick and an ancient, moth-weary Union Jack flag. These new treasures gave me fresh perspective on the cottage: it was still an achingly blank canvas, but with loads of potential. I'd set to work, beginning with my library card. The living room coffee table and the cabinet beside my bed now sported tempting piles of browse-worthy books. Next, I had risked a criminal record by helping myself to some of the late summer grasses in the lane outside the cottage. These were now dotted about in old jam jars and in front of the fireplace was a jug of rose-hip stems.

As planned, I had accompanied Lorraine on a Cambridge shopping trip for bed and breakfast accessories. I had touched, measured, squinted and checked her opinion time and again, until I had a firm idea of her budget and taste. My creative juices were flowing again: exploring autumn designs in the English stores made an interesting change from the summer stock I'd seen in Crate & Barrel and Pottery Barn.

Inevitably, I'd started mentally transporting bits and pieces to my own cottage. Returning the following day to make Lorraine's purchases, I'd bowed to the inevitable and had splurged on a few things for myself. My living room now boasted an abstract wool rug, bright cushions and chunky candles on the mantelpiece. The stark, transitory rental was now a cosy sanctuary.

'Probably a sign you're feeling better,' Nancy smiled, and sipped her mug of tea. She still took it black, with lemon, but at least she'd stopped asking for Lipton in public. Not that it was anything to do with me, but I'd much rather my new American friend embarrassed herself by messing up the pronunciation of Peterborough than drank something that no self-respecting Brit would order.

'I am,' I agreed. 'At least, the fog is wearing off.'

'Will you launch an interior design business here?' she asked. 'You'd be awesome.'

'I dunno. I don't think so. Amelia said I should consider home staging, but ...'

'But?'

'Well, there's just so much pressure, once someone's paying you for something.'

'But I thought Lorraine and Peter paid you?' Nancy was at her most bird-like, fixing her clever, sharp eyes on me. 'Was that pressure?'

'Well, no, but most of it was so obvious to me. I couldn't charge a lot for telling people things that are staring me in the face.'

'Well, honey, they weren't staring them in the face. I think you should put your rates up.'

'You talk like I have a business.'

'You could, if you wanted, I bet.'

'I don't think so. Anyway, they might both be bankrupt within a month and chasing after me with a pitchfork.' Nancy's prodding was making me uncomfortable. I'd only been helping a couple of friends, after all. 'Right,' I said, changing the subject. 'Let's go and show this beef who's boss.'

The meat had made it into the oven unscathed and early aromas suggested it wasn't a total disaster. Mungo, at any rate, had stationed himself firmly in the middle of the kitchen, so he didn't miss anything crucial. We had peeled and parboiled the potatoes for roasting and I was now attempting to explain Yorkshire puddings to Nancy.

'No, they're not dessert, we eat them with the beef,' I told her.

'You mean, like we put maple syrup on our bacon? Sweet and savoury together?' She was trying to keep a culinary open mind.

'No.' I furrowed my brow. 'They're not sweet. More like a ...' I was sure I'd had something like them, somewhere in the States. 'A popover!' I finally declared, dredging up a memory from a trip to Vermont. 'A little baked batter roll thingummy.'

'Oh, a *popover!*' Nancy laughed. She stole a raw carrot to munch, then gave me a quick one-shouldered hug. 'Thanks, Grace, this is great. Elijah's so into his food.'

'Umm?' I was busy trying not to get spattered by the beef as I squeezed the tray of potatoes into the narrow oven. My stove in Menlo Park had been twice this size.

'Yes, he's mentioned a couple of times how great his wife's cooking is.'

'Is it?' I kicked shut the oven door, then turned slowly as her words filtered through. 'Sorry,' I said, 'whose cooking?'

Instantly, Nancy looked uncomfortable. 'His wife's,' she repeated softly.

I put my hands up to my face and wondered if I was about to pass out, as the room went black. But no, I just had navy oven gloves on. I threw them down on the counter and bit my lip.

'This is Elijah, right?' I asked her carefully.

She nodded.

'The man you've been seeing for, what, six months? The man you moved continents to be with?'

'Grace –'

'And he's *married?*' I couldn't have been more upset if Nancy had told me she was shagging the prime minister.

'Grace, he is, but his marriage is over. He and his wife –

they're practically separated.'

'Oh, he told you that, did he?'

'He has an apartment in Cambridge; he hardly sleeps at home any more. He's just waiting for the right time to start the divorce.'

I let out a squawk. 'How could you? You fool!'

Mungo lifted his head in concern as Nancy took a step towards me and I took one back.

'Grace, I know this is awkward, what with –'

'You're sleeping with another woman's husband,' I hissed. 'Have you considered what that makes you?'

'It isn't like that. I told you, the marriage is toast.'

'Has anyone told his wife that? Have either of you thought about how she feels?'

Nancy folded her arms and looked at the kitchen floor. 'I get it, you're upset. I don't blame you.'

'No, I'm not upset,' I bit out. 'I'm disgusted. Take it from me, his marriage *isn't* over. His wife *doesn't* know and he *isn't* thinking about divorce.'

Nancy had turned white, her voice a whisper. 'But he said he loves me.'

Mungo looked alarmed and jumped up to visit each of us. Nancy's pat was limp so he turned instead to me and nudged my hip with his velvet nose.

My glare disintegrated and I began to cry. 'I can't believe you have a PhD but fell for this. He's stringing you along – you're better than that.'

'Well, I sure appreciate your vote of confidence.' She went into the living room and gathered up her bag and jacket. I sagged against the kitchen sink, partly because Mungo had snuggled up for reassurance and was pressing his weight against my knees.

'Not sure I'm in the mood for beef.' Nancy touched me briefly on the arm, then opened the back door and headed out into the rain.

Chapter 16

'So Mungo got the best supper of his life,' I told Jem ruefully on the phone a couple of days later. I was in bed unusually early, tired and listless.

'Roast beef, lucky hound,' she replied. 'And how about you, did you eat anything?'

'I skipped the beef and put golden syrup on the Yorkshire puddings,' I admitted. 'I was so churned up by the whole thing. Do you think I should have just held my tongue?'

Down the phone line, I heard Jem suck her breath through her teeth. 'I don't know,' she said. 'Everyone's situation is different. And you've never actually met what's-his-name, have you?'

'Nope,' I conceded. I'd never laid eyes on Elijah.

'But I don't blame you for being upset. She doesn't exactly come out of it smelling of roses.'

'Nope,' I repeated eloquently, concentrating on tucking the duvet more tightly around my feet.

'What matters now is, what are you going to do? Will you apologise, or just let it be?'

'I don't feel much like apologising,' I said. 'But I could use a few friends here. Besides, I like Nancy. I was just so shocked she would willingly be a part of it.'

'Love is blind, and all that.'

'Hmph. Love should get some contact lenses. There seems to be an awful lot of cheating in this world.'

'I know, Grace,' Jem said quietly. After a few moments, she added, 'But it's not up to you to sort it all out.'

She was right. I had enough on my plate. 'Anyway,' I said, changing tack, 'I've got a slightly more pressing problem.'

'Oh yes?'

I could hear my brother in the background, helping to

keep Seb occupied so that Jem and I could talk. He'd never been that obliging when he'd lived at home.

'Something really bad has happened.' I could feel my palms getting sweaty, just thinking about it.

'What? What's wrong?'

'I've been asked to speak at the parish council meeting.'

'Whatever for?'

I pulled the petrifying letter from my bedside table, where I'd stuffed it hastily in the back of a library book and hoped it might disappear. 'They're doing a special meeting on new opportunities for village businesses. Something about promoting Saffron Sweeting to a diverse population.'

There was a pause while Jem translated this. 'You mean, selling stuff to the Americans?'

'Precisely,' I said.

'And they think you know about that?'

'They do. Seems that Peter – he's the antiques guy, if you remember – has been singing my praises.'

'But that's great! You'll be brilliant!'

Argh, she just wasn't getting it. 'But, Jem –'

'But what?'

'You know I'd rather chew my own leg off than speak in public.'

~~~

Try as I might to think of a way to say *No* tactfully, I didn't seem to be able to wriggle out of the talk. Led by Peter, Brian and Lorraine had formed an unofficial fan club and had been whispering in influential ears. Brian was even planning to say a few introductory words on the difference in his bakery. Worse, I discovered that businesses from the neighbouring villages were also invited. This meant the audience would swell into double figures, at least. What on earth have I started, I thought.

Amelia, of course, was all for it. 'I think it's marvellous, darling! You certainly made a terrific difference here.' She waved a bejewelled hand around the office. 'Anyway, it's only a few shopkeepers – not like you're giving a speech to the UN.'

Well, she wouldn't see the problem, I thought moodily, as I began stapling a stack of property details with far more force than was necessary. She would love to be centre stage for an evening. I bet she could be caught by a BBC news crew in her pyjamas and say something witty and eloquent.

A moment later, I felt ungrateful as she offered to help me practise my talk and choose something 'captivating' to wear.

'If you'd like ...' She eyed me carefully before sticking her neck out further.

I planted a neutral look on my face. Was she going to offer to get me hammered, so I wouldn't have to talk while sober?

She wasn't. 'We could do a bit more with your make-up too.'

~~~

That's how, a few evenings before the meeting, I found myself seated at Amelia's dressing table for a trial run.

I hadn't known what to expect from her home. Would she inhabit a sleek, modern pad? Or the penthouse of a converted manor? Or maybe she would prefer five-bedroom luxury, with an in-and-out driveway.

It turned out to be surprisingly small, by a sharp bend in the river on the edge of the village. I guessed there were just two bedrooms, one for Amelia and one for her son, Oscar. I'd met him only once and he'd just gone back to boarding school for the new term.

'Michael got the house, I got the business, darling,' she told me. 'I bought this a couple of years after the divorce and re-did it. It used to be the fire engine house.'

So that explained the single storey and huge patio doors in her living room. She had used a lot of natural materials –

stone, slate, wood – but the overall effect was clean and contemporary. In her bedroom, the wall behind the bed was papered in a beautiful bronze metallic. The curtains, a shimmering shade of coffee, appeared to be silk. A bank of fitted wardrobes ran along one wall. I wondered if they housed her clothes, or only her shoes.

'You haven't told me what caused your divorce.' I hoped we knew each other well enough for me to be nosy.

Amelia was unscrewing a tube of foundation but stopped and looked at me in the mirror.

'We grew apart,' she said, frowning at the memory. 'I was so young – I'd only just finished at Cambridge when we met. I was temping, saving money. I was going to move to London and try my luck as an actress.'

'But you met Michael?'

'Yup. He was older, charming, so smooth. He persuaded me to work for him, instead.'

'And?'

Amelia started to dab foundation around my nose. 'And for ten years or so, it was lovely. But things changed after Oscar was born. I think Michael had a midlife crisis – he was almost certainly playing around.'

I sighed. Was this how every marriage came unstuck?

'When he talked about escaping it all and moving to Spain, well, we didn't last long after that.'

'Oh.' I digested this. 'So he went to Spain?'

'No. Turned out he just needed to escape from me.' She wiped her fingers on a tissue before inspecting my face.

'How long ago was this?' I asked.

'Gosh, I dunno, eight, nine years.'

'But you seem ... fine, now.'

'I've had my share of dark moments.'

Did she mean the alcohol? I waited for more, but she didn't elaborate. Instead, she started selecting make-up colours. I wriggled nervously in front of the mirror, wondering if I had been right to agree to this. I was a minimal make-up wearer, who liked to put it on at eight in the morning, then forget about it.

'Relax,' Amelia said, 'I'm not going to make you look like a clown. Let's try this eyeshadow and see what you think.'

I took a glug of the red wine I had brought. I'd purchased it at the post office and it was evident that Violet was not one of the world's great vintners. In fact, it was only really fit for sangria. Still, it dulled my nerves as Amelia dabbed, brushed and blended.

She was shockingly quick and I was half disappointed when, after only about ten minutes, she stood back and said, 'Gorgeous.'

Not quite the words I would have used, but I had to agree I looked good. She had brushed tawny eyeshadow on my lids, with some kind of highlighter on my brow bones and cheekbones. Dark brown mascara made me look more awake than usual. And rather than heavy lipstick, she had skimmed my mouth with a gentle rose lip gloss. I resisted the urge to lick if off immediately. The overall effect was healthy and flirtatious.

'Do you like it?' she asked me, looking confident.

'I do.' I peered at myself again while the surprise wore off. 'I don't know how to say this modestly, but I really do.'

I wondered what James would think if he could see me, then reminded myself sternly that I shouldn't care.

'Excellent!' Amelia clapped her hands fleetingly, like a girl forty years younger. 'Well, that was fun. Now, come through to the kitchen and we'll have a proper drink.'

I settled myself at the island in her sleek and stylish kitchen, surreptitiously checking out my surroundings. I loved the black and white tiles behind her stove, but didn't fancy keeping the inky granite counters free of smears. Then again, I suspected she rarely cooked.

'Tomorrow,' Amelia said, bringing out a bottle of vodka, 'we can look at your clothes. That still gives us late-night shopping on Wednesday if we have to get you something new.'

'Okay,' I said meekly, declining the booze. I was starting to feel this council meeting might not be the end of the world. Amelia had already made me prepare a set of reminder index cards to hold, in case my mind went totally blank.

Amelia poured herself a generous splash of vodka, adding a thimbleful of orange juice for garnish. Then she perched on a stool at the island, sweeping a pile of paper to one side. I knew she worked hard, but had no idea she brought quite this much home with her.

'What is all this stuff?' I asked. 'New listings?'

'Most of it's for an investment I'm considering. And some industry reading, which of course I always fall asleep before I get to. Oh, and the odd deal for a client.'

I was impressed. My idea of an investment these days was a moth-eaten Union Jack flag.

Amelia looked at me carefully. 'Grace,' she started, 'I didn't want to tell you this sooner because I thought you'd get in a tizz about it.'

I sucked in my cheeks.

'You know you tend to worry about things that might never happen,' she continued, extracting some papers from the pile. 'But it does look now as if it's going through.'

'What's going through?'

She passed me the papers and I saw they were from her scary solicitor friend. It took me a few moments to process the legal mumbo jumbo. I pushed them away from me with a sigh.

'Well, that's all I need.' I ran my tongue around my teeth, remembering my beautiful lip gloss a fraction too late. Then, I added stoically, 'I don't suppose you've got any ice cream?'

'I'm sorry, darling.' Amelia shook her head and reached for my hand.

I don't know whether she was apologising for her badly-stocked pantry with its dearth of frozen desserts, or for her imminent success in selling my cottage.

Chapter 17

Just as the parish council request had overshadowed my fight with Nancy, so the prospect of becoming homeless took my mind off the talk.

I was surprised how rattled I was at the prospect of losing the cottage. After all, I'd lived there less than three months. But, ever since I was a kid, my surroundings had been important to me: around the age of thirteen, I remember begging my mum to change the wallpaper and bed linen in my room to a Laura Ashley print. And the recent small improvements I'd made to the cottage had made it feel like mine. It was the anchor point in my new life and I looked forward to coming home each night.

I didn't blame Amelia for not telling me sooner. She was right: I would have tortured myself with what-if scenarios. As it was, she'd told me the sale was still being negotiated and would take at least a month to become final. At that point, she promised to throw her considerable influence behind finding new digs for me.

'Just go with the flow, Grace,' she'd said. 'It'll all be fine.'

~~~

September was delivering a shaky Indian summer and the evening of the parish council meeting was humid. When we arrived at the village hall, I was dismayed to see so many sweaty bodies crammed into the dark, musty space. Had they got the wrong night? Did they think this was the thrilling alternative of Neighbourhood Watch?

I was wearing flowing silky trousers in a quiet shade of mushroom, purchased in John Lewis the day before. On my feet were bronze sandals with a chunky heel, loaned by Amelia to make me look taller but hopefully not in danger of 'taking a tumble'. We'd also found a stretchy top in a green and cream print, slightly ruffled around the neckline. The ruffles had the surprising side effect of enhancing my chest size, and I'd been reluctant to wear it for a business meeting.

Amelia, though, had brushed this objection aside. 'Don't be daft! You look fabulous and the colours bring out your eyes.'

She had done my make-up again and so far I had kept my nervous teeth away from the lip gloss. In fact, my anxious molars had been greatly helped by a large glass of Sauvignon Blanc before we set out.

So now, all I had to do was talk. Simple, right? I sat at the end of the front row and tried to listen as Brian introduced me. But my ears couldn't process his words. My insides were churning like a butter factory and my tongue discovered that my mouth was as dry as plain toast. Did I have time to make it to the loo and throw up?

I did not. To scattered applause from the audience and a cheerful poke in the ribs from Amelia, I stood, turned and faced a sea of expectant faces. In reality, there were probably only thirty people present, but in the little hall, I felt as if I were facing several hundred. There was no stage and no microphone, and I was grateful to my employer for her choice of shoes.

'Thank you for inviting me,' I began. I paused, coughed, and instantly forgot all I had planned to say. In a panic, I looked down at my first index card.

'My name is Grace Palmer and I've just returned from four years in California. Nonetheless, England is my home and always will be.'

'Speak up,' someone hollered.

I tried again. 'I'm enormously grateful for the welcome given to me by the kind residents of Saffron Sweeting.' That was louder and better. I swallowed and remembered to exhale. Risking a look at my tormentors, I discovered friendly faces amongst the mob. Brian was there, of course. Lorraine and Marjorie were sitting in the third row, as was

Violet, although she looked more sceptical than supportive. Standing at the back, apparently a late arrival, was Peter. He waved at me and gave me his big grin. I smiled back and felt my jaw relax a little.

'I've been asked to talk to you this evening because it seems a fresh perspective may be useful. I don't have too much expertise in this area –'

'Rubbish,' Brian heckled cheerfully.

'– but I'll be happy to offer some suggestions on attracting new customers to your business.'

I glanced at Amelia, who was nodding encouragingly, like a proud mother at a school nativity play.

'It's no secret that the population of Saffron Sweeting is growing,' I continued. 'And I think that's a good thing. The opportunities from the newcomers from America are huge. However, with new customers come new expectations. I encourage you to consider adapting to these new demands. Go with this new tide and see where it takes you.'

My own nervous tide was still swooshing around in my stomach, but it was more gentle now. And at least they were listening. 'The topic you've given me is tricky to cover, without making sweeping generalisations.' This had been my biggest fear: how to talk about both Yanks and Limeys without offending both groups horribly. I had agonised over the right choice of words. Words which had now deserted me.

I thought about the little tables and umbrellas outside the bakery, and pressed on. 'Some of the principles apply regardless of who you think your customers are. Some are more targeted at our cousins from across the Atlantic.'

I caught Lorraine's eye and she gave me a thumbs up. Violet was fanning herself but at least she hadn't walked out. In fact, nobody had. I remembered my index cards and realised I had reached the meaty part of my talk. Right, Grace Palmer, *here goes.*

Fifteen minutes later, as I sat down to enthusiastic applause, I found I had been concentrating so hard on getting my message across, I had forgotten to worry about how they were receiving it.

I had talked about the importance of personalising the product or service: 'Spotted Dick shouldn't always have to come with custard'. I had waxed lyrical on the need to be found easily online, along with the possibilities presented by social media. I had been passionate in my request that they listen to their customers: 'Ask them what they think. Your average American is more forthcoming than your average Brit: I bet they'll tell you. And when they do, thank them and tell them to Have a Nice Day!'

And I had told them of my belief in beefing up their product or service: 'Add some value. Give something for nothing. For the bakery, free refills seem to be working already. For the antiques store, it means free delivery. At the pub, give them a free glass of water.' The landlord looked horrified. 'Go on, I dare you,' I'd insisted, my nerves, by this time, melting on the floor beside me. 'But when you do improve your service or make it a little special, don't forget to put your prices up.' A murmur skittered through the room and I jumped on it. 'These people have money. Forget competing on price: compete on value.' It was hardly rocket science, but apparently it was a message they hadn't heard before. I hoped the principle would hold as true in Saffron Sweeting as it did in Silicon Valley.

For my parting shot, I had thrown out a challenge. 'Ladies and gentlemen, members of the parish council, all these ideas are worthy of your attention and I hope they prove useful. But as a community, we must seize a short-term opportunity.' A rustle ran along each row, which I hoped was the audience sitting up to take notice, rather than getting ready to lynch me. 'In seven weeks' time, it's Halloween. If you have ever visited the States in October, you might be aware that this is huge.'

Briefly, I had asked them to imagine American families spending their first autumn in Europe and their expectations of this 'holiday'. I had stressed the good-natured, family-friendly aspects of Halloween, which were a million miles away from the teenage egg-throwing which took place in many of Britain's suburbs. I had explained the importance of pumpkins, of costumes, of trick-or-treating and candy bowls. I had suggested a parade, a party, a pumpkin carving contest. I had challenged each business to come up with some reason for every little princess or pirate to visit their shop or office, with parents firmly in tow. In short, I'd begged, 'Don't let them wake up disappointed on the first of November.'

~ ~ ~

The chairman of the council, who resembled an octogenarian Galapagos tortoise, thanked me and adjourned the meeting. This triggered much discussion and debate in the crowded, clammy hall. I was surrounded by my cluster of supporters, who were effusive in their praise. Amelia hugged me and said 'Jolly good show. Nice sandals too.'

Lorraine told me the plumber had already visited and that work would start next week. Even Kenneth from the library shook my hand. 'Most intriguing,' he said gallantly, then intercepted Violet as she headed for the exit. 'What did you make of it, Violet? Intriguing, no?'

I braced myself as Violet adjusted her handbag on her arm. Was she about to take a swing at me? However, she gave a tight smile and said, 'Very interesting, Grace. Very interesting.'

Kenneth nodded amiably, but the insult wasn't lost on me. My mum uses that same adjective for my cooking.

I was propelled the short distance to the pub, where I was teased mercilessly by everyone demanding a free glass of water. To my relief, they all seemed to be ordering real drinks too. With my trauma out of the way, I was enormously thirsty. I perched happily on a velvet-covered barstool, watching the game of darts in the far corner.

'Do you give consultations?' A man in a bow tie

approached me hesitantly.

'She does,' Amelia interrupted, beaming. Then she named an hourly rate which would more than cover the cost of my new outfit.

'Thank you,' said bow-tie man. 'I'll keep that in mind.' He wandered off.

I nudged Amelia in the ribs and hissed, 'What are you *doing?*'

'Sorry, darling, but you have to walk the talk. You just told them all to offer a quality service and charge accordingly.' She drifted away, Pimms in hand.

I pondered my glass of iced juice and conceded privately she might have a point. Brian breezed up to say hello and I thanked him for his introduction, even though I hadn't internalised a word of it. Across the room, Peter was giving out fliers. Within a few minutes, he arrived at the bar and presented one to me with a flourish.

'Your launch party!' I was delighted to see he was going ahead with the idea.

'Next month,' he smiled. 'Let's hope the weather holds.'

'May I have a few more? I'd like to put them out in the estate agency.'

'With pleasure.' He gave me a stack. 'Bring me some of these infamous Americans and I'll be your friend for life.'

'I'll do my best.' The ice cubes in my glass clinked as I swirled it.

'You gave a super talk, Grace.' Peter waved to someone, then turned back to me. 'Even my mother couldn't find a bad word to say.'

'Your mother?' I was lost.

'Yes. Mum. Violet. She runs the post office.'

Uh-oh. I had no idea Peter was Violet's son. He was so amiable, and she was so scratchy. My brain raced to remember whether I'd said anything bitchy about her.

But before I could recall and apologise for any wayward remarks, a fair-haired man in a crisp blue shirt appeared beside Peter. I felt a jolt I couldn't explain as I recognised

Scott. Then, seeing him order them both a pint, it crossed my mind he might be competition for Giles.

'Have you met Scott?' Peter asked me. 'Scott, this is Grace.'

'Yes,' I said. 'Hello again.' Not witty or original, but at least this time my clothes were dry and I wasn't bidding on random houses.

Scott passed one of the beers to Peter, then nodded and crinkled his blue eyes at me. 'I enjoyed your talk,' he said. 'Very revealing.'

How did he make that simple word sound so suggestive? And was he really checking out my appearance? If so, the ruffled stretchy top was to blame. This guy was certainly *not* competition for Giles. Incapable of saying anything remotely clever, I blushed and gazed at the ranks of inverted bottles behind the bar.

'Scott lives in London.' Peter came to the rescue. 'But we're old school friends.'

'I do a lot of business in East Anglia,' Scott added, navigating the foam on his beer with skill. 'I like to harass Peter when I'm passing through. Sometimes, I let him win at golf too.'

'No, you don't,' Peter said amiably. Then, not knowing Scott had already seen me with Amelia, added, 'When Grace isn't giving speeches, she works at the estate agency.'

'And what is it you do?' I recovered enough to ask Scott. Was it my imagination, or had he been staring more than he needed to? It had been such a long time since James and I had got together, I was rusty at reading the signs. But in any case, after my horrendous mistake with Peter, I was determined to assume a business demeanour with every new acquaintance, especially the good-looking ones.

'I'm a property developer,' he said.

That explained why he'd been at the auction and knew Amelia. I wasn't entirely sure what property developing was, but I had a feeling it meant buying up green-belt fields, evicting the cows and cramming in carbon copy houses.

Saving Saffron Sweeting

Cambridge residents were always hungry for new housing, despite then sitting bumper to bumper in traffic each morning to get into the city.

'And we're thrilled to see him circling around Saffron Sweeting,' Peter said with heavy sarcasm.

'That's not much of a welcome, is it?' Scott looked at me, eyes twinkling once again. As I had noted at the auction, the only flaw in his handsome face was a nose that wasn't quite straight. I wondered whether he'd broken it, and if so, how. Perhaps a brawl with a love rival?

I slurped the last of my juice inelegantly, but my throat was still parched. What was wrong with me? I decided it must be the happy outcome of my talk, hot on the heels of acute fear which had nearly asphyxiated me. A big mug of tea would calm me down. I looked for Fergus in the hope of persuading him to make me some Typhoo.

My discomfort was alleviated by a blonde head bobbing through the throng. Marjorie greeted me like an old friend and we found her a stool. She was wearing a black jacket, black skinny jeans and spiky heels, which made me think of Olivia Newton-John's final scene in *Grease*. Marjorie, of course, was considerably older and much rounder, but she rocked the look, even so.

'Well, what a breath of fresh air you were,' she enthused. 'Got those old fuddy-duddies talking, I can tell you.'

'In a good way, I hope?' Scott asked.

'Oh, I think so,' Marjorie noticed him now, looked away, and then sat up straighter. Involuntarily, she patted her hair. So, I wasn't the only one affected by nice teeth and a suntan. 'Things have been pretty dismal around here – someone has to shake the village up a bit.'

'Well,' said Scott, leaning closer to Marjorie, but looking straight past her towards me, 'I can imagine Grace would shake them up *very* successfully.'

That was it. I couldn't sit there like an overheated lemon any longer. I fled to the cramped ladies' loo, where I ran cold water on my wrists and prayed that my faulty thermostat would recalibrate. I leaned on the sink and breathed carefully as I examined my flushed reflection in the mirror.

What an evening. I had faced one of my biggest fears and come out the other side. I had delivered my suggestions and sparked some positive discussion. And yet, I knew that of all the people in the village hall tonight, the one who had received the most vigorous shaking was me.

Chapter 18

'You're awfully quiet this morning.' Amelia had been on the phone since I arrived in the office, but now she peered at me over her mug.

'Hmm? Sorry,' I said. 'Still recovering from last night.' I had been pretending to update the Hargraves website while I mulled things over.

My brain had a lot to process, but it was moving through the preceding day's events slowly, like an elderly visitor to an art gallery. I was so relieved the talk was over. But if it was helpful to the village, then good. Maybe someone would run with the idea of Halloween festivities. And if we discovered butternut squash soup on the menu at The Plough, even better.

As for Scott, I had learned my lesson with Peter. I wasn't going to leap to conclusions: probably, he'd been flirting harmlessly. And even if he had intended more, it was still way too early for me to contemplate a new relationship.

Yesterday had been one of those strange days that occasionally punctuate life, but serve only as the spice, not the main dish. I had done enough pondering recently. From now on, I was going to live in the moment and focus on my work.

'Argh, I completely forgot!' I tapped myself on the forehead with my knuckle.

'What?' Amelia looked up. She'd been reviewing the August accounts and seemed to welcome a distraction.

'I've been meaning to ask you since I visited Peter's barn.' I saved my web edits and turned to her. 'I was thinking, it would help the village if we put together a pack for new house buyers, with information on the local shops and services.'

Amelia put her head on one side. 'A welcome pack, you mean?'

'Yes. We could include some special offers, maybe.'

'Hmm. And Peter wants to be part of that?'

'I didn't ask him directly. I wanted to talk to you first. But I think he would, yes.'

'How much do you think he'd pay?' She fiddled with her calculator, turning it in circles that echoed the twirling of her shoe.

Pay? I hadn't expected this. 'Er, I didn't think we'd charge. Just put a packet together to help promote the other businesses.'

Amelia chuckled. 'Well, I'm not providing free advertising from the goodness of my heart, Grace.'

'Oh.' I paused. 'But it'd be great for the village. These new families – they have money to spend.'

'All the more reason Peter and friends can cough up,' she said crisply. Then, seeing my face, 'All right, I'll think about it,' and turned back to her accounts.

I sighed and started phoning anyone who'd viewed a house recently. Now that the school holidays were over, we were telling buyers that if they got a move on, they could be in their new home for Christmas. If they were American, I shortened the timescale to Thanksgiving.

Later that afternoon, Amelia took a call.

'Yes, she's here,' she said, 'I'll transfer you.' With the caller on hold, she said to me, 'It's Bernard somebody.'

Bernard? Had I shown a house to anyone called Bernard? I didn't think so.

'Hello, Grace speaking.'

'Ah, yes, good afternoon. We met last night after the parish council meeting,' said a plummy accent. 'This is Bernard Pennington-Jones. I'm the general manager of Saffron Hall.'

Could this perhaps be bow-tie man? He had certainly looked like a Bernard.

'Are you familiar with Saffron Hall?' he continued.

'Er, not really.' Was that the rather austere-looking place, further up the road past Nancy's house?

'We're a manor house on the road to Soham. Grade II listed. Privately owned. We open for tours a couple of times a month and do weddings in summer.'

'I see,' I said politely, not seeing at all.

'And I was wondering if you would give us some of your business expertise.'

Holy cow. Was this a wind-up?

'Miss Palmer?'

'Sorry,' I said, pulling myself together and wiggling my mouse to wake up my computer. 'Just looking you up on the internet.'

I found it. Wow, it was huge. There must have been twenty windows in the front facade alone. Peach-coloured brick: a boxy, elegant building. Gorgeous.

'And you're asking us to sell Saffron Hall for you?' I asked. If so, he shouldn't be talking to me. Amelia was without doubt the best woman for that job.

'No, no – ha, ha!'

I don't know how it's possible to laugh with a posh accent, but he managed it.

'Goodness, no.' He seemed entertained. 'Not yet, at least. But we're having a spot of bother and I found your talk last night fascinating.'

'Okay,' I said, to show him I was listening.

'You see, we have a great deal to offer visitors, yet we never seem to attract enough of them. I'm afraid we operate rather in the shadow of Anglesey Abbey.'

I knew Anglesey Abbey, of course. A centuries-old priory, owned by the National Trust, with extensive gardens and a working watermill. Oh, and let's not forget the tearoom.

'So I'd like your advice on increasing visitor numbers.'

This was way out of my league. 'Mr –' What was his name? 'Mr Pennington-Jones, I'm flattered, but I can't help.'

'Oh. That's a shame.' He sounded disappointed. 'Yes, well, I understand.'

'I'm sorry,' I said. 'I'm just not sure I have the expertise to tell you how to run your stately home.'

'That's very honest of you, Miss Palmer. I appreciate your integrity.' He paused for a moment. 'Nonetheless, may I offer you a free tour? Perhaps a spot of lunch in the orangery?'

'Oh.' I thought about the peach brick and the sweeping driveway. There wasn't any harm in just going for a snoop round, was there? 'That's really kind of you,' I said. 'When would be convenient?'

~~~

It had been at least six weeks since I'd seen Jem.

'It's like you've disappeared off to Brigadoon,' she'd complained. 'What do I have to do to see you – wait a hundred years?'

As a result, she was driving up with Harry and baby Seb for lunch on Sunday. This was a fine plan, until my hapless brother let it slip to my parents on the phone. At that point, I'd been volunteered to host a family reunion.

'You've chosen a perfect spot between here and London,' said my dad, ever practical. 'Suits me – can't stand that North Circular.'

My mum was more effusive. 'Poppet! What a lovely idea! We haven't all been together since you came back. And I'd like to see this little village of yours.'

I knew better than to attempt to cook. On Thursday, I placed an order with Brian that was almost big enough to finance his eldest through university. On Saturday, I picked up two quiches, ready-to-bake garlic bread and a Black Forest gateau. Then I made a guilty trip to Waitrose in Newmarket for the rest of the groceries, which Saffron Sweeting couldn't supply.

Harry and Jem arrived first, with Seb asleep in his baby seat. I hadn't seen Harry in nearly a year, since before he became a father. We hugged awkwardly – the Gilling family not being good at outward affection – and he disappeared into the living room in search of sport to watch. He re-emerged in annoyance when he found I didn't own a television, but then settled for the general knowledge crossword.

'He's on duty with Seb,' Jem said in a hushed tone, looking appreciatively at her husband. 'He promised we could have some girl time before your parents arrive.'

While the kettle boiled for tea, I brought her up to speed on the parish council meeting. 'I thought I was going to die of fright, but actually, it turned out okay.'

'Good for you – another dragon slain.'

'And ...' I glanced towards the living room to check my brother's ears weren't waggling, 'there was this guy. I think he was flirting.'

'Ooh la la! Tell me more!'

I described Scott and how he had let his gaze linger.

'This could be a sign.' Jem poured our tea. 'Oh, you used a bag. I wanted to look at the leaves.'

'What do you mean, a sign?'

'That it's time for the next Chapter. You know,' she said in an undertone, 'move on from James.'

'I'm not sure I want to move on,' I replied instinctively. 'I mean, it's just so soon.'

'Perhaps,' she said. 'Perhaps not. Depends how nice his bum is, I suppose.'

I considered pretending I hadn't looked at Scott's backside, but she knew me too well and smirked confidently. I sipped my tea demurely but smiled nonetheless.

'Woo-eeh! Here we are!' A cry pierced the thick stone walls of the cottage. Moments later, my mother erupted through the back door. She was wearing a floppy straw hat – as if she were off to the Chelsea Flower Show – a linen shirt and trendy white jeans.

'Halloo! And where's my gorgeous grandson?' She almost bowled Jem over in her haste to shower Sebastian in ardent kisses. Seb woke obligingly and started to squawk, then shut up as he presumably recognised grandma. I saw

Jem sag a little and gave her a sympathetic smile. It wasn't that mum meant to be rude, she just tended to overlook Jem's role in creating and nurturing the twenty pound bundle of bliss she was now cuddling. In fairness, she pretty much glossed over Harry's role in it too.

I went outside to see if dad had suffered collateral damage from the maternal maelstrom.

'Hello, Gracie. Good to see you, love.' He was lifting a box out of the car boot.

'And you, dad. What's that?'

'Ah, it appears to be for you. From James.' Poor dad, he didn't like conveying awkward news. 'He's phoned a few times, you know ... but your mother's forbidden me from telling him anything.'

So, James had been calling my parents as well as Jem. Given the situation, that was brave of him. I eyed the box. Sure enough, it had come via FedEx and was plastered in customs stickers. 'Thanks, dad. I'll open it later.'

I busied myself sorting out drinks. Mum was now strolling around happily with Seb in her arms and he seemed equally entranced by her hat. My father and brother were talking animatedly about cricket, the Middle East, or possibly cricket *in* the Middle East. Jem had her head in the fridge, pulling out boxes and packets in preparation for lunch.

This was the most people I'd ever entertained in Pothole Cottage. Even though they were my family, it felt strange. Had I become so insular and protective of my bolt-hole? With the FedEx box out of the way, I wondered how long it would be before someone dared mention James.

As it turned out, we made it most of the way through lunch, squeezed around my kitchen table. We talked politely about Harry's two-dimensional banking job and dad's work in progress – a calculus textbook, no less. So that took all of five minutes. Mum shared news of the chickens, the din of their neighbour's Harley Davidson, and the 'dreadful' organisation of the golf club's charity fashion show. I decided that must be the origin of the white jeans, since she surely didn't have the sartorial initiative to have chosen them on her own.

Jem was interrogated on her plans for going back to work, including 'But Jemima dear, you'll go simply dotty at home all day,' from my mother; 'Norah was always there when you two got home from school,' from dad; and a jokey 'As long as my dinner's ready, I don't mind,' from my brother. This earned him an airborne napkin from me and a withering stare from his wife. Had they talked properly about their situation?

'So, Grace.' My brother had been given the important role of dividing up the chocolate gateau. 'Is it completely kaput with James?'

Silence fell around the table, and we all watched as Harry manoeuvred a tall slice of gooey cake, cherry and all, onto my father's plate. I twisted my feet under my chair and hoped someone would change the subject. No one did.

'I would say so.' Perhaps a brief, dignified answer would suffice.

'What's in the box, poppet? Some of your things?' Despite two sherries before lunch, mum had the sensitivity to bring her exuberance down a notch.

I nodded.

'Nice of him to do that. Must have cost a bit to send,' Harry said.

'Considering he slept with someone else, it's the least he could do.' Jem threw a warning glance in Harry's direction.

'So that's it, then?' my brother persisted. 'End of the road?'

'When a husband cheats, it usually is.' Jem was either sticking up for me, or firing a shot across Harry's bows, or maybe both.

My mother surveyed the differing wedges of gateau on each of our plates and apparently needed no calculus textbook to deduce that she had been cheated out of a cherry.

'Don't be so sure of that,' she said, and reached over to steal dad's.

He didn't even blink, much less object, but just sat there looking sorrowful.

~~~

Eight helping hands professed themselves eager to help tidy up the meal, so I escaped to the living room where Seb was dozing in his little seat. I tried to think of him growing up, going to school, getting married, perhaps cheating on his wife. My imagination failed me: I just couldn't picture this innocent baby inflicting that amount of pain.

'You've got it so easy,' I told him. 'Keep it that way, little buddy.'

Dad had fallen asleep in the big armchair by the fireplace, so the rest of us decided to take a stroll round the village. Everywhere was closed for Sunday afternoon, but I showed them the malt house, Hargraves & Co and – proudly – a couple of houses I had helped sell.

'Yes, it's all very nice,' mum pronounced. By that, I think she had decided that Saffron Sweeting probably voted Conservative, or, worst case, Lib Dem.

Harry was eyeing up property prices in the Hargraves window. 'Not cheap round here, is it? Sorry Jem, I don't think we'll be buying a weekend home in Saffron Sweeting.'

Jem, in charge of Seb in his pushchair, shrugged as she watched the bees on a nearby lavender bush warily. She's always been more of a city girl.

'Grace, you've done all right with your cottage. Nice place,' my brother continued.

'Well, my days there may be numbered.' I told them about the skirmish over land access, but that a sale now seemed likely.

'Shame,' mum tutted, as we reached Mary Lou's house and turned left. 'Although of course, you're always welcome back home, you know that.'

'Thanks, mum. I'll, um, keep that in mind,' I replied. There was no way I could deal with both my parents and a daily dose of Harley-riding chickens.

We had nearly walked back up the track to the cottage when I realised a car was inching along behind us. I turned to see a dark blue sporty convertible.

'Oh my God. It can't be.' I was as shocked as if the baby had launched into a Puccini aria.

'What?' Jem was slower to turn, as she'd been watching to make sure that Seb's pushchair wheels didn't fall into a pothole. 'Oh, lookee here,' she said.

I was already lookee-ing here. In the driver's seat was Scott, blond hair tousled, dark glasses glinting and white teeth smiling.

Mum was taking off her shoes on the back-door mat and hadn't noticed the handsome arrival or my panicked expression. My brother, however, clocked the car, then the speculative grin on his wife's face and finally my slack jaw. Had he overheard what I'd told Jem before lunch? In any case, for once in his life, he did the tactful thing and hustled our mother inside.

'We'll put the kettle on,' he called, and shut the door.

Scott parked his car behind dad's and got out. 'Grace, hello again.'

'Hi,' I said, wondering how scruffy I looked in comparison to the other night.

Jem, bless her, busied herself in reaching down to unbuckle Seb and lift him out of his pushchair.

'You live here?' he asked.

'That's right.' This was awkward. 'Did Amelia give you directions?'

'Yes. Yes, that's right. She did.' He nodded slowly and then seemed lost for words.

'This is Jem,' I said. 'My sister-in-law.' Jem freed a hand to shake Scott's, then went back to jiggling Seb and patting his back.

'The rest of the scary clan are inside,' I went on.

'Visiting for Sunday lunch.' Oops, I was in danger of babbling.

'I've come at a bad time. Sorry. I'll leave you to it.' Scott made as if to turn round.

'No, no, that's okay, I need to change this little monster,' Jem interrupted brightly. 'You two carry on.' She made a lunge for the nappy bag from the bottom rack of the pushchair. 'Nice to meet you, Scott.' She disappeared inside.

Scott looked up at the white walls of the cottage. 'Attractive place,' he said.

'Isn't it?' I looked again at the climbing roses, the tiled roof and wonky chimneys. 'I fell in love, the first day I saw it.'

He smiled at me and I allowed myself to smile back. He certainly was good-looking. Today he was in jeans with a faded red checked shirt. I should have been reminded of a steakhouse tablecloth, but on him it looked just fine. He took his sunglasses off and polished them on the hem of the shirt before looking at me again. His blue eyes really were incredible. Today, in the soft September sunshine, they seemed to have an inner ring of gold too.

'I'm glad I bumped into you,' he said.

That struck me as strange, since he'd clearly been on his way to visit me. I smoothed down my T-shirt surreptitiously.

'I enjoyed chatting the other night.' He seemed more confident now, more like he had been in the pub. Again, he was holding eye contact just a fraction longer than necessary.

I held my tongue, despite my racing thoughts. To distract myself, I began nudging a loose stone with my toe.

'So, if you have any free time next weekend, I was wondering, can I take you out to lunch?'

I'd be lying if I said I was totally floored by this. After his flirting in the pub, then showing up in my driveway, I'd had a few minutes to compute the likelihood of him asking me out.

I kicked at the stone, thinking about the FedEx box

which had travelled five thousand miles to bring me the remnants of my old life. And I realised, I couldn't come up with a single good reason to decline.

'Oh ... thanks.' I gave the loose stone a final kick. It landed with a soft thud in the nearest flowerbed. Then I looked him in the face. 'Yes, I'd love to.'

Chapter 19

'And how long is it since you were measured for a bra?' The saleslady, tall, bony, with no bosom of her own that I could see, flexed her tape measure.

Surely this was a question like your dentist asks, *how often do you floss?*, which nobody ever answers honestly. I pretended to think. The saleslady peered over her bifocals at me and waited.

'Oh, quite a while,' I muttered, trying to look as if it might have been sometime last year. In reality, I'd been wearing the same size since I was twenty. It was one of the few clothing sizes which hadn't needed translation when I moved to California. This had struck me as odd. Britain and America couldn't agree on shoe sizing, dress sizing, weight, distance or temperature measurements, but on the scale of breasts, we were of one voice. Was this the true nature of the 'special relationship' which leaders in the White House and Downing Street were so proud of?

I didn't know whether I was going to have to take my top off and whether it was okay to get the giggles if her hands were chilly. I glanced nervously at the five short-listed bras on their dainty hangers. All had multiple little tags hanging off them. In my experience, the more dinky tags on a piece of clothing, the higher the price. I wondered how much this free fitting was going to end up costing.

The shopping trip had been Amelia's idea. On hearing about my date with Scott, she'd been uncharacteristically quiet at first. I waited for her to tell me he was gay, married or dying of a terminal disease, but she didn't drop any bombshells. She simply looked thoughtful for a few minutes.

'Is something wrong?' I'd asked. Was there some history between them? He was a tad young for her, but that didn't rule anything out. With her limitless energy and strong fashion sense, she could pass for fifteen years younger. I formed a new theory. 'Oh, I get it. You think it's too soon for me to start seeing someone.'

'Hell, no!' she'd responded instantly. 'The sooner the better. After things fell apart with Michael, I dated so many men it was hard to keep them straight.'

'Really?'

'Yes, darling, I think it's terrific. And you like Scott?'

'He seems very nice,' I said – a blatant understatement.

'He's also very ambitious.'

Well, takes one to know one, I thought. 'You think I'm not ... dynamic enough for him?' Nobody has ever called me the life of the party, and I hadn't been on a date this decade. Did I even still know what to do?

'I didn't mean that,' Amelia back-pedalled. 'Just that he's driven by his work, you know?'

I was silent, conflicted. My cowardly half was looking for an excuse to wimp out of the date with Scott. The other, flattered, half wanted to have some fun.

'Look,' said Amelia. 'No one's talking about marriage. Just go out with him, have a blast, and you'll feel better.'

'Fair enough,' I nodded. How come everything was always so simple when Amelia said it, but so complicated inside my head?

Scott had phoned to delay our date until the following weekend. I told myself to read nothing into this and said that would be totally fine.

'Do you like horse racing?' he asked. 'I thought we might go over to Newmarket.'

I had never been. Something told me that student-era visits to the greyhound track, where four of us had risked one bet each and shared a bag of chips, were best not mentioned.

'Well, I like horses,' I said, which was perfectly true. As a nine-year-old, I had begged unsuccessfully for a pony. Harry and I had been given a pair of gerbils instead.

'Great!' he said. 'Shall I pick you up at twelve?'

'Okay. Do I need to wear a hat?'

He laughed. 'Only if you want to.'

Amelia, however, had been adamant. 'We need to go shopping again. We'll go to London on Sunday.'

'But he said hats are optional.'

She laughed at me. 'I'm not talking about a hat, Grace. I'm talking about the rest of it.'

Since her sartorial advice had helped me land the date with Scott in the first place, I decided I'd better listen to her. Still, it irked me slightly: why did she get to be the glamorous one? After all, I had spent time in America, while she lived in an English backwater. Then, I'd had to admit that the jeans and flip-flop uniform of Silicon Valley was hardly on a par with the catwalks of Manhattan. And I hadn't had a pedicure, let alone a manicure, since touching down on English soil.

So now, I found myself in Selfridges on Oxford Street with a tape measure firmly around my ribs. Amelia had wanted to go to Harvey Nichols, I had pressed for Marks and Spencer. This was our compromise. My protestations that Scott wouldn't be seeing my underwear had been swept aside. Amelia had given me a playful look and told me there was no sin in being prepared.

'34B,' pronounced the saleslady.

'Oh. Okay.' I had been wearing 36A. Did this mean I was now smaller but chestier? I thought it unlikely, considering the number of cream teas I had consumed recently. Or was she on commission and trained to tell me a different size, so I would immediately buy seven new sets of undies?

I emerged from the plush fitting room with a couple of pretty white bras and showed them to Amelia, who was lounging on a sofa, thumbing through a magazine. She tutted and sent me back in with a darker, lacier and racier selection. Then, she waited until I was at a perilous stage of undress, before snaking her hand around the curtain to waggle the matching knickers at me.

'Okay, okay, you win,' I sighed. The cost per square inch

of this stuff was breathtaking: my credit card was going to need CPR.

Despite my outward protests, I enjoyed shopping with Amelia. Apart from my new haircut and the outfit for the parish council meeting, it had been a long time since I'd spent money on my appearance. I knew this was a problem for many interior designers, who kept falling in love with house accessories and ending up with no budget for socks. In any case, I'd thought James didn't care whether I looked fashionable. That complacency had apparently cost me dear.

Satisfied with my underwear purchase, Amelia had allowed me a quick canter around John Lewis before treating me to lunch in their cafe. No doubt the glass of wine with my toasted sandwich eased the afternoon's decision-making: I shimmied without complaint into and out of cotton, silk and jersey by Monsoon, East and Phase Eight.

'Good,' Amelia declared finally, on the pavement at the corner of Bond Street. 'That should save you from complete embarrassment.'

With that, she thrust out her arm. 'I'm off to see a sweet friend in Hampstead,' she said, as a black cab swooped to a halt at the curb. Probably, the driver had been blinded by the glint of her cocktail ring. 'Do you want me to drop you at King's Cross?'

'No, thanks, I have plans,' I said, mainly to prove I did have a social life outside the Saffron Sweeting pub.

'All right, bye for now, then. See you on Tuesday, yes?'

I nodded and steered myself and my shopping bags down the escalator and onto the Tube to Ealing.

~~~

'So, tell me if this is too nosy, but what was in the box from James?'

Jem and I were sitting on her bed, while Harry watched *Match of the Day* in the living room. I had warned him that if I fell asleep before he vacated the sofa, he would have to spend the night there. Seb was asleep in his cot in his tiny bedroom, faint breathing and the occasional gurgle coming through the baby alarm. Their easy domesticity was like a comfortable sweater and I was happy to slip into its sleeves.

I stirred my mug of Ovaltine, trying to get the last lumps of powder to dissolve.

'Oh, just silly personal things. My favourite mug, some clothes, a few of my beloved issues of *Domino*.'

Jem looked puzzled.

'It is – was – a design magazine. No longer published, but widely worshipped.' I didn't mention Eeyore, who had also made the journey across the Pond. I loved Jem, but she didn't need to know I liked to drool on a donkey at night.

'That was all?' She seemed a bit disappointed.

'Pretty much. Some chocolate from Trader Joe's. A short note; nothing you can't guess.'

Jem gave me one of her slow, kind smiles and didn't press further.

I knew the letter pretty much by heart.

Dear Grace, I hope this finds you well and happy, also that I've done okay at sending the things you asked for. I'm so sorry again for what happened and have been searching for the right way to explain and apologise to you. I want to talk to you more than ever, but can understand that you don't want to see me right now. If and when you are ready, I will be on the next plane. Much love, James.

He had also sent a couple of our wedding photos, which I didn't know how to interpret. I had considered those and the letter for some time, wondering if he was keen to 'explain and apologise' so that we could both move on. And why did he want to talk 'more than ever'? Eventually, I resolved to stop stewing and enjoy being reunited with Eeyore. And, looking on the bright side, at least the box didn't include divorce papers.

~~~

I was chaotically nervous by the time horse-racing day arrived. How was I supposed to make interesting conversation for several hours with a man I hardly knew, who clearly wasn't lacking in self-confidence and could flirt for England? Was I going to be a riding school pony at the Grand National?

Still, at least I looked good. If, as I'd previously fretted, I'd let myself go, then I was thrilled to be mostly back. Amelia had loaned me her sandals again and taught me her make-up tricks in the tiny loo in the back of the Hargraves office. That morning, I had nipped into Cambridge to treat myself to a blow-dry. My dress, however, was the bee's knees: feminine but sophisticated. In a fifties shape, with a fitted sleeveless top and full skirt, the colour was a gentle shade which Amelia called mink. Swirly cream embroidery clambered over an organza base. We had decided the matching coat was too much – 'It's not a wedding, after all, darling' – but had hedged our bets with a cropped cashmere cardigan in an impractical milky colour. As a result, I had resolved only to eat beige food on my date. My little handbag was ivory snakeskin, also borrowed from Amelia. I hoped it was fake, but in view of her generosity, not just in fashion but in letting me have a Saturday off too, hadn't liked to ask.

Scott was unexpectedly right on time. For some reason, I had imagined he would keep me waiting. He jumped out of his car as I came out of the cottage and came around to the passenger side, where he kissed me fleetingly on the cheek and opened the door for me. I folded myself as elegantly I could into the low leather seat, proudly remembering to check my ample skirt wasn't trapped in the door.

'Ready?' he asked.

'I hope so.' I smiled gamely, hoping my hair would survive the open-topped experience.

'You look lovely.' He paused to let the compliment sink in and then started the engine. It gave a mighty purr and saved me from responding.

He was wearing a navy blazer, fawn chinos, immaculate white shirt and a silk tie patterned with what seemed to be daisies. Good, my outfit was definitely on a level playing field.

We made small talk on the short journey to Newmarket. I was thankful for heavy race day traffic, which kept our speed down and thus saved my hair from being whipped into a Medusa-like mess.

'So, you're working with Amelia?' Scott asked me.

'Yes, part-time. She's so busy, she needs the help.'

'She's doing well,' he replied. 'From what I hear, her business has thrived since she went solo.'

'Have you known her long?' I asked casually, looking at the giant sausage rolls of harvested hay in the fields.

He shook his head. 'Not really. We met through business. But she's clearly very sharp.'

Did he mean *sharp* as in clever, or prickly? Amelia didn't suffer fools gladly.

'Tell me more about what you do,' I prompted.

'Well, it's simple. I look for land and buildings which would be more profitable if they were turned into something else. Then I buy them and convince someone to build for me.'

We'd hit the back of the traffic queue on the edge of Newmarket.

'Is there a type you specialise in?' I was treading carefully, discussing a topic I knew nothing about.

'About twenty per cent of my deals are for vacant land. Agricultural, usually, where the farmer finds it uneconomic to keep growing wheat or pigs or whatever. But I like it best when I take old buildings and convert them.'

'What do you turn them into?'

'Depends, obviously. Retirement flats are often a safe bet. If it's an urban area, offices sometimes. Mixed use is becoming hugely popular. The planning authorities love that.'

'Mixed use?'

'Where you have, say, flats on the top and shops on the bottom. Commercial and residential together.'

'So, do you do barn conversions, that kind of thing?'

He laughed and turned off the main road, following the signs for premier car parking.

'Barns have been a bit overdone. All the good ones were snapped up long ago. At least, the ones in East Anglia. And generally, I'm on the lookout for larger projects.'

'Amelia lives in a converted fire engine house. Really stylish,' I said, then wondered if he already knew that.

'Does she?' he said. 'Good for her.'

I analysed his neutral tone and decided there was probably no romantic history between him and my boss.

We parked and I managed to extricate myself from my ludicrously low seat. As Scott delved in the tiny boot, emerging with a pair of binoculars, I looked at the car and found it was a Jaguar. Did he know the shiny dark blue paint was a wonderful complement to his eyes? No, that would be outrageously vain and he didn't seem like a peacock. I felt myself smiling and relaxed a little.

'So,' I asked him, 'what now?'

He looked at his watch. 'We have a little over an hour before the first race. How about we get something to eat and then check out the runners?'

I wasn't enormously hungry, for which the only explanation was nerves. Nonetheless, I followed willingly as we entered the Premier Enclosure and made our way to a bistro. The facilities were already busy and there was a festive atmosphere as excited race-goers, all dressed to impress, milled around. People greeted each other noisily and there was much laughter and anticipation in the air. The general scene was much like a wedding, at the part before the guests get drunk and disorderly. I could tell that some were diehard enthusiasts, here for the horses, but others were guests or hangers-on, like myself. I tried and failed to think of an original way to ask Scott if he came here often.

'You'll have to guide me on how this works,' I said

Saving Saffron Sweeting

instead, as we sat down in the crowded restaurant with our sandwiches. Scott had offered me champagne and I wondered whether that was first date panache, or a regular tipple for him. In any case, I had determined to stick to orange juice until I saw how the day developed. I didn't want to get giggly even before the first race was under way.

'Well, you unwrap it and take a large bite,' he said, seriously, then broke into his wide smile, which surely belonged on a toothpaste poster.

I smiled back at him. So far, this had been easier than I thought. I hadn't said anything stupid and being in such a busy, public place took the pressure off. We didn't have to fill every moment with meaningful conversation, and the venue was so packed that some physical contact was inevitable. He had put his hand on my back or elbow a couple of times already. I found I liked it.

'I mean the racing,' I said. 'I don't know what I'm doing.'

'You don't need to know,' he replied. 'We'll go and look at the Parade Ring, and maybe even the saddling boxes if we have time. That's where you pick out who you think is going to win. Once the jockeys come out and mount, the horses go down to the start line and we place our bets.'

'So I have to gamble?' I said pleasantly.

He shook his head. 'You don't have to, but it's fun. We can stick with the Tote if you want to start small. It's less intimidating than the bookies.'

I liked the sound of the Tote, whatever that might be. I had seen a few television dramas featuring street-wise bookmakers in grubby brown raincoats. Their world seemed a bit seedy, not to mention mathematically impossible to understand.

'The Tote's pretty straightforward,' Scott continued. 'They won't tell you odds or anything, but if your horse wins, you get a share of the bets placed.'

'Fine,' I said. 'Let's do that. Then what?'

'Then, they start the race. Your job is to cheer like mad,

jump up and down and generally scream your head off.'

I grinned and shook my head. 'I don't think so.'

He leaned in across our little lunch table and ran his index finger over the back of my hand. I looked down, surprised that I could feel this simple touch deep in my stomach too. Then I glanced up at his face.

'Trust me.' He held my gaze boldly, eyes playful. 'You'll scream.'

Chapter 20

He was right. Innuendo aside, the sight of a horse on which I'd staked a princely five pounds, moving gradually from fourth place to third as she hurtled round the final bend, was more than enough to get me on my feet and yelling. The noisy energy of the race crowd, their laughter and cheering, was infectious. I guessed some had large bets riding on the backs of the glossy fillies, but the excitement was uniform across old and young, male and female, those in the Premier Enclosure like us and those next door in the Paddock. I totally understood why Eliza Doolittle lost her new-found decorum and hollered at her horse to *move yer bloomin' arse.*

Scott had tried to get me to study the previous form of the horses and whether they did best on soft turf or firm, but I was far more interested in picking my winners based on their name or the colours the jockey was wearing. Teal and turquoise were my favourites and if their silks were spotted, so much the better.

My method was severely flawed. I'd lost my money on Golden Gate. PBJ Sandwich disgraced me by finishing last. So, in the third race, I switched my allegiance to Blighty and placed an each way bet on Lovely Jubbly. Bobbing up and down to see past the unruly group in front of us, I lost sight of her.

'I can't see!' I was up on my tiptoes despite Amelia's heeled sandals. 'Where is she?'

Scott was a good eight inches taller and was glued to his binoculars. 'Er, fifth. No, wait – that's not her.'

I clutched his arm and bobbed some more.

'There she is! She's second!' he called out.

I whooped as she came back into view, thundering down the home straight. The leader was a length clear, but two other horses were nudging alongside my pick.

'Hang in there! Come on!' I yelled.

A blur of colours whizzed past us, to deafening shouts and cheers from the crowd.

'What happened?' I cried. 'I couldn't tell. Did she do it?'

'I think so.' Scott was grinning at me. 'Let's go and see.'

When we reached the Tote and I found I'd made all of nineteen pounds, I did a little jig.

'Champagne!' I announced. 'My treat!'

Scott laughed. 'You won't have any winnings left.' But he looked pleased for me nonetheless.

'I don't care,' I said. 'That was brilliant.'

He laughed again, shook his head and gestured to the bar.

~~~

'So, is this a good time to ask if you're enjoying yourself?' Scott smiled as we clinked glasses.

'Well, obviously the first couple of races were dire, but I might rethink that opinion now.' I sipped my champagne and reminded myself that bouncing up and down like a sugar-fuelled eight-year-old at a birthday party wasn't ideal first date behaviour. This guy was sophisticated and my winner's jig had not been cool.

He nodded and said nothing, watching my face.

I was tempted to just sit there and gaze back, but blamed that on the champagne. Instead, I added, 'Yes, it's really fun, thank you.'

'You're welcome,' he said.

There was a pause and then he waved at someone behind me.

'Will you be okay on your own for a few minutes? There's someone over there I need to talk business with.'

'No problem.'

He made a tilting gesture with his glass. 'I'll text you if I can't find you.'

'Sure thing.'

I was curious, but had no particular wish to be introduced to his business colleague. Instead, I took a quick peek as Scott made his way across the bar and greeted a paunchy older man in a grey suit. A city fat cat, perhaps?

I'd taken careful note of Scott's betting behaviour so far, as it had occurred to me he might be a hard-core gambler. But from what I could see, he was treating the afternoon lightly and was a good loser. True, he placed larger bets than me, but that wasn't hard, and after all, this wasn't his first rodeo. Whether it was his preference, or to keep me company, he'd stuck mainly with the Tote for his betting. Only once did he head for the bookmakers, when he said he was intrigued by the long odds for a horse called Beach Belle. That flutter had resulted in a fistful of twenties, which he had pocketed with a grin and a careless shrug. Overall, he didn't seem to be displaying addictive gambling tendencies.

I, on the other hand, was hooked. This was so much more fun than feeding ten-pence pieces into the waterfall machines at the beach in Lowestoft. Harry and I had done that on every family holiday, until he'd reached sixteen and abandoned me for the delights of the disco.

Now, I ran my eye down the list of runners for the next race. American Dream jumped out at me as the obvious choice. Still riding high from my recent win, I almost ran to place my bet, then drooped over the railings with my hand in front of my eyes as the hapless horse ambled around the track so slowly he might as well have gone backwards.

Jem, no doubt, would declare this to be a sign, and for once I was inclined to agree.

Enough of this foolishness. James had broken my heart, and now I was starting over. I was on a date with an incredibly attractive man and I had no intention of blowing it. My life was in England now.

~ ~ ~

After his short absence, Scott rejoined me and apologised for being rude.

'No problem,' I said cheerfully, 'I was quite happy losing all my money on a terrible horse.'

'I get the picture,' he responded. 'Don't worry, that happens to me all the time.'

I'm not sure it was true, but it was gallant of him to say it. He really was a decent bloke.

'So, I take it you're quitting while you're behind?' he asked. 'Do you want to leave?'

'No, no, I'm fine. But I might get a cup of tea while I calm down a bit.'

'Told you it would work you into a frenzy,' he said.

He was totally flirting with me and I didn't need to blame the champagne for my willingness to flirt back. We watched a couple more races, standing closer than the crowd required, his arm around my waist as he pulled me nearer to point out something on the far side of the course.

It was late afternoon when Scott turned to me. 'So, Grace, last chance. You either win back all your money, or we leave now and beat the traffic.' He consulted the race card, then said, 'Decision made. To hell with the traffic. Let's check her out.'

We made our way to the Parade Ring, and there, in beautiful turquoise silks with white spots, a diminutive jockey was being hoisted onto Grace Under Fire.

'Up for this?' he asked me.

I paused for a split second, then smiled up at him. 'Absolutely.'

~~~

It was dark when Scott bumped the Jaguar back up the track to my cottage.

My final race winnings had been more than enough to pay for dinner at the quiet country pub he'd chosen, but Scott had insisted that today was on him.

'Perhaps I'll let you pay next time,' he said, as he'd scooped up our bill.

Forgive my anti-feminist treachery, but I was impressed. We'd shared a lovely meal, and I had felt sufficiently tired from the afternoon to relax properly in his company. I liked the sound of *next time* too.

During dinner, he'd asked what had brought me to Saffron Sweeting.

I'd set down my fork and taken a glug of wine. I was unprepared for this topic and the longer I stretched the pause, the bigger deal it would become.

'My marriage ended a few months ago.' When in doubt, keep it brief.

'I'm sorry.' His reply was equally simple. He looked away and I couldn't begin to guess what he thought.

'And the village? Why there?' he asked.

I shrugged. 'It was either Saffron Sweeting or move back home to mum and dad's.' I made sure to smile, to show him I was at ease. 'No-brainer.'

He'd nodded, then topped up my wine. 'Well, then.' He raised his glass. 'Here's to Grace under fire.'

My cottage was in darkness but I thought I could make out Mungo's black and white shape, sitting on the doormat.

'Your dog?' Scott asked.

'No, he just thinks he lives here,' I said. 'Don't get out, you'll only get slobbered on.'

'You make it sound so tempting.' He turned the engine off anyway.

'Thank you, that was a lovely day.' I was formal now, feeling shy. The low bucket seats of his car were hardly conducive to smooching and in any case, I had no idea of current etiquette at the end of a first date.

'Thank you for joining me.' As before, he ran a single finger down my forearm and over my hand. I felt the tingle from my ears to my toes, then froze like a rabbit as he leaned across the gearstick. Yet, when he brushed my cheek with the briefest of kisses, I was disappointed. Was that his secret, to leave me wanting more?

Inside, the cottage felt chilly and it crossed my mind I'd have to investigate how the heating worked. Mungo sat optimistically next to the empty fireplace, as I paced between the kitchen and the living room. I wasn't sleepy, but couldn't settle to do anything useful.

In the end, I flopped on the sofa and fondled Mungo's ears as he arrived, tail waving, at my side. His doggie identification tags made a tuneful clinking as I scratched him under the chin with my left hand and let my mind run over the day.

This small noise from Mungo's collar brought me back to the present. I stilled my hand and paused, looking down at my fingers. Mungo sank with a sigh at my feet and the only sound now was the rhythmic tick-thud of my antique clock.

Slowly, carefully and before I could change my mind, I took hold of my platinum wedding ring. Then I tugged, twisted and wriggled, until it was off my finger.

~~~

On Tuesday morning I stopped at the bakery, in search of Amelia's favourite custard tarts.

Brian was wiping crumbs off the counter. 'They're only just out of the oven. Can you come back in ten minutes?' he said cheerfully, adding, 'You look well, Grace.'

I was indeed feeling upbeat after Saturday's horse racing and heart racing, but I wasn't going to share that with Brian.

'Thanks. How's business?' I asked.

'My accountant's still finalising the August numbers, but fingers crossed, things are looking good.' He seemed pleased. 'Some of us are meeting tonight to plan Halloween.'

'Really? That's great.' I was thrilled to hear it.

To kill the time, I reluctantly took myself to the post office for stamps. Generally speaking, I tried to avoid Violet.

My instincts had been right. As I turned to leave, she stopped me.

'What's going on with you and my dog?'

'What do you mean?' I stalled for time, but knew full well what she meant.

'Seems to me, you've been holding him hostage. He's up at your place more often than not.'

'I haven't been holding him hostage,' I retorted. 'Mungo shows up of his own free will. You shouldn't let him out if you don't want him to roam.'

She glared at me. I realised that squabbling over a canine's affections was pretty lame.

'Look,' I said, 'I'm sorry. I know he's your dog. But for some reason he likes the cottage.' I took a breath. 'And when he first arrived, I didn't have any other friends here.'

Violet folded her arms. 'So you made friends with my dog?'

'It was a difficult time for me. I'd just left my husband.' I felt tears beginning and kicked myself. What was I thinking, to reveal that to her? Now she'd make mincemeat out of me.

'Why?' she asked.

For heaven's sake, I thought. That's too personal for the post office. Can't we talk about the weather, or something a bit more British?

I lifted my chin. 'He cheated on me.' Great, now my shame would be all over Saffron Sweeting by lunchtime.

Violet, however, looked awkward and began tidying the newspapers on the counter. Then she sighed. 'Well. His loss, dear.'

It took a few seconds for this veiled compliment to sink in. I blinked back the threatening tears and edged towards the door.

'Is there anything you'd recommend?' Violet asked suddenly.

'Sorry?' What did she mean? A brand of tranquilliser? A tactic for dealing with errant husbands?

'Anything you think I should stock, which the Americans would like?'

'Oh. Right.' I looked around as my brain scrambled to catch up. Her selection was uninspiring at best, but I had no retail experience to call on. I struggled to think back to last autumn and what I'd seen on sale in the States. Violet waited, her expression softer than usual but still wary. Asking me for advice was obviously an olive branch.

'Right. Um, well.' *Orange*. I had seen a whole lot of orange. 'Well, at this time of year, they get really excited about Halloween.'

'Which means?'

'If you can find supplies of pumpkins, and put them outside, that would attract folks in. And orange things. Black and orange, those are the Halloween colours. Oh, and candy – I mean, sweets. People give out sweets. Can you get some big bags of individually-wrapped small sweets?'

She made a slight nodding gesture. 'Thank you, Grace.'

'Sorry,' I said. 'I'm not thinking clearly just now. If I come up with anything else, I'll let you know.'

'Okay. You do that.'

We parted, certainly not friends. But we had each shared a problem and revealed a chink in our armour, and the other had passed up the opportunity to stick the sword in. The truce was palpable.

I headed back to the bakery, glad to have an awkward conversation out of the way, and feeling much in need of strong coffee and the promised tart. What I didn't need was to run straight into Nancy.

Chapter 21

Nancy and I both went into reverse, like two nervous drivers on a single-track road. Then we both seemed to realise that avoidance was futile.

'Hi.' I spoke first.

'Hey there.' She had just come out of the bakery, a white paper bag in her hand.

'How are you?' This is pretty much what the English say to everyone, whether best friend or sworn enemy.

'Doing great, thanks – how about you?'

'Yes, fine, thanks.' I paused, thinking it was strange to bump into her on a weekday. 'Not at work today?'

'Working from home.' She smiled. 'Allegedly. Big report to write, so I figured I'd ease in gently, with some pastries.'

'Look,' I blurted, 'I'm sorry I jumped down your throat. It was none of my business.'

I saw her relax.

'Got time for a quick coffee?' she asked.

Was this to be my morning of making truces? I looked at my watch. 'Okay, just a quick one.'

Brian had packaged up the custard tarts and he poured us two coffees. In the interim, Mary Lou had arrived in his shop. Thankfully, her fiendish boys were absent: they must finally have started school. She was talking earnestly to Brian and scribbling on a yellow notepad. Perhaps he was giving her baking tips.

Nancy and I settled ourselves at one of the outside tables. It was still just warm enough, but summer was fading fast. The morning had an autumnal nip and the trees by the church were displaying the first hints of gold.

'I meant to come see you, Grace,' Nancy began. 'You sure hit a nerve with what you said ...'

'I'm sorry,' I said again. 'I do realise that just because my husband was cheating, it doesn't give me the right to stick my nose into your affairs.' Oops, bad choice of word.

She shook her head rapidly. 'Well, I'm kinda glad you did.'

I looked at her tentatively over the rim of my coffee and waited tactfully.

'I was a schmuck. I'm kicking myself for pinning my hopes on a married man.' Nancy tore off the ends of two sweetener packets at once and poured them as a pair into her mug.

'Has something happened?' I picked up on her use of the past tense.

'Well, we had a big fight, and I gave him an ultimatum that he has to tell her and move out by the end of the month.'

'Really?' It was October next week. 'I read somewhere it's not usually a brilliant idea to give ultimatums,' I said carefully.

'Only if you're not prepared for the outcome.' She gave a wobbly smile. 'I'm ready to end it. At least, I think I am. But anyway, thanks, Grace. I wasn't acting smart and I needed a push.'

'Okay ... wow.' I wasn't sure I was ready for this catalytic responsibility on my shoulders. What's more, I seemed to be making waves everywhere I went. The plan of hiding away and licking my wounds wasn't quite panning out. 'Well, I admire you for that. I really do,' I told her quietly.

She shook her head, looking gloomy. 'Better late than never.'

'It seems to me,' I said, 'all kinds of smart women end up looking like complete idiots where men are concerned.'

'Amen to that, sister. But when October rolls around, I need you to hold me to my word.'

'I can do that,' I said. 'In fact, I can't think of anyone better to nag you.'

'That's a deal, then. Now I guess we should both get to work.'

We hugged briefly and I watched her walk purposefully off along the pavement, paper bag swinging from one hand.

~~~

I wasn't quite giddy enough to spend that week walking on air, but the date with Scott did put a certain spring in my step for the next few days. Amelia hadn't asked for details, which struck me as odd, and I still wondered if they had some history. However, we didn't have a lot of time for chit-chat. Hargraves & Co was pleasantly busy and I had to make time for my promised visit to Saffron Hall.

The white Beetle was no stranger to extravagant houses, but even so, I considered parking it somewhere other than the sweeping driveway outside the Hall. My humble vehicle definitely didn't belong amongst such grandeur.

Having crunched self-consciously across the deep gravel, I looked in vain for a doorbell and had to settle for the heavy brass door knocker instead. I then stood like a wally, waiting for somebody to appear. After counting to ten, I decided to risk a gander through the downstairs windows.

I was inching my way off the doorstep when the door was thrown open by bow-tie man.

'Miss Palmer! Good morning to you!'

'Hello.' I shook the hand that was offered to me, sure now that this was Bernard Pennington-Jones.

'So good of you to come.' He ushered me into the entrance hall.

'Thank you for inviting me.'

Bernard's careful manners verged on formal as he gave a little cough before running through a brief speech on the history of Saffron Hall.

Inside, the house didn't feel as big as I had expected. It was impressive, but not forbiddingly grand, in the way a real stately home might be. Instead, it felt more like someone's residence: comfortable, practical and a little battered around the edges. There was wood panelling, of course, some chandeliers and the occasional oil portrait. However, most of the downstairs rooms made me feel that somebody's rich grandmother had just popped out to the shops.

'Does the family still live here?' I asked Bernard.

'No. There's just my wife and me, in our self-contained flat. Nobody's lived in these rooms for a couple of years now.'

'And you host wedding receptions? Where are they held?'

We were standing in the middle of a small library. The smell of hundreds of leather-bound books blended with wood panelling and old carpets. I was reminded of Peter's antiques store.

'Here,' Bernard replied, leading me through a modest connecting hallway. 'In the ballroom.'

We were at one end of a large, high-ceilinged room, empty except for a couple of wooden chairs. A dozen tall windows ran along one wall, flooding the room with light. The other walls were painted burnt orange and held enormous paintings of Cambridge colleges. The floor was an intricate parquet pattern, in a wood I couldn't identify.

'This is stunning.' I was still taking it in. 'I see why people would want their wedding here.'

'It looks super when the caterers bring in all their gear. Oh, and flowers, of course.'

'I'll bet.' I tried to picture the scene: bride, relatives, over-excited kids ducking under tablecloths. Cake, speeches, the first dance.

'Has it ever been used for film or television?' Despite myself, I was getting ideas for the house.

'Not that we know of.'

'Shame.' I wanted to suggest he registered with a film location website, but stopped short. I wasn't qualified to meddle here. Then I wished I had spoken: it might have disguised the growling of my stomach.

'Gosh, look here,' said Bernard, 'I'm forgetting my manners. I promised you some lunch.'

'Sorry,' I said. 'Ignore it, I'm fine.'

'No, no, it's time we ate. On we go, last stop on our tour.'

We retraced our steps to the hallway, and from there went through some double glass doors and down a couple of steps. I found myself in the most beautiful long conservatory. Its windows, made up of multiple white-framed panes, were arched. Sitting majestically on the terracotta-tiled floor, generous wicker chairs gave a colonial feel. Tall potted palms reached up to the peaked ceiling, which seemed to be made entirely of glass. Some of the roof panes were open, by means of a complicated system of levers. My nose told me that citrus bushes were thriving in here.

Sure enough, 'And this is our orangery,' Bernard told me proudly.

'I love it,' I breathed. 'I could spend all day in here, with a book.'

'Many of our visitors feel the same way. I've arranged a spot of lunch for us.' He gestured to some wicker chairs drawn up to a round table, which was set with a cloth and cutlery.

'This is lovely,' I said, as I sat down and shook the linen napkin into my lap. 'You didn't have to go to all this trouble.' I hoped he wasn't going to make some kind of pass at me. Lunch for two in the orangery looked terribly romantic, but he was almost my dad's age. With foolish relief, I saw the table was set for three.

'Not at all,' he replied. 'My wife is the housekeeper – she'll join us in a minute.'

'Super,' I said. Scott's flirting had clearly gone to my head, if I had doubted Bernard's intentions.

I liked Daphne Pennington-Jones instantly. She bounded with gracious ease into the orangery, unhindered by a tray of sandwiches and a pitcher of elderflower cordial. I put her at close to seventy, but her silver hair was cropped in a trendy cut and her eyes, the colour of sapphires, twinkled merrily.

'Grace!' She shook my hand heartily. 'I've heard heaps about you! Bernard's so glad you came.' She waved me back into my seat. 'Egg and cress or cheese and tomato?'

For every ounce of Bernard's stiff formality, Daphne compensated with double helpings of warmth. She asked endless questions, and I found I was comfortable explaining that my marriage had ended and I was in the village by chance. We talked about my parents, their chickens, Amelia's business and my hopes for Halloween in the village.

'Bernard!' His wife grabbed his arm. 'We should have a Halloween party!'

'Oh, I don't know about that, dear. Sounds rowdy.' He looked distressed.

'Do you do the catering for the events here, Mrs Pennington-Jones?' I asked.

'Call me Daphne, please. Goodness, no, what a lot of bother that would be. We use one of the Cambridge firms.' She turned to her husband. 'Bernard, Halloween would be brilliant. You're always saying we need new ideas for this place. I don't know how we're going to pull ourselves out of the doldrums if you won't try things.'

Bernard sighed, looking down at his lap. 'Just not quite what I had in mind,' he said glumly.

There was a pause. I opened my big mouth, purely to fill the gap. 'Never mind, there's always Thanksgiving.'

'Pardon?' Bernard put down his sandwich and looked at me.

I had taken a bite and was chewing politely before I answered. Too late.

'Thanksgiving!' Daphne repeated. 'You know, Bernard, they have a sort of Christmas dinner. Don't they, Grace?'

'Sort of,' I confirmed, beginning to feel uneasy.

'That's it!' Daphne threw her hands wide in delight. 'Thanksgiving lunch, in the ballroom. We'll advertise to all the Americans. When is Thanksgiving, Grace?'

I furrowed my brow, basing my calculations on Harry's birthday. 'It's early this year. November twenty-third, I think.' My mind was racing, torn between potential and fear of what was unfolding. The ballroom, with its scale and foliage colours, would look wonderful. The house was impressive and might be a huge hit with our friends from the States. But surely, the cost of an event like this would be enormous? I knew nothing about planning large parties.

Daphne evidently shared my vision but not my fears. 'This is it. I know it. Grace, that's a splendid idea.'

'Uh, hang on, I didn't have an *idea*,' I backtracked. 'I wasn't actually *suggesting* anything.'

Daphne and Bernard weren't listening. Her head was on one side as she looked expectantly at her husband. He was rubbing his chin thoughtfully.

'Thanksgiving ...' he said slowly, then gave a tiny nod.

'We love it!' Daphne clapped her hands and beamed at me. 'Now, if you'll be a sweetie and help spread the word, we'll do the rest.'

'Oh, I don't know –' I floundered. 'This isn't my area.' I looked at Bernard pleadingly. He'd remember our phone conversation, surely?

'Nonetheless, Grace,' he said, 'I think you're onto something marvellous.'

So there it was, two against one. I had meddled again, without even trying.

~~~

Worse was to come. The three of us finished lunch: two animated and the other wondering what she'd got herself into. They even bullied me into taking a small percentage of the profit from Thanksgiving as my 'marketing fee'.

As they walked me to my car, I agreed to help Daphne with menu choices and other details. She was even bouncier than she'd been before lunch.

'Now, don't get carried away,' Bernard said to her. 'It'll

take more than just one event to turn this place around.'

'I know that,' she said, 'but if we can get eighty Americans here and excited about it, that's a start. Keep our greedy son at bay for a bit longer.'

This comment intrigued me. I looked at Bernard for his reaction, but didn't like to ask what she meant.

He saw my glance and ran his hand through what remained of his hair. 'I told you we're in a bit of a pickle,' he said, in a way that made me guess it was in fact quite a big pickle. 'The Hall is managed by a trust – Daphne and I are both trustees. Trouble is, so is our son.'

None the wiser, I unlocked the white Beetle.

Daphne tutted impatiently. 'Scott's a property developer. Keeps trying to convince us to turn Saffron Hall into flats. We argue about it all the time.'

As my ears rang with alarm, the blood left my fingers. My keys landed with a clink in the gravel and I scrabbled to pick them up. When I stood again, I was sure my face was flushed.

'Scott ...?' I took a gulp of air. 'Umm, I think Amelia's mentioned him ... Scott Jones?'

'That's right,' his mother nodded. 'He dropped the *Pennington*.'

'Said it sounded pretentious,' Bernard huffed. 'Silly boy.'

Indeed, I thought. And silly me. Without knowing it, I had just met the parents.

Chapter 22

When Scott called a few days later and suggested we go out for dinner in Cambridge, I played it cool. On Jem's advice, I'd decided the parental thing was an irrelevant detail.

'Should I challenge him?' I'd asked her on the phone.

'I wouldn't,' Jem had replied. 'It's not a big deal, is it?'

'I just think it's odd he didn't mention it. Now I think about it, I reckon I saw him talking to Bernard at the council meeting. But I assumed he was there because he's friends with Peter.'

'Well,' she said, 'you're not exactly joined at the hip to your family. I wouldn't mention it unless it comes up.'

'It might come up,' I said gloomily. 'I've got to work out how to find eighty mouths for Thanksgiving turkey.' Daphne and I had moved the meal to early evening, thinking this would make it easier for working people.

'Sounds like fun,' Jem said wryly. 'What are you doing, putting up posters?'

'Yes, actually,' I said. 'And I took a stab at a press release, but I don't know if we'll get any coverage. I can't believe I let them talk me into it.'

'I'm sure you're doing fine,' she said. 'Anyway, sounds like you can't lose. Either it'll be a disaster and Scott will be happy, or it'll be a huge success and your future in-laws will love you.'

'Don't call them that,' I groaned. 'If I muck this up, they'll probably all end up hating me.'

'I doubt it,' Jem replied. 'Still, you might not want to mention on your second date that you're in cahoots with his mum and dad.'

So, my tactical dinner plan was to look good, eat my food and not say anything that could get me into hot water. I liked Scott enough to try not to scare him off.

I liked him even more once we'd climbed the last few

steep steps to the roof terrace of the Varsity Hotel. We had just missed the sunset, but the colleges and churches of Cambridge were laid out around us, bathed in the last, gentle light of day.

'I thought we'd have a drink up here before dinner, if you're warm enough,' Scott said.

'How could I get cold with a view like this?' I shook my head in wonder. I'd never seen the city look so mellow and lovely. No wonder scientists and poets alike had been inspired to change the world from Cambridge. 'I had no idea this place existed.'

We settled down on one of the outdoor sofas and ordered drinks. I had repeated my outfit from the parish council meeting, adding my new cashmere cardigan on top. I was glad of the cardigan; the early October evening was mild but by no means balmy.

Noticing me buttoning my cardigan, Scott murmured, 'May I?' and slipped his arm around my shoulders.

Not daring to move in case he thought I was shrugging him off, I caught my breath and held it for a full ten seconds before I concluded that I had to exhale at some point during the evening. Nonetheless, I sat very still and enjoyed the changing colours of the buildings below us, as they sank from gold and rose into earthy charcoal. The peacefulness of the city and just-glimpsed River Cam settled me and I realised how content I felt in Scott's presence. It should have been weird, having another man's arm around me after five years of marriage, but instead being with him felt natural. I wondered whether further physical contact would feel as right. Chewing my lip, I blushed, grateful he couldn't see my face. At this rate, I wouldn't be able to eat any dinner.

'Either you're quiet because you're bored or you've frozen to death,' Scott said quietly, after we had sat in silence for a few minutes.

'No, just relaxing. It's beautiful here.' I glanced up at him as I spoke and found he had chosen the same moment to look at me. In the low evening light, his eyes were the colour of slate, his gaze intense. His face was mere inches away and I could feel his breath on my cheek. He smelled faintly of citrus: fresh and exciting.

With the slightest tilt of his head, Scott brushed his lips softly over mine, then pulled back to check my reaction. I leaned in for more, my eyes on his mouth. He wrapped his other arm around me and pulled me tight as we kissed deeply. My hand found the back of his neck and I sighed as I explored his skin for the first time. This kind of heat had been missing from my marriage for months. I had forgotten I could feel this level of anticipation, and certainly not just from kissing.

But, after all, this was Cambridge, not Cannes. British couples don't indulge in steamy tangles on hotel sofas. By mutual consent, we pulled a little way apart. I let out my breath slowly and tried to remove the lust from my features. I hoped I didn't have *wanton wench* glowing on my forehead.

'Well,' I said.

'Well, yourself,' he echoed, as I sat back a little and smoothed out the wrinkles in my trousers.

'Hungry?' he asked, his voice so silky that he attached at least two meanings to the question.

I made an awkward little nodding gesture. 'Are you?'

'Ravenous.' He grinned now. 'I hope you like steak.'

~~~

Mungo was absent from my doorstep when we got back. Considering I was carrying a foil parcel of leftover fillet steak, this was his bad luck. Despite leaping butterflies, I'd been able to eat most of my meal. Scott had no problem at all in polishing off a venison pie, followed by lemon cheesecake. After a good-natured tussle over the bill, he'd allowed me to pay.

'That doesn't seem right. I chose the place.' He'd shaken his head.

'Humour me, it makes me feel useful,' I'd said firmly.

'I'm sure you're very useful.' He winked and pushed both of the complimentary chocolates in my direction.

I hadn't intended my comment to be flirtatious. Was this a good time to mention his parents and their expectations that I'd promote Thanksgiving dinner? Not wanting to rock the boat, I'd chickened out.

'Would you like some coffee?' I asked him now, as he turned off the car engine.

'Thanks, yes, but I can't stay long. I have a breakfast meeting in the city.'

If he'd dropped that piece of information to help me relax, I was glad. Kissing him was one thing, but now we were alone, I was nervous.

Inside my cottage, I busied myself with the kettle and apologised for the instant coffee.

'Sorry,' I told him, 'I haven't bought much stuff. No coffee maker yet.'

'That's okay.' Scott was looking around the kitchen: high, low and in all the corners. If my mum had walked in and done the same, I would have told her off for being nosy. Still, I guessed he spent a lot of time looking at houses and the cottage was certainly charming.

'Explore, if you want,' I told him.

'Really?' He seemed surprised.

'I don't mind,' I said, smiling casually, but thanking my organised genes which had led me to hide Eeyore, my tampons and other girlie items before I'd gone out. I was also wearing some of my new undies and there were clean sheets on the bed. Still, I was relieved he wasn't staying. Being prepared was one thing, taking action was another thing entirely. No matter how much I'd enjoyed kissing him or how comfortable his arm felt around me, I was nervous of going further.

After roaming around the living room and peering at the fireplace for a while, he gestured upstairs.

'Go ahead,' I said, sitting down with my coffee to make

it clear I wasn't throwing myself at him.

I heard his footsteps overhead and called out, 'But don't go falling in love with the place. Amelia tells me it's probably going to be sold.'

He didn't answer and I assumed he couldn't hear me. I debated taking my sandals off, but decided that was too casual. There certainly was a lot to navigate when dating. Momentarily, I missed the ease of curling up on the sofa at the other end from James, wriggling my toes under his thighs to keep them warm.

'I never get sick of looking at old places,' Scott said, as he came back downstairs. 'You've made it very comfortable.'

I smiled and he hesitated before choosing an armchair.

'I didn't think you'd be here in the middle of the week,' I said. 'I assumed you'd be mostly in London.'

'Nope,' he said, adding milk to his coffee. 'I get around a fair bit.'

'How do you find the places you buy?' I thought this would give him the chance to mention Saffron Hall.

He didn't take that path. 'It varies. Friends and contacts give me tips. But I keep my ear to the ground too.'

'Do you always go and look at stuff in person?'

'Always. Yes. I look at the analysis, obviously, but gut feel is crucial.' He stretched his legs out in front, crossing them at the ankle. 'Would you like to join me one day?'

So, our fragile relationship had survived the instant coffee granules. 'Sounds fun. That is, if you're sure I won't be in the way.'

'You won't be. I need to look at a couple of places next week actually, north of Ipswich. Does Amelia give you a day off?'

I nodded. 'Monday, usually.'

'Monday it is, then.'

~~~

'Did you sleep with him?' Amelia looked me up and down

the next day.

'I'm not telling you that!' I said indignantly, then, as her eyes gleamed, 'No.'

'*No*, or *No, not yet?*' Amelia swivelled her chair from her desk towards mine and twirled a foot. She had been shopping for the new season and was wearing gorgeous Carvela court shoes, in camel with a dark brown toe.

'I'm not sure,' I sighed. 'I really like him ... but I'm a bit spooked about things going that far.'

'So, did he mention Saffron Hall, or ... anything?' she asked, a bit too casually.

I shook my head. 'Nope. I still find it a bit odd. But I avoided asking him directly.'

Amelia sucked the end of her pen, unusually thoughtful. Then she shrugged. 'You may as well go with the flow, darling. Just enjoy it without searching for hidden meaning.'

I shuffled some property brochures. 'Do you think it's too soon ... to go to bed with Scott?' I felt awkward, but after all, she had been the one forcing me to buy new underwear.

'Too soon since you've known him? Or too soon since you broke up with James?'

She'd seen right through my question. The issue wasn't whether I was ready to be with Scott, it was whether I was ready not to be with James. I hadn't heard from him since his letter in the FedEx box. The obvious conclusion was that he was moving on with his life. I rubbed my temples and didn't answer.

'All I can say is, casual flings saved my sanity after Michael left. Sex with someone new can be a lot of fun. You never know what you might learn.'

'Okay, okay, I get the picture.' We were getting into the territory of too much information. What kind of sex games had ignited in Amelia's fire engine house? And, scary thought, what had Scott been thinking, as he'd eyed up the ancient beams and banisters at my place? I coughed in my most business-like manner and picked up the phone to schedule some client viewings.

~~~

On my way home from work, I decided to call at Nancy's house. We were now well into October and I'd promised to act as her conscience in her dealings with Elijah. Still, I was nervous of the reception I'd get. It wasn't until I'd rung the doorbell that the horrible thought occurred to me: what if he'd moved in with her and I disturbed them both? I didn't want to meet him: I was afraid of what I might say.

'If it's a bad time, I'll go,' I blurted, as soon as she opened the door. Then I saw her red tartan pyjamas and orange Princeton sweatshirt and concluded she was probably on her own.

'Hey.' Nancy opened the door wider and gestured for me to enter. I'd been inside her house before, when we first viewed it. Now, it was much messier. I took in the piles of books and old newspapers, shoes kicked off randomly, and dirty dishes piled on the coffee table.

'I brought wine,' I said, 'and chocolate. I wasn't sure which you'd prefer.'

Without make-up, her face was sallow. Her bird-like movements were dull as she sagged beside me on the sofa.

'We might need both.' She let her head loll backwards and closed her eyes. 'Have you come to say *I told you so*?'

I shook my head. 'No ... I wanted to see how you're doing.' I was pretty clear by now that she was not on the brink of a new life with Elijah.

'Oh, Grace,' she began, 'I don't know whether I'm more pissed with him or with myself.'

'So ...?' What on earth to say at this point? *Congratulations* hardly seemed appropriate.

'So, it's over. We're done. Toast.'

'He wouldn't leave his wife, then?'

'No. You were right.'

She started to cry and I passed her the tissues from the coffee table. The box was almost empty.

'He was a total jerk,' she said, between sobs. 'Like he

had nothing to do with me moving to England. Asshole.'

I patted her hand awkwardly. 'I'm sorry,' I said. 'Really, I am. He doesn't deserve you.'

'But – I wanted – kids,' she gulped out. 'I've worked my ass off for years and now I'm running out of time. I'm –' sob 'thirty-eight.'

'You still have time,' I said, fervently hoping it was true. I hadn't made up my own mind yet about children and now I was husband-less, I needed to believe I still had some runway ahead of me too.

Nancy dropped a tissue on the carpet and snuffled into another.

I changed the subject to distract her. 'But now that you're in England, you'll stay, won't you?'

'You bet,' she sobbed. 'I'm so happy here.'

Funny way of showing it. I went to the kitchen to hunt down a corkscrew and wash some glasses. When I came back, she'd discovered the Galaxy chocolate and was holding a piece between thumb and forefinger.

'This is good stuff.' Nancy licked it carefully. 'It's smoother than Hershey's, I think.'

I made a mental note to introduce her to Maltesers, Crunchie bars and possibly Curly Wurlies.

'Try it with the red wine,' I suggested.

The combination was pretty awful, but we didn't care. When we'd annihilated all of the chocolate and most of the wine, I made us some cheese on toast. Then we watched *Coronation Street* and *Doctor Who*. Neither of us had a clue what was happening in either programme, but it didn't matter. We sat there in mutual melancholy, punctuated by the Daleks and some cheap red plonk.

Chapter 23

'Antiques aren't really my thing, but I wasn't going to turn down free cheese and wine.'

Amelia clinked her glass against mine and shrugged innocently.

'Fair enough,' I told her. 'I'm just pleased there's a big crowd here to support Peter and Giles.'

Already, a high volume of chatter was floating up to the rafters of the antiques barn, and a few people were even examining the merchandise.

I saw Mary Lou through the throng and waved at her. She had helpfully invited her friends to the party.

'And it's nice to have something social in the village,' Amelia continued. 'Too bloody quiet around here.'

Peter joined us. 'Ladies, hi.' He was wearing a gorgeous striped lavender shirt, which I would have been happy to own myself.

'How's it going so far?' I asked him. The responsibility for suggesting the party was weighing heavily on me and I nibbled anxiously on a cube of Wensleydale.

'I think it's going well,' he said, looking around. 'Several people have said they never knew there was a shop here, so that's a start.' He lowered his voice. 'And, Grace, you did brilliantly at getting the Americans to come.'

'Watch out, here's another one,' said a female voice behind us. 'Grace hassled me mercilessly, until I promised to show up.'

I turned and found Nancy smiling bravely. Dressed in a chestnut trouser suit, she had seemingly come straight from work. She looked much brighter. We hugged and I checked that she knew Amelia and remembered Peter from the pub.

'How's your house?' Amelia asked her. 'Everything okay?'

'Just great, thanks. I love it,' Nancy replied.

'Could you use some antiques?' I joked. 'Peter has a few spare.'

'Actually, I'd love to get something. Just so long as it's small enough to ship when I go back.'

'How long are you here for?' Peter asked her.

'I'm not sure yet. At least a year, though.'

'Well, I'll be happy to show you around.'

They moved off together, already deep in discussion.

'Does she know he's gay?' Amelia murmured to me.

'No problem there,' I replied. 'She's heartbroken over some spineless tosser who wouldn't leave his wife.'

~~~

'Sorry about that,' Scott said, as he got back in the Jaguar. 'It'll get more interesting from now on.'

'And I had been thinking your job was glamorous,' I replied. I kept my voice cheerful, but I was thinking that picking Monday morning for our next date had been a big mistake.

Scott's car was parked outside a disused factory on the outskirts of Ipswich. The building was a grey, soulless shape from the sixties, windows broken, litter flapping in the chilly breeze. Even the graffiti was uninspiring. I had declined the tour politely, waiting instead in the car with the doors locked.

'Was it any good?' I asked.

'I doubt it,' he said. 'Even if we could sort it out – which would cost a bomb – I can't see people wanting to live in this apocalyptic wasteland.' He started the engine. 'Let's get out of here.'

He headed north on the A12 and within minutes, the scenery improved, with the landscape an autumn mix of greens, yellows and some rusts. I stole a look at Scott as he drove. So far today, he had been business-like in his behaviour to me, but that made sense as he was effectively at work. He had picked me up from Ipswich station, greeting me with nothing more than a 'Good morning'. I was losing my nervousness at being with him, but was wondering if and when we'd repeat our kiss of the other evening.

'I could do with a coffee,' he said now. 'Okay if we stop off?'

'I'd love one,' I said. Unusually for me, I'd skipped breakfast in order to catch an early train. It hadn't helped that I'd changed outfit twice, finally settling for black jeans, boots and Amelia's tan leather jacket.

He turned onto a minor road and before long we were in a charming historic town. Scott parked his car in the market square.

'Where's this?' I asked. 'I like it.'

'Woodbridge,' he replied. 'I actually own a small cottage here.'

'Oh, for weekends?' The town seemed pleasant, but I had pictured Scott preferring something more cosmopolitan for his Saturday nights.

'No,' he smiled and shook his head. 'It has tenants. I bought it as an investment.'

Oh. So, whereas my interior design work tempted me to buy cushions, his job had led to a whole cottage. My impulse buys could hardly be considered wise investments. No wonder he drove a purring Jaguar and I owned a crumbling Beetle.

The little cafe had bleached pine tables. On its walls were Suffolk landscapes by local artists. We were alone except for two young mothers and their babies. Scott sat opposite me at our table in the window. He was looking expensively smooth in a dark suit, his shirt open at the neck. If he'd spent the weekend partying hard, it didn't show.

'Do you usually work alone?' My bandwidth for eloquent conversation was restricted by my assault on two thick slices of granary toast and a pot of tea. I should have known better than to miss breakfast; lack of food always makes me sag.

'Pretty much. At least, initially. Obviously later there

are meetings, investors, all that stuff. It's nice to have company for a change.' He was stirring a large latte and watching me with some amusement.

'Sorry,' I said, adding more honey to my toast. 'I know this looks piggy. No breakfast.'

'You go ahead. I'm glad it's doing the trick. Nothing worse than a woman who doesn't eat.'

Inevitably, I imagined a recent girlfriend: tall, wafer thin, probably a model or a public relations princess. Glamorous, high maintenance. And here I was, noshing greedily on toast and honey. Well, too bad, I couldn't be captivating on an empty stomach.

I gave Scott my best smile and was rewarded with his own slow grin. Really, his eyes shouldn't be allowed out before the cocktail hour – they were too sensuous for this time of day.

'So, what's next?' I tried to get my thoughts back to business, but was derailed when Scott reached over and poured more tea for me. The gesture was endearingly familiar.

'There's an old school just north of here, which I'm keen to scout out. Some canny old codger's been hanging onto it, but I think his kids have convinced him to sell.'

'Kids can be so persuasive,' I said meaningfully, offering him another chance to mention his parents.

He glossed right over it. 'After that, there's a hotel in Aldeburgh that's just come on the market. Thought it might be worth a look. It's in a great location.'

Okay, so he didn't want to talk about Saffron Hall. No big deal. I wiped my mouth carefully, keen to eradicate lingering crumbs and honey.

The waitress brought our bill and we both reached for it at the same time. His hand landed on mine and he curled his fingers around mine. I glanced up nervously as he began stroking his thumb over the inside of my wrist, then had to look away as longing heated my insides. Or it could have been the tea, but if that was the case, they should have charged a whole lot more for it and recruited Meg Ryan as their celebrity sponsor.

'You're not wearing your wedding ring,' he said quietly.

Finding nothing to say, I shook my head. I didn't think men noticed that kind of thing. Did this mean Scott had spotted it, in the pub or maybe at the races? If so, he'd known he was chatting up a married woman.

'So ... it's over then?' he asked.

I looked out of the window. On the other side of the street, an old couple, bent with age, were passing slowly. He was in a brown tweed cap, relying on a walking stick, she wore a bright headscarf and pulled a small wheeled shopping bag behind her. Her free arm was tucked through his and each careful step they took was in perfect timing.

'I think so ...' I caught Scott's gaze and exhaled. 'Yes. Yes, it's over.'

~~~

It was amazing the difference that tea and toast made to my spirits. From then on, the day just seemed to get better and better.

En route from the cafe back to Scott's car, we passed an estate agency. Without a word between us, we both ground to a halt so we could steam up the windows. I imagine I was looking for the fun of it and to see which living room photo I liked best, whereas Scott was on the hunt for his next deal. I got a kick out of our shared interest, anyway.

It wasn't far to the old school. As we drove, I wondered idly whether his residential projects would need an interior designer for the show homes. For a few seconds, I allowed myself a pleasant daydream that we could work together, or at least that he'd pass me lots of lucrative design work. With a decent budget and interesting architecture, I could create some stunning spaces. Teaming up with Scott would be a neat solution to both my personal and professional limbo.

Fortunately, I had the presence of mind to know I was

getting ahead of myself and I made sure I was back on earth before he parked opposite the school.

This time, I joined willingly in the tour of the brick building with steeply pitched roof. It even had a little bell tower on top, although the ivy covering half the school was threatening to claim that too.

'What would you turn it into?' I'd asked as we waited outside for the agent to arrive.

'Either flats or offices,' he'd replied. 'Probably flats. The residential market is strong round here.'

'Is it listed?' I asked, proud that I knew this could be a barrier to conversion.

'No, thank God,' he said, reading through the information he'd downloaded. 'I think the biggest problem will be whether the old git wants to sell.'

He'd shut up quickly as a silver Volvo drew up and I surmised that insulting the owner wasn't in the game plan.

As we looked around the school, I kept an eye on Scott, trying to guess what he was thinking. Clearly, he'd make a good poker player: he showed no emotion at all. That said, the windows had been boarded up, so the light was dim and I had to concentrate to avoid a face full of cobwebs. Scott took photos and measurements and I tried to picture the space divided into flats, but couldn't see how the windows might work. It seemed whoever built the original school didn't believe that daylight was necessary in the care and nurture of children.

'Okay, I'm dying to know what you think,' I said, only restraining myself until the agent drove away and we were alone again.

'Might be worth some further research.' Scott was looking up at the roof, then reached for his camera to get a few more pictures.

'It'd make a lovely tearoom,' I suggested, imagining the gentle vanilla scent of cakes fresh from the oven, the waitress in her starched white apron and perhaps an array of local crafts for sale too.

He laughed. 'Sorry, Grace. Tearooms don't make me much dough.'

~~~

My expectations of cobwebs and broken windows were pleasantly shattered when we pulled up outside the hotel which was for sale. The place was still very much open for business, and although not exactly thriving on a Monday in October, it didn't look close to bankruptcy, either.

Inside, we found it was furnished in traditional style. We ambled through the peach damask reception area, stuck our noses into the quiet residents' lounge, and found ourselves outside the dining room. Each table boasted white linens and multiple glinting wine glasses.

'I don't mean to be tactless,' Scott turned to me, 'but have you any room for lunch after all that toast?'

I could hardly object to his teasing. 'I could manage a salad,' I said coyly, knowing full well I would probably order something more substantial.

'Excellent.' He nodded in approval. 'Fish and chips – with salad – for two.'

~~~

'I wasn't expecting it to be this nice,' I said, as the nervous eastern European waiter cleared our plates carefully. I had been restrained and had declined Scott's suggestion of battered fish. Instead, chicken salad and two glasses of Chardonnay left me feeling relaxed but not stuffed.

'Me neither,' Scott agreed. 'The photos don't do it justice.'

I was glad the derelict school was still a possibility. I didn't want him to look back on a day spent with me as a total waste. 'Will you ask to look at the rooms?' I said.

He looked up at the ceiling of the dining room, with its cornices and ornate mouldings. 'I doubt it,' he said. 'It's not run down enough to give much room for profit.' He shrugged. 'I get more excited when I see cracks and flaws.'

'Right ...' I inclined my head knowingly. 'I guessed there had to be a reason you're hanging around with me.'

He flashed me his sexy grin. 'Yeah, you have great potential.' He narrowed his eyes speculatively, dropping them to my neckline and then lower. 'But I haven't had the full tour yet.'

'Yet..?' I showed him I could flirt back.

Scott rested his elbows on the table and lowered his voice. I found myself nudging closer, to hear him.

'Well, obviously, I need to check things out really carefully,' he said slowly. His gaze was firmly on my face now, travelling from my eyes to my lips and back again.

'How carefully?' I barely recognised the sexy tone in my voice.

'I'd say ... inch by inch.'

His words hung in the air and neither of us spoke.

'Madam, sir, would you be liking dessert?' The unfortunate waiter coughed beside us.

Scott raised his eyebrows at me wordlessly, but I had no interest in trifle and Pavlova. The only taste I was craving was his mouth on mine. I licked my lips and tried to speak, but had to settle for shaking my head.

'No, thanks, just the bill.' He hadn't taken his eyes off me.

The waiter scuttled away. Scott reached out his hand and placed it gently on the side of my neck, just under my ear. I leaned into his touch and closed my eyes briefly.

'I think ... I've changed my mind,' he said slowly.

I frowned, not catching his meaning. By now, I was light with lust.

He let out a long breath. 'I think we should go and see what their best room looks like.'

Chapter 24

My embarrassment at checking in without luggage evaporated as Scott kissed me urgently while we waited for the ancient lift. Impatience got the better of us: we gave up and dragged each other up three flights of stairs instead. Breathless, we reached our room. I fumbled the key card and Scott took it from me, dropping it, cursing, finally achieving the little green light.

Normally, when I arrive in a hotel room, I inspect the sheets, the view, the thermostat and the fake leather binder of guest information. I examine the plan on the back of the door which shows the fire exits and then I use the bathroom, careful to unwrap the miniature soap before I get my hands wet.

I did none of that. Clothes were already coming off as we tumbled into the suite. Scott kicked the door shut and two jackets, two shirts hit the carpet. Shoes, socks, boots followed. Neither of us said a word: we were too busy kissing, touching and exploring. My arms were around his neck and my eyes were closed as he backed me over to the bed. When the mattress hit the back of my knees, he lowered me down gently but insistently.

I opened my eyes to look into his, finding them bluer than ever. He touched his thumb to my lips and then bent to kiss my neck. His hands moved over my hair, my shoulders, my ribs and stomach. I curled my fingers around his lightly tanned forearms, giving a tiny moan as I stroked hungrily over the tense muscles of his biceps, chest and back.

But when he started to tug at my jeans, I froze. A sudden image of James flashed into my mind, so piercing that I dug my teeth into my lip. Scott leaned away from me, eyes intense but wary.

'Are you all right?' he asked in a low voice.

I swallowed. 'Sorry.' Had I ruined this?

'It's okay,' he said, stroking my cheek with measured gentleness. He found my hand and kissed the palm, then kissed each finger in turn. 'It's okay,' he repeated, kissing my forehead and stroking my hair.

When I gave the slightest of sighs, he started to stroke my shoulders and collar bone. When my tension dissolved through my toes and I let out a slow breath, he began to kiss me through my bra. When I began to kiss him back, he dispensed with the rest of our clothing. As I finally arched up towards him, he framed my face with both hands and asked me a silent question.

And when I responded with one small, needy word, he covered my body with his.

~~~

'For someone who's late for work, you look awfully pleased with yourself.' Amelia put down her phone and gave me a stern look. Still, I spotted the smile that was drawing at the corners of her mouth.

'Sorry.' I pressed my lips together and tried to look demure, but the grin escaped anyway as I slid into my seat.

'So, I take it you had a nice day looking at decaying sugar factories?'

'His job's actually pretty fun,' I said, blowing at the dust on my computer screen.

'Hmm. And how about Scott? Is he fun?' She failed to keep a straight face.

I stretched my arms above my head. 'Indeed he is.' For once, my croissant lay forgotten.

We had left the hotel at dawn that morning. Scott had broken several speed limits driving me back to Saffron Sweeting, which was chivalrous, as he was supposed to be in London.

'Are you going to be very late?' I'd asked, as we grazed a roundabout in fourth gear.

'I'll call them,' he shrugged.

'Sorry.'

He squeezed my thigh, then changed up to fifth. 'I'm not.'

As Suffolk whizzed past us, I'd pushed my guilt about James to one side. Surely, this didn't count as being unfaithful, if your husband had cheated first?

When I'd eventually got round to inspecting the fire exits – functional – and sea view – beautiful – from our hotel suite, it had been almost dark. The amazing sex had been followed by room service cream tea, supplemented with champagne and extra sandwiches. Feeding each other scones had led to some delicious fooling around with the clotted cream, and the generous pot of tea was stone cold by the time we drank it.

'I just realised, I've never actually done that before,' I'd said, as he slowed the Jaguar in deference to the bumpy track to my cottage.

'Which part?' He winked. 'You didn't seem like a beginner to me.'

'Stayed overnight somewhere, without planning it.'

'What –' he replied, 'you've never got drunk and crashed on someone's sofa?'

I shook my head. 'No. Or missed the last train. I'm too organised.' Or maybe just too dull, I added silently.

'Well, in that case,' he'd grinned, 'I think we should do it again.'

Now, Amelia inhaled the scent of her coffee. 'So you didn't spend much time talking, then.'

'Of course we talked,' I replied. 'We looked at a factory, and a school, and the, um, hotel.'

'I get the idea,' she said pointedly as I wriggled in my seat, glowing a little from embarrassment, but mostly just glowing.

Amelia walked over to the coffee table and began to rearrange the glossy property magazines. 'So, you feel you know him pretty well?'

'Uh – well enough, I think. Why?'

Saving Saffron Sweeting

'I know I told you to go and have fun, but, Grace ...'

'What?' Something in her voice made me nervous.

'Don't get me wrong, I'm thrilled you're seeing someone.' She was definitely uncomfortable.

'So? What are you getting at?'

'Just ... well, that he might only be your rebound guy. You know that, don't you?'

'Well, of course I know that.' I had reminded myself of it frequently. I became suspicious. 'Why have you shuffled those magazines, like, six times? Is there something between you and Scott?' Okay, I was paranoid, but given my recent history, it was a reasonable question.

Nonetheless, I was startled that she looked so guilty. Her phone started to ring but she sank down on a chair and ignored it.

'Amelia? For Christ's sake, what's going on?'

'Grace, keep your hair on. I can see you like him, and that's lovely.'

I watched her fiercely, seconds away from implosion.

'But ... I kept hoping he'd tell you himself. And I'm dreadfully cross that he hasn't. You do have a right to know.'

'Know what, for crying out loud?'

She made a defeated gesture, both palms up.

'Grace, Scott's just bought your cottage.'

~~~

I was so angry, I didn't return any of his phone calls.

So, it wasn't a total surprise when I got home from work on Friday night to find a blue Jaguar parked outside. Both Scott and Mungo were waiting on the doorstep. They seemed to have formed an uneasy alliance, each suspicious of the other's intentions. Mungo wasted no time in showering me with physical affection, to prove he was my number one guy.

'Hey,' I said, trying to ignore the fresh dog slobber on my best trousers. Perhaps sensing my unease, Mungo

~ 204 ~

growled as Scott moved towards me.

Scott stopped in his tracks, eyeing Mungo with dislike. 'I was worried,' he said. 'You didn't call me back.'

'I'm fine.' I locked the Beetle and folded my arms.

'Right. Okay.' He looked surprised and I guessed this was a new experience for him. He was so charmingly gorgeous, his other girlfriends probably returned his calls before he'd even hung up the phone.

'So, are you here on business or pleasure?' I asked acidly.

He was watching me carefully. 'Well, pleasure ... obviously ... I came to see you.'

'Oh, really?' I looked at the cottage. 'I thought you might have come to serve an eviction order.'

'Grace ...' He squeezed his eyes shut, then opened them skywards, as if seeking assistance. 'I'm an idiot,' he said.

I waited, tight-lipped. But I tilted my head to one side to show I was listening.

'Look, I should have told you. I'm sorry. There just didn't seem to be a good time.'

'There were plenty of good times,' I shot back. 'Right before we got a room would have been a *really* good time.'

He shook his head. 'I couldn't help it. I'm sorry. I didn't want to wreck things.' He was half smiling, looking sheepish but sexy.

'I'm sure.' A thought occurred to me. 'That Sunday, when my family was here? You hadn't come to see me, had you?' What a mug I'd been.

He didn't answer, but dug his hands in his pockets.

'You'd come to check out my cottage, hadn't you?' Oh hell. And he'd covered up by asking me on a date. 'You weren't interested in me at all.'

'That's not true. Yes, I did come to have a peek at the cottage. But you were a delightful bonus.'

I looked at him in horror. *Bonus?* I'd been a fool to get involved with another man so quickly.

He saw my expression and tried again. 'What I'm trying

to say is, I didn't expect to like you so much.' He was wrinkling those blue eyes at me now. 'By the time your horse won that race, I was hooked.'

Hooked? I didn't answer, but hope flared within me.

'Look,' he said gently, 'can we go inside?'

'Do I have the legal right to refuse?' I huffed, but he could tell I was softening.

Mungo, traitor that he was, started to paw at the door.

We sat awkwardly at opposite ends of the sofa. Mungo lolled happily in front of the fireplace, but still kept a lazy eye on Scott.

'So, how long have I got?' I asked with a sigh.

'What do you mean?'

'Before you evict me.'

He laughed. 'Grace, I'm not going to evict you.'

'You're not?' I searched his expression for confirmation.

He shook his head slowly. 'Absolutely not. The cottage is just an investment. Like the other one. I told you about it, remember?'

'Oh.' I was quiet for a moment and he watched me, a smile playing on his face.

'You should have told me about this one too,' I said, still grumpy but thawing fast.

'I know. I know.' He scooted along the sofa and touched my thigh. 'I'm sorry.'

I sighed. 'It's just ... I really like it here.'

'That's good,' he said. Then he raised his hand to play with my hair. 'I really like it here too.'

I looked up at him and was defeated.

As Scott leaned me back on the sofa and began kissing me carefully but deliciously, a wet canine nose was thrust under my elbow.

'Bugger off, Mungo,' I muttered. 'Can't you see we're busy?'

~~~

The following Tuesday morning, a dozen white roses were waiting for me at Hargraves and Co.

'Wow, he's totally fallen for you,' said Jem on the phone that evening. 'Not that that's surprising,' she added hastily.

'I'm having a hard time believing it,' I said, looking at the tall blooms in their vase.

'So, you spent the weekend together?'

'Yes. Sunday and Monday, I mean. We went to Southwold.'

Scott had picked me up after I'd finished work on Saturday evening and we'd driven to an upmarket boutique hotel. This time, I'd made sure I had clean undies and a toothbrush.

'Southwold? Not quite Paris, is it?'

'Have you ever been? It's gorgeous. Adorable painted beach huts – they change hands for tens of thousands of pounds, Scott says. And the shops were cute too.'

'Was he trying to buy a beach hut, then?'

'I don't think so.' Scott had, in fact, mixed some business into our trip but I didn't mind. So what if he was deducting me from his taxable income? I was having a great time and while he wasn't completely flashing money around, he'd made sure I experienced the luxury end of Suffolk. Being chauffeured in a Jaguar and feasting on gourmet meals made a welcome change from the white Beetle and a Waitrose curry. The days were getting chilly and I was a sudden fan of heated leather seats.

As we'd been eating a late dinner on Saturday night, I'd said to him, 'There's something else we need to talk about.'

He'd flinched slightly, in the way men often do when they hear the word *talk*.

'You didn't tell me about your parents and Saffron Hall.'

In fact, he hadn't shared a single thing about his family. Yet, he knew my mother kept chickens, that my dad had once played cricket for Lancashire and that my brother's wife was nicknamed Puddle-Duck in college. I'd kept quiet about the Gruffalo, though.

'I didn't think it was worth mentioning.'

I was determined not to make a scene and scanned the dessert menu before continuing. 'But you do know I'm helping them plan a big Thanksgiving event? Can we share the bread and butter pudding?'

He didn't blink. 'Yes to the pudding and yes, I know about the turkey dinner.'

'And?'

'And what? It's no big deal. I think you're all bonkers.'

Bonkers? That didn't sound like a term of endearment.

'Look, the Hall's mortgaged up to the nines. It's inevitable they'll have to sell it sooner or later. But if the three of you want to play at party planning for a bit, I'm not going to get in the way. You'll be lucky to break even, though.'

'Oh.' I didn't pursue the topic, but I was disappointed.

Now, to Jem, I confessed, 'It wasn't quite the reaction I'd been hoping for.'

'Well, it sounds like he might have a point,' she said.

'Maybe he does, but a bit more faith in me would be nice.' Then again, James had shown unswerving faith in my business abilities, and look where that had landed us.

'So you just made mad passionate love in a hotel in Southwold all weekend?' Jem teased me.

'I'm not going to dignify that question with a response,' I said, but she could hear the huge smile in my voice. 'Let's just say, all that outrageously expensive underwear doesn't seem such a waste now.'

'Oh, lucky you,' she replied wistfully. 'I can't remember the last time we – well, you know. And certainly not in expensive underwear.'

'Are things okay?'

She sighed. 'Fine. You know, it's just ... just everything. So tired the whole time.'

I didn't know what to say to make her feel better. I had no words of wisdom for juggling nappies and nookie.

'But I want to hear about the rest of your weekend,' Jem

said loyally.

'There isn't much more to tell. He took me to a place called Snape Maltings. We should meet up there some time, you'd like it.'

'Snape what?'

'Maltings. It's an old malt house, like the one here, you remember? Only this one isn't falling down, it's been converted into a huge concert hall, and there are shops and cafes and luxury holiday flats. It's very cool.'

I had, in fact, been in absolute heaven browsing the blissfully stylish home decor shop at Snape. Scott had sensibly realised I wasn't listening to a word he said and had wandered off somewhere. By the time he came back, I'd bought new bed linen, a duck-egg-blue milk jug and a set of French glasses embossed with bees.

Jem laughed. 'I think I'll just live vicariously through you, Grace.'

'What do you mean?'

'Look at you – new job, cute cottage, sexy man who sends you roses. I'm so happy for you.'

I was happy for me too. Of course I was.

I said goodnight to Jem and tucked the vase of roses under my arm to take upstairs. I wanted them next to my bed, to make sure I saw them as soon as I woke up in the morning.

Chapter 25

I confess, I was so busy seeing the world through Scott-tinted glasses that Halloween sneaked up on me. But in the last week of October, I suddenly realised that the village had made a herculean effort to get into the ghostly spirit.

Outside the pub were straw bales and pumpkins, and what looked like a stolen scarecrow hastily transformed into a witch. The little library sported hairy black spiders in its window, and inside I spotted a display of spooky books suitable for reading to children. Brian had gone all out in the bakery: cookies and cupcakes were decorated with bats, cats and orange icing. He was also taking orders for pumpkin pies.

I got the biggest shock, however, when I popped into the post office and encountered a human skeleton, which was clutching a telescope and wearing a pirate's hat. Next to him, a fake hand reached out of an old sailor's trunk.

'Good grief!' I said to Violet, in admiration. 'Where on earth did you find him?'

'Peter helped me,' she replied, looking proud. 'He dug around and found me a couple of bits he hadn't sold.'

'Can't think why,' I murmured. After all, every stylish home needs a skeleton next to the television.

I noticed she had a prominent display featuring plastic witches' hats, black and orange party supplies and even a tall basket filled with broomsticks.

'It looks great in here,' I told her.

'Did you see my pumpkins?' At her age, she could ask that kind of question without people snickering.

I nodded: there was a fine display of pumpkins outside the door.

'I've sold an entire crate already. That's the second batch and more are coming from Wisbech this week.'

'That's wonderful,' I smiled.

She pointed out a large poster on her noticeboard. 'The kiddies' parade starts at four o'clock. I assume Hargraves is taking part? If you are, you have to put orange balloons outside, so people know.'

'Orange balloons. Right. Absolutely.'

I bought three small pumpkins and fled, arms full, back to the office, where I fell down our step.

'What's the matter with you?' Amelia had just returned from viewings and was hanging keys back up.

'I've goofed!' I yelped, picking up the two pumpkins that I'd dropped. 'It's Halloween in four days and we haven't decorated!'

'Why do we have to decorate?' she asked calmly.

'Because I told the whole village how important Halloween is to the Americans. There's going to be a parade and all the kids will want free candy – I mean sweets. We need to have orange balloons outside. Oh God, and costumes. You and I have to dress up.'

'You're pulling my leg.' Amelia smirked and smoothed down her grey leather skirt.

I shook my head. 'I'm deadly serious. There are posters everywhere, haven't you seen them? This is a big thing for the village.'

She looked sceptical and started typing.

'It'll bring in new people,' I said, having no idea if this was true. But I remembered the reception I'd got from Amelia last time I suggested something to benefit the village. This time, I was going to be more devious. 'People who might not have considered living here.'

Amelia's head swivelled sharply, like an owl's. 'Really?'

Good, I had her attention. 'Oh yes, definitely,' I said confidently.

She put her elbows on her desk, making a steeple of her fingers as her eyes narrowed.

'Okay,' she said, 'you do decorations, I'll sort out costumes. You can spend a hundred pounds, but keep the receipts.'

I leaped up and tried to hug her but she batted me off. Undeterred, I grabbed my car keys and headed out of the door.

~~~

'Holy crap!' Amelia said in a loud whisper. 'Where are they all coming from?'

I shushed her in case any of the pirates, pixies or princesses overheard. 'I think maybe they're bussing them in.'

It was only twenty past four and we had already been deluged by children. Some were shy, and barely knew whether to accept the free sweets or not. Others tried to grab fistfuls and had to be reminded by their video-camera wielding parent to *say the magic word*. All, however, were enormously cute. So far, we had seen a bumble bee, a flamingo and even a television set, as well as the more predictable pirates, ghosts and witches. As far as I could make out, both British and American families were out in force.

My jester costume was comical, verging on ridiculous, but at least it was warm. Dressed in a purple and red velvet tunic, with long sweeping sleeves, matching curly hat and bottle-green tights, I had risked an earlier trip to the bakery for snacks to sustain us through the evening.

To my concern, I found Brian had put on twenty pounds and changed gender. Happily, the figure behind the cat mask, dressed entirely in black Lycra, turned out to be Marjorie.

'Brian's along at the malt house, setting up,' she told me. 'I'm just minding the shop and giving out sweeties to the kids, then I'm closing at four thirty.'

I didn't ask what kind of setting up he was doing as I was busy choosing the least gruesome cookies left in the cabinet.

On my way back to the Hargraves office, I'd looked up

the High Street. The clocks had changed the previous weekend and it was already dusk. I spotted several clusters of orange balloons, and outside the pub, a trio of buskers were unpacking instruments. They were wearing university gowns and mortar boards, which might or might not have been their regular busking attire. It was one of those days when it was extremely dangerous to compliment someone on their costume.

I was in no doubt, however, that Amelia had changed her outfit. She was also a jester, but I noticed with envy that her costume was far sexier than mine. She looked classy but racy in black and white diamond spandex, complete with black gloves and a sparkly face mask. Unlike my awkward booties with curled up toes, she was wearing tall black stilettos. I noticed she'd even managed to get one of her cocktail rings on over her glove.

'Where on earth did you get these?' I'd asked her, not liking to enquire whether she was wearing any underwear.

'Years ago, when I was a student, I was in the drama club,' she said. 'Footlights, you might have heard of it?'

'You mean *the* Footlights, where a gazillion famous people got started? Stephen Fry, Emma Thompson?'

'Yes, yes,' she said briskly. 'Anyway, I called an old friend and he recommended a costume supplier.'

'Wow.' I felt better about my jester get-up, knowing there was a chance it could have been worn by a great thespian.

Even if I looked a little bizarre, the office was fabulous. In my panic that Halloween was upon us, I had worked until midnight gathering supplies and then decorating. I had repeated the orange balloons inside, and nearly broke my neck climbing on our desks to hang matching paper streamers. Black cut-out ghosts floated in our window, while obligatory spiders dangled from the ceiling and perched on our computers. A Cambridge party store had yielded a cavernous plastic cauldron, which now contained the necessary candy for the trick-or-treaters.

Best of all, I had taken inspiration from Violet and persuaded Peter to let me raid his antiques barn. A huge doll's house now claimed our coffee table. Populated by mini witches and thumb-sized black cats, it glowed from battery-powered lights covered in orange paper. Beside it, an old half barrel was filled with packing straw and lucky dip gifts.

Now, seeing the hammering it was taking from eager little paws, I hoped we had enough trinkets. Perhaps I should make a mercy dash to the post office to see if Violet had any stock left.

Amelia was having a wonderful time, shaking her jester bells at the children, flirting with their fathers and generally hailing all visitors with 'Trick or Tree-heat!' I hoped she hadn't been at the emergency brandy we kept under the kitchen sink. She was collecting business cards in a separate cauldron, ostensibly a raffle for a bottle of wine, but I knew she'd be calling everyone in the next few days to see if they had any real estate needs.

At five, we locked up and made our way down the High Street in the direction of the noise and merriment. There were cars parked everywhere, and small family clusters straggled along in the growing dusk, buckets of candy dangling from little fingers. Under the tall black swan-necks of the Saffron Sweeting street lights, the bustle of wizardly figures made me think we had been transported to Diagon Alley.

The student buskers had moved on from the pub, so we followed the sounds of their music – currently, 'The Sorcerer's Apprentice' from *Fantasia* – to the crowd clustered in the field next to the malt house. There, we found temporary lighting had been strung up in the beech trees, and some enterprising soul had brought in a cart to sell candyfloss and popcorn. The adults, meanwhile, were flocking around an old ice cream truck, which seemed strange until I approached and saw it had been commandeered by Brian to sell both cider and mulled wine.

Amelia spotted it too and made a beeline for the queue.

I joined her and when we got to the front, was surprised to find Brian being assisted by none other than Mary Lou.

'Grace!' She seemed delighted to see me. 'Isn't this awesome?'

'It's great,' I said.

'What's it gonna be? We have hot dogs and pretzels, as well as drinks.'

Perfect. I bought mulled wine for Amelia and cider for me. I hoped the American families knew the crucial difference between our cider and theirs. They'd get pulled over on their drive home, if not.

'How come there are so many people here?' I asked Mary Lou.

'Well, you know, word just sorta spread,' she grinned.

'I love that you're working with Brian.'

'We got plans, honey. You ain't seen nothing yet,' she replied.

I would have asked what she meant, but the orderly British queue behind me was starting to rustle and mutter, so I moved aside.

The evening was chilly, but not so inhospitable that people couldn't stand around and chat. By the malt house – where someone had hoisted up fake ghosts – I saw bales of straw arranged as circular seating. Curious, I went over and found none other than Kenneth, reading ghost stories to a cluster of children. He peered intermittently over his spectacles, to make sure they were listening.

'Grace, congratulations!' Peter appeared from the throng and raised his paper cup to me.

I shook my head. 'What do you mean?'

'This is all thanks to you, you know.'

'Oh no, not me,' I protested. 'I didn't do this.'

He bit into a hot dog held in a paper napkin, and waved it as he spoke with his mouth partly full. 'You started it, at least. It's fantastic to see what the village can do, when people get inspired.'

'Well, that's true,' I said. 'But I can't take the credit.' I felt guilty for being so wrapped up in Scott recently, but nonetheless was thrilled to see my new friends enjoying themselves.

From the ice cream truck, Nancy waved at us and then threaded through the crowd. She wasn't in costume, but was wearing a beautiful rusty orange coat and big amber earrings. The colours suited her.

'This is awesome!' she said, hugging me and giving Peter a friendly squeeze on the arm. I hadn't realised they'd become friends.

'Jeez,' she gasped, as a sudden loud pop drew our attention. 'Is that Giles?'

I followed her surprised gaze and sure enough, saw Peter's partner knee-deep in children. He was making balloon animals for them.

'That's so sweet,' I said.

Peter nodded. 'Giles loves kids.' I thought he looked wistful, and wondered if the authorities would entertain the idea of them starting a family. I had a feeling adoption might be trickier here than in San Francisco. And what on earth would his mother say?

Nancy nudged me. 'I haven't seen you in a while,' she said, meaningfully.

I bowed my head in acknowledgement. 'I know,' I said. 'I barely realised it was Halloween, until this week.'

'And then Thanksgiving! I love this time of year.'

I groaned. 'Don't remind me.'

'Why?' she asked. 'Aren't you planning a big party?'

'Umm, yeah, but it's not going so well.'

I told her how few tickets we had sold and how my press releases seemed to have landed in recycling bins.

'At this rate, we're heading for a big loss. I feel awful – I'm letting Bernard and Daphne down.' I sighed. 'Then again, Scott did say we were wasting our time.'

'Did he? Why?'

'Well, he'd like it to fizzle, then he'd be able to persuade the trustees to sell Saffron Hall. But his parents are so excited. And they're lovely people, I like them.'

'So, he doesn't think you can make it work? That's not very supportive.'

I shook my head and shifted from one curly jester foot to the other. I had, in fact, talked to Daphne about Scott's belief that the Hall should be sold for development.

'It was hard for him as a little boy,' his mother had said. 'We were squeezed into our couple of rooms and I kept having to explain to him we didn't own the whole house. He didn't understand why he couldn't play wherever he wanted.'

'But now he's on a mission to sell the Hall, not save it,' I'd pointed out.

Daphne had sighed. 'Scott believes in fitting his own oxygen mask first. His own financial security is uppermost in his mind. He bought his first flat when he was twenty-one and hasn't looked back.'

If his investment properties and Jaguar were anything to go by, Scott's financial security was in the bag. Perhaps he just didn't know when to stop. And to be honest, I wasn't putting up much of a protest at his generosity in sharing his lifestyle.

To Nancy, I said in a subdued voice, 'I think part of me might want Thanksgiving to fail, so as not to rock the boat with Scott.'

'Grace, that's pretty lame.' Nancy tutted.

'I know.' I finished my cider and shrugged, then realised she was still waiting for a response. 'What?' I said defensively.

'You shouldn't let him intimidate you,' she said. 'Swing for the fences.'

'Easier said than done,' I grumbled.

'Grace, wake up! How many families are here tonight?'

I looked around. 'I dunno. Thirty?'

'More like eighty. Do you have any fliers?'

I nodded. 'They're at home.'

'Well, don't just stand there! Go fetch them!'

When I got back to the malt house, Nancy and Peter were still chatting. I'd had to park the Beetle a quarter of a mile away and arrived, breathless, jester bells jingling and hat askew.

'What now?' I panted.

'Cars,' she said. 'Windshields.'

'Can I help?' Peter asked.

'Sure thing.' Nancy handed him a pile of leaflets. We set off down the High Street, me on one side of the road, the two of them on the other, putting our literature under windscreen wipers.

'Good,' Nancy declared, as the cars finally petered out by the vicarage. 'That should help.'

The three of us began walking back together. 'How are you selling tickets?' she asked me.

'People send a cheque to the Hall,' I replied.

'That sucks, if you'll excuse me saying. Why aren't you doing it online?'

'I don't know how,' I said. 'I've never done anything like this before.' The uncomfortable truth was, I hadn't given it a whole lot of thought. I'd been too busy gazing into Scott's eyes and being swept off my feet.

'Right,' she said. 'Leave that to me.'

~~~

When I arrived home, after ten o'clock, the novelty of being a jester was wearing thin. In fact, I was looking forward to a long bubble bath and maybe getting the edges of *Good Housekeeping* soggy.

Most of the families with children had drifted away by seven. It had started to get really cold and the remaining grown-ups, myself included, had trooped by mutual consent to the pub. We made a funny group: two jesters, three witches, at least four vampires and Marjorie as a feline.

Bizarrely, Fergus, the pub landlord, had been dressed as Cleopatra, complete with black wig.

'It was on sale,' he told us cheerfully.

We hadn't been there long when Brian and his wife came in. Everyone greeted him enthusiastically, praising his initiative and hot refreshments.

'To be honest, it was Mary Lou's idea.' He wouldn't accept the compliments. 'She's got a heck of a zeal, that one.'

'Where is she?' Fergus asked.

'Taking those wretched kids home to throttle them, I hope,' Brian said. 'Talk about sugar overload.'

'What did she mean about more plans?' I asked, then looked at Brian's wife in case I'd put my foot in it. Thankfully, her pretty face remained calm as she drank her shandy. Whatever the deal was with Mary Lou, she wasn't bothered.

'You'll like this, Grace.' Brian paused for effect, then said, 'Mary Lou and that friend of hers are going to open a shop. Second hand children's stuff. Or toys, or something.'

'Really? Where?'

'In the old bank building. It's been empty for months now.'

I wondered if Amelia had been part of this plan. Then again, she didn't seem to bother much with commercial property.

'They're going to have space for a cafe. They seem to think mothers – or moms, as they keep saying – will love it.'

'Gosh.' I processed this. 'But won't a cafe compete with you?' Now it was autumn, Brian's outdoor tables weren't getting much use, but his takeaway coffee still seemed popular.

'Hah! That's the best part. I'm running it. I've got an ad in the paper for staff.'

'See, Grace.' Peter had been listening and chimed in. 'You really have started something rolling.'

I had shrugged it off, but privately, I was thrilled to hear of a joint American–British venture. If Mary Lou could pull it off, I could see that her shop might attract mothers from outside the village too. It couldn't be easy, moving continents without all the paraphernalia that accompanies kids. I'd thought about Jem and Harry's tiny flat and the sheer amount of gear they seemed to need for Seb.

I started to run a bath and then perched on my bed to look at the day's mail. There wasn't much, but a chunky envelope from Norfolk caught my eye.

This arrived for you, said a short cover note on lavender paper. *I thought it might be important. Love Mum. PS: Will you be coming for Christmas?*

It contained another envelope. I needed only a glance to ascertain it had come via the US Postal Service. James's careful writing was on the outside.

I felt sick. Was this what divorce papers looked like? I turned the envelope over in my hands, then remembered the bath. I scuttled to turn off the taps before I caused a flood. As I straightened up, I caught sight of myself in the bathroom mirror. I was still wearing the ridiculous jester's hat. I pulled it off and threw it on the floor, then looked myself bravely in the eye.

'Whatever is in here, Grace Palmer, you can deal with it,' I said firmly. 'Things are going fine. *You're* doing fine. You have a new life now.'

Nonetheless, as I located my nail file and ran it along the short edge of the envelope, I couldn't help wishing Mungo was there to keep me company.

Chapter 26

All the information was in English, but my brain still struggled to make sense of it. I had been so ready to read the official words signalling the end of my marriage to James, I couldn't comprehend why I was seeing pages with a conference agenda and travel itinerary. An Information Security summit in Kensington held zero interest for me. On the other hand, ethical hacking and cryptography seminars would be a total magnet for James. Light dawned. I fumbled the sheets and realised I'd been reading back to front.

His note was brief.

Dear Grace, I haven't come to England before now, because if you don't want to see me, there didn't seem to be much point. But work are sending me to this conference in London (see info). I've added a couple of nights on the end of my stay and hope you'll agree to meet me. I miss you so much and want to see how you are. I would love to get together. I can meet you anywhere. Please let me know. All my love, James.

I let the papers flutter onto the bed and drifted, unseeing, through to the steam-filled bathroom. I didn't even swear when I stubbed my toe on the edge of the bath. Shedding my jester gear in a trance, I sank into the snug embrace of the water.

That was two *loves* in one short letter. And the second one said *All my*. This was the exact opposite of what I had expected and he would be here next week.

I added yet more hot water and closed my eyes.

~~~

The village, meanwhile, was on a roll. Less than a week after Halloween, we found ourselves in warm clothes and wellies again, huddled in the dark to celebrate Guy Fawkes night.

November the fifth was a Sunday, so the fireworks were held the night before, in the field behind the malt house. Unlike the Fourth of July, this time there was no grumbling about the noise: the whole village seemed to be there, determined to enjoy themselves despite the weak drizzle.

Violet and I had come to an amicable understanding that Mungo was to be locked securely in her utility room with his dog bed and – my gift – a fresh bone. This would ensure there was no repeat of Independence Day's terrified gallop round the village. Having reached this truce, I didn't try to avoid her when I saw her near the bonfire, after the brief but much lauded fireworks display.

'Does Saffron Sweeting have fireworks every year?' I asked, as we found the right distance from the flames to warm our hands.

'No – only alternate years,' she replied. 'We don't have the funds. But tonight's were some of the best I can remember.'

'There's a huge crowd,' I said.

Over by the main gate, a couple of parish councillors were holding donation buckets. They seemed to be doing pretty well. Once again, families were out in force, kids whirling sparklers in rapt delight.

Violet nodded and shuffled her feet to keep them warm. 'Lots of folks from outside the village. Again.'

In the firelight, I could only just see her face. The darkness gave me courage. 'Do you resent that?' I asked quietly.

I thought she hadn't heard me over the crackle of the flames. Then, as the bonfire started to caress the bottom of the wonky chair on which the guy sat, she said, 'No, of course not. Their ways just take some getting used to, that's all.'

'You mean the Americans?' I wiggled my fingers towards the glowing heat.

'Not just them. Although some of the Yanks are too loud for their own good.'

I couldn't entirely refute that, even though most of the families were lovely. Tonight, they were confused about why we were burning an effigy and most thought celebrating the near destruction of our Parliament was a little subversive. In general, though, they seemed happy just to enjoy the occasion. The pub had been dishing out bangers and mash non-stop since lunchtime.

'Everything's changing so fast,' Violet continued. 'I'm having trouble keeping up. I can't see the post office surviving much longer.'

The guy was in even more imminent danger than the Royal Mail: the flames had reached his booted feet.

'But wouldn't you like to retire?' I said, hoping this wasn't too rude.

'Daft question,' she said. 'I was born in the last year of the War.'

That meant she was close to seventy. Even though she seemed to be in perfect health, she deserved to take things a bit easier.

'My father was American,' she said suddenly.

'Really?' I hadn't seen that coming.

'I never knew him. He never even saw me. My mother told everyone he was killed. But before she died, she confessed she never knew that for sure. He could have simply gone back to Kansas and left us to it.'

'Crumbs,' I said, sensing an incredible story here. Politely, I added, 'I'm so sorry. That's hard.'

She smiled, her face half orange, half shadowed. 'Well, obviously it was a long time ago. I've pretty much stopped wondering whether every newcomer to the village is my half-sibling. But I would like to know whether he went on to have another family.'

I nodded. No wonder she found the inbound Americans a little unsettling.

The wind changed direction slightly; we were getting smoked and would have to move soon. Violet waved at someone across the field. I looked through the haze, and saw

Peter in the queue for the hot dog van. Nancy was with him.

'He's been spending a lot of time with her,' Violet said.

'Who? Nancy?'

'Yes.' She shrugged. 'I'm getting used to the idea, slowly.'

'Oh. Well, I think she just likes antiques,' I offered.

'Humph. That's not all she likes, I'd say.'

This was truly cryptic. I took a breath to ask why it mattered, since Peter was clearly so happy with Giles, but before I could speak, the guy fell off his chair. Amid cheering, he tumbled head first into the roaring fire, sparks shooting in all directions.

'But I suppose it's good that Peter's learning to trust again,' his mother continued. 'He hasn't been out with anyone since his fiancée dumped him last autumn. Nasty girl.'

Coughing from both smoke and shock, I thanked the bonfire gods for saving me from putting both feet in my mouth. This was way too much new information for one evening. My main question now, was whether Nancy knew that Peter was straight.

~~~

Scott and I had arranged to meet for Sunday lunch at a pub on the South Bank of the Thames. He'd mentioned 'hanging out' for the afternoon and then suggested casually that I stay over at his place. I'd jumped at the chance, mainly because I was dying to see where he called home. And since he'd not only toured my cottage but had deviously gone and bought it when I wasn't looking, I thought it was only fair that I got to sticky-beak in return.

He'd arrived twenty minutes late. Stomach growling, I'd waited outside the pub, watching pigeons pecking around on the path. I'd been up for hours: Sunday train service was poor at the best of times and today we'd been delayed due to leaves on the line. How long should I give it before phoning him? This was unfamiliar dating territory for me.

'Really sorry ... Couldn't park ... Sorry.' Scott's hurried arrival, black winter coat flapping out behind him, had scattered the pigeons. I forgot my irritation as he wrapped me in a warm hug. We kissed, but briefly, as by that time my nose had started to run.

Even with the patio heaters blaring, it wasn't warm enough to sit outside. We'd found a table near the window instead. Despite the dreary day, the view across the river to St Paul's Cathedral was wonderful.

'You know all the cool spots,' I'd said, remembering Amelia's remark that Scott kept trendy company. He knew several of my friends but I had not yet met any of his. I was nervous of my ability to come up to scratch. At least I knew his parents, if only by coincidence.

'The first time I came here, I'd been to the Tate Modern and was starving. Just fell in by chance.'

'You like modern art?' I'd asked, hoping we weren't heading there after lunch. I get bored fast in museums, much preferring the gift shop and cafe. On the other hand, I can spend hours ogling in a contemporary show home that's had a heavy dose of interior design.

'It's okay. Why, did you fancy going?' He'd glanced at the menu and was now tapping his fingers on the reclaimed planks of our table top. Was he getting impatient with me? I'd missed great pub food in California and was wondering if I was hungry enough to tackle the steak and ale pie.

'I'd rather relax at your place,' I'd said, doing my best to look flirtatious despite my glowing nose. Was I coming down with a cold? I hoped not. And since I'd already kissed him today, Scott was going to have to take his chances with getting ill.

'Now, that does sound appealing.' He held my hand now and smiled at me.

Catching his look, I'd decided I'd better have a light lunch. It looked like I might be getting some exercise later.

~~~

Scott lived just a couple of miles away, near Tower Hill. I was unfamiliar with this part of London but I knew that large numbers of riverside commercial buildings had been redeveloped in the eighties and nineties.

'When we get back, remind me I need to book a flight for tomorrow,' Scott said, as he inched the Jaguar out of a painfully tight parking spot. I held my breath, not wanting to be present if he dented either his car or the neighbouring Renault.

Once we were safely clear, I asked, 'Where are you going?'

'Manchester. Just for one meeting.' He glanced at me. 'I know I suggested you stay over, and that still works. I'll get a mid-morning flight – meet them at lunchtime.'

'Fine,' I said. I would take myself back on the train and spend a quiet afternoon pottering in my cottage. Between work, all the time I'd spent with Scott and the village festivities of the past week, I was behind on laundry and cleaning. 'You're buying something up there?'

'Yup. It's looking good. The local authorities are much less snooty than down south, I can tell you.'

We were crossing the river and I craned my neck to see the Tower of London.

'Doesn't all that bloody history trouble you?' I asked.

'No,' he laughed, shaking his head as if I were just beyond hope. 'Location, location, location, Grace.'

I understood his point when I saw that, in his case, *location* meant a converted brick warehouse with private marina, a heartbeat away from Tower Bridge. I may actually have squeaked in awe when Scott opened the heavy door and I found myself in an enormous, loft-style living space. The windows were elegant wide arches, the floor seemed to be slate and the walls were either snowy white or a beautiful pale brick.

'Oh God,' I said. 'I think I just died.'

Scott put the kettle on, which, in such a glamorous space, seemed sexily domesticated. 'Make yourself at home,' he said. 'I'm just going to sort out this ticket.'

'Can I look round?'

'Course. Don't get upset if you find my porn, though.'

I wasn't sure whether he was joking, but I was too busy drinking in the surroundings to worry. In fact, at that point he could have introduced me to his blonde Swedish housemates and I don't think I'd have cared.

My eyes out on stalks, I explored greedily. The ceilings were also arched and of brick, as they might be in a Napa wine cave. They were high and the space was so well lit, the balance of intimate and impressive was perfect. His furnishings were modern – no surprise there: chocolate leather sofas, abstract art, luscious cream rugs. The kitchen was L-shaped, white and glossy with stainless steel.

On one long wall were framed architectural plans and I guessed these might be for favourite projects he'd worked on. Sure enough, a couple of architecture award certificates were hanging in the little hallway outside the bedroom. For a man who loved his work, I was relieved they weren't in the master bedroom itself. I felt too awkward to linger in there, but I saw that it was entirely grey and white, furnished sparsely. The bed was large, low and pristine.

Finally, I discovered the apartment's best feature: a covered balcony, also with brick ceiling, offering a partial view of the dock below. Luxury boats were nestled there and I was going to tease Scott about which one was his, but bit my tongue in case he did, in fact, own one.

'Dammit. I don't believe it.'

I was brought back to earth by this exclamation from one of the long sofas, where Scott was studying his laptop.

'What's wrong?' I lingered in front of a bookcase, which was at least fifteen feet wide and contained a mammoth flat screen television.

He tutted again. 'Tomorrow's flights are full.'

'Really?' The kettle had boiled but despite my scratchy

throat, I wasn't sure I should start rummaging in his cupboards for mugs and teabags.

Scott sighed. 'Serves me right.'

'Can you drive?' I suggested.

'To Manchester, on a Monday morning? Not likely.' His tone was snappy.

'Oh.' I perched side-saddle on the sofa at the far end.

'I'll have to go tonight.' He shook his head in annoyance. 'I'm really sorry.'

'Tonight? When?'

He consulted the screen. 'There's a flight at nine. I'd have to leave here about seven. That would work. We can still spend the afternoon together.'

'Okay,' I said, although really, it wasn't, and I was too polite to say so. 'I'll head back to Cambridge tonight.'

'No,' he said, reaching for me along the sofa, 'stay.'

I gave him a sceptical look.

'I can call them and make it a breakfast meeting.' He rubbed his chin as he thought. 'It'll only take an hour. I'll hop straight on a plane – I can be back for an early lunch.'

'What, stay here on my own?' I asked. That was weird. It felt too early for me to be roaming his home unsupervised. And yet, I was tempted by getting to know him better through nosing around his apartment.

'Why not?' He put the laptop on the coffee table and moved to put his arms round me. 'I'm so sorry, this is cutting into our weekend. But at least this way, I get to see you tomorrow too.'

He wanted to see me tomorrow. That was flattering.

'There are films,' he continued, gesturing at the huge array of DVDs. 'And books. And lots of shops down on the dock. You could get a massage or a manicure or something. My treat, obviously.'

He was smiling at me confidently, but I hesitated. Still, at least he wasn't suggesting I did his ironing while I waited.

'You don't have to decide now.' Scott was playing with my hair with one hand, while the other rubbed my thigh in a way that was much more than companionable. He started to kiss my neck, nuzzling at my ear. 'You can decide later.'

'Well, okay, maybe,' I said, thinking that a lazy morning and beauty treatment were more appealing than my housework.

'Great.' He slid his fingers inside my shirt.

I smiled and squirmed, but covered his hand with mine. 'Do you think we could have that cup of tea first? I'm gasping.'

~ ~ ~

By eleven the next morning, I had made the most of my luxurious surroundings, but was more than ready for company again.

The previous evening, after Scott left, I had looked in all the kitchen cupboards and scanned the title of every book on his shelves. I had examined every piece of art and decorative accessory, and thumbed through his collection of CDs. I even allowed myself a quick peek in his wardrobe, which revealed lots of dark suits and tailored shirts, with a preference for Ted Baker and Paul Costelloe. In the hall cupboard I'd found skis and a substantial set of golf clubs.

Beyond that, however, I didn't pry. Even by my nosy standards, it felt too personal to explore bedroom drawers or the office. But I noticed there were no photos in Scott's home. Not one.

I'd made myself toast and Marmite for supper, phoned Jem for a chat, and then found that if I stood on the balcony and leaned out as far as I dared, I could just see a fireworks display from the direction of Blackheath.

Scott had left me a key to his loft, which had triggered an awkward exchange as we both confirmed I was only borrowing it, not keeping it. On Monday morning, I'd found an eye-wateringly expensive delicatessen and stocked his fridge with milk, bread, eggs and organic cheddar. Too late, I realised I didn't know how often Scott was at home and whether he even liked to cook. Then, I'd browsed the shops next to the marina, and ended with a manicure and blow-dry at the beauty salon.

Allowing for an early meeting, journey to Manchester airport, flight and then the motorbike taxi from Heathrow, I calculated Scott might be back by about noon. I settled myself on one of his leather sofas, Starbucks latte in hand, and waited.

And waited. Noon became one, one became half past.

'I'm not the type to call every five minutes,' he'd said the previous evening, throwing a shirt and underwear into a Samsonite laptop case.

'No problem.' I'd been naked under his sheets, stretching luxuriously and sleepily.

At two, I texted him: 'Should I wait?'

His reply: 'Sorry, took longer than expected.'

This told me nothing. At two fifteen, stomach growling from lack of lunch, I followed up with: 'Where are you?'

'Just finishing up,' came the response, a few minutes later.

What a pain. He'd dodged the question. Was he still in Manchester? Not even at the airport, let alone boarding a flight? I could either sit here indefinitely, or send a nagging text every fifteen minutes. Neither option appealed.

I jumped up, stuffed my overnight things into my bag and placed Scott's spare key on the kitchen island. Then, pausing only to make a grab for the designer cheese, I let myself out.

~~~

It was an easy journey by Tube from Tower Hill to Liverpool Street. Once a train turned up, I figured I'd be there in a jiffy.

I'd waited a good five minutes before I realised I was on the wrong platform. Kicking myself for such an elementary mistake, I consulted the map. The last thing I wanted was to go the wrong way round the Circle line, via Victoria and South Kensington. I started to walk towards the steps but stopped abruptly, causing a throng of Japanese tourists to flow, babbling, around me. An uncomfortable thought had occurred to me: had I been as wrapped up in my design business as Scott was now? Had I shut James out, undermining us by being remote and unreliable?

Kensington was ringing a loud bell and I had just worked out why. I suddenly saw that I might be on the right platform, after all.

I put my bag down, took out my phone and called my husband.

Chapter 27

I was pathetically unprepared for the triad of familiarity, love and pain which swirled over me when I saw James. I recognised him as soon as I entered the marble hotel lobby, and would have known him as easily at fifty paces or even five hundred. Every mannerism, from the way he was standing with one hand in his pocket, to the lift of his head when he saw me, to the way his red shirt wasn't fully tucked in, was exactly the same. I didn't even know I knew these things, apparently absorbed into my subconscious memory through years of routine living.

The second emotion was pure delight, as my heart recognised the man I had thought was my soulmate. We exchanged the look you sometimes see between lovers at parties, when they're in the same room but not standing together: just a fleeting second of eye contact where both acknowledges a connection stronger than steel. The tug at my lips was purely involuntary.

When I saw the matching smile on his face, my heart leaped, then crashed as the pain hit and I remembered why we were here, in a smart London hotel with shiny floors and assertively yellow walls.

'Hi.' James had crossed the lobby, made as if to hug me, but stopped short and squeezed both my arms lightly instead. He looked down at me, smiling awkwardly, surveying me cautiously.

'Hi.' I held my overnight bag as a barrier in front of me, gripping it with both hands. By now, my lips were firmly clenched so that they betrayed neither smile nor wobble.

'I'm really glad you came,' he said, putting both hands in his pockets and coughing. 'How are you?'

'Fine.' I nodded more than was necessary, glad of that morning's hairdresser visit, as my hair settled obediently. At least I was looking great. 'You?'

'Fine. Yep.'

Neither of us spoke for a moment and when I risked looking at him directly, I saw his eyes had softened. I looked away in a hurry. He had definitely lost weight. Ever since university, he'd been slender, but once we'd moved to California, swimming and cycling had beefed him up a bit. Now, though, his face seemed pinched and there were blueish shadows under his eyes.

'So ... how was the conference?' I asked.

'Oh. Good. Yes, fine.'

Great. Everything was officially 'fine'.

'Shall I take that?' He gestured at my bag.

'Oh.' This was awkward: I had shown up with luggage. I spoke quickly. 'I'm not staying. I was in London last night. I'm on my way home.'

'Okay,' he said. 'But we can put it in the storage room for a bit.' Seeing me hesitate, he continued, 'We could go for a walk, if you'd like.'

A walk. Yes. That was a good plan. Fresh air would be nice. I still suspected I was getting a cold and my head felt muzzy.

We left my bag and walked north from his hotel. Within minutes, we crossed the main road and entered Hyde Park. The air was damp and far from fresh, due to all the bonfires of recent days. Leaves were falling, joining others lying soggy on the path. Still, I was glad to stretch my legs. I guessed we had about an hour of decent daylight left.

James asked after my family; I asked after his mum. He asked where I was living, and I was deliberately vague in saying I had found somewhere nice and had made friends. He asked whether I was working, and I admitted I was helping out at an estate agency and enjoying it.

'That's great,' he said. 'I bet you're really good at that.'

We reached the Serpentine and turned right, to walk around the lake.

'And, um, how's work for you?' I wasn't being polite, I desperately wanted to know. I looked at him out of the corner of my eye to get clues from his face as he answered.

'It's okay,' he said. 'Not much new.'

I gave a tiny snort.

'What?' he asked.

'You have to give me more information than that,' I said pointedly, stopping for a moment.

'Like what?' He stopped too and seemed genuinely puzzled.

'Well.' I dug my hands in my coat pockets and looked at the geese on the water. 'Well, like, how's Rebecca?'

'Rebecca? She moved to Seattle,' he said. 'Months ago.'

I stiffened and my mouth formed a silent 'Oh.'

'Didn't I tell you?' He shook his head and looked surprised.

For heaven's sake, I thought, I would have remembered that. I had been torturing myself for five months and forming painful pictures of their cosy daily life.

James brought a hand up to the back of his neck and kneaded the muscles there. Then he spoke carefully. 'Grace, I don't think you believed me, but I was being honest with you when I said the – thing – with Rebecca, it just happened one time.'

I looked up at him. My nose was starting to run but if I reached for a tissue now, he might think I was crying. I shook my head silently.

'One lousy mistake, in Vegas,' he said. 'On my mother's life, I swear to you.'

Did I believe him? I couldn't think what he would gain from lying to me, but I still remembered the way Rebecca had looked at him. Her devoted expression didn't seem to fit with one quick shag in Las Vegas.

'But you saw her bedroom,' I muttered, thinking of the treacherous purple accent wall.

'I gave her a lift home one day, when her car was getting fixed. She wanted to show me your work.' James shook his head emphatically. 'That was it – that was all, I *promise*.'

Sod it. I found a tissue and wiped my nose.

'Grace, say something.'

'I think I'm getting a cold.'

He sighed. 'Let's walk.' The murky light was fading and other people in the park were starting to thin out. It wasn't yet four o'clock and it occurred to me that California winters had turned me soft. We picked up our pace a little and continued in silence for a few minutes.

'Look.' James was staring fixedly at the path in front of us. 'I know I hurt you terribly. I'm so sorry. I'd give anything to undo that. But ...' He stopped again and turned to me. His face was absolutely intent, the little frown lines clear on his forehead. 'This is awful. I love you and I want you back. Just tell me what I have to do and I'll do it.'

I swallowed hard, staring back at him. Rebecca was gone; he was asking to try again. These were the eyes I had gazed into on my wedding day, the day we'd promised better or worse, come what may, as long as we lived. I felt a magnet pulling me to him. James was my North. All I had to say was *Yes*, and I could walk straight into his arms.

Neither of us moved. James looked at me, trusting and waiting, scanning my face for an answer.

'I'm seeing someone,' I said, and my voice seemed to come from another person entirely.

He stared, blinked, turned half away. Then he turned back to me and reached for my arm. 'But, Gruff –'

'Don't,' I said, overwhelmed by how much was wrapped up in that nickname. I started to cry.

He shook his head and gave a brief ironic smile, before biting his lip. 'Is it serious?'

I wiped my eyes and hugged myself from cold and confusion. 'I don't know.'

James gazed out across the lake, where the wind had started to make gentle ripples. He let out a long breath and then looked at me. 'We should walk back.'

I nodded, shivering slightly. We turned to retrace our path around the eastern end of the Serpentine. For five minutes, we walked in silence, then the mist in the air turned to insistent London drizzle. I ducked my head and pulled my coat collar up around my ears. So much for my hairdo.

Without a word, James stepped closer to me and put his arm around my shoulders, giving me a hint of warmth and shelter. At the same time, he adjusted his long stride so that our progress was more comfortable. A stab of longing went through me as I felt his familiar body pressed against mine. After a few seconds, I remembered to breathe, and matched my pace to his. We walked on.

~~~

James let me go as we climbed the steps of his hotel. The warmth of the bright lobby was welcome, but I was embarrassed by my red nose and ratty hair.

'Are you hungry? Want something to eat?' he asked.

These innocent words were a conciliatory overture in disguise. As a three-meals-a-day guy, James couldn't understand my reliance on snacks. He got by on water from the reusable aluminium bottle he carried everywhere.

Remembering that my lunch had been a four-inch wedge of cheese, I said, 'That would be great.' Surprisingly, I wasn't all that hungry, but I was thirsty, wet and cold.

'The hotel does afternoon tea. It's famous, I think.'

He went to the front desk and came back with a menu. It boasted savoury skewers, taster spoons and cakes which had allegedly been inspired by Gucci and Valentino.

'My treat,' James prompted, nodding at me encouragingly.

Jem and I would definitely have to come back here, but today I was in no mood for fussy. I was also aware that inflicting herbal infusions and a cherry bavarois on James was somewhat mean.

'It looks a bit fancy.' I wrinkled my nose apologetically. 'Can we just go to a cafe?'

Our marriage might be as flat as a day-old soufflé, but I

had read him well. He looked relieved as we retrieved my bag and trudged back out into the rain.

~~~

Mungo welcomed me home that night but I wasn't up to playing or patting. Not pausing to draw the downstairs curtains, I headed straight for bed, dumping my now dry but wrinkled clothes on the bedroom floor. I felt sick, headachy and miserable. The heating was on but I was shivering. I found my warmest pyjamas and added socks and a thin jumper.

My phone contained four apologetic texts from Scott, plus two voice messages, which I hadn't listened to. Before I climbed under the covers, I shook his brown-tinged roses into the bathroom bin and rinsed out the vase. I wasn't making a grand gesture, it was time for them to go in any case. And I needed somewhere to put the freesias from James.

Apart from a couple of solitary souls with laptops, the coffee shop near the Tube station had been almost deserted. On a wet Monday afternoon in November, Londoners had found somewhere better to be. We claimed two armchairs in the corner and waited for the bored-looking barista to concoct our drinks. In another show of solidarity, James had ordered a hot chocolate, an indulgence he usually reserved for ski trips to Tahoe.

Neither of us had said much since leaving the park. I was a bit surprised he hadn't simply packed me onto the nearest Tube train, but was feeling too miserable to analyse this. As soon as our order had been brought to us, I wriggled my damp feet out of my boots and tucked them up under me, glancing around furtively as I did so.

'Maybe we should have got you a brandy, instead of tea,' James said, stretching out his legs and blowing on his drink.

'I'm okay,' I said, my attention temporarily on a plump

teacake, which was dripping butter onto my plate.

By the time I had polished that off and drunk some tea, I felt brighter. 'Just a cold coming, I think,' I said. 'I hope I haven't given it to you.'

Funny, I hadn't given much thought to infecting Scott, but I didn't want to make James sick.

'If you have, I'll just pass it on to the other three hundred people on my flight.'

'When do you leave?'

'Tomorrow,' he said. 'So it's lucky you phoned today.' He gave a half smile.

After another pause, I said, 'Thank you for the parcel you sent.'

'No problem,' he replied. 'Do you have everything you need?'

I nodded.

'Are you ... staying in England for good?' he asked.

I lifted the lid on the teapot to add more hot water, then agitated the bag with a spoon. 'Dunno. I haven't decided.' Then I saw he was waiting for more and added quickly, 'Do you need me to move my stuff out?'

'No. No, not at all.' He shook his head. 'That wasn't what I meant.' He leaned across and put his hand on mine, where it rested on the arm of my chair. 'I'd much rather you came back to Menlo Park.'

I looked down at his fingers covering mine. His touch was warm and inviting. Then I noticed he wasn't wearing his wedding ring. If he'd seen I wasn't wearing mine either, he hadn't said anything.

I paused, as the significance sunk in. 'I don't think I can do that,' I said sadly.

'Will you at least tell me where you're living?'

I shrugged. 'It's a nice village. Near Cambridge. It suits me.'

'And ... you're okay for money?'

'Yup.' I was making ends meet, but only just. Still, that wasn't his problem and considering I'd confessed to a new relationship, it was a generous question. He really was being kind. Then I remembered he was the one who'd got us into this mess in the first place.

I looked at my watch. 'I always seem to hit rush hour,' I said.

'How are you getting back?'

'Liverpool Street. Or maybe King's Cross.'

'I'll come and see you off.'

'You don't have to do that. I'm fine.'

'I'd like to.'

So we wedged ourselves onto a packed Circle line train, strap-hanging in near silence with dozens of strangers, the combined body heat drawing wisps of steam from our damp clothes.

At Liverpool Street, we found I had twenty minutes before the Cambridge train.

'I'd better spend a penny,' I said, leaving him beside the escalator.

In fact, my visit cost me an exorbitant thirty pence. Britain was becoming an expensive place to live.

When I returned, James was standing in the same spot, but was now holding a large bunch of freesias wrapped in pink tissue paper.

He gave them to me awkwardly. 'I wanted to get you something,' he said. 'I don't know why, but these just reminded me of you.'

I took them, said a simple thank you, and swallowed down the invading lump in my throat.

'Well. Bye then,' he said.

'Bye.'

After hesitating, he kissed me on the cheek. I ducked my head and walked away quickly, through the ticket barrier and onto the platform. As I boarded the train, I looked back, and saw he was still there. My husband raised his hand in a simple wave, and then I lost sight of him in the commuter crowd.

I hefted my bag onto the luggage rack and folded myself

into a seat, the freesias on my lap. Gingerly, I sniffed, and as the deep, sensuous scent floated up, I let the tears stream down my face.

James wasn't good with girlie stuff; he wouldn't remember details like this. I'm sure he had absolutely no idea he'd just given me the same flowers I'd carried on our wedding day.

Chapter 28

'I owe you big time,' I said to Nancy, two weeks later. 'This was a disaster until you stepped in.'

The Thanksgiving meal at Saffron Hall had just finished, most of the guests had gone home, and the catering staff were beginning to pick their way through the vast mounds of debris on each table.

Nancy surveyed the ballroom. 'It looks like a whole new disaster now.'

I smiled. 'I'm glad I'm not clearing up.'

Over a hundred people had squeezed into the space at round tables of eight, and had been served a traditional Thanksgiving dinner including turkey, sweet potatoes and green bean casserole. For dessert, apple pie or pumpkin pie – or both – had been offered. There had been much talking, laughing and, naturally, giving gratitude for blessings big and small.

'I still don't know how you did it,' I said.

Nancy grinned. 'I just spread the word a bit.'

She had done much more than that. Moving the ticketing online had been a master stroke, and she had also persuaded the human resources director at her company to give us a plug in the staff newsletter. A couple of families told me they had been in the village for Halloween, and four whole tables had been sold to American military personnel from the Air Force base at Lakenheath.

'I'm amazed,' I had said, upon learning this. 'Don't they have free turkey at the base?'

'I guess they wanted something different,' Nancy had replied. 'Our venue is more special.'

Needless to say, Bernard and Daphne were over the moon with the income – and more importantly, awareness – the day had generated.

'Here she is!' Bernard cried, shaking my hand

enthusiastically.

Daphne bounded up behind him, looking twenty years younger than she was.

'Grace, dear, this has been absolutely marvellous,' she said, hugging me.

'I can't accept responsibility.' I meant it. 'Please meet my friend Nancy, she really turned this around for us.'

Bernard shook Nancy's hand. 'Did you enjoy your dinner, my dear?'

'It was swell,' Nancy replied. 'It was so great not to be alone this evening.'

I knew that feeling, and how hard special days in the calendar could be. As well as raising money for the Hall, we'd offered something valuable to those who were thousands of miles from home.

'So, Grace,' Daphne said brightly, 'we were wondering about doing mince pies and carols on the Sundays leading up to Christmas. What do you think?'

'Sounds wonderful,' I said. 'We can send an email announcement to everyone who was here tonight.'

'Gosh, how flash,' said Bernard. 'I was going to draft something on my typewriter.'

Daphne poked him in the arm. 'Don't be a clot, dear. It's all on Facebook these days, isn't it, Grace?'

We laughed.

'Have I missed the party?' called a voice from the other side of the room.

'Scott, darling!' His mother was the first to claim a kiss, and I was surprised to see Bernard hug his son briefly too. I had been under the impression they weren't close.

'Hi Grace,' Scott said to me, but with no attempt at a physical greeting. He was in a dark business suit, looking tired, somewhat creased, but absolutely delicious. The loosened tie and five o'clock shadow suited him. I hadn't seen him since his trip to Manchester, although we had spoken on the phone.

'I understand you were delayed,' I'd said, 'but why

didn't you let me know?'

'The meeting was pretty intense,' Scott had replied. 'I was caught off guard: I thought the deal was in the bag. I'm sorry, I lost track of time.'

'I've got better things to do than sit around waiting for you.'

'I know, of course you do, I'm really sorry. I hated not being able to get back and see you.'

His words were smooth, his tone sincere, but I just couldn't shake the feeling that if I had been anywhere near the top of his priorities, he wouldn't have left me hanging.

Upon being introduced to Scott, Nancy fixed him with her appraising, bird-like look. Not only did she know about his dismissal of our Thanksgiving efforts, but I had told her about him disappearing to Manchester.

'So, I hear you were hoping tonight would fall flat on its fanny?' Nancy said pointedly to him.

Bernard was clearly shocked and even Daphne took a step backwards.

'She means *bottom*. Sorry,' I said hastily.

Scott, however, was grinning. 'No,' he said slowly, 'but I *was* hoping there would be leftovers.'

Nancy raised her chin, ready to engage, but Daphne spoke first.

'Oh, sweetheart, haven't you eaten yet? There's lots of pie and coffee.'

Scott was still looking as though he would enjoy a sparring match with Nancy. And was he actually assessing her legs in her short tweedy skirt and high-heeled boots? Perhaps he wasn't as tired as I had assumed.

'I wouldn't mind a forage,' he said.

I was relieved that his hungry gaze was now directed at the dessert buffet. He still hadn't made any attempt to kiss or hug me.

'Where are you staying tonight, dear?' his mother asked. She knew we were an item and that Scott had slept over at my cottage on previous visits to the village.

'I'm not sure.' Scott glanced at me now and waited.

I paused. He was gorgeous and eligible, and had apologised sincerely. More flowers had arrived, this time stunning orchids. They were providing some much-needed wow factor in my living room. Even so, I had left the freesias beside my bed.

I shook my head. 'It's getting late, we've had a long day. I should go.'

Daphne nodded briskly to Scott. 'I'll put some sheets on the sofa bed.'

She and Bernard went off together, arm in arm, and I imagined them in their little flat, making Horlicks and watching the ten o'clock news before bed.

Nancy patted her stomach. 'I'm so full, I need to go home and lie down. I don't think I'll eat for a week.'

'Thanks again,' I told her as we hugged. 'You were incredible.'

'I wish our relationships were as easy,' she whispered to me, before bidding us goodnight.

Scott took his tie off, stuffing it in his suit pocket. At last, he put his arms around me and kissed me briefly on the lips. 'Stay for a coffee, at least?'

His eyes were bloodshot and I wondered how far he'd driven that day. His hands were pressing gently in the small of my back. It felt nice to be close to him. 'Okay then,' I said.

Scott helped himself to several slices of pie and I poured coffee for us both. We looked around the chaos of the ballroom; the caterers were making good progress in swishing everything away.

'How about the orangery?' he suggested.

'Perfect.' I needed no encouragement to chill out in my favourite part of the Hall.

We settled in the wicker armchairs and I sipped my coffee while Scott ate. The orangery felt completely different in the darkness, more intimate, and the scent from the citrus plants was delicious. Designed as a room for daytime use, the old electric lights were inadequate and bathed us in a gentle, flattering glow.

'I wasn't sure if you'd forgiven me,' Scott said, when only crumbs remained on his plate. His confident, sexy smile, on the other hand, suggested he felt very certain indeed.

'What for? Abandoning me in London, or for your complete lack of faith in tonight?' My tone wasn't unfriendly, but I didn't plan to be a complete pushover.

'Ouch. Well, as for London, I am truly sorry and I promise to make it up to you. As for you and my parents hoping to save Saffron Hall one party at a time …' He pulled a face.

'What?' This wasn't fair: the dinner had been a smashing success. Did I have to show him the profit and loss sheet?

'Grace, honey, it's very sweet that you're all trying, but honestly, this place is on death row.'

'Why?' I propped my elbows on the table and cupped my chin on one hand.

'Have you seen the grounds? The stables are crumbling, the swimming pool should be condemned. The house itself needs rewiring.'

Right on cue, the orangery lights flickered. This was such a romantic setting, but I was feeling more irritated with him than I'd ever been.

'And don't get me started on the plumbing,' he went on. 'Most of it's probably lead.'

This rattled me. I hoped the hundred Americans who'd eaten here tonight didn't know their water had come through poisonous pipes. If they did, we'd have a class action lawsuit to add to our troubles.

'But it's so beautiful,' I said, sitting back and gazing at the glass roof. It was a cloudy night, threatening rain, but I could just make out the moon overhead. 'How can you not want to save it?'

'Grace, you're adorable.' He shook his head. 'Just because it's beautiful doesn't mean it's viable.'

I liked being called adorable, but had a feeling it wasn't meant as a compliment.

'Anyway,' he smiled at me, 'if you and the parentals are determined to keep trying, I have another project to keep me out of trouble. One that would mean I could spend quite a bit of time in the village.' He looked at me meaningfully, his confidence bubbling just below the surface.

'Oh?' Naturally, I was now super-curious. 'What?'

'The malt house.' He leaned back in his seat, pleased. 'Or, I should say, the land it's on.'

'What about it?' I narrowed my eyes.

'This area desperately needs short-term corporate accommodation. It's all very well for the bio-tech staff on long contracts, but what about the ones only coming for a month? They need luxury executive housing.'

'And you want to convert the malt house?'

He shook his head. 'Not convert. Demolish. It's a brilliant location.'

'Oh – my – God,' I said slowly. 'Please tell me you're pulling my leg.'

'Er – no.'

'But it's the heart of the village!' I said. 'It's how we got our name.'

'No, it's a decaying heap of wasted space.'

I too sat back, but in dismay, not in complacent satisfaction. 'I just don't know what to say.'

Scott was looking at me in wide-eyed puzzlement. 'You have a problem with it?'

I blew out slowly. 'Hell, Scott, yes, I do. And if you can't see that, then that's a problem all of its own.'

~~~

Word travelled faster than a celebrity divorce on Twitter. The villagers were furious. From the post office to the pub and even in the bakery, I was met with tight lips and waspish comments.

'I'm not conspiring with him,' I told Brian as he wrapped up two Chelsea buns. 'I hate the idea of the malt house being demolished.'

'Maybe you do.' He sighed. 'But it doesn't help that people see you riding around in his flashy car, smiling at him.'

'What can I do?' I asked.

'There's a meeting tonight at the pub. Come to that, and get your thinking cap on.'

'Okay. Absolutely.'

'Oh, and another thing.' Brian leaned over the counter. 'Bring Amelia. Round here, she's the sharpest knife in the drawer.'

~~~

Brian was wrong. Amelia certainly was a shrewd, strategic thinker, but I had never seen anything like the organisational power of the Americans, once they got worked up about something. Mary Lou had rallied her troops and they were thirsty for blood. I was amazed at the sense of ownership they were displaying in protecting Saffron Sweeting's heritage.

'I grew up with strip malls and four lane highways,' said a woman with a Scarlett O'Hara accent. 'I don't want that for my kids. We came to England for your history and your countryside.'

'Agreed,' came a male voice. 'We moved here to escape the billboards. What's next, KFC?'

Fergus looked alarmed at the thought of competition for the pub and started giving out free bags of crisps.

Aware of my precarious position, I sat quietly in the corner and observed proceedings. Amelia and Mary Lou had emerged as natural leaders of the small but passionate group. The former, I suspect, was simply flattered that so many of the villagers were looking to her for advice, but to her credit, she got them organised into task forces. One group was to start a publicity campaign under the banner of *Save Saffron Sweeting*. A second group was to research legal options for protecting the malt house. And a third group was in charge of approaching conservation charities, in case one could be persuaded to step in and help.

'Grace, which committee do you want to join?' Amelia singled me out.

For a moment, I wondered which of the options would infuriate Scott the least. Then I realised I didn't care. Saffron Sweeting was my home now, and these people were my tribe.

'I'm not sure,' I said, ignoring the nudging around me. 'But I think we should talk to Snape Maltings. They seem to have a booming business and their malt house is intact.'

'Right,' said Mary Lou briskly. 'Put Grace down with non-profit liaison.'

My shoulders sagged slightly and I caught an icy look from Violet. It looked like it might be time to pick which side I was on.

Chapter 29

'No, mum, definitely the navy.'

We were Christmas shopping together in Marks and Spencer and my mother was eyeing up a scarf set for Harry.

'But the red is more festive,' she protested.

'Precisely.' Harry would be a hundred times more likely to wear the blue than the garish red. I placed the navy version firmly in mum's basket.

We didn't often shop together, and as long as I wasn't looking seriously for things for me, I quite enjoyed it. My mother was an impulsive shopper and easily distracted, but in short doses she was fun.

'What are you getting for dad?' I asked.

'Oh, he's so tricky.' She shook her head in irritation. 'Socks and a chocolate orange, I expect.'

I looked around the menswear section of the store for inspiration. If I had been buying a gift for James, he would be more than happy with something from here, but I knew that Scott had more exclusive tastes. And I wasn't even sure I wanted to get him anything, since he had stood me up squarely last night.

Our weekend escapes had been fun, but they'd left me with the feeling, now impossible to ignore, that I didn't really know him. I had thought that a dose of real life might help, and had suggested I cook us a special dinner at my place. I'd chopped, browned, simmered and seasoned to create a rich boeuf bourguignon, my only error being to mix up the cooking wine with the one we were supposed to drink. For appetisers, I'd attempted individual soufflés, which were ready to go in the oven the moment Scott arrived. Not only that, but I had dusted, vacuumed, lit candles and taken a long, sensuous bath in preparation for our romantic evening. I'd even managed to get a fire going without smoking the cottage out.

Mungo hadn't got the memo that this was to be a private party. He'd shown up around six and by seven, as tantalising smells engulfed the cottage, he was drooling all over the kitchen floor. When Scott still hadn't pitched up thirty minutes later, I broke into a bag of Quavers and shared them with my canine companion, nibbling slowly so as not to spoil my appetite. At eight, I stirred the beef anxiously, noticing how dry it was getting around the edges of the pot. Mungo sat up in anticipation, his tongue lolling out.

Gloomily, I took a large glass of the remaining wine to the sofa, where I stared into the fire. Was I so pathetic, I was destined to be with men who messed me around? After last time, surely Scott realised that if he was going to be late, he absolutely had to call? Feeble or not, I was too proud to text him.

Finally, my phone rang.

'Where are you this time?'

'Glasgow. We're fogbound. I'm so sorry.'

'Right.' So much for three hours of cooking and cleaning.

'You're livid, I can tell.'

'It would just be a bit more convenient if you could confine yourself to East Anglia, when I'm slaving over dinner.'

'Well, if you weren't making it so hard for me to find projects, I wouldn't have to go further afield, would I?'

'That's not fair.' I played with Mungo's ears as he nudged his chin onto my lap.

'Look ...' Scott sighed and paused to let an airport announcement finish. 'Can I see you on Sunday evening?'

'If you want reheated beef stew, then yes, I suppose so.'

'Good. I have something to ask you.'

Needless to say, Mungo got a fine dinner that night, and he didn't seem to care that his soufflé sagged.

'Don't you dare go home to Violet and throw it up,' I'd told him as he flopped down by the fire with a sigh of doggy contentment.

I hadn't told my family about Scott, so I wasn't going to mention the dinner disaster to my mother. And I couldn't imagine what kind of question he might have up his sleeve.

By now, mum was scrutinising some V-neck jumpers with Argyle diamonds on the front.

'That's a bit trendy for dad, isn't it?' I said doubtfully, as she held up a lilac jumper with a bold yellow pattern. My father didn't like to wear anything that wasn't navy, beige or maroon.

'Not for your father, silly. For me. I was thinking it would look quite natty on the golf course.'

'Mmm,' I replied. 'Lovely.'

Amelia had given me Saturday afternoon off as we were so close to Christmas, nobody was looking seriously at houses. I suspected she was using the time to plot her efforts to save the malt house. Considering there was no obvious profit to be made from the project, she had become impressively committed to the cause.

Not only that, but without me mentioning it again, she had quietly started to put together welcome packs to be given to all new residents along with their house keys. The bakery, antiques barn, Oak House bed and breakfast and even The Plough had promotional offers in there.

'Never thought I'd see this,' Brian had said to me, and personally delivered half a dozen custard tarts for Amelia.

Mum added the sweater to the growing pile in her basket, then stopped and looked at me. 'So, how are you doing, love?'

'Fine.' I met her eye, but looked away quickly.

'You look brighter, I'll say that much.'

After a hearty portion of beef and two big glasses of wine, I had slept remarkably well, despite the indignity of my no-show date. I tried to change the subject. 'Does dad need more socks?'

I was unsuccessful.

'It's none of my business ...' she said, and I braced

myself for what was inevitably going to be a pointed question.

'... but have you heard from James?'

I blinked. Yes, totally nosy. Still, what did it matter? 'Not since I met up with him in London.'

'Oh, I didn't know you'd seen him.'

I filled her in briefly on his conference trip and Hyde Park, but not the freesias.

'And how do you feel, now you've had some time ... to yourself?'

I shook my head, not because I was unwilling to talk, but because I didn't know what to say. I feigned interest in the fabric composition of a pack of rainbow striped socks.

'Gracie.' Mum took the socks out of my hands and put them back. 'Marriage can be very hard.'

I grunted in acknowledgement.

'Especially these days. Young people now have such high expectations.'

'Er, mum, I expected my husband to be faithful.'

She nodded. 'I know you did. We all do. It's just ... well, sometimes, Grace, you have to wonder whether it's better, in the long run, to compromise.'

I put my head on one side. 'Compromise?'

'There are thousands of happy marriages which haven't always run smoothly. That's all I'm trying to say.' She added a three-pack of boring navy socks to her haul.

What point was she making here? 'You're not saying I should take him back, are you?'

'That's up to you, love. I'm just suggesting you think about your long-term happiness. Be sure you're not cutting off your nose to spite your face.'

'Easy for you to say. You've got dad.'

She smiled softly and gave a tiny shake of her head. 'Nobody's a saint, Grace.'

'Maybe. But I'm not going to let a man make a fool of me again.'

'I just want you to be happy. And there's more than one

path to get there.'

I watched as she fished in her handbag for her shopping list, surreptitiously slipping the happy rainbow socks into my own basket. Then, as she looked at me again, I plastered a Christmas smile on my face and said brightly, 'Fancy a coffee?'

~~~

The next day was a Sunday. Amelia, Nancy and I took a field trip to Snape Maltings, claiming it was for research. Actually, it was a girls' festive outing, before Nancy headed back home for Hanukkah and Amelia went to her parents in Bournemouth. Shopping, eating and gossiping were high on our agenda. As such, we'd only been there an hour when we decided brunch was a necessity. The three of us clattered upstairs to the charming white-walled cafe with its scrubbed wooden tables and thick overhead beams.

'I'm so impressed with what they've done here.' Amelia's eyes lit up as she spied bacon sandwiches on the menu. 'I knew about the music festival, but not the rest of it.'

'Agreed.' I was tempted by the full English breakfast but decided that was too piggy, even for me. I hoped Nancy wouldn't mind both Amelia and me tucking into bacon. 'And the shops are fantastic. I plan on getting all my Christmas gifts in one fell swoop.'

'Ooh, there's a whole building of antiques.' Nancy consulted the Snape map on her phone.

'Are you allowed to fraternise with the competition?' I asked her.

She winked. 'I won't tell if you won't.'

'Won't tell what?' Amelia said.

'Tell Peter that Nancy's been buying antiques without him.'

'Why, has he got some kind of monopoly on you?' Amelia asked.

'Well, not quite.' Nancy was looking exceedingly

pleased.

Amelia frowned. 'I don't get it.'

'You know.' I tilted my head towards Nancy and attempted to waggle my eyebrows. 'The dishy and delightful Peter.'

'Er, the gay Peter?' Amelia said loudly, cocktail ring glinting as she made a camp gesture.

I shushed her as our food arrived.

'Peter's not gay,' Nancy said evenly.

'Yes, he is,' Amelia daubed HP sauce on her sandwich. She took a huge bite and looked at me to back her up.

I caught her eye meaningfully and shook my head.

'No, he's *not*,' said Nancy definitively. She grinned and picked up her fork to tackle her scrambled eggs.

'Holy crap!' Amelia choked on her bacon butty.

Nancy thumped her on the back, smiling. 'Nothing's happened yet,' she protested.

'Yet? Wow.' When she could talk again, Amelia raised her cappuccino cup to Nancy. 'Here's to you, darling.'

After we'd munched for a few minutes, I looked at our stylishly simple surroundings. 'Do you think we can save our malt house and create something like this?'

Amelia puffed up her cheeks. 'I dunno,' she said. 'It would be amazing, but I'll be honest, it's a long shot.'

'They've really got it together here,' I sighed. 'No wonder Scott was sniffing around.'

'Was he?' Nancy asked.

I nodded. 'He brought me here on a date: I thought he was just trying to make sure I had a good time. Silly me. It was obviously a business visit for him. He already had his beady eye on the Saffron Sweeting malt house.'

'Except he wants to demolish ours, not convert it,' Amelia pointed out.

'It probably costs more to preserve something like this than just to start again,' Nancy said practically.

'Yes, well, money isn't everything,' said Amelia as she fished in her Mulberry handbag for a Dior lipstick, then crossed her legs and accidentally kicked me with her new Coach boot.

I threw her an ironic look, which she missed completely. She was totally behind this malt house project; perhaps her altruistic side had surfaced at last. And although she said our chances of saving it were slim, I felt more hopeful. We'd stirred up a little publicity and the previous week, a dishy journalist from the local Cambridge paper had interviewed several of us.

'Anyway,' Amelia narrowed her eyes at me, 'if anyone's fraternising with the enemy, it's Grace.'

'Oh, c'mon,' I said. 'I didn't know what Scott was up to.'

'But you do now,' Nancy said crisply.

They were both looking at me unflinchingly. I gazed down at my lap.

'He stood me up on Friday,' I said, after a pause.

If I was looking for sympathy, I didn't get it.

'Where?' Nancy asked.

'My place. I cooked dinner.'

'And he didn't show up?' said Amelia.

'No. Fog in Glasgow. Flight was cancelled.'

Nancy and Amelia exchanged looks.

'How many times is that now?' Nancy said.

'How many what?' I asked.

'That he's blown you off.'

Amelia looked momentarily confused, but I knew what Nancy meant.

'Only twice,' I said.

Nancy snorted. 'Only? How many times does it take?'

I made a little pile of the sandwich crumbs on my empty plate. 'What are you saying?'

Nancy wrinkled her nose and blinked at me through her glasses. 'Just that he's not treating you real good.'

I glanced at Amelia, who had her elbows on the table and was resting her chin on top of interwoven fingers.

'Actually, darling, he's not behaving very well in general, is he?' she said.

'No.' I screwed up my napkin and ran a weary hand through my hair. 'He's not.'

~~~

Nancy and I had left our cars in Saffron Sweeting, so Amelia took us back to the Hargraves office in her green Mercedes. We were almost at the shortest day of the year. Despite leaving Snape in the early afternoon, it was now dusk. As we passed the malt house, I was sure I spotted a Jaguar through the gloom.

So far, December had proved damp and foggy. As I transferred my shopping bags into the Beetle's boot, I thought the village looked almost Dickensian.

Ignoring the welcoming promise of the pub, I trekked back in the direction of the malt house. The long building was in shadow, of course. It looked doomed and mournful, like the Titanic after her lights went out. Beside it, the beech trees were now bare. As I stood looking up, an owl hooted, making me jump and reminding me why I was here. Yes, there was the Jaguar, with Scott sitting in the driver's seat, fingers moving over his iPad. I tapped on the window and now it was his turn to jump.

'Hello, gorgeous.' He smiled in surprise as the window slid down. 'I was on my way to see you.'

I shrugged wordlessly, shoving both hands into my coat pockets and hunching my shoulders against the damp chill.

'Hop in,' he said. 'It's cold out there.'

I shook my head. 'I'm okay.'

Scott looked surprised, then turned to grab his coat from the passenger seat. He got out of the car, sliding his arms into his jacket. Then he gave me a quick hug and lowered his head for a kiss. I turned away.

'Are you hungry? Would you like to go out for dinner?' He settled for brushing the hair off my face.

'There's leftover beef, remember?' I couldn't believe he'd forgotten.

'I'm so sorry about Friday night,' he said. 'I mean it.'

I nodded dubiously and gazed at the chunky zip on his trendy navy jacket. It said *Barbour* in tiny letters.

'What was it you wanted to ask me?' I said.

Doubt crossed his face. 'Can we do this at your place, where it's warmer?'

I looked up at the malt house, looming above. I had the impression it was protecting us from the wind. I shook my head. 'Ask me here.'

'Well, okay. I know it's been difficult spending time together recently.' He smiled. 'I'm busy, you're busy.'

I wasn't too busy to whisk egg whites into a soufflé and whisk myself into fancy underwear, I thought. But I said nothing.

'So I was thinking, if you'd like, we should go away properly together. For Christmas. No work, no distractions, just you, me and a five-star hotel.'

'Somewhere else you're buying?' I lifted my chin in irritation.

'No. Gosh, no, definitely not. I was thinking maybe Prague. Or Vienna?'

I couldn't help it, my eyebrows climbed of their own volition. 'Wow.'

This was serious stuff. I had visited Prague years ago on a backpacking trip, but never Vienna. I pictured snow-dusted castles and glossy horses pulling carriages. I saw string quartets and a roaring fire in an ornate, gilded hotel suite. Oh, and I saw elegant tiered plates of delicate European pastries. It was hard to imagine anything more romantic.

Scott put a gloved finger under my chin and tilted it so he could see my face. 'Well?' In the darkness, his face was shadowed, but he looked as charming and confident as ever.

I licked my lips to say *Yes* and kiss him, but was stalled by a new vision. I saw myself, on Christmas Eve, dressed in a new coat and snug fleece-lined boots. I was standing in a check-in hall at Heathrow Airport, with one eye on the flight departures board and one eye on my silent phone, as throngs of hurried travellers swarmed around me. I was waiting for a man who wasn't going to show up. Again.

I took a step backwards and said a reluctant goodbye to the ride in a horse-drawn carriage.

'Grace? Will you come with me to Vienna?'

'No,' I said. 'I'm sorry. I won't.'

Chapter 30

Christmas was grim. Having turned down the festive allure of Austria, my next best option was to spend it with my parents in Norfolk. Sometimes, the familial hearth can be the loneliest place in the world.

The creations of the Gilling kitchen were worthy of an international culinary festival. For three days before Christmas, ingredients were seared, simmered, sautéed and steamed. Smells which would have driven Mungo insane wafted through the house, from fresh bread in the morning to herb-laden soups at lunchtime. By afternoon, cinnamon and vanilla scents could be detected, and each evening, slow-roasting meats thrilled our noses with their promise of juicy tenderness.

My parents, competitive in the kitchen at the best of times, were in heaven. Between them, they lugged in mounds of vegetables and visited the butcher's shop daily. Their narrow fridge couldn't cope, so an extra one was rigged up in the garage, beside the golf clubs and long-forgotten camping gear.

Since I was so clearly single, I decided I might as well eat to keep warm. The relentless heat of the kitchen meant the central heating was turned down and the rest of the bungalow was nippy. Most of the time I was wearing two jumpers and a scarf, even indoors. Yet, in spite of the extra layers, I can't ever remember feeling so cold at this time of year. I helped half-heartedly with the food preparation but mostly stared mindlessly at repeats on television. Whenever Radio 2 played 'Last Christmas', I left the room before I began crying.

Jem, glowing so much that I wondered if she might be pregnant again, arrived with my brother and Seb the day before Christmas Eve. But no: she said, 'This time of year just suits me. I'm thrilled to bits to get my meals cooked for five days.'

She was right; the season, with its gold, crimson and teal, did suit her dark colouring.

'Don't you miss being with your family?' I asked.

'No,' she laughed. 'There are so many of us, I always wonder if Seb's going to get trampled underfoot. They won't miss three.'

'Are you sleeping better?' I wanted to know. I, for one, was not, and the sofa bed in dad's study wasn't helping.

She smiled. 'Not much. But I seem to have more energy. Getting past Seb's first birthday was a milestone.'

'That's great,' I said.

'Didn't I tell you? I've started doing a bit of freelance work.'

'Really? Like what?'

'I'm calling it HR consulting, although between you and me that's a bit of a grand title. But I can do it from home, answer questions, give policy advice, that kind of thing.'

'That's fantastic!' I hugged her.

'So far I'm only doing it for one company – they're small and don't want a full-time person.' She started attacking the bowl of nuts on the living room table, shelling them with the nutcrackers that we only saw at Christmas time.

'Still, I'm impressed.'

'Yup. It beats minimum wage at Tesco. I woke up one morning and decided to just try and create the life I want.'

'Good for you,' I murmured, moving my feet out of the way of flying nut shrapnel, while noting it was the second time this week I'd heard that concept.

'And how are you doing?' Jem asked quietly.

I had called and told her that Scott and I had broken up, but hadn't shared details. I'd simply said, 'He lives life completely on his own terms. I don't think he gives any thought to the people around him.'

I made out I was okay, but in reality I was angry with myself for getting swept up in a hollow relationship. Amelia was right: Scott had been a total rebound guy, and I was beginning to think his only purpose had been to soothe my shattered ego.

Even so, I couldn't help thinking wistfully of that hotel in Vienna, romantic, snowy walks, and warm arms around me at night. But as I mooched around the house, observing my parents' gentle harmony and Harry and Jem's joy at Christmas with Seb, I wondered whose arms I was really missing.

'C'mon, Grace,' Scott had said when I told him I wouldn't go to Austria. 'I said I was sorry. What's the problem?'

I'd backed away from him and folded my arms. 'I just don't think we share the same values.'

'Like what? Pretending a village that's stuck in the last century isn't going down the pan?'

'It's not stuck in the last century. It's a way of life. You grew up here, for heaven's sake!'

'Which is precisely why I can see the writing on the wall. You're being naive.'

'And you're being mercenary.'

He laughed. 'No, I'm just going after what I want. You should try it, rather than drifting around playing nice the whole time.'

I'd glared at him.

'So you won't come away with me?'

'No thanks.'

'Fine.' He turned to get back in his car. 'I know plenty of other women who'll do the Viennese Waltz.'

That had been a cheap shot. Had he ever really cared about me, or had I just happened to be around buildings he fancied? I thought back to his loft apartment, where pride of place had been given to framed blueprints, not framed faces.

~~~

Not counting tiny Seb, there would be six mouths to feed on Christmas Day: mum and dad, Harry and Jem, me, and Aunt Dotty.

My father's sister and a retired traffic warden, Dorothy Gilling lives in King's Lynn and has acted eighty years old for the past three decades. She makes much drama of the weather and considers the thirty-five mile trip to Holt to be equivalent to crossing the Himalayas. Dressed accordingly in a sensible tweed skirt, walking boots and thick woollen socks, she allows at least two hours for the journey and grips the wheel of her Ford Fiesta with unblinking intent. Despite all that, she's fun to have around, especially once she's had a couple of sweet sherries. A colourful character, I was relying on her to take the burden of the family's curiosity off my shoulders.

Still, as I sat at the Christmas lunch table wearing a lopsided paper hat and a fake smile, I couldn't help gazing at Dotty over my glass of Sauvignon Blanc and wondering if this was how I was going to end up: eccentric and alone.

We had feasted royally and quaffed even more. Smoked salmon salad was followed by turkey, stuffing, parsnips, roast potatoes, Brussels sprouts and sweetcorn. Secretly, I liked the bacon-wrapped mini sausages the best, but I tackled the bird with as much gusto as I could manage, grateful we weren't feasting on one of mum's chickens.

Crackers had been pulled, silly jokes told. I tried not to think about last year when James had been here. He knew all the cracker jokes off by heart but had humoured my father by playing along. He'd also peeled five pounds of potatoes without a word of complaint and had been first on hand with a damp tea towel when it looked as if the flames around the Christmas pudding might take out the dining room curtains.

This year, there were no pyrotechnics, at least, not visible ones.

Dotty waved her spoon, laden with pudding and brandy sauce, in Jem and Harry's direction. 'I like to see the next generation looking so happy,' she pronounced.

Harry raised his glass to her. He, too, seemed more relaxed than usual, confident that the banking world could do without him for seventy-two hours. He had been buried in the *Radio Times*, plotting how many classic action films he could fit in. Now, he looked at Jem and smiled. She leaned her head into his shoulder for a moment, before glancing at Seb, docile in his bouncer seat. My mother looked as if she might get teary and even dad nodded proudly.

Dotty turned her wizened gaze to me. 'And what about you, Grace? You're awfully glum for Christmas Day.'

'She's fine,' mum said quickly.

'I noticed your wedding photo's been relegated to the loo,' Dotty said, with a meaningful twitch of her head.

I had seen that too, and remembered thinking it would have been easier if my mother had hidden it completely. But now, I just shrugged, unable to craft a witty comeback about my marriage going down the toilet.

'Terrible shame.' My aunt, bossy at the best of times, had had far too much to drink. 'Throwing a good man away, just because he had a fancy woman.'

'That's enough, Dot,' my father muttered, as I gazed down at my red paper napkin and started tearing its corners off.

'Well, Geoffrey,' his sister popped more pudding in her mouth and continued cheerfully, 'it's not as if she'd be the first Gilling to pick up the pieces and carry on.'

I was so mortified, her words didn't register immediately. By the time I looked up, Harry was staring fixedly out of the window, my father's eyes were huge as he glared at Dorothy, and Jem was gazing at me in disbelief. I turned in slow motion to my mother, who had gone white except for two small blotches of red burning on her cheeks. She stood up and started gathering bowls, even though most of us hadn't finished our pudding.

'Right,' she said, clattering her best china as though it

had come from the bargain bin at Oxfam. 'Who wants cheese?'

~~~

Nobody dared say anything further, right through the Queen's speech, the inevitable *Two Ronnies* repeat and most of *Titanic*. Dotty sat in the best chair, first looking pleased with herself, then rubbing her stomach for indigestion, and finally nodding her head in gentle slumber.

As Rose and Jack's new-found love faced the looming iceberg, I followed Harry and Jem to the kitchen where the carnage was breathtaking. Exuberant and creative cooks, my parents didn't believe in tidying up as they went along. While Jem busied herself transferring mountains of leftovers to Tupperware, Harry bravely rolled up his sleeves at the sink. I squeezed a few more things into the dishwasher then picked up a Royal Wedding tea towel – Charles and Diana, not William and Kate.

'Will you say something?' I said to Harry, after he'd sudded and scrubbed diligently for a few minutes.

'What?' He pretended not to know what I meant.

'You know what. Dotty. That stuff she said, about picking up the pieces.'

I saw Jem glance at Harry's back but she said nothing and carried on spooning sprouts into a container.

'You and James are none of my business,' my brother said, working on the crystal wine glasses.

'What about mum and dad?' I said. 'Was that what she meant?'

'I don't know anything about mum and dad.' Harry adopted a blank expression.

'Yes, you do,' I said. 'Is it – them – that Dotty meant?'

'Look, Grace, I honestly don't know.' Harry started on the stainless steel serving dishes which Jem had piled up beside him. Then he gave me a sideways look. 'There might have been something around the time we moved to Norfolk.

But I don't know anything for sure.'

I processed this. I had been fourteen when we moved from Cambridge. I didn't remember anything special about it, although I had stayed with Dotty for most of that summer. Harry was two years older; he'd had a temporary job or something. Quickly, I did the maths. This was twenty years ago. Who knew what wounds had opened and healed?

Jem came over to me now, putting her arm around my shoulders. 'She was awfully tipsy, you know.'

I nodded. 'I know.' I looked at Harry again. 'I just wonder what she meant.'

He wouldn't meet my eye.

~ ~ ~

It was on Boxing Day morning, after Dotty had left, that I finally cornered my mother outside the chicken run. She was whispering sweet nothings to her brood.

'I'm surprised you can still eat poultry,' I said to her. I was out of my pyjamas, but feeling crummy in tracksuit bottoms and a jumper stolen from Harry. The extra guests and limited bathroom facilities meant I hadn't yet had a shower today.

'Yes, chicken nuggets are certainly off the menu,' she replied.

I watched, surprised, as she broke a banana into pieces and offered it to them. A white chicken and a pinky-brown cousin competed fiercely for the treat.

I worked up my courage. 'Is there anything you want to tell me?'

'Poppet ...'

I twisted my hands in the too-long sleeves of Harry's sweater. 'Well?'

'Dotty had no right to say anything.' My mother threw the banana skin at the compost heap and wiped her fingers on her trousers.

'So, there was something to say?' My voice was barely

audible.

Mum turned to me and took both my hands in hers to stop me fidgeting. 'Love, it was a long time ago. We can't dwell in the past.'

'Did dad ... did he cheat on you?'

She looked at me steadily, her face showing only the slightest shadow of pain. Then she reached out a hand and gently smoothed my hair. 'Gracie, I love my life. I love my husband. And I love my family very much.'

I opened my mouth to protest, got as far as 'But, mum –' before she silenced me with a resolute shake of her head.

'No,' she said. 'No. Look to your future, Grace.'

~~~

Next afternoon, Harry, Jem and I were making half-hearted efforts to get our stuff together in preparation for departure, when the doorbell rang.

'Oh gawd,' said my mother, trundling to the front door in her slippers. 'I hope it's not the Smythes and another of their impromptu drinks parties.'

It wasn't social neighbours: it was FedEx with a box for me, origin California. Was this a late-arriving gift? There had been nothing under the tree for me from James, which didn't surprise me. I hadn't sent him anything, either. After all, what would one buy for an estranged spouse? I took myself to the far end of the living room where mum and dad had laid out tea things so we could all have a snack before our journey.

First, I found the card, a simple hand-written note which read, *Grace, I didn't know what you would like but I know you feel the cold. Happy Christmas. All my love, James.*

Inside a badly wrapped package I found a beautiful pale grey cashmere blanket, which, if I couldn't snuggle up with a man, was certainly the next best thing. Mungo would have to keep his grubby paws off this.

As I flapped the blanket open to admire it, a small square box slipped to the floor. I exchanged a silent look with Jem, and reached to pick it up. The outside read *Astley Clarke, London*, and inside was a beautifully simple pair of stud earrings.

'Ooh.' Jem peered from the other end of the sofa. 'Yummy.'

I wasn't sure, but I had a feeling I was looking at diamonds set in white gold. James wasn't stingy, but by his usual standards, these were a beautiful gift. He must have bought them during his recent trip to London. The earrings glimmered as I tilted them back and forth.

There was something else in the box: a large, thin envelope. After diamonds and cashmere, divorce papers seemed unlikely. Puzzled, I delved inside. There were several sheets of paper, with a sticky note on top: *I wanted you to see these, in case they help. Sorry, I couldn't get them before now. J.* The pages looked like log files from a computer program. I had to look closely before I could make out I was reading system-stored email correspondence.

May 18. From McMahon, R to Palmer, J: So excited for my bedroom. It's going to be great. You should see it! Rebecca.

May 19. From Palmer, J to McMahon, R: Glad to hear it. Grace is very talented. James.

May 19. From McMahon, R to Palmer, J: I'm so looking forward to Vegas! It's gonna be a blast. Can you stay on after for the workshops? Rebecca. xo

May 20. From Palmer, J to McMahon, R: I don't think so, I need to get back. Regards, James.

There were more like this, upbeat, hopeful, a little flirtatious from Rebecca to James; brief and business-like from him to her. I read on, until I found:

May 29. From McMahon, R to Palmer, J: Just checked in! Room 955. View is great. Come see it! R. xo

May 29. From Palmer, J to McMahon, R: Still have

some work to do for tomorrow. I'll see you all at dinner. James.

May 30. From McMahon, R to Palmer, J: You were awesome today! The investors loved you! So privileged to work with you. Congrats and hugs, Becca. xoxo

May 30. From Palmer, J to McMahon, R: Thanks. You too. ;)

Then, this. I bit my lip hard as I read on, not caring that, for once, the Gillings had gone as quiet as mice.

May 31. From McMahon, R to Palmer, J: Good morning ... xxx

May 31. From Palmer, J to McMahon, R: I feel terrible about what happened. We have to talk. James.

May 31. From McMahon, R to Palmer, J: Last night was amazing. Meet you later for cocktails? Becca xxx

May 31. From Palmer, J to McMahon, R: I'm sorry, I made a big mistake. I was horribly drunk. I want to apologise to you. I'll find you at lunchtime. James.

Finally, there were these:

June 4. From McMahon, R to Palmer, J: I know we're trying to hide this from the office, but I can't keep pretending. You're amazing. I want to be with you. Can't wait to pick up where we left off in Vegas. My place tonight? Hugs and kisses, Becca. xxx

June 4. From Palmer, J to McMahon, R: If I ever gave you reason to think I have feelings for you, I apologise unreservedly. I made a terrible, one-time mistake. I love my wife. Please stop these notes. James.

My tea in its white china cup was cold and murky. I realised I'd been gripping the cashmere blanket as I read, holding it to my chest like a shield.

I looked up at Jem and Harry, not caring that my eyes were full of tears. 'Guys, I need a favour.'

Jem nodded immediately. 'Sure thing,' she said.

'If I drop my car in Saffron Sweeting, can I get a lift to your place for tonight? I need to be at Heathrow first thing tomorrow.'

Harry stretched his arms above his head and glanced at my parents before replying. 'Where are you going?'

I stood up to finish packing. I didn't want to lose a single moment. 'San Francisco.'

Chapter 31

After the dreary British weather, I had trouble adjusting to the bright afternoon sunlight as I drove south on US101 from San Francisco Airport. Traffic was light and the temperature was several degrees warmer than in England. I turned up the radio in my rental car and felt a joyful purpose which had been absent for a long time.

My wallet, by contrast, was feeling the pain of a last-minute ticket purchase, but it seemed a small price to pay to see James. Completely unable to sleep on the plane, I had twirled my wedding ring and watched the map on the seat-back television, counting down the miles as we made absurdly slow progress across remote parts of northern Canada. This had, at least, given me time to settle my thoughts.

After my encounter with mum in the garden, I'd escaped for a walk, tearfully refusing Jem's offer of company.

Far from being crisp and sunny, Boxing Day had been overcast and damp. To counteract the creeping cold and my tumbling thoughts, I'd set a punishing pace, aiming for Kelling Heath.

For the first couple of miles, I'd seen nothing of the countryside. My head was down, my hands jammed in my pockets, my thoughts swimming with doubt and self-pity. But as my body warmed up and my brain cooled down, I'd found myself thinking about Mungo, wishing he were here to explore and meet new rabbits.

I'd wondered how James had spent Christmas, and whether he was on his own. Then, as sudden, mournful emptiness threatened to invade my chest, I'd pushed those thoughts aside and contemplated my parents' marriage.

Granted, they no longer behaved like besotted lovers, but their relationship seemed comfortable, respectful, solid.

The two of them were like wheels on a bicycle, hard to imagine the machine functioning without both front and back. So if – and I still wasn't sure – dad had cheated on mum, did that mean infidelity was a puncture that could be repaired? Sure, you had to take the whole inner tube out, find the hole, patch carefully and allow time for the glue to set. But then, with care, you could pedal on. I had been unshakable in my assumption that an affair meant the end of the road, but here they were, twenty years later, cooking up a Christmas feast and blithely sharing the wishbone.

~ ~ ~

I figured it was too early for James to be home from work, but I didn't care. I headed to Menlo Park to wait. Fully expecting to have to park myself on the wooden steps leading up from the street, I knocked on the door, just in case. Strangely, my ears detected music from inside the apartment but, deciding they must still be unreliable from the flight, I turned away and prepared to wait.

The door opened behind me and I swung around to find not my husband but a tall, slim young woman. I took in a terrifying expanse of brown leg before my eye was arrested by pink workout shorts and a skimpy Nike top. Her face was girl-next-door cute and her blonde hair was cut short, like a pixie. She didn't look a day over twenty-five.

'Hey?' she greeted me blankly.

Battling a mouth that was full of tongue and drier than an airline sandwich, I asked if James was home.

'James? No, he's not. Are you a friend?'

'Uh-huh. From England.'

'Oh jeez, that's too bad. I think he left town.'

'Left town?' What could she mean?

She nodded her pixie head. 'He sublet the place to me, for three months. Sorry, I don't know where he went.' She chewed on a finger, thinking. 'I have an email address for him, if you want.'

'That's okay. I have it.' At this point, I remembered to breathe. 'Er, so, you're not his ... girlfriend?'

'Hah! No, totally not. I think he's married, actually. He put this place on Craigslist and I got lucky. It's really nicely decorated, for a guy.'

Reversing my initial opinion, I decided I liked her. But that still left me with my sails fully rigged and no wind. I'd crossed eight time zones and he'd left town?

'Are you okay?' She looked at me as I sagged against her – my – doorway.

'Yeah. Sorry. Just jet-lagged.' I stood straighter and rubbed my eyes. It was getting on for midnight in the UK. 'I guess I'll head to my hotel.'

I thanked her and made my way back down the steps, holding on carefully to the banister as I didn't trust my legs.

In the car, I pulled out my phone to call James, but got only a generic voicemail message. Could he really have gone away?

~~~

The last time I had visited James's workplace, I had been spilling both tears and purple paint, so I was nervous about making a reappearance. Nor was I looking my best, after being processed through the sausage machine of economy-class travel. But it couldn't be helped. I brushed my hair, left my unflattering duffel coat in the car and lifted my chin as I walked into his Palo Alto office.

I sensed the company was doing well. The clock on the wall told me it was almost five, but that was still early in start-up land. More desks were filled than in the summer, and some framed magazine features were displayed proudly on the wall. They even had a receptionist, a rusty-haired, freckled young thing wearing scruffy jeans and an eager smile. But I couldn't see James at his old spot.

'Hi,' I spoke confidently, even though my insides were like a technology stock on the day after the IPO. 'I'm here to see James Palmer.'

'Oh.' The receptionist looked confused, darting a glance over to the area where I knew the engineering team sat. 'James doesn't work here any more.'

Even though I was half expecting this, I still felt the thump of disappointment in my stomach.

'Do you know how I could reach him?' I made sure to speak clearly, hoping my British accent would lend some credibility and authority without giving me away as his wife.

'Sorry.' She shook her head. 'But Duncan might.'

Duncan was just passing the front desk, enormous Starbucks cup in hand. Wearing thick glasses and a Google polo shirt, I suspected he had already made his millions and only worked here to keep his brain entertained.

I turned to him and smiled engagingly, holding out my hand. 'Hello. I was expecting to meet with James Palmer.'

The light glinted off Duncan's glasses as he looked at me suspiciously. 'Are you a headhunter?'

'No – goodness, no. I'm Gr-' Whoops, that wouldn't do. 'I'm Greta Gilling. From the British CISSP.' My face turned pink as I faked a name and threw out an acronym I'd heard James use. I had no idea what it stood for and hoped desperately it would provide sufficient cover.

Duncan sipped his coffee through the lid of the paper cup. 'James left us right before the holidays. Let go, in actual fact.'

Let go? Did he mean sacked? I couldn't believe that: James had always shone at work and the company was obviously growing.

I smoothed the surprise off my face and tried for a neutral tone. 'Do you know where he is now?'

Duncan shook his head. 'No. You could try Microsoft. We've lost a few good guys to them recently. James was one of our best too.'

'Microsoft?' I didn't think that was likely. Bill Gates had never been one of my husband's heroes. He preferred the romantic nobility of the Linux crowd.

'Yeah. Not here, though. Seattle.'

Seattle? Oh no, please no. I knew of someone else who had recently moved to Seattle. She signed her emails *Hugs, Becca.*

'Right. Thanks.' My chin drooped.

'But if you do see James, can you get him to give me a call? I'd like to talk to him about unauthorised access of our email server.'

'Okay.' My ears threw this information away immediately; they were too busy helping me keep my balance, as the oxygen evaporated from the atmosphere around me.

I didn't start crying until I was outside, sitting in the rental car. Then I let my head fall to the steering wheel and I sobbed. How could I have got this so wrong? I'd come five thousand miles and had missed the boat.

The glowing December sun had dipped below the Stanford hills and the mild winter air felt suddenly brisk. Around me, the Christmas lights of downtown Palo Alto twinkled, palm trees wrapped with tiny white stars. Yet Silicon Valley, home of so many dreams, had never looked less appealing.

I looked at my watch. There didn't seem to be anything left to do. If I got a serious wiggle on, I might just catch the last British Airways flight of the day.

~~~

With typical British joie de vivre, there was a forty minute queue for passport control and London's taxi drivers were on strike.

'Welcome home,' said the immigration officer as he examined my passport with leisurely interest and scrutinised me for signs of terrorist tendencies.

I looked back at him blankly, struggling even to find a courteous smile. I suspected the only story on my face was shell shock, brought on by two days' non-stop travel and managing to lose the same husband twice. Oscar Wilde would no doubt deem this most careless.

Having been allowed back into my own country, I took one look at the seething bowels of Heathrow's transportation system and gave up. Desperate international arrivals were trying to fathom their transit options, buy Oyster cards with foreign currency and cram themselves onto the churning platforms for either the Piccadilly line or the Heathrow Express. Deciding to take my chances on the M25, I headed wearily for the National Express coach station.

~~~

The taxi from Cambridge dropped me on the road outside Grey Stoke House. It was already pitch dark and all I wanted to do was crawl into bed and sleep.

I picked my way over the perilous, potholed obstacle course to my cottage, assisted only by a wafer of moon. For once, it was a relatively clear night and a few flakes of snow fell on the back of my neck.

As I came nearer to home, I realised that as well as my faithful Beetle, another car was parked in the shadows. My heart lifted, Hollywood-style, as I saw a male figure huddled by the front door. For one tiny moment, time froze and hope flared as I jumped to the irrational conclusion that James was waiting.

The joy crumbled as I saw the car was a Jaguar, and the man was Scott. And he wasn't huddled like a desperate romantic hero, he was putting something through the letterbox.

'Well, that's lucky,' he said brightly, as I coughed to announce my presence behind him. He spoke as if no animosity had happened between us.

'What are you doing here?' I was five minutes away from the oblivion of my duvet and had no interest in being delayed.

'I just put a copy through your door, but I think I'm supposed to hand one to you too.' He paused and squinted at me in the darkness. 'How was your Christmas?'

'Best ever,' I muttered bitterly. I sure as heck wasn't going to enquire about Vienna. 'What is it?' I looked down at the envelope he'd put into my hand.

'Er, it's a Section 21 Notice.'

'A what?' I tucked the envelope under one arm and started to dig in my bag for my door key. I couldn't find it amongst all the random rubbish which had accompanied me to San Francisco and back again.

Scott looked fleetingly uncomfortable, but he settled on an expression of bland innocence. 'Don't go flying off the deep end,' he said. 'By law, I have to give you at least two months.'

'Two months what?' Where was that wretched key?

'Notice to vacate.' He shifted from foot to foot as if to keep warm, or perhaps just because he was shifty.

'Sorry? What?' I was definitely going to have to get my ears tested. 'Did you say *vacate*?'

But as I finally found my key and looked up at his face, I realised my ears were absolutely fine.

I had eaten nothing but meagre airline rations for two days. The last of my savings were now lining the velvet coffers of British Airways. The only man I ever wanted to be with had given up on our marriage and disappeared.

And now, I was being evicted from my cottage.

Chapter 32

'Oh bugger!' exclaimed Amelia. Her shoe twirling stopped mid-circle as she looked at me in sympathetic horror.

'That sums it up nicely,' I agreed in a low voice.

It was the morning of the second of January and I was too weary even to switch on my computer. I had told Amelia about the emails between James and Rebecca, my fruitless escapade to California and Scott's unapologetic arrival at the cottage.

'But I thought he said he wasn't going to boot you out?'

'It seems that was only the case while I was shagging him.' I hugged myself, coat tugged tightly around me. The Hargraves office hadn't yet warmed up after being closed for more than a week. 'Now, all bets are off.'

Scott was behaving perfectly logically. Still dead keen to develop executive accommodation in the village, his eye had fallen on Grey Stoke House. Uninspiring and relatively modern, it was unlikely to trigger the fierce feelings swirling around the malt house. And it stood on a hefty plot of land. He had made the owners a generous offer just before Christmas, which they'd accepted. By now, they were probably celebrating with rum punch in Barbados.

'I feel awful,' Amelia said. 'I should have paid more attention to your rental agreement.'

'You weren't to know this would happen.' I paused to rub my aching temples. 'The house is going to be demolished for corporate flats. Apparently, my cottage is destined to be the fitness centre.'

'Oh, darling, I'm sorry. How are you feeling?'

I raised my red-rimmed eyes from the carpet to consider the question, but then let them sink again as I shook my head.

'I'm not sure I care,' I said dully.

And I truly didn't. My capacity to feel, to worry, to hurt

was wiped out. Over the last few days, I had learned that chocolate ice cream tastes better swimming in Baileys, that Mungo was a warm but smelly bed companion and that Pot Noodles were the most depressing food on earth. I had spent the two remaining days of last year and the first day of the new year under the duvet, staring blankly at my bedroom ceiling. The alarm clock had ticked relentlessly beside me, and with the passing seconds and minutes my shock and denial had turned to hollow apathy.

Amelia watched me for a moment, then got up to microwave my cold coffee. She returned holding both my mug and a slim glass bottle. 'I think it's time for the emergency brandy,' she said.

~~~

I trudged through the workday motions, still numb but soothed by checking emails, taking messages for Amelia and placing our next advert with the *Cambridge Evening News*. Despite my claims that I wasn't hungry, by early afternoon my stomach was grumbling and I was grateful when Amelia went to the bakery. Normally, this was my job, but she sensed I didn't feel like village chit-chat today. She returned with sandwiches and mince pies.

'I hope these haven't been sitting there since before Christmas,' she said, prising up the pastry lid of a pie and sniffing the dark, spicy contents cautiously.

'Doesn't matter. I don't think they ever go off,' I said. 'And if they do, I can add food poisoning to my list of triumphs.'

'Talking of triumphs, I forgot to tell you.' Amelia went over to the coffee table by the door and started digging through the newspapers. 'You didn't recycle any of these yet, did you?'

I shook my head, feeling boosted by strong cheddar and crunchy pickle on soft poppy seed bread. 'Nope.'

'Here it is. That sexy journalist got his piece published. It was in the paper a few days ago.'

She was clearly thrilled and I took the article obligingly. Under the headline 'New Year, New Hope for Malt House' I read about our *Anglo-American alliance to save local heritage*. There was a flattering photo of Amelia with some of her groupies outside the malt house, and an inane quote from me on different nationalities rallying round a cause.

'Nice.' I folded it up and gave it back.

'I think I might frame it.' Amelia squinted at the prime wall space by the door.

'Okay.' I had just messed up the printing of some double-sided house details. Sighing, I dumped the whole lot in our recycling bin.

'Grace,' Amelia went back to her desk and began thumbing through her piles, 'I know things seem pretty dire right now, but on the professional front, stuff is looking good for you.'

'Hmm?' The mince pie would probably be nicer warm, but I couldn't be bothered to heat it.

'One of the bio-tech companies asked me if we could provide full relocation services to their people.'

'Uh-huh.'

'It'd be a whole new sideline. We'd help with orientation tours and schools, as well as the obvious stuff like housing.' She had polished off her own mince pie in two bites, whereas I was dissecting mine slowly. 'I thought you could manage it as a separate business. Maybe offer interior design too,' she continued, eyeing me beadily.

'Oh. Heck, I dunno. Sounds scary.'

Amelia sat back and folded her arms. 'I get it. You're too deflated just now. But keep it in mind, Grace. You'd be brilliant and I bet we can charge a fat rate.'

I sighed again and said I'd think about it.

'And I was copied on that email from Visit Britain. That could be super too.'

'I think I deleted it.' Some pushy man from the tourist

board wanted me to write a guide for small business owners about marketing to American guests. I had zero intention of responding. 'So, um, has the Hobbs sale started yet?'

Amelia was not to be distracted. 'If you don't call him back, I'm coming after you with a hockey stick.'

'Okay, okay. I'll give him a buzz tomorrow.' Anything to get her off my back.

'All right,' she said. 'I know you're tired. But take it from me, when your personal life comes crashing down around you, that's when work can be a relief. It's either that or the bottle.'

I nodded so she wouldn't think I was completely ungrateful. But right now, the only relief I wanted was to find a dark cave and crawl into it with my new cashmere blankie.

~~~

Within a couple of days, I saw grudgingly that Amelia might have a point about work as an antidote for personal pain. The sheer necessity of getting out of bed in the morning, showering, finding something to eat and getting to the office, prevented me from descending into complete senselessness. Business was still quiet, but I had at least acknowledged the request from Visit Britain and arranged to meet with them. I had also agreed to take down the Hargraves Christmas decorations, before we reached Twelfth Night and tempted yet more bad luck by leaving the tinsel hanging.

With considerably less enthusiasm than I had felt at Halloween, I started in the back corner of the office. Amelia was at her desk so I didn't bother to turn as I heard the door open and her standard client greeting of 'Hello, I'm Amelia, how can I help?'

'Hi. Well – I'm looking to buy a house,' answered a familiar male voice.

And that's how it came about, that I was balanced on an eight-foot ladder with a mouth full of fake holly when I realised that my husband had found me.

~ ~ ~

To Amelia's credit, she was quick to catch on. It could have been the way James was looking straight past her at me, his face a picture of last-ditch hope. More likely, though, it was the way I gasped, yelped and promptly fell off the ladder, bursting into tears even before I hit the floor.

'Bloody hell, darling, are you all right?' Amelia swivelled on a pointy zebra-print ankle boot, but James was faster.

He knelt down beside me in the holly-strewn corner, and from my humiliated huddle against the wall I looked into the kindest pair of brown eyes I'll ever know.

'Grace?' He touched me tentatively on the arm.

'I'm okay. Ouch.' I reached for my ankle as a needle of pain shot through my foot, but by now I was smiling as well as crying. 'Sod. I'm fine, really. I'll just sit here for a minute.'

I wiped my eyes with the back of my hand. Great, another clumsy triumph. No doubt I was doing a good impression of a dog's dinner.

Amelia leaned over my desk to peer down at the pair of us. Satisfied no ambulance was needed, she retreated to the edge of her own desk where she perched with an expression of rapt bemusement.

'How did you get here?' I asked between sniffs.

'I drove,' James said.

I shook my head. 'No – I meant, how did you – ' sniff ' – find me?'

'Ah. Well, your name was in the Cambridge newspaper. It came up on Google.'

Presumably, he was talking about the article by the journalist Amelia fancied.

'After I saw you off at Liverpool Street,' James

continued, 'I had an idea of where to look. But it turns out I was barking up the wrong tree in Saffron Walden.'

I wondered how many trees he'd barked up, and for how long.

'You sublet the apartment,' I said, a hint of accusation in my voice.

'Yeah.' He sighed, then inclined his head to one side. 'How did you know that?'

I couldn't answer, pressing my lips together and shaking my head slightly as I gazed at him, having trouble meeting his eyes. He was looking surprisingly non-scruffy, in inky blue jeans and a black zip-neck jumper.

James rocked back on his heels and pondered my ankle for a few seconds. I was still massaging it with both hands.

Then he said softly, 'You're wearing your wedding ring again.'

I finally managed to look at him and in that moment we both saw in the other the mirror of our brittle hopes.

'Gruff ...' James put his arms around me and I felt the firm reassurance of his chest as I leaned my head against him. I breathed out, a long sigh that felt like it had been churning inside me for the last six months. As he rubbed my shoulder and kissed my forehead, I let the tears roll down unchecked onto his lambswool sweater.

We sat like that for several minutes, before James pulled away slightly. He waited for me to look up, then kissed me gently on the lips. Ankle forgotten, I began kissing him back, and I'm not sure where that would have led had we not been disturbed by a politely assertive cough from Amelia.

'Sorry to interrupt, you two.' She didn't look sorry at all, grinning down at us from on high. 'But did you say something about buying a house?'

~~~

The pub had just opened for the evening, so James and I were able to tuck ourselves away in a secluded corner. Amelia had shooed us out of the Hargraves office, suggesting that as we were clearly in no fit state to buy a home, James could start by buying me a drink.

I had remembered to comb my hair and wipe away the tear streaks, but I still felt shy and awkward. Once again, my name was proving ironic.

'Do you want to talk about it?' James asked, as he returned from the bar with a glass of red wine and a pint of pale ale.

'I don't know where to start.' I gave a hesitant smile.

'Were you in Menlo Park?'

I nodded. 'Where were you?'

'Well, with my mum, for Christmas. Then I made a quick trip up to Holt.'

'To my parents?' I hadn't seen that coming.

'Don't worry, they were very loyal. But they did say you'd left for Heathrow in a hurry. I didn't know what that meant, so I decided I'd just have to visit all the estate agents in Cambridgeshire.' He grimaced. 'I've been shaking eager hands ever since.'

I drank some wine, careful to sip although I wanted to glug.

'Then,' he continued, 'I got lucky. Your name and something about a malt house came up. So here I am.'

I frowned. 'Your office said you don't work there any more.'

'No. Did you get the emails I printed?'

'I did. They – um – they helped. I wish I'd seen them sooner.' I couldn't manage more. My feelings were still complex, multi-layered, but reading the messages between him and Rebecca had reduced my inner storm. It still wouldn't fit in a teacup, but a bucket might now be big enough.

'I'm kicking myself for not thinking of them before.' James took a drink of beer. 'The thing is, I'd deleted my own copies. So to get them, I sort of had to access the central mail server.' His tone was sheepish.

'What do you mean, access?' I had been married to him long enough to know when to dig further.

'I hacked it. Totally worth it, though,' he added, as he read the dismay on my face.

'And that's when they fired you?'

He nodded, with a what's-a-guy-to-do type shrug.

'Oh no.' I forgot about sipping my wine and took a big gulp. 'Do you think they'll prosecute?'

'Nah, I doubt it.' He genuinely didn't seem bothered. 'Once they check the system logs, they'll realise I was after personal emails, not their precious source code. It'll be okay.'

I was silent, amazed and alarmed that he would do something like that to salvage our marriage.

'Sweetheart, don't panic,' James said after a minute or two, covering my small hand with his much larger one.

'When did you put your wedding ring on?' I asked.

He looked down at the platinum band. 'I always wear it.'

'No. You weren't wearing it the day I saw you in London.' I tried to pull my hand away.

'Yes, I was.' He added his right hand to our pile of fingers, keeping mine trapped. 'But – well, I took it off in the park, after you said you were seeing someone.'

I swallowed. 'I'm so sorry,' I said in an undertone.

James looked at me carefully. 'Are you still ...?'

'No! Hell, no. No, I'm not.' I told him the basics about Scott. 'So, as our American friends would say, he's a jerk.'

'He sounds like it, if he's kicking you out of your cottage.'

'Yep.' I gazed down at our matching beer mats.

'Shame,' James said casually. 'I was hoping you might have room for one more.'

I shook my head, but caught his meaning. I leaned in to kiss him, magic and heat flaring inside me as his hand stroked my face and he rubbed his thumb over my lip. We sat for a minute, foreheads touching.

'Well, there's nothing else for it.' James sat back and finished his beer, setting the empty glass down purposefully.

'What?' I smiled at him and drank the last of my wine.

'We really will have to look at buying a house.'

'Don't be daft. You've got no job and prices are insane. We'd be lucky to get a chicken shed.'

'That's what I love about you, Gruff.' He pulled me to my feet and into his arms, pushing a strand of hair behind my ear. 'You always look on the bright side.'

Chapter 33

'We have to get up,' I said.

It was a Saturday evening in late January, and we were due at the first fund raiser for the malt house. It had been dark for hours and the cottage bedroom was lit by a single soft lamp. From the bedside table, my diamond earrings winked knowingly. I had dropped them there in a delicious hurry.

'No, we don't.' James stretched out beside me in bed and then pressed his long legs against me. He reached around and wrapped his hand over mine, kissing my naked shoulder as he did so. I sighed and let him nuzzle the back of my neck, enjoying the heat of his body and the quiet rhythm of our breathing. I felt as though I'd been dipped in melted chocolate, my whole body bathed in warm, sensuous pleasure.

My breath grew more shallow as the nuzzling became kissing and James ran a lazy hand down over my arm, then hip.

'Mmm.' I closed my eyes and enjoyed the bliss of the two of us hiding from the world. Reluctantly, I shifted. 'That's lovely. But we have to get up.'

'We can't get up,' James murmured. His warm fingers had reached the top of my thigh.

'Why not?' I wriggled and turned over, trying to sit up.

Mungo, who had been snoozing on the rug at the bottom of the bed, got to his feet lazily and stretched. He and James had become firm friends and had spent happy hours exploring the countryside while I was at work.

My husband propped himself on one elbow and leaned over me, preventing my escape. 'Because,' he said, eyes bright with tenderness as he looked into my face, 'I haven't told you how much I love you.'

~ ~ ~

Unsurprisingly, we arrived late.

'You look stunning,' James said, as we scurried from the car towards Saffron Hall, where the fund raiser was being held. We'd had to park almost in Suffolk.

'Thank you, sir.' Clinging to his arm for safety, I was making a valiant effort to trot in strappy heels. My hired cocktail dress was dusky lavender, beaded and slinky. I made a swishing sound as I walked. 'You look pretty hot, yourself.' I couldn't remember the last time I'd seen James in a suit. He certainly hadn't owned one in laid-back California, but here he was, smoothly groomed in charcoal grey. To my amazement, he'd even polished his shoes.

We ran into Bernard and Daphne as soon as we entered the ballroom. I held my breath, but their faces were pleasantly neutral as I introduced James. Probably a sign of their impeccable breeding.

'Thank you for hosting tonight,' James said, his hand pressing gently into the hollow of my back. 'It's really important to Grace.'

Bernard, charming as ever, inclined his head. 'And Grace is very important to us.'

Daphne said nothing but smiled and touched me lightly on the arm. I smiled back.

'You're a very lucky man, if I may say so.' Bernard nodded to James, as if he were merely making small talk.

'I know.' James glanced at me fondly.

'Thank you,' I said to them both, and blushed as Bernard reached to kiss my hand.

'No, Grace,' he said. 'Thank you.'

I looked around the room, wondering if an awkward encounter with Scott was on the cards. But of course, he wasn't there. He was hardly likely to pay fifty pounds for a ticket to help save the malt house.

The rest of the village, however, was getting stuck into

the sparkling wine and canapés as if they hadn't eaten since Christmas. Violet came over and kissed James warmly on the cheek. She had been a fan since he'd rescued her home computer from a virus last week.

'Are you well?' I asked. I hadn't seen her for ages.

'Never better,' she said cheerfully, twinkling at James. 'I'm surfing the net and plotting my retirement.'

This was news to me and I murmured something non-committal, in case I put my foot in it.

'They're thinking of moving the post office into the antiques barn,' James told me, after Violet had wandered away to inspect the raffle prizes.

'Really? That's creative.' I made eye contact with a waiter and scored two glasses of wine. 'I guess it makes sense, if Peter's there all day. And she probably likes the idea of handing over to her son.'

Amelia sashayed up. She was looking gorgeous in a green silk trouser suit with a plunging neckline.

'Good evening, Mr and Mrs Palmer.' She hugged us both. 'Nice dress, Grace.'

'Thanks,' I said. 'You too.'

'Well.' Amelia clearly wasn't on her first glass of wine. Her eyes were shining and she was beaming widely. 'This is all looking rather hunky dory.'

'You think so?' I asked.

'Yes, darling. *Lots* of the right people.'

I looked around, recognising several American families. Mary Lou was in a black cocktail dress and looked like she meant business.

'Oh, not just them,' Amelia said, following my gaze. 'Although they're important, of course. See the spindly woman over there, who looks like she's swallowed a wasp?'

'Yes ...'

Amelia put her hand on my shoulder and leaned in conspiratorially. 'I have it on good authority, she's from the *Independent*.'

'Nice,' James said.

'Uh-huh. And the twin stooges by the door?' Amelia jerked her head at two men in black suits. I nodded. They did indeed look like hired bouncers.

'English Heritage,' she said proudly.

'Wow, that's great. Are they getting involved?'

'I'm not sure, darling. There's still a long way to go. But I have to say, things are looking promising.' Amelia took a mouthful of wine, then seemed to spot something, or someone, in the crowd. 'And that ... is even more promising.' She stood up straighter and placed a hand nonchalantly on her hip.

James caught my eye and raised one eyebrow. Over his shoulder I saw the handsome local journalist approaching. We all said hello and I watched as he pulled out his notebook, but not before he'd checked out Amelia's cleavage.

'Excuse us,' I said, trying not to giggle. 'We haven't bought our raffle tickets yet.'

James and I exchanged a knowing look, then made our way to where Mary Lou was forcing people to part with large amounts of cash.

'Do you take dollars?' James smiled, reaching for his wallet. Considering he was newly unemployed, he was being a great sport about chipping in.

'Hell yeah, you betcha!' Mary Lou winked at me. 'Great guy of yours, Grace.'

'Thanks. I think so too.' Other people had been saying that to me, ever since James showed up in Saffron Sweeting. Brian had said I looked like the weight of a London bus had been lifted off my shoulders. Then he'd commented that love was making me skinny, and sent me home with a free treacle tart.

Our transaction complete, Mary Lou tugged on the sleeve of the man beside her. 'Have you met Ross? Honey, this is Grace and James.'

I had met Mary Lou's husband just once before. He was the size of man who looked like he played football – the

American kind, with helmets and shoulder pads.

'Why the dollars?' He shook James's hand vigorously and I hoped all his fingers were still intact. He needed them to type. 'Isn't your accent British?'

'It is,' James said evenly, 'but I was working for a company near San Francisco.'

'Oh yeah? What field are you in?'

'Computers,' James replied, his usual answer for our English friends.

'Duh. Obviously.' Ross frowned. 'I meant, what *field* are you in?'

'Network security and cryptography.'

'Who knew?' Mary Lou had robbed another willing villager of a twenty pound note and tore off their raffle tickets. 'Ross is CSO at Fairmont Pharmaceuticals.' She placed a finger under my elbow and steered me firmly away. 'Grace, can I borrow you for a second?'

'What's a CSO?' I muttered, as she walked me over to a high cocktail table, where a platter of crostini was unattended. 'Mmm, yummy.' I tasted one and reached for another.

'Chief Security Officer.' Mary Lou winked for the second time that evening. 'You might want to let them chat for a few minutes.'

I shook my head at her, smiling my thanks. 'You're brilliant. Please let me know if I can help with your shop.'

'That's a deal. We open next month, I hope. Now, excuse me, I'm off to find my next victim.'

Alone, I surveyed the room and took the chance to waylay the waiting staff, who were circulating with tasty morsels. The caterers had done a fine job and the mood in the ballroom was enthusiastic.

'Hey, Grace' said a voice, and I turned with delight to find Nancy. Peter was just behind her.

After greetings and compliments on everyone's outfits, I said to Peter, 'I hear you might be taking on the post office?'

'It's a possibility,' he replied. 'Don't see how it can

survive unless we combine it with another business. Might get a few new folk into my place too.'

'Sounds ideal,' I said.

'And how are you?' Nancy asked. 'Is the honeymoon over yet?'

I smiled and coloured. 'I'm fine, thanks.'

'Any luck finding somewhere to live?'

I wrinkled my nose. 'Not yet. But we're having fun looking.'

Two nights after James had arrived in the village, it had snowed. Delighted, we had found suitable boots and gone for a long walk along the river the next day, from Anglesey Abbey to Quy.

En route, we had discussed our future.

'I've only been here six months, but it feels like forever,' I'd said.

The snow had settled prettily on all the hedges and branches, but now that the sun had come out, it would disappear fast.

'You definitely want to stay?' James kept his voice light.

I didn't answer for a moment, listening to the chirp of finches and the muffled crunch under our feet.

Then I said, 'Yes. I really do.' The East Anglian countryside lacked the glamour of the San Francisco Bay, with its mountains, bridges and wide Pacific Ocean. But it felt like home to me, and now that James was here, I was awash with contentment. I stopped to look at him. 'Is that asking too much?'

James had one of my gloved hands in his already, and now he took the other one too. 'No,' he said, brown eyes serious. 'We can make that work.'

I reached up for a quick kiss, but was waylaid by reality. 'You've got no job.'

'Something'll turn up.' James shrugged as we began walking again. 'This is Cambridge, after all.' He was confident his skills would find a use.

He'd also been perfectly serious about buying a house,

cryptically mentioning that his mum might help with the deposit. Even allowing for that, and assuming he found a great job, we would be on a painfully tight budget. Still, it had been a good excuse to visit some of the smaller properties on Amelia's books together.

'Ooh, that was nasty,' I'd said after the first, experiencing an unpleasant flashback to my early days in the village, looking for somewhere to rent.

'Agreed, the smelly carpets weren't a big turn on.' James took big gulps of fresh winter air. 'But if we're buying rather than renting, we can rip the whole lot out and start from scratch.'

'Hmm, that might be fun.' There was definite appeal in starting with a blank slate and designing it all myself.

'Or maybe we'll find someone with a spare chicken shed, after all.'

I laughed. 'I'll keep my ears open.'

In fact, Amelia already had both ears open and I suspected the other villagers could be persuaded to do the same. Something told me they'd rather tip off James and me about a vacant property, than Scott.

Now, I put my head on one side and looked at Peter. 'Um, if you do move the post office into the antiques store, what happens to the existing building?'

The current post office was housed in a narrow, quirky cottage, in prime position on the High Street.

'No idea,' Peter said. 'I imagine it would be sold.'

'I think I see where Grace is heading with this,' Nancy said.

I blinked at Peter with mock innocence. 'Maybe you could let me know, when you know?'

Peter smiled meaningfully. 'I'll keep you *posted*.'

'Hi, all.' James arrived, bearing a plate laden with mini quiches and bite-sized scotch eggs. 'Thought you might be hungry,' he murmured, passing the bounty to me.

'You treasure.' I nibbled happily while he chatted with Nancy and Peter. We were interrupted by Amelia tapping a

Saving Saffron Sweeting

spoon against a glass.

'Ladies and gentlemen ...' She smiled confidently as the room hushed. 'I have the great pleasure of welcoming you all to the official launch of the Save Saffron Sweeting Campaign.'

We clapped proudly.

'We all know how much work is ahead of us to preserve the unique charm and character of our village, and especially its malt house. However, I'm delighted to see so many of you here tonight to support this vital endeavour.' Amelia paused, comfortable in her role, no doubt knowing she looked fantastic. 'Now, please make sure you have purchased your raffle tickets from Mary Lou, as we'll be starting the draw in just a few minutes.'

A murmur of anticipation ran through the attendees. Presumably, they were excited at the prospect of winning a case of wine from Tesco or dinner at the pub. A fresh crowd of purchasers formed around Mary Lou.

James surveyed the scene with amusement, then bent to speak into my ear. 'Want to get some air?' he said in a low voice, running his hand up and down my back.

'What about the raffle?' I said, surprised.

'Good point.' He looked around the room. 'I think they'll manage without us.'

I smiled and tipped my head in agreement.

'Here, would you two mind doing the honours?' James offered our strip of orange tickets to Nancy and Peter. 'We're just going to step outside for a few minutes.'

He led me through the elegant French doors of the ballroom to the shadows of the covered terrace.

'It's a great party,' he said, 'but I fancied a few minutes alone with my wife.'

I turned to snuggle into his warmth as he wrapped both arms around me.

'You're a big hit with everyone,' I said, grinning up at him. The height gap was less than usual, due to my impractical shoes.

'No,' he said. 'If they like me, it's only because they're smitten with you.'

I shook my head in protest.

'It's true,' he said. 'I should know.' His gaze was soft but sincere.

I reached my hand up and played with his tie as I waited for the wave of emotion to calm. In the pause, clapping floated out to us from the ballroom.

'They're really getting into it,' I said, seeing the fever of raffle winning on the villagers' faces. They were taking no notice of the couple in the frosty shadows outside, who were holding onto each other as if they had scooped first prize. 'I think Saffron Sweeting might bounce back better than ever.'

James looked at them, then at me. 'Tough times make you stronger,' he said gently.

He didn't just mean the village. I felt tears welling.

'I'm so sorry, Grace.' James hadn't taken his eyes off my face.

'It's okay.' I swallowed. 'We'll be okay now,' I whispered, and let myself sink into his soft, sweet kiss.

The road behind us couldn't be changed, but I was eager to walk the path ahead.

From the Author

Independent authors like me rely on reviews from readers to help spread the word about our work. Please consider adding your review of *Saving Saffron Sweeting* to Amazon, Goodreads and other online forums.

I love to connect with readers through my website and social media. Visit *www.paulinewiles.com* for news, bonus materials and special promotions.

Made in the USA
Lexington, KY
27 September 2013